Virtually Perfect

Virtually Perfect

PAIGE ROBERTS

KENSINGTON BOOKS
www.kensingtonbooks.com

This book is a work of fiction. Names, characters, places, and incidents either are products of the author's imagination or are used fictitiously. Any resemblance to actual persons, living or dead, events, or locales is entirely coincidental.

KENSINGTON BOOKS are published by

Kensington Publishing Corp.
119 West 40th Street
New York, NY 10018

All Kensington titles, imprints, and distributed lines are available at special quantity discounts for bulk purchases for sales promotion, premiums, fund-raising, educational or institutional use.

Special book excerpts or customized printings can also be created to fit specific needs. For details, write or phone the office of the Kensington Sales Manager: Kensington Publishing Corp., 119 West 40th Street, New York, NY 10018. Attn. Sales Department. Phone: 1-800-221-2647.

Kensington and the K logo Reg. U.S. Pat. & TM Off.

eISBN-13: 978-1-4967-1010-9
eISBN-10: 1-4967-1010-X
First Kensington Electronic Edition: October 2017

ISBN-13: 978-1-4967-1009-3
ISBN-10: 1-4967-1009-6
First Kensington Trade Paperback Printing: October 2017

10 9 8 7 6 5 4 3 2

Printed in the United States of America

For my mom

CHAPTER 1

Lizzie Glass didn't consider herself a liar. Or at least not a born liar. She hadn't made up stories in kindergarten about how she was secretly a princess in disguise, even though she wanted nothing more than to be just that. As a teenager she never pretended to have smoked pot or made up a fake boyfriend, even when doing so would have saved her a lot of embarrassment. For the most part, any lies she'd told had been crimes of omission. And, okay, yes, some of those omissions had been bigger than others. Some had been pretty massive, actually. Nevertheless, she wasn't in the habit of making declarations she knew were patently false.

And yet here she was: dressed in a toga in the New York Botanical Garden, handing out free samples of "cottziki," and lying.

She'd been hired by Queensridge Dairy to help with their #FitForAQueen campaign to give cottage cheese a face-lift, and she'd spent the past month trucking around New York and New Jersey trying to convince people cottage cheese wasn't merely diet food for old ladies and health nuts. Today was Mother's Day, the final day of the campaign, and Queensridge had arranged for Lizzie to camp out next to the food trucks on Daffodil Hill, hoping to snag some hungry families taking part in the Botanical Garden's annual Mother's Day party.

"Cottziki?" Lizzie offered cheerily, extending a tray of dill-and-cucumber-flecked curds toward a group of passersby.

The truth was, Lizzie hated cottage cheese. *Hated* it. For someone who cooked for a living, despising a food with such passion was awkward, if not unusual. The sour smell, the lumpy texture . . . she always felt as if she were being asked to eat someone else's vomit. Every time she looked at the samples of cottage cheese tzatziki in those little plastic cups, she cringed. She had no idea why she'd taken this job.

That wasn't true. She knew why. It paid, and she needed the money. And as long as someone out there was willing to exploit her former fame, she was happy to cash the check. There had been far fewer of those checks lately, as her television days drifted further into the past. Recently, even her personal chef gigs had started drying up, leaving her with a single client, who was demanding and impossible but who paid on time and in full. And of course there was the monthly column with *Savor,* but her contract was nearly up, and the magazine had recently appointed a new editor in chief, who'd spawned rumors about a "total magazine makeover."

So it had come to this: pushing a food she couldn't stomach onto strangers, telling them it was healthy and glamorous and they absolutely had to try it.

"Cottziki?" Lizzie repeated as another crowd walked past. This time a mother and her twentysomething daughter slowed their step to survey Lizzie's offerings.

"Cott what?" the mother asked.

"Cottziki. Like tzatziki, but with cottage cheese instead of yogurt."

"Why not just use yogurt?"

Lizzie smiled and trotted out her practiced spiel. "Cottage cheese is an excellent source of protein and vitamin A, and with its unique flavor profile, it takes dishes like tzatziki to the next level!"

"But isn't it loaded with sodium? And those lumps . . . ick."

You're right! Lizzie thought. *It's gross! But I can't afford my rent anymore, so I'm pretending it's not!*

"Give it a try," Lizzie said. "I think you'll be pleasantly surprised."

The mother and daughter eyed each other warily. "Here goes nothing . . ." the daughter said.

Lizzie watched as they both reached for a cup and brought the small plastic spoons to their lips. The daughter's expression was unreadable, but the mother looked as if she'd sucked on a lemon.

"Not for me," she said, and tossed the cup into the trash bin.

Lizzie smiled politely and adjusted her toga. Why was she wearing a toga, anyway? The whole costume only seemed to emphasize that what she was serving was emphatically *not* authentically Greek and that she was trying way too hard.

The mother and daughter began to walk away, when the daughter stopped and turned around. "Hey, didn't you used to be on that show a few years back? *Healthy University* or something?"

"*Healthy U.*"

"Yeah, that's it. What happened? I never see it on anymore."

"It got canceled. A while ago, actually."

"Oh." She took in Lizzie's costume and the electric-blue Queensridge Dairy food truck behind her. "So is this what you're doing now?"

"Among other things."

"That's . . . cool." She tried to sound enthusiastic, but Lizzie knew better. "Good luck to you."

The daughter turned around and joined her mother down the walking path, and Lizzie told herself there was no reason to feel embarrassed, even if, deep down, she knew that was another lie.

An hour later, Lizzie had made little progress in her cottziki crusade. Apart from a handful of enthusiastic cottage cheese fans (whose sanity Lizzie couldn't help but question), people generally didn't see why they needed to try a lumpy riff on a Greek dish when they could get the real thing from the Greek food truck fifty feet away.

"This stuff any good?" asked Emilio, the Queensridge truck driver for the day. There seemed to be a different one every time.

"It's okay," Lizzie said. "Not my favorite."

Emilio grabbed a cup and took a bite. "Eh. Not bad. Who made it?"

"Me."

"And you say it's just 'okay'?"

"I'm my own biggest critic."

That was true, but it also killed Lizzie to serve up a dish she could barely recommend. When she'd first taken the job, she pitched recipes that disguised her most hated food in dishes she loved: her grandmother's noodle kugel, lasagna, deep-fried dumplings (because she figured pretty much anything tastes delicious if you dip it in batter and deep-fry it). But the #FitForAQueen campaign manager told Lizzie the point was to showcase the company's product—not to hide it under so many ingredients the customers wouldn't know it was there (which was, indeed, exactly what Lizzie was trying to do). Besides, healthy cuisine was Lizzie's calling card, and things like fried food didn't fit with her image.

So Lizzie came up with a battery of healthy, cottage cheese–centric recipes: herbed cottage cheese dip, cherry-and-oat cottage cheese breakfast parfait, honey-vanilla cottage cheese pudding. She could tolerate those recipes, and she even developed a chocolate–peanut butter "Snickers" protein shake she quite liked (though she was certain it would be better with yogurt). But then as Mother's Day approached, the campaign manager got it in his head that a Greek-themed dish was essential, as if somehow togas and motherhood went hand in hand, and her riff on a Greek classic was born.

Lizzie stared across Daffodil Hill, taking in the bright yellow and white blooms, their fluffy petals fluttering in the warm spring breeze. After a cold April that had felt more like autumn, May had ushered in a spell of warm weather that had awakened all of the flowers and shrubs from their winter slumber. The vibrant fuchsia and white azaleas reminded Lizzie how much she missed her mother's garden in Philadelphia, where her flame-colored azalea bush probably looked as if it were on fire right now.

Instinctively, Lizzie reached for her phone, only to realize she'd left it in the truck because her toga didn't have pockets. There was a momentary lull in foot traffic, so Lizzie took the opportunity to rest for a few minutes in the front seat of the truck, where she'd left her phone on the dashboard.

She had a missed call and message from her mom. Lizzie had

tried her earlier in the morning to wish her a happy Mother's Day, but the call had gone straight to voice mail. She'd assumed her mom was still sleeping, but part of her worried, like she always did, that something was wrong. A few years ago, a friend had told Lizzie about his former neighbor, who died when she choked on a piece of chicken in her kitchen. The woman was divorced and lived alone, and all Lizzie could think was how easily that could happen to her own mother.

Lizzie listened to her mom's message while she sat in the passenger seat, playing with a chestnut strand of hair that had come loose from her faux Greek updo.

"Hi, sweetie, it's Mom." Lizzie smiled at the sound of her mother's voice. It had a gravelly quality, with a slight New York accent that betrayed the nearly four decades she'd lived in Philadelphia. "Sorry I missed your call earlier—if you can believe it, I only just woke up! But give me a ring when you get this. You said you might be able to take a late train to Philly? I know better than to get my hopes up, but . . . it would be great to see you. Anyway, hope your event is going well. Cottage cheese? Are pigs flying?"

Lizzie grinned.

"Hey, traffic's picking up again," Emilio called. "You should probably get back out here."

"One sec'," Lizzie called back as she quickly scrolled through her in-box. She scanned through the usual junk—sales at Williams Sonoma and the Gap, recipes from various food sites—but her smile tightened when she reached an e-mail from Jonah Sun, her editor at *Savor*:

> Hey, Lizzie,
> Thanks for the latest column. Looks great. Can't wait to try those baked apples.
> This is probably a good time to tell you that as much as I've really loved working with you the past few years, it looks like the magazine will be making some changes. The new editor is doing a total reboot, and so a lot of content is being replaced with fresher, newer stuff. It's an exciting time for sure,

but unfortunately, this means we won't be needing a regular column from you anymore. You're totally welcome to pitch ideas whenever you want, but they'll be judged on a case-by-case basis and won't be a regular thing. So sorry to be the bearer of bad news. Given that your contract was up anyway, the timing sort of works out for everyone.

I'll make sure we get the check out to you for your last column ASAP. Best of luck with everything!

Cheers,

Jonah

Lizzie stared at the message, the world around her fading to silence. She read it two more times just to make sure she hadn't misunderstood anything. So that was it. Over. Like her show, like her book deals, like everything else. Over. Okay, so she wasn't fresh and new. She understood that. But she was only thirty! Surely she was still fresh-ish. People still loved her columns, or at least that's what the e-mails she received led her to believe. Granted, there had been fewer of those e-mails lately, but she hadn't received any telling her otherwise—that her recipes didn't work or that her recipe for kale chips was *so* ten years ago.

"I'm still . . . *somebody,*" Lizzie said to herself, her phone clutched in her hand.

"You won't be for long if you don't get out there," said Emilio, who'd snuck up behind her. "The boss will be pissed if he hears you were hanging in the truck all afternoon."

"Sorry. Coming." Lizzie slid the phone back on the dashboard, grabbed the tray of Greek curds, and tried to tell herself everything would be okay, even though at the moment she couldn't see how that could possibly be true.

CHAPTER 2

The problem was this: Lizzie was broke. Not properly broke, as in she had zero dollars in her bank account and nowhere to live, but "New York broke," in a way that was becoming increasingly unsustainable.

Six years ago, she never would have dreamed she'd be in this position. Looking back on it now, she realized that was probably part of the problem. But she'd had a successful show on the Food Network and a two-book cookbook deal with Clarkson Potter, and she was making good money—not millions or, frankly, anywhere close, but enough to live a comfortable life in a hip Brooklyn neighborhood. She'd been invited to openings of some of the coolest New York restaurants and went to all sorts of parties and events, where people recognized her and everyone she met wanted to be her new best friend. She'd buy those new friends rounds of drinks and at the end of the night could take cabs home without worrying too much about the cost.

What she soon discovered was that comfort in New York had no buffer. Her life was like a shaky tower built of Popsicle sticks, and removing just one caused the entire structure to collapse. Gone were her carefree days of meals out and regular taxis. She started scrimping and saving, eating nearly every meal at home and keeping only the essentials in her pantry. She invested in a good pair of sneakers and walked everywhere she could reach in forty-five minutes or less on foot and used buses and the subway for the rest. She couldn't remember the last time she'd bought a new article of clothing. Yet even with all of her commitment to frugality, she was still barely scraping by.

And now she was in even bigger trouble.

"Hey, what's with the sour puss?" Emilio asked as they packed up the truck. The event was over, and not a moment too soon.

"Nothing. Long day."

"Hey, at least they're paying you for this. It's not like you're working for free."

"Thank God for that."

Emilio laughed, but Lizzie didn't find any of this very funny. What was she going to do without the monthly check from *Savor*? They didn't pay her a fortune, but the thousand dollars she received each month helped defray the cost of her rent, which she was having more and more trouble paying.

Would she have to move to Queens? She'd already moved from her apartment in Park Slope to a smaller, cheaper place in neighboring Greenwood Heights, and even that rent was a stretch. Frankly, she was barely in Greenwood Heights. She was really in the northern part of the predominately Mexican and Chinese neighborhood of Sunset Park. But nearly everyone she knew lived in Brooklyn these days, and the prospect of moving away from them—not just physically but also financially—made her feel like an even bigger failure.

"Got any Mother's Day plans after this?" Emilio asked.

"I was thinking of taking the train to Philly to see my mom, but it kind of depends on the train schedule." *And the ticket price,* she added to herself.

"No kids of your own then?"

Lizzie flinched. "Of my own?"

She'd only met Emilio this morning, and she was pretty sure she hadn't said anything that would imply offspring of any kind.

"Yeah, I thought maybe . . ." He trailed off, clearly rethinking whatever he'd been about to say.

"I'm not married," Lizzie said, waving her left hand.

"So? Doesn't mean you couldn't have a kid."

"Emilio, how old do you think I am?"

As soon as she spoke the words, she wished she hadn't. She wasn't ready to hear the answer, unless it was a number less than thirty.

"I dunno . . . thirty?"

Lizzie's shoulders relaxed. He didn't think she was forty-two. *Thank God.*

She stiffened again, though, when she realized the implications of his answer: that thirty was a perfectly reasonable age to have a child. Because it was. Her mom had been thirty-one when she'd had Lizzie, and her aunt Linda had given birth at twenty-seven. Every day, it seemed, Lizzie was bombarded with images on Facebook of swaddled newborns in those little pink-and-blue-striped hats, the progeny of one of her classmates somewhere along the line. Every time she saw one of those photos, she had to fight the instinct to call one of her high school friends and exclaim, *Oh my God, did you know Katie Allen got* knocked up? In Lizzie's mind, they were all still so young—certainly too young to be parents. Parents were old. Parents were responsible.

But gradually Lizzie realized everyone else was growing up, while she was being left behind. She didn't even have a boyfriend, much less a baby. Right now she barely had a job. At least if she were still hosting *Healthy U* she could point to her high-flying career and fast-paced lifestyle. But instead, she was hawking cottage cheese with some guy named Emilio and had just lost yet another source of income.

"Good guess," Lizzie said as Emilio sealed up the truck. "For a minute there you had me worried."

"I was right? You're thirty?"

"Yep," Lizzie said, and as she did she sounded almost as surprised as he did.

As soon as Lizzie reached her apartment building, her phone rang. It was her mom.

"Mom, hey—sorry, I'm only just getting back from this job."

"I guess that answers my question, then."

"Which was?"

"Whether or not you were on a train."

"Oh. No. Sorry."

"No need to apologize. I wasn't expecting it. Just hoping."

Lizzie opened the front door to her building. It was a three-story walk-up, sandwiched between brick row houses of varying shades of red, beige, and cream, all of which seemed to bear tin awnings over their front doors.

"I didn't expect the day to last this long. What time is it now? Five something?"

"Almost six."

"Seriously? I swear, no matter how long I've lived here, I can't get over how big this city is. It took me almost two hours to get home from the Bronx."

Emilio had been kind enough to drop Lizzie at the subway on his way to the truck depot, but the D train ride lasted a good hour and when she factored in the time to and from the subway stops the journey seemed downright Odyssean.

"How'd the event go?"

"Okay," Lizzie said, trying to sound upbeat. She wasn't lying. The event *was* okay—not brilliant, not disastrous, just . . . okay— but she didn't want to belabor the "just okay–ness" of the day because she didn't want to alarm her mom. Lizzie knew how anxious she was about her daughter living alone in a so-so neighborhood in Brooklyn, and she didn't want to add to her angst. For as long as Lizzie could remember, she had tried to ease her mother's worries. That was partly down to Lizzie's guilt over her parents' divorce and partly down to her eternal desire to fix things, and also, she supposed, partly down to a lifelong attempt to make up for the death of her brother, Ryan, when he was a baby.

"So I guess there's no chance you'll make it to Philly tonight, huh?"

"I don't think so," Lizzie said as she let herself into her apartment.

Her mom sighed. "Ah, well. Maybe next Mother's Day."

"Hold on a sec'; I didn't say I wasn't coming at all. I said not tonight."

"Oh!" Her mom's voice brightened. "You might come this week? When?"

"Well . . . I wanted to run an idea by you first."

Lizzie took a deep breath. She'd thought about this the entire journey back from the Botanical Garden. At first, she'd started crunching the numbers, trying to figure out how many new clients she'd need to pick up for her personal chef work to make up for the lost magazine column and dwindling cookbook royalties. But when she started factoring in transportation costs and travel time, she wasn't sure she could accommodate as many clients as she'd need.

And then she started wondering: *Why the hell am I doing this?* For years she'd convinced herself she needed to be in New York, and for many of those years that was true. She'd shot her show in New York, and her agent, editor, and publisher were all there, too. And the food and restaurant scene in New York couldn't be beat. Why would she live anywhere else?

But numbers weren't adding up anymore. She wasn't shooting a show, and her agent barely returned her e-mails, much less invited her for lunch or drinks. For a while, she got by on her former fame, but the Queensridge Dairy gig was the first promotional opportunity she'd had in a long, long time (and from what she heard, she only got it after a long list of other talent said no first). The fact that someone recognized her today had actually come as a surprise. Most people had figured she was simply another millennial looking to pick up extra cash on the weekend. She couldn't remember the last time someone had asked for her autograph. Certainly not in the last two years.

And so she had made a decision.

"What if I moved home?"

"Home? With me?"

"Just for a bit, until I figure out what I'm doing."

"What you're doing with what?"

"My career."

"But . . . I thought things were going well. Queensridge Dairy hired you to make cottage cheese seem hip! And you have that client with the Fabergé egg collection and gold wallpaper. . . ."

"Mrs. Sokolov? Yeah, she's crazy. Nightmare client. And the other stuff isn't . . . well, as regular as I'd like."

"But for someone like you, who has such a strong background, who went to Penn." She stopped abruptly. They both knew why.

"I'm not planning on sleeping until noon and sponging off you for months. I just think it's time for me to pull the plug on New York, at least temporarily. I feel like I'm paying for the privilege of living here and not getting much in return."

"Oh, believe me, I hear you. Why do you think your father and I decided to stay in Philly? It's just . . . I worry about you."

"I know. But you shouldn't. I'm fine. And I think this is the right decision."

"Well, if you're sure, then I'm sure. I guess you can write from anywhere. And there are plenty of people in Philadelphia and the surrounding area looking for a personal chef."

"Exactly."

"I'll need to get your room in order . . . and the pantry is an embarrassment. . . ."

"Mom, all of that can wait until I arrive. I'll help you."

"Oh! And I'll have to stock up on oatmeal and yogurts. And eggs! And those honey-almond granola bars you used to buy all the time. You still eat those, right?" Her voice was brighter now.

"Sure."

"Oh, good." She hummed into the receiver. "My baby is coming home. I can't believe it."

Lizzie smiled to herself and held her breath, not wanting to admit out loud that as much as she stood by her decision, she couldn't believe it either.

CHAPTER 3

Linda,

Are you sitting down? Because I've got some pretty big news—Lizzie is moving home! I know. I was shocked. Apparently NYC isn't going as well as I thought, so she's decided to stay with me while she figures things out. I'm trying not to worry too much, but you know me. She has a good head on her shoulders, so I'm sure she'll work everything out, but sometimes I wonder. . . . She gave me the same reassurances when she left Penn to move to New York for Healthy U, and look how that turned out. But I do understand how hard it can be in the city. I told her, why do you think your dad and I stayed in Philly? I can't believe I brought Frank into it—what I should have said was, why do you think your aunt Linda and I both ended up here?

Anyway, I'm sure she'll work it all out, but I thought I'd check with you to see if you knew of anyone at CC Media who might need a personal or private chef. I realize it's a huge company (did you see that article about how it's the biggest cable company in the country now?!), but since you have the ear of the number two over there, I figured you'd be more likely to find someone needing a personal chef than I would. Even just a summer job would be a big help. Doesn't your boss go down the shore every weekend to that ridiculous house he built? I'm still dying to see pictures. It sounded obscene. From what you've told me about his family, I'm not at all surprised.

In other news . . . I saw Gary again last night. I think I really like him. He's so different from anyone I've ever dated, especially Frank. But then Jessica and I are polar opposites, so maybe that's what Frank and I needed to move on after Ryan (never mind that Frank got there a few decades before I did . . .). Gary and I are getting together again this week, so we'll see. He wants to take me to some talk on "cleaning up your lifestyle." Sounds a little New Agey for me, but I'm trying to keep an open mind.

Okay, gotta run. I meant this to be a three-line e-mail, but you know me—when I get going, there's no stopping me, especially when it comes to Lizzie! Let me know if you hear of any potential job leads. I'll try not to hold my breath, but honestly, who am I kidding?

xxoo
Susan

CHAPTER 4

Lizzie turned onto Waverly Road, feeling more confident than she'd expected. When her aunt Linda called her with a potential summer job—a private chef gig at the beach house of CC Media's chief operating officer—Lizzie wasn't sure she wanted it. She'd heard strange stories about Jim Silvester and his family over the years, mostly from her aunt, who'd been his executive assistant for more than a decade. And Lizzie knew that working as a hired hand for extremely wealthy families came with a surfeit of potential hazards: esoteric requests, inflated expectations, complete lack of personal time.

But as Lizzie drove down the road in her mother's Honda Accord she sighed in relief as she surveyed the houses around her. These weren't the twenty-thousand-square-foot manses she'd imagined when she heard the Silvesters lived in Gladwyne, the crème de la crème of Philadelphia's Main Line. She'd once read an article that listed Gladwyne's residents as some of the wealthiest in the country, along with those of Beverly Hills and Greenwich, Connecticut. But from what she could see, the houses around her looked . . . well, normal. Bigger than her mother's quaint redbrick colonial in Glenside, a thirty-minute drive from here, but not gargantuan. Not *obscene*.

"You will reach your destination in two hundred yards," the GPS told her. "Your destination is on the left."

Lizzie looked to her left. Okay, so the homes were beginning to look a bit more . . . stately. In fact, for a minute she thought the one she just passed was a hotel. But it wasn't the Silvesters' home. Theirs might be like the others she'd seen earlier—big but reasonable. That's what she was hoping for in general: a family that had a big income and a big personality but that was also reasonable. After so many years cobbling together a living from different sources, Lizzie was ready for a summer of steady income and predictability, with an employer who didn't shout at her in Russian while dressed in a gold lamé duster jacket.

"You have reached your destination," the GPS said.

"Oh," Lizzie said as she looked to her left. "*Oh*."

She gulped as she took in the tall wrought-iron gate that stretched across a cobblestone driveway, both sides framed by tall stone-and-brick pillars. The lip of the driveway was framed by two flower beds, each of which was filled with perfectly pruned boxwoods and white and violet impatiens. The black mulch looked as if it had just been laid that morning, and the plantings were all spaced with scientific exactitude.

She turned in and stopped in front of the gate. There was a small call box to the left, so she lowered the car window and pressed the button.

"Hello?" said a woman with a slight foreign accent of indeterminate origin.

"Hi . . . yes . . . it's Lizzie Glass. About the summer job? I'm . . . here."

Obviously, you idiot, she thought. *Where else would you be? Hong Kong?* She hadn't been for a job interview in ages, and she was suddenly very nervous.

"Yes. Okay. Please come in." Lizzie thought the accent sounded Spanish, but she couldn't be sure.

The gates juddered open, and Lizzie pulled through them and continued along the driveway until she reached a large parking area in front of the house.

"Holy stromboli," Lizzie whispered as her eyes crawled up the building's gray stone façade. The house rose four stories to a gabled roof, whose points and peaks were lined with limestone bricks. The footprint seemed to stretch on forever—for miles, it seemed—and she couldn't believe only one family lived here. She was terrible when it came to estimating distances or square footages by sight, but she knew her mom's house was about two thousand square feet, and, from the outside at least, she guessed she could fit about eight of her mom's houses in this one. *Eight*. She shook her head in disbelief.

She grabbed her knife case and bag of ingredients and made for the front door. When she'd talked to Mrs. Silvester on the phone earlier in the week, they'd discussed the interview format. Mrs. Silvester would ask Lizzie a series of questions, and then Lizzie would cook a sample meal in the Silvesters' kitchen to showcase her skills and style.

Lizzie pressed the buzzer beside the elegant walnut door and peered into one of the small windows that lined either side. Before she could glimpse more than the twinkle of the crystal chandelier in the foyer, her view was blocked by a demurely dressed Hispanic woman with a narrow face, dark hair, and striking dark, round eyes.

The door swung open. "Hello," the woman said, ushering Lizzie into the foyer. "Mrs. Silvester will be down in one minute. You can wait here."

"Great," said Lizzie. "Thanks."

The woman smiled and disappeared into the next room, and Lizzie took a moment to size up her surroundings. The foyer was vast, surrounded by white paneled walls and thick white columns that lined the doorways to the rooms on either side, as if she were about to enter a Greek temple. Above her hung a crystal chandelier that Lizzie thought was big enough to constitute its own solar system. It was matched by another of the same size fifty feet away, which dangled beside a stately turned staircase with bright white spindles and a dark cherry banister, which matched the shiny Brazilian cherry hardwood floors. Lizzie had never seen a house like this before, except maybe in the pages of *Architectural Digest* or on TV. It was so big. And so *clean*. She could hardly believe someone actually lived here. Where was all of the stuff? The sneakers and the jackets and all the little signs that real people ate and slept here and that this wasn't just a museum of good taste?

As Lizzie studied the thick Persian rug beneath her, she heard footsteps on the broad staircase. She looked up and saw a petite woman coming toward her, her shoulder-length blond hair shimmering in the light of the chandelier. Everything about the woman screamed wealth: the highlights, the haircut, the nickel-size diamond on her hand, the impeccably tailored clothes and red-soled shoes. She had that well-maintained look Lizzie had encountered so often in New York, when she found herself on the Upper East Side or at an event for prominent Wall Street executives. Not a hair out of place, not a frown line in sight.

"You must be Lizzie," the woman said with a smile. Her voice was high and bubbly, just as it had been on the phone. "Kathryn Silvester."

She extended a hand, and Lizzie tucked her knife kit under her arm so that she could shake it.

"So nice to meet in person," Lizzie said. "You have a beautiful home."

"Thank you," Kathryn said in a way that indicated she was used to this sort of compliment. And why wouldn't she be? The house was amazing. "So, I was thinking we could talk for a bit in the kitchen, and once we've gotten through the basics, you can start cooking. Work for you?"

Lizzie smiled, trying to seem as friendly and can-do as possible. "Works for me."

Kathryn led Lizzie from the foyer into the dining room, whose walls were lined in purply-gray grass cloth and whose ceiling featured two more crystal chandeliers, of smaller proportion than those in the foyer but of equal grandeur and sparkle. From there, they walked through a broad doorway flanked by open French doors into the kitchen.

The kitchen was decorated in a French country style, with white-washed cabinetry, cream granite countertops, and ornate wrought-iron pulls and knobs on the drawers and doors. Lizzie counted not one but two refrigerators, each more than three feet wide, the exteriors bearing the same painted wood as the cabinets around them. Like the rest of the house Lizzie had seen so far, everything in the kitchen was perfectly arranged, as if it had never been used: a massive bowl in the middle of the triangular island filled with just the right amount and variety of fruit; vintage glass candy jars filled with a rainbow assortment of jelly beans, striped taffy, and gourmet lollipops; and crystal vases brimming with fluffy pink peonies. What struck Lizzie most of all was how tasteful everything was. Clearly the Silvesters had spent a fortune decorating this house, but they hadn't gone crazy with chinz and gold leaf and marble statues. They'd done it the way Lizzie might have done herself, if she'd had many millions of dollars to spare.

Kathryn pulled out one of the upholstered chairs around the kitchen island. "Why don't you sit here, and I'll sit next to you, and we can talk a bit about your past clients. You don't have to name names—although I won't stop you, if you feel like dishing! No pun intended." She winked as Lizzie climbed onto the chair and rested her bags on the counter. "Anyway, I'm most interested in what sort of special diet experience you have. Can you talk a little about that?"

Lizzie sat up tall. Aunt Linda had mentioned that Lizzie's background in healthy cuisine had helped land her the interview, so she was prepared for this question.

"My last client couldn't eat gluten, soy, or dairy, so I created menus that omitted those ingredients but were still exciting and innovative and met with her tastes. And other clients have ranged from vegan to kosher, so I'm able to accommodate any dietary restrictions you might have."

"What about a range of restrictions? For example, I am currently experimenting with the Paleo diet—which, by the way, has been amazing so far—but my husband, Jim, shouldn't eat red meat and doesn't love most vegetables. He's also allergic to garlic. And then, of course, there's Zoe. . . ."

"Zoe?"

"My daughter. She's been traveling in Europe since she graduated from GW last June, but she'll be joining us for the summer. Or at least most of it."

"And she has special dietary needs as well?"

"She's . . ." Kathryn paused, choosing her words carefully. "She's very particular about what she eats."

"A little picky?"

"No, not picky. Particular."

"In what way?"

"Well, she's vegan, but she also only eats food that's . . . what is the word she's always using . . . ? 'Clean.' You know—organic, seasonal, nothing processed, that kind of thing."

"Oh, okay. That's fine."

"But you see what I'm saying—we all have slightly different needs. Would you be able to make a meal that suits all of us?"

"Sure. Like one night I could make a chicken dish for dinner for you and your husband and the side dishes could all be vegan so that your daughter could eat those, along with a legume-based dish for protein."

"Good. Excellent. That will make her happy." She ran her hand against the edge of the counter. "Zoe has . . . a lot of opinions about food. She runs some sort of food blog—I forget the name. Apparently it's pretty popular. She takes meals and snacks very seriously. A little *too* seriously sometimes, if you ask me, but . . . well, there you have it."

Lizzie already had an idea of what Zoe might be like, and she wasn't sure they'd get along at all. For starters, on some level she blamed people like Zoe—young whippersnappers with an Internet connection, an expensive camera, and a moderate interest in food—for torpedoing her TV career. Lizzie knew that wasn't entirely true or fair, but she couldn't help but feel that the proliferation of beautiful and free content on the Web—content that rivaled her own in sensibility and style—helped tip the scales against her. Why should the Food Network pay her to tell twenty-year-olds how to eat healthily when someone who was *actually* twenty was happy to do so online for free?

Aside from a personal grudge, Lizzie was also wary of Zoe's obsession with so-called clean eating. Lizzie liked to eat healthily, but the main reason she'd started *Healthy U* was because she saw an opportunity, not because she was a health food zealot. These days, people seemed to take themselves so seriously, as if eating an Oreo cookie were tantamount to shooting heroin. She worried what it would be like to subject herself to that mentality for an entire summer.

"Anyway!" Kathryn chimed, cutting through Lizzie's thoughts. "What about your experience with large parties? Can you cater for large groups?"

"Definitely." This wasn't so much a lie as it was an aspirational truth. Technically, Lizzie had never cooked for a group larger than twenty, but she felt confident she could handle something bigger.

"Oh, good, good—we love throwing a good party! It's sort of what we're known for. Well, among other things."

Lizzie wasn't exactly sure what those other things were, other than making a lot of money, but before she could ask more about their celebrated fetes Katherine jumped in.

"There's so much more to discuss, but first why don't you start on the sample meal? We can talk about everything else while you're cooking."

Lizzie reached for her bags and hopped off the stool, feeling Kathryn's eyes on her as she walked to the other side of the counter.

"I was so relieved when Linda passed along your name. Our chef quit unexpectedly, and by the time he did, all of the good people we knew were already booked for the summer."

"I'm glad she was able to connect us."

She looked Lizzie up and down as Lizzie pulled a filet of salmon and a bunch of leeks from her bag. "So how does a former Food Network star end up here? I mean, *something* must have gone wrong. This couldn't have been part of the plan, right?"

It was the question Lizzie dreaded most, and the one for which she didn't have a good answer, or at least an answer a potential employer might receive in a positive light.

I got old.

I wasn't cool anymore.

People got bored.

But mostly . . . I screwed up.

None of those answers would do. So instead, she replied with her standard, vague response.

"It's a changing industry," she said.

"I read about that somewhere. In the *Times*? Or maybe it was *InStyle*. No, that doesn't seem right. *Vogue* maybe? I can never remember where I've read things these days, especially if it was online. Someone sends me a link, and I click on it, but most of the time, I'm more interested in the article or pictures than what site I'm visiting. That isn't always true, of course, but in this case I guess it is, although—" Kathryn cut herself off as she glanced at the leeks. "Oh! Leeks! I love leeks. Such a random vegetable to love, I know, but I've had a thing for zucchini leek soup ever since I tried it at Canyon Ranch a few years back. What are you planning to do with those?"

Lizzie felt her confidence return, relieved they'd moved on from a topic she didn't want to discuss and moment in her life she didn't want to relive. She couldn't guarantee it wouldn't come up again. It almost always did. All she could do was hope that the next time Kathryn asked she'd already have the job and she could deflect her again or, at the very least, come up with an answer that wouldn't get her fired.

CHAPTER 5

Linda,

Thank you, thank you, THANK YOU!!! Your boss may be a nut, but he is also a savior. Lizzie starts work next weekend (how is it Memorial Day already?!), and she's thrilled. Or maybe that's just me. She's relieved, at any rate. Whether that's because she won't have to live at home with me all summer or because she'll have a job working for a multimillionaire, I'm not sure. Probably a little of both. I've told her she has to snap as many photos as possible of that house (without being rude or seeming nosy, obviously, but I mean, come on— 14,000 square feet??? I need to see this!).

Anyway, the talk Gary took me to was really interesting! I had no idea how much harm I've probably been doing to my own body. The shampoo I've been buying, foods I've been eating, the stuff I've been using to clean the house . . . It's all so toxic and terrible! Gary said he'd come by this week and help me clean out my refrigerator and pantry (and my medicine cabinet too, but I'm thinking one step at a time—I'm not ready for him to see how many wrinkle creams I own . . . hahaha). He's already recommended a few supplements I should start taking, so once we've cleared out all the bad stuff in my kitchen, we'll probably take a trip to the grocery store and stock up on all the healthy things I *should* be eating. I know—a date at the grocery store? Is this dating in the 21st century? Or just dating at 61? (Can we pretend it's the former?)

Oh, and as for the lunch offer—I'd love to, but I have my mammogram that day (bleh), so I can't make it downtown. Maybe the following week? Let me know what works for you.

xxoo

S

CHAPTER 6

Lizzie arrived in Avalon the Friday before Memorial Day, at nearly four o'clock in the afternoon. A drive that was meant to take only two hours had taken five, and Lizzie was sure she'd left her sanity somewhere on the Garden State Parkway. She'd known the holiday traffic would be bad and that the bad traffic might sour her mood, but she hadn't expected to be borderline psychotic by the end of the journey. Kathryn hadn't specified an arrival time—technically, Lizzie didn't begin working for them until tomorrow, and the Silvesters' annual Memorial Day barbecue wasn't until Sunday— but Lizzie had hoped to arrive by one, and so aside from having been trapped in a car for five hours, she now felt as if she were late. Late, stiff, and flustered: not how she'd hoped to start a new job.

She tried to bring her anxiety under control as she drove along Avalon Boulevard and turned onto Dune Drive, putting herself in the heart of Avalon's business district. *You're here,* she told herself. *You're here, and you have a job, and you will be able to pay your bills. That's all that matters.*

Was it really all that mattered? No, she supposed it wasn't. But as Kathryn had outlined it, the job seemed manageable, ideal even—a position from Memorial Day until Labor Day, with one day off per week, that would mostly involve cooking for Kathryn and her friends. Her husband, Jim, would come Friday and stay for the weekend, but during the week he would be back in Philadelphia, and so most of the time Kathryn would have the run of the house. In mid-June Zoe would arrive, having just returned from Nice, but Lizzie wasn't sure how long Zoe would be staying or how many meals she typically ate with her family. Given Kathryn's interview questions, Lizzie assumed Zoe would partake in at least some of the meals, but Kathryn had been uncharacteristically light on those particular details once she offered the job. She'd been even lighter on details when it came to Nate, Jim's son from his first marriage, who apparently planned to visit for a week in July.

Lizzie slowed the car as a family of four scurried across the street, chairs and umbrellas in tow as they made their way back from the beach. Lizzie had always loved the Jersey Shore's relaxed vibe. She and her family had stayed in different towns over the years—Ocean City, Cape May, Sea Isle—all with different personalities but with the uniting characteristic that, at least during the daytime, there was no dress code or timetable or requirements of any kind. People rolled out of bed when they wanted, threw on a bathing suit, cover-up, and flip-flops, and made their way to the beach.

Lizzie stopped at the red light across from Uncle Bill's Pancake House, a shore institution with outposts dotting the southern Jersey coast. When she was eight, her parents had rented a small house in Ocean City with her uncle, who happened to be named Bill, and his wife and three kids. The entire crew would pile into Uncle Bill's at breakfast time and fill up on silver dollar pancakes and pork roll. Lizzie's uncle would ask the kids how they liked "his restaurant" and to let him know if they had any complaints because he would get back in the kitchen and handle it.

But Lizzie never had any complaints because the pancakes were impossibly fluffy and tender and her parents let her cover them in more syrup than they ever did at home. One morning, she just kept pouring and pouring, her eyes trained on her mom and dad, who were staring in opposite directions and didn't seem to notice. When Lizzie finally put the syrup down and goaded them into looking, her dad frowned and her mom sighed, but neither of them told her off in the way she'd expected.

"This vacation *rules!*" she'd said as she shoveled the sopping, sticky pancakes into her mouth. She didn't realize her parents' permissiveness stemmed from the dissolution of their marriage and a correlated willingness to do anything to keep Lizzie happy. When they sat Lizzie down once they returned home and told her they were getting divorced, a part of Lizzie wondered if only she hadn't used *so* much syrup maybe they would have stayed together. She knew now, of course, that had nothing to do with it, but seeing the Uncle Bill's logo brought back a torrent of memories she'd happily packed away.

The light turned green, and Lizzie carried on along Dune Drive, the cafés and sandwich shops giving way to one beautiful house after the next. Her recollection of Avalon was hazy—she'd gone once with her parents two years before their divorce and once with her mom and Aunt Linda a year after—but Lizzie somehow remembered the houses being more subdued. She'd heard that many of the quaint beach cottages had been replaced by large, expensive homes, but by the looks of it "many" meant "most." As she drove along, she spotted the occasional one-story cottage, but those homes looked out of place and a little shabby compared to the sparkling three-story manses surrounding them. Given how few of the older, smaller homes remained, Lizzie knew it was only a matter of time before they'd all be sold off, torn down, and replaced with buildings three times their size.

She glanced up as she passed the water tower just before 39th Street: AVALON . . . COOLER BY A MILE. She rolled down the window and let the sea air fill the car. She wasn't a beach person per se (she burned easily and didn't really like swimming in the ocean), but she loved the smell of the shore. The air was thick and salty. It had texture. New York air had texture, too, but it was unpleasant and sticky and often smelled of sewage. Here she could stick out her tongue and almost taste the freshness of the ocean.

Within a few blocks, the side streets on Lizzie's left gave way to a thicket of Japanese black pine, bayberry, and white cedar trees. Every few blocks, there would be a break in the dense vegetation, where a walking path would lead to the beach. But otherwise, this particular area along the coast was devoid of houses or shops and was instead overrun by nature.

Lizzie knew these must be the high dunes she'd read about when she Googled the Silvesters and their beachfront mansion. Avalon's high dunes were a lush two-mile stretch of maritime forests and grasslands that soared thirty to fifty feet above sea level, providing a protective buffer between the town and the sea. A few years back, the Silvesters bought a parcel of land on this formerly undeveloped area and won approval to build a fourteen-thousand-square-foot home, which set off a firestorm among locals and long-time Avalon enthusiasts. They worried the Silvesters were ruining the character of the beach town they'd known and loved and were putting other residents at risk by compromising the dunes' protective nature. But ultimately the detractors lost and the Silvesters won, and soon other McMansions followed on the last untouched stretch of Avalon's coast.

"You will reach your destination in two hundred yards," the GPS alerted her.

Lizzie narrowed her eyes as she tried to read the house numbers as she crossed 51st Street. All of the homes built on the high dunes were hidden away, ensconced by trees and shrubs, as if people were trying to keep a secret that they'd built where they shouldn't. When the GPS announced that she'd reached her destination, Lizzie turned into a driveway lined with brick red pavers and stopped when she reached a closed wrought-iron gate.

She gasped. The house . . . it couldn't even be called a house. It was a palace. A sand castle brought to life. The sprawling edifice was even the color of sand, a muted buttery yellow that was offset by rust-colored shutters and windows wreathed in bright white paint. She counted three porches visible from the front (and was that a fourth?), each covered by a roof held up by thick white columns. If someone had told her it was a hotel, she would have nodded and said, *Sure,* and assumed she wouldn't be able to afford a room.

It was just so . . . big. Maybe a hair smaller than their Gladwyne home, but that was their primary residence. This was a second home—a third, actually, if she was counting the apartment in New York she'd read about. Did it really need to be so big? On the one hand, the Silvesters had the money and the necessary parties had approved the building plans, so why not? The Silvesters had the right to build whatever house they wanted to build. But knowing the particulars of their family arrangement—that Jim was only there on weekends, that they had only one daughter, that the only time they really used the house was for three months in the summer—Lizzie couldn't quite understand why they needed so much space. Did the gardeners and other staff live there too? Or did the Silvesters dislike one another so much that they needed to put thousands of square feet between them? And if the latter was the case . . . what had Lizzie gotten herself into?

She pressed the buzzer on the call box, and a woman's voice answered, similar in accent but different in tone to that of the housekeeper Lizzie had met in Gladwyne.

"Hi, it's Lizzie Glass," Lizzie announced into the receiver. "Sorry I'm late—traffic was terrible."

"Not a problem," the woman replied. "Park your car in the lot on the left, and I'll come out to meet you."

The lot? Lizzie shook her head in disbelief. She'd never seen a house with its own parking lot before. The gates opened, and Lizzie pulled the car up the broad, paved driveway. It was her mom's car—a well-maintained Honda Accord that she'd been kind enough to lend—and although Lizzie was grateful, she was suddenly conscious of its mediocrity when compared to the Silvesters' lavish estate. Ahead of her, she saw a small fountain surrounded by black-eyed Susans, hot-pink impatiens, and daylilies. To her left was a flat, rectangular area that looked as if it could accommodate a dozen or so cars. She parked in the far corner, next to a crepe myrtle.

She had popped the trunk and stepped out of the car when she saw a middle-aged woman with tan skin and cropped auburn hair walking toward her. She was dressed in white from head to toe: polo shirt, belt, pants, sneakers.

"Hi," the woman said, smiling as she extended her hand toward Lizzie. "I'm Renata. Welcome."

Lizzie shook her hand. "Thank you. Sorry again about the delay."

"What delay? You are perfectly on time. Traffic is always terrible, especially Memorial Day weekend." Her eyes landed on the contents of Lizzie's trunk. "I'll get someone to help with your things, yes?"

"Oh, that's okay—it's only a few bags."

Renata clicked her tongue. "Please. It's my job to make sure everything is taken care of. Come, I'll show you inside and help you get settled."

She grabbed one of Lizzie's bags, and Lizzie took another and followed Renata toward the house.

"How long have you worked for the Silvesters?" Lizzie asked as they passed the water feature. It was even more beautiful up close, with sheets of water cascading down two circular stone discs.

"Ten years," she said. "First in their old house, then in this one."

"Old house?"

"The one they built before this one. It was smaller."

I'm pretty sure Independence Hall is smaller, Lizzie thought.

Renata led Lizzie toward the front steps, a steep curved staircase made of stone that climbed so high Lizzie needed to tilt her head back to see the front door. Did the Silvesters really climb these steps every day? It seemed like a punishing journey to make even once, much less multiple times a day. Maybe that's how they kept the riffraff out. If someone managed to break through the front gate with the intention of robbing the place, he'd take one look at those steps and say, *Fuck it. I'd have an easier time climbing Everest.*

Before they reached the steps, Renata veered to the right and approached a keypad, into which she punched a code that opened a disguised garage door.

Lizzie sighed in relief. "For a second, I thought we were going to have to climb those stairs."

Renata smiled. "No, we come in and out through the garage. The front stairway is for guests."

Lizzie nodded as if this made total sense, even though it struck her as ridiculous. What kind of dinner invitation was that? *Please, join us, but first—behold!—the Feats of Strength.* Did they make their guests walk on hot coals through the foyer? Were dinner parties like episodes of *Survivor*?

Renata led Lizzie through the garage door and into a small reception area that, in a normal house, might be considered a mudroom but here looked like a waiting area to meet a member of the royal family. Sandy-beige marble covered the floors from end to end, glistening in the light of the oval wrought-iron chandelier hanging from the ceiling. A series of wrought-iron hooks dotted the walls, serving as resting places for a variety of beach-related accoutrements: a white metal beach bucket with a rope handle, a brass shovel, a wicker beach hat. Like many of the objects in the Silvesters' Gladwyne kitchen, these items seemed more ornamental than functional, and if Lizzie had to guess, neither the bucket nor the shovel had ever made it to the beach. Kathryn didn't seem like the type of woman who built sand castles, unless it was one she could live in.

"The laundry room is back there," Renata said, pointing to the closed door at the end of the room. "I wash on Mondays and Thursdays, and whenever Mr. and Mrs. Silvester ask. If you need something washed on another day, I will try my best, but it may need to wait."

"Don't worry about me—I can do my own laundry."

Renata looked surprised. "Oh. Well, that's fine too, I guess. I'll need to show you how the machines work."

Lizzie wondered if she looked like the kind of person who didn't know how to operate a washer and dryer. She'd been doing laundry since high school, when she'd come back from a party smelling like smoke and booze and would change her clothes in the car and throw the smelly ones in the washer as soon as she got inside. She was never the one doing the smoking or drinking, but somehow the odors from other people's cigarettes, pot, and alcohol wove themselves into the fabric of her clothing, and she knew her mom would have a meltdown if she suspected Lizzie had driven while drunk or high.

"Drunk driving kills," her mom would repeat again and again, often apropos of nothing while they were doing something random, like cleaning out Lizzie's closet. "It's reckless and irresponsible. You could die."

Losing Lizzie was her mom's greatest fear, and not one Lizzie took lightly. *News flash: Dying isn't on my To Do list,* Lizzie always wanted to say—and did once when her mom laid out the dangers of drunk driving for what felt like the five thousandth time. Her mother blanched, and in the tearful tirade that followed, Lizzie realized she should have kept her mouth shut and nodded like she always did. She should have known that after losing Ryan as a baby, her mom wouldn't find much humor in the death of a child.

Renata led Lizzie down a long hallway lined with closed doors. It looked like maids' quarters, which, if Lizzie had to guess, was exactly what it was. They stopped when they reached the last doorway on the right.

"This will be your room," Renata said as she rested her hand on the knob. She twisted it and led Lizzie inside. The floors, like the rest of the house Lizzie had seen so far, were covered by beige marble tiles, on top of which sat a twin bed, a nightstand, and a dresser. The furniture was all very simple—dark walnut, simple brass handles and knobs—and the curtains and bedspread were an understated cream linen. The walls were white and mostly bare, with the exception of two small paintings, both beach scenes wreathed by distressed gold frames.

"Who sleeps in the other rooms on this hall?" Lizzie asked.

"Me. And when the Silvesters have parties or visitors, the support staff sleep down here as well."

"Support staff?"

"Maids, waiters—that kind of thing. We will be fully staffed for the party this weekend."

"Speaking of . . ." Lizzie had almost forgotten about the party. She was supposed to sit down with Kathryn at some point today to finalize the menu. "Is Kathryn upstairs?"

Renata shook her head. "She's at the beach with Jim. He arrived late this morning."

By helicopter? Lizzie wondered. Because otherwise, she couldn't fathom how he had arrived so early. Frankly, given the size of the house, she wouldn't be surprised to learn there was a helipad on the roof.

"Okay. I just want to talk to her about Sunday's barbecue. She hadn't decided on the food last time we talked."

"She'll be back soon. They've been down there awhile. And she will want to discuss tonight's dinner anyway." Renata glanced quickly over her shoulder. "Ah, here comes Manuel with your bags."

A stocky man scooted past Renata into the room, Lizzie's luggage slung over every free limb and body part. Had he really managed it all in one trip? Lizzie had never seen anything like it. He looked like a circus performer. She half-expected him to leap in the air and land on a beach ball to raucous applause.

He extracted himself from the assortment of duffels and totes and stashed them in the far corner. He then gave both Renata and Lizzie a quick nod and left without uttering a word.

"*Gracias,*" Renata called after him. She clasped her hands together. "I have to talk to the gardener about the hydrangea by the front steps, so unless you have any questions for me . . ."

Only about a million, Lizzie thought. "None that I can think of right now. I'm sure I'll have plenty once I talk to Kathryn."

"Great. I will leave you to settle in, then. If you need me for any reason, just press this button and page me." She pointed to an intercom to the left of the door. "In the meantime . . . make yourself at home."

Renata turned and left, and moments later Lizzie heard an eruption of rapid-fire Spanish at the end of the hall, none of which she could understand. She took a deep breath and reached for one of her suitcases, determined to make the room feel like her own, even though, at the moment, she felt farther from home than ever.

CHAPTER 7

"Lizzie—welcome!"

Lizzie jumped up from the bed as Kathryn appeared in her doorway, dressed in a black gauzy cover-up and a huge floppy black beach hat. Kathryn somehow already looked tan, which made the blond hair framing her face and peeking from beneath the hat look even more sparkly. Lizzie had started unpacking her things but at some point decided to test out the mattress and pillow, and apparently that test had morphed into a nap of indeterminate length.

"Sorry, I must have fallen asleep. That drive took it out of me."

"It's the absolute worst. That's why Jim always books a chopper for holiday weekends. There's no other way."

There was another way, and that way was driving, which Lizzie had spent the bulk of her day doing. But more to the point, Jim *had* taken a helicopter. Lizzie felt both vindicated and amazed. Was she also right about the helipad on the roof? She didn't have the nerve to ask.

"So, dinner," Kathryn continued, her hand clasped around a pair of Jackie O–style sunglasses. "I'm thinking scallops."

"Scallops. Right. Okay." Lizzie tried to bring her mind into focus. She was still groggy and was having trouble processing her whereabouts, much less a dinner menu. "Where do you tend to buy them around here? I haven't had a chance to scope out the town yet."

"I think our cook last year used Avalon Seafood. Or maybe Sylvester's? No relation, by the way." She smiled. "I don't know. Ask Renata. She'll know. She knows everything about everything when it comes to keeping this house afloat."

"Okay. Any preference on what to serve with the scallops?"

"Jim will want corn, but I shouldn't have it because of the Paleo thing. It's a little early for corn anyway. Tomatoes won't be in yet, but they may still have decent asparagus. Or maybe some peas or spinach—whatever looks good. Again, ask Renata where to go. She'll know."

"And what about the barbecue Sunday?"

"Ah, right." She tapped her sunglasses against her lips, which looked smooth and plump in a way that made Lizzie question their authenticity. "I like the idea of grilled chicken—only could you leave out the garlic? Jim can't do garlic. He'll want potato salad for sure. Make the French kind, though. No mayonnaise. I'd love some grilled shrimp, too. Jim can take or leave shrimp, so you can go crazy with the garlic on those. And then just do a bunch of veggie salads—green beans, asparagus, beets. You get the idea. I shouldn't have dairy because of my diet, but not everyone has gone Paleo—at least not yet!"

The suggestions came out at rapid speed, and Lizzie started making mental lists before she forgot everything Kathryn had said.

"And for dessert? What did you think about mini strawberry shortcakes?"

"Perfect. I mean, I'll only have the berries, but other people will love them, and they will look fabulous. And that's really the point, isn't it?"

Lizzie wasn't sure if Kathryn was referring to other people loving them or the shortcakes looking fabulous, so she just nodded politely.

Kathryn clapped her hands. "Right. So that's that. Oh, and for tomorrow—Jim and I tend to get up early and go for a long walk, and when we get back we'll have breakfast. My juice shipment came in this morning, so I'm set, but Jim will want bagels and cream cheese and fruit, so just make sure the refrigerator is stocked. A nice salad for lunch should do it. And then we're going out for dinner, so you can have the evening to prepare for Sunday."

"Got it." Lizzie wished she had a pen and paper, but she was pretty sure she hadn't missed anything. Kathryn's requests weren't particularly obscure or strange. Compared to some of the clients Lizzie had worked for in New York, Kathryn was relatively easygoing and tame. When it came to conversing with Kathryn, it was more an issue of volume than content.

Kathryn glanced at her watch. "I should let you get to it. But like I said, any questions, ask Renata. And in the meantime, I hope you're settling in okay."

"I am. Your house is really lovely."

"Thanks." She rested her hand on the door frame and took a deep breath as she scanned Lizzie's room. "If you even knew half the drama that went into building it . . . Nightmare."

Lizzie wondered if Kathryn truly didn't know that her shore drama had been splashed across the pages of the *Philadelphia Inquirer* and *Philadelphia* magazine, along with numerous local shore papers, or if she was saying this merely for effect. Lizzie also didn't know whether this was a cue for her to ask for details so that Kathryn could tell the full tale in all its messy, unabridged glory. Lizzie decided mute acknowledgment and sympathy was the best way to avoid a thirty-minute story time.

"Anyway, I'll stop holding you up. I always do this . . . go on and on with the staff and then wonder why nothing gets done. Jim always tells me, if I weren't such a talker . . . But it just gets lonely in this big house, and you're all here, and there are so many details to discuss to make sure everything is the way he likes it." She shook her head. "Here I go again! I'm leaving now. For real. We can talk later! Or not. If I'm ever keeping you, just tell me, *Kathryn, I have work to do.* I won't be offended. Or if I am, remind me of this conversation. All right? Okay. I'm going. For real this time!"

She backed out of the doorway and scampered down the hall, and Lizzie wondered if she was in for a summer of Kathryn's endless chatter and, if so, whether and how she would survive.

* * *

Before Lizzie left to do her shopping, she met Renata at the bottom of the stairway at the far end of the hall. She noticed the rooms on the front side of the house had windows that looked on to the driveway or, in one case, the pool equipment, whereas the rooms like hers that technically faced the ocean had no windows or views at all. She hadn't seen more than the bottom floor, but she guessed that the steep slope of the dunes accounted for her room's cave-like quality. Her room was probably built into the sand, whereas the room directly above her was probably level with the ground.

"So where am I going?" Lizzie asked. It was already six o'clock and the Silvesters wanted to eat at eight, so Lizzie needed to hustle if she had any hope of serving dinner on time.

"Avalon Seafood. Twenty-ninth and Ocean Drive. There's a small market next door that sells vegetables and other odds and ends you can use to get started."

Lizzie tried to do the math in her head. "That's . . . what, twenty blocks or so from here? Could I walk?"

"Not if you want to make it back before the sun goes down. It would take you a half hour each way. You should drive." She glanced at her watch. "Do you want to take a quick look at the kitchen before you leave?"

"That would be great."

She followed Renata up the stairs, her knife bag and purse slung over her shoulder. She was dying to see what the whole house looked like, but she knew they wouldn't have time today to tour a house bigger than Monticello. She would need days to explore the Silvesters' palace, or whatever parts of it she was allowed to trespass in, but in the meantime she was content to size up the room where she'd be spending the bulk of her time.

They reached the top of the stairway, which emptied into a two-story great room unlike anything Lizzie had ever seen. The room was surrounded by floor-to-ceiling windows, providing unobstructed views of the ocean as it crashed into the shore. Lizzie noticed that one of the windows was actually a disguised door, which led to a patio outfitted with a pool, lounge chairs, cabanas, and a large dining table. Inside, the room featured a large glass coffee table surrounded by two couches, a love seat, and two armchairs, all covered by the same blue-and-white Ikat upholstery.

"Wow," Lizzie said. She looked at Renata, who simply nodded, as if to say, *Yes. Wow.*

The room continued to her right, where there was a long glass dining table surrounded by—Lizzie counted them—twenty chairs, each with a high back made of woven reeds. A large metal bowl sat in the middle of the table, filled with sand dollars, starfish, shells, and sea glass. Running parallel to the table sat a long marble island, longer than any island Lizzie had ever encountered, outfitted with a double sink, a huge metal knife block, and a six-burner Viking range. The way the room was arranged, as one vast open space, cooking here would be like a performance, where the kitchen island was the stage and the dining and living rooms were the VIP seats.

"The kitchen," Renata announced, as if there were any question.

Beyond the island, Lizzie counted two double ovens, two oversize refrigerators, a wok station, a second sink, two dishwashers, and too many cabinets to count. Above the second sink, Lizzie noticed a bookshelf with a few stacks of books, all carefully arranged, and a smattering of cooking tools and molds, all of which looked brand-new. As she got closer, she noticed the books were actually cookbooks, though none looked used. She slowed her step as she approached the shelf and scanned the titles. They were either classics such as *The Art of French Cooking* or weighty nouveau tomes such as *Modernist Cuisine.*

"Martha Stewart's *Entertaining,*" Lizzie said, running her finger down the spine. "The book that made her."

"It's Kathryn's favorite," Renata said.

"*Kathryn's?*" Lizzie tried not to sound shocked, but Kathryn hadn't indicated even the slightest interest in cooking.

"She won it at an auction. It's a signed first edition."

"Wow. Does she ever cook from it?"

"Oh, no, no, no. It's really just for display."

So, it seemed, was everything in the kitchen, Lizzie thought. Nothing looked used. It was all so clean.

Renata gestured toward the door beside the bookshelf, and they walked through together into a room with yet another island, sink, stove, refrigerator, and dishwasher.

"You can use this area for prep," Renata said.

Lizzie nodded. This was the backstage area, where she'd do all the grunt work before the main event. The Silvesters and their guests wanted to see a chef in action, but they didn't want to see the unpleasant tasks, like peeling shrimp or spatchcocking a chicken. They wanted the prettied-up performance of what they thought a chef's job entailed, rather than the reality of what was involved.

"This is where we keep groceries." Renata pointed to the cupboards lining the walls. "Baking ingredients here. Canned goods there. Onions and garlic there. Pasta and grains here."

She walked to the end of the row of cabinets and pointed to the one at the very end. "This one is for Zoe's things."

"She has her own cupboard?"

"She is very particular about what she eats."

"So Kathryn says."

"I wouldn't mess with her food, if I were you. Last year's chef used a bit of her cider vinegar, and it didn't end well."

"Got it. Her stuff is off-limits."

Renata nodded approvingly and clapped her hands together. "Right. Ready to shop?"

Lizzie slid her knife bag onto the counter, clasped her purse in her hand, and followed Renata out of the room, giving Zoe's cupboard one last look and wondering what inside could be so precious.

CHAPTER 8

The scallops were perfect: huge, sugary sweet, and bathed in nutty brown butter. Lizzie put the finishing touches on the plates—an extra asparagus spear here, a dash of flaky salt there—and brought them to the table.

When she'd returned from the market, Kathryn was in the shower and Jim had yet to make an appearance, so Lizzie had begun prepping and cooking in the butler's pantry. But now, as she entered the kitchen, she saw the two of them sitting across from each other at the end of the dining table. It looked odd, two people seated at a table for twenty, as if he were Louis XVI and she were Marie Antoinette. Lizzie half-expected to stumble into Kathryn's ladies-in-waiting.

"Ah—perfect timing!" Kathryn chimed as she laid her eyes on Lizzie.

Jim peered over his shoulder. He looked just as he did in the CC Media headshot Lizzie had seen in articles and on the company Web site: a stocky build with broad shoulders, a wide nose, and a thick crown of gray hair. He had a ruddy complexion, which looked pinker in the light of the sunset shining through their windows, and was dressed in a salmon polo shirt, which Lizzie thought was an unfortunate color choice, given his skin tone.

"Jim, this is Lizzie," Kathryn said as Lizzie laid the plates in front of them.

"Pleasure," he said, reaching out to shake Lizzie's hand. He glanced down at his plate. "Looks great. Let's eat."

His tone was abrupt—not rude but unadorned. Efficient. Lizzie sensed he was the kind of man who fielded many questions a day and, short on time, conveyed the answers in as few words as possible. His linguistic economy stood in sharp contrast to his wife, who more than made up for his apparent disinterest in chitchat.

Lizzie shuffled back to the kitchen and began tidying her workstation, catching the odd bit of conversation between Kathryn and Jim. From what she gathered, it wasn't so much a conversation as it was Kathryn jabbering on for several minutes and eventually catching her breath, at which point Jim would respond with a sentence or two, and then Kathryn's deluge of speech would resume. Lizzie wondered if this is what it would be like most nights for the next three months, the two of them sitting at an enormous table while Kathryn prattled on for an hour. Then she remembered that, with the exception of a week in July, Jim would only be visiting on weekends. Would Lizzie be the one listening to Kathryn's monologue all week long? *Oh, God.* Lizzie's ears went numb just thinking about it.

When she went to collect the plates, she noticed Kathryn had left a few scraps, but Jim hadn't left a single bite.

"There's a little more of everything in the back," Lizzie offered. "I also picked up a pie."

"Oh, no pie for me," Kathryn said, even though Lizzie had been speaking to Jim. "Unless it's Paleo, which I'm guessing it isn't. It isn't easy to find Paleo desserts."

"Because they taste like dirt," Jim said.

"They don't taste like *dirt*. Some are actually delicious! Remember those 'noatmeal' cookies I found? They were grain-free, dairy-free, and refined-sugar-free but tasted just like real oatmeal cookies!"

"No, they didn't."

Kathryn clicked her tongue. "Oh, stop being such a negative nelly. They were delicious."

Lizzie was inclined to side with Jim on this one, even though she'd never tried the so-called noatmeal cookies. The few Paleo desserts she'd eaten had been texturally strange and digestively problematic. She'd never understood why people voluntarily on restrictive diets created recipes to imitate the allegedly evil foods they'd given up. If you truly believed it was healthier to eat like a caveman, then you shouldn't have a problem giving up muffins and cookies. Lizzie highly doubted her prehistoric ancestors sat around their cave fires making grain-free s'mores.

"Anyway," Kathryn continued, as she always seemed to do, "as I said, none for me, but Jim loves pie, don't you, sweetheart? Blueberry is his favorite, tied with cherry. And he loves peach too, although I hear it can be hard to find good peaches these days. They can be so mealy. No flavor at all. He once had a slice of bourbon peach pie—in Sea Island, *Georgia,* of all places!—and said all he could taste was the bourbon, which I figured for Jim would be a good thing, but he said if he wanted bourbon, he'd drink it in a glass, thanks!"

It went on and on. Lizzie found it odd how Kathryn spoke for Jim, as if he were in the other room and not five feet away. Odder still was the fact that Jim just sat there while Kathryn rambled on. Lizzie conceded that pie wasn't exactly a riveting topic for the average corporate executive, but didn't he want to tell his own stories, rather than have Kathryn tell them for him? Perhaps he didn't have a choice. Or perhaps, after many years of marriage, his only means of coping with her verbal diarrhea was to go temporarily deaf and so he actually had no idea what she was saying.

"It's strawberry rhubarb," Lizzie said.

"You like that, don't you, honey? Isn't that the kind you had on that trip to Hilton Head? Or was it Pinehurst? I can't keep track. Jim is a golfer. Always jetting off to a different course. And then there's little old me, the golf widow. I don't mind, although I joked with Jim that if he keeps disappearing on golf trips I'll have to take up the sport myself so that I can join him!"

Lizzie couldn't tell if she saw pure terror in Jim's face at this suggestion or if she was just imagining it. From what very little she'd seen, Jim and Kathryn had a good marriage—she doted on him, and he could actually tolerate her endless chatter, which probably set him apart from 99.9 percent of men in the universe—but

Lizzie suspected golf was his sanctuary, a few hours of preserved quiet. For Kathryn to intrude would defeat the entire purpose.

Jim jumped in before Kathryn could continue with some story she'd begun about private jets. "A small slice," he said.

Lizzie nodded and collected their plates, thankful for Jim's brevity. How would she survive on the nights he wasn't here? She was beginning to dread the prospect.

She cut Jim a piece of pie, the juicy ruby-colored fruit spilling onto the plate. The perfume of sweet, ripe strawberries filled the air. Lizzie took a deep breath. She would definitely be cutting a piece for herself later.

She grabbed a clean fork from the drawer and carried the dessert into the dining room, where Kathryn and Jim were now speaking in hushed tones.

"*Again?*" Jim said. He sounded exasperated. "I thought you talked to her."

"I did," Kathryn said in a loud whisper. "But you know how she is. It was only a few thousand dollars."

"Only? We talked about this."

"I know, but remember what Dr. Stephens said. When Zoe gets like this—" She stopped abruptly as Lizzie approached the table. "Oh, Jim, would you look at that pie!"

He glanced casually at the plate as Lizzie placed it in front of him. "Don't change the subject," he said.

Kathryn forced a smile. "What subject? We're eating dinner. We can talk about all this later."

Jim sighed as Kathryn began telling him about the Memorial Day barbecue, and Lizzie headed back to the kitchen, glad to escape a room whose air had become tense, sour, and, unless Lizzie was imagining it, tinged with a hint of danger.

CHAPTER 9

The Memorial Day barbecue began Sunday at four o'clock, and by the time the first guests arrived Lizzie was already sweating through her chef's coat. Every burner on the stove in the butler's pantry was blazing, elevating the temperature in the room by at least ten degrees, and Lizzie could feel beads of sweat at the base of her neck cutting loose and trickling down her back. She hoped the Silvesters didn't expect her to spend much time with guests, because she was pretty sure she looked and smelled like a wild animal.

Renata shuttled between the butler's pantry and living area, directing an army of servers who had appeared that morning, as if by magic. There were at least a dozen of them, all dressed in pressed white pants and white polo shirts, and they all seemed to know where to go and what to do, even though Lizzie had never seen them before.

"*Rellenar el guacamole, por favor,*" Renata said to one of them, pointing to the refrigerator, where Lizzie had stashed the extra guacamole and salsa. She surveyed Lizzie's workstation. "How are you doing?"

"Good," Lizzie said as she chopped a bunch of chives to use as garnish. She wiped the sweat off her brow with the back of her forearm. "Is the grill ready?"

"Preheating. Manuel turned it on about ten minutes ago."

"Great. Thanks."

Renata nodded at one of the servers, who'd come in with a tray of empty glasses, directing her toward the sink, where a man with a dishcloth stood at the ready. In addition to the servers, the Silvesters had hired a dishwasher and two prep cooks, who were there to help Lizzie get the food on the buffet in a timely and presentable fashion.

Lizzie wasn't used to having so much help or, frankly, cooking for such a large group. In New York, her personal chef work involved preparing weekly meals for clients and leaving the food in their refrigerators, all of which was done on her own. And even when she'd done promotional events as a Food Network personality, she'd really only had help on the entertainment side—producers and assistants who were there to make sure Lizzie was effectively marketing her brand. She'd catered the occasional dinner party, often an "Evening with a Food Network Star" that a wealthy lawyer or banker had won at a charity auction. But she'd never run the equivalent of a catering operation. It was a little overwhelming.

Lizzie slipped out the side door to the grilling station, which was located at the side of the house, just before the dunes dropped precipitously toward the driveway. The station was perfectly positioned so that the smoky aroma could waft toward the pool and porch without subjecting the Silvesters or their guests to the heat and mess of the flames. The area featured not one but three gas grills, along with four simmering stations, a large prep counter, and a wood-fired pizza oven. Lizzie couldn't wait to experiment with the pizza oven—not just to make pizza but for roasting chicken and meat and vegetables—but she figured her first official party wasn't the time to screw around with fire. Given her luck, she'd burn the whole place to the ground.

One of the prep cooks brought out the tray of marinating chicken, and Lizzie quickly divided it among two of the three grills. She'd use the third for the shrimp. The meat sizzled as it hit the hot grates, the smell of charred skin mixing with the heady marinade of lemon and rosemary. Smoke poured out from the grill, dousing Lizzie in its scent, her already damp chef's coat now sopping.

She shuffled down the line of grills, the smoke pricking her eyes until they filled with tears. Before her parents divorced, her dad was the one who did all the grilling in their house, usually with a bottle of Rolling Rock in his hand while he flipped the steaks or burgers with the other. Once he'd moved out, Lizzie's mom took up the mantle, or at least tried. The truth was, neither Lizzie nor her mother liked cooking over open flames all that much. They both called themselves feminists and didn't want to admit that, deep down, they considered grilling a man's job. Lizzie would never say it out loud, and every time the thought danced across her consciousness she felt embarrassed and guilty (*So old-fashioned! So unprogressive!*), but it didn't change the fact that she'd rather leave the grilling to the menfolk.

Nevertheless, here she was, cooking with fire. Because, of course, she *could* do it; she just preferred not to. She poked and turned the chicken until the skin was blackened and crispy and the meat was tender and juicy and then piled the breasts onto two serving platters, adding a few sprigs of rosemary and lemon slices as garnishes. She handed them off to Manuel, who passed her a plate of garlic-marinated shrimp. By the time the shrimp were the desired combination of pink and singed, she was so drenched she looked as if she'd jumped in the Silvesters' pool.

Could she jump in their pool? The thought suddenly sounded like the best idea she'd ever had. Maybe once the guests left. The prospect of a cool, refreshing swim was the only thing that would get her through the next few hours.

Once all of the dishes had made it onto the buffet on the patio, Lizzie poured herself a tall glass of lemonade and scooted back outside to have a drink and catch her breath. She'd never smoked, but she understood now more than ever why many chefs did. Her need for a break was extreme, and she could imagine the peace brought by leaning against a wall and taking a long drag of a cigarette. Given that she had no intention of starting a bad habit she'd have trouble breaking, a cold drink would have to do. Maybe next time she'd add a splash of vodka.

As she took a long sip of the cool, tart juice, she heard a familiar voice on the other side of the stone wall separating the grill station from the pool area.

"Yep, back in Philly," the voice said. "I always said I'd never move back, but the job was too good."

Lizzie froze. It couldn't be . . . What would *she* be doing here?

"Not since college," the voice continued. "I can't believe how much the city has changed. If it had been like this ten years ago, maybe I wouldn't have left."

Lizzie inched closer to the wall. It definitely sounded like her, but her presence here . . . it didn't make any sense. The Silvesters were old. Not nursing home old but *older*. Old enough to have a thirtysomething son from a first marriage. Old enough to have a daughter who recently finished college. Most of the guests Lizzie had seen at the party were their age. Kathryn appeared to be about ten to fifteen years younger than Jim, but she was still at least fifty. This wasn't a party for thirty-year-olds.

"Just for the day," the voice said. "Too much work to take off a whole weekend."

That velvety timbre . . . Was she here with her parents? That wouldn't even make sense. Last Lizzie heard, they'd moved to Florida. Not that Lizzie had been in touch enough to know this for a fact. These days, most of what she knew about any of her old friends and acquaintances was through social media: a photo on a Caribbean beach, a short video of a wedding reception, a meme about motherhood. From these snippets, Lizzie would piece together what she knew—or what she thought she knew—about people's lives. She knew these portraits were carefully curated to present people as they wanted to be seen, not necessarily how they actually were, but as she'd drifted away from more and more of her friends these simulacra were all she had.

Lizzie moved closer to the doorway leading to the patio. She didn't intend to walk through it. No one needed to see her sweat-slicked face or tangled hair. But she thought maybe she could catch a glimpse of the face attached to that voice, just to confirm it wasn't her. Lizzie didn't like to dwell on her own past, and she'd conveniently distanced herself from the unpleasant parts of it she'd rather forget. To have a figure from her past appear here, after all this time . . . no thank you.

She attempted to peer through a space between the wooden door and stone wall, but all she could see was the fringes of the Silvesters' landscaping. She rested her hand on the doorknob. If she cracked the door an inch or two, she could see who was standing close by without drawing attention to herself.

"Lizzie?"

She whipped her head around to see Renata emerging from the house.

"Kathryn is looking for you. Do you have a minute?"

"Sure." She pulled her hand from the doorknob. "Be right there."

She threw back the rest of her lemonade and, just as she turned to go back inside, she heard it.

"April Sherman," the voice said. "Nice to meet you."

Lizzie was right. It was her.

Kathryn met Lizzie in the butler's pantry. She wore a wicker hat with a broad, floppy brim and black satin sash and was dressed in black capris and a stiff black-and-white sleeveless top.

"Everything is fabulous," she said. "That chicken—Jim is in heaven! And the green bean salad. I'd ask for the recipe, but who am I kidding? Jim says I can barely make toast. Not that I would anyway these days, unless it was Paleo toast, but you get the idea. People have been raving about the potato salad, too. I am so thrilled Linda passed along your name!"

"Me too."

Kathryn clapped her hands together. "Anyway, I'll let you get back to it. I just wanted to let you know how happy we are with the food. Last year's cook . . . well, no. That's not fair. Bob was good. He was. We had no complaints about the food. It was really more of a . . . personality issue, I guess. And he and Zoe—well, don't get me *started* on all of that."

Lizzie was tempted to remind Kathryn that she hadn't gotten her started on anything. This entire pinball game of a conversation had been Kathryn's doing, and she was the one careening from one topic to the next.

"I will say this," Kathryn continued, apparently unable to stop herself. "I blame him for the predicament we were in when we hired you. All these chefs know each other, and I know—I *know*—Bob blabbed around his story to other people in the trade, and when it got back to our hire for this summer, the whole story had gotten blown out of proportion, and he quit out of fear. I tried to tell him half the story was made up and the other half had gotten completely distorted, but he was having none of it. And by then everyone had heard, or at least everyone we called, and it was just . . . ugh. Like I said, don't get me *started*."

Again Lizzie wanted to remind Kathryn that she'd spoken a mere two words since she reentered the house. But of greater concern was this alleged story—a story damaging enough that Kathryn had difficulty filling the position Lizzie had so eagerly taken. Clearly it had something to do with Zoe. Had they slept together? Pretty young college girl . . . edgy older chef . . . it seemed like an entirely possible, if clichéd, scenario. But it also wasn't the kind of situation that would put off other chefs. If anything, certain potential employees would see that as a perk. *Super-rich folks with an easy, hot daughter? Where do I sign up?*

No, it had to be something worse. Something that would deter a range of private chefs, male and female, from wanting to live in a palace for the summer. Something that would put off a class of people who are usually desperate enough for work and a steady paycheck that they are willing to overlook a lot of serious bullshit. Something that, even if half of it was made up, the other half was still bad enough to leave the Silvesters in the lurch.

Dear God, Lizzie thought. *What the hell* happened?

The party was still going strong some five hours after it began, and Lizzie wondered if and when these people would ever go home. She understood the appeal from the guests' perspective: lots of good food, open bar, a beautiful mansion right on the beach. Why would you want to go anywhere else? But Lizzie was exhausted, and she just wanted to go to bed.

With the staff's help, she finished cleaning up the last of the mess in the butler's pantry, stashing the leftover ingredients in the refrigerator and cupboards. There weren't many leftovers, even with the extra purchases halfway through the party, when Kathryn decided they needed beef kebabs ("I can't believe I forgot to ask for the kebabs! What was I thinking? It isn't too late, is it? Oh, Jim will be so disappointed if we don't have the beef kebabs!"). In a panic, Lizzie had sent Manuel to Avalon Market, where he picked up some beef and peppers and extra onions, and Lizzie went back to the grill to fire off three platters of beef on a stick.

Lizzie had wiped down the cutting board and slid it into the appropriate cabinet beneath the island when Kathryn popped back into the room. She'd had several drinks by this point, which made her even chattier than normal.

"Ah, there you are!" she said as if she were surprised to find Lizzie in the kitchen. "You are officially dismissed."

Lizzie's shoulders relaxed.

"For the evening!" Kathryn added quickly. "Not for good. Just for the evening. God, can you imagine? Firing the chef the first weekend? We'd be screwed for the whole summer! That's not the only reason we're keeping you on, obviously. Like I said, the food was fabulous! I told you that, right? Of course I did. Right in this room." She smacked her forehead. "My brain is not what it used to be. Can I blame the mojitos? Let's blame the mojitos. Though let's be honest—I'm not getting any younger! Wouldn't that be nice, aging in reverse? I wonder if the Paleo diet can do *that!*"

Lizzie searched for a figurative floatation device as she drowned in the sea of Kathryn's speech. There was nothing obvious to latch on to. The words . . . there were so many of them, and they came so fast.

"Anyway, the rest of the evening is yours. Renata will make sure the staff cleans up what's left. You're free to do whatever you like!"

Lizzie wanted to jump in the pool, but she couldn't do that in front of the remaining guests, of whom there was a substantial number. So instead, she planned to take a long shower and curl up in bed with a juicy thriller she'd plucked from her mom's nightstand before she left.

"Oh, but before you go," Kathryn cut in, "there's someone I want you to meet. Do you have a quick second?"

She waved Lizzie into the main kitchen area, where Lizzie could see groups of five or ten clustered throughout the dining and living areas. Music was still humming through the speakers—a peppy mix of salsa and mambo—and the party showed no signs of winding down.

"Lizzie, this is Barb, a dear friend of mine. She *loved* your show on the Food Network."

A tan, slim woman with long sable hair reached out to shake Lizzie's hand. Like Kathryn, she was well-groomed and well-dressed, and also a bit tipsy.

"*Loved* it," Barb said with a husky smoker's voice. She swayed as she leaned in and gave Lizzie's hand a limp shake. "What *happened?* I used to watch you all the time, and now I never see you *anywhere.*"

"The show got canceled."

"Why-y-y-y?" she moaned. She was more than a bit tipsy, Lizzie decided. She was thoroughly drunk. "All I see nowadays is that freaking...what's his name...with the blond spiky hair....I mean, do I really need him telling me where to find a dive? *Hello.* I live in Phila-freaking-delphia. If I want a dive, I think I can find one myself, you know what I mean?"

Lizzie forced a smile, but she was more embarrassed for this woman than she was for herself, which, when discussing her career history, was a first.

"People seem to like him," Lizzie said.

Barb made a gagging gesture. "Those people need some taste. You were great. I loved your show. Kids these days need more of that kind of thing, you know what I mean? The healthy thing. It's all processed stuff now, and GMOs and carbs and all that crap." She took a sip of her mojito, which was nearly empty. "So why did you get canceled?"

If ever Lizzie didn't want to get into her backstory, it was here, now, with this drunk woman, who either wouldn't remember their conversation tomorrow or, if she did, would trot it around like a prize, as if she'd gotten some scoop from a celeb at a fabulous party. Lizzie also wasn't sure who else was listening.

"Oh, you know..." she'd begun when she heard a voice over her shoulder.

"Lizzie?"

She turned around, and there was her college roommate, April Sherman. Her coffee-colored skin was luminous, as it always had been, and her dark, copper-flecked hair spilled in long waves over her shoulders. She wore a gauzy peach dress that hit at mid-thigh, showing off her toned legs. She looked fabulous.

"April—hi," Lizzie said, catching her breath. "How are you?"

"I'm great." She sized up Lizzie's ensemble. On a good day, Lizzie wasn't half as beautiful or stylish as April, but today, with her tangled hair and stained chef's coat, she looked particularly bad.

"What are you doing here?" April asked. "Are you . . . cooking?"

"I am. I'm working for the Silvesters for the summer."

"Oh. Wow. That's . . . great." Lizzie thought she detected a smirk.

"We were just talking about Lizzie's fabulous show," Barb chimed in, waving her empty glass in the air.

Lizzie flushed. *Oh, God,* she thought. *Not in front of April. Please don't discuss the show in front of April.*

"Former show," April said. "It got canceled. Isn't that right?"

Lizzie nodded, her cheeks burning. Like April needed to ask.

"That's what she was saying. Isn't that terrible? I just loved, loved, loved her show. I mean, I didn't watch it all the time. But if I flipped by and it was on . . . When was it on, again?"

"Saturday mornings."

"Exa-a-a-actly. I'd watch it when I was at the gym!"

"Me too!" Kathryn chimed in. "It's been a while, though—since I've seen your show, not since I've been to the gym. I go every day! Not that I have far to go. We have a wonderful setup in our basement—weights, elliptical, treadmill, Reformer, TVs, the works. I also recently started Zumba, and it's wonderful."

"The one in Ardmore?" Barb asked. She waved over a waiter and swapped her empty mojito glass for a full one.

"No, Bryn Mawr. On Lancaster. You should come sometime! You would love it."

Lizzie had never wanted to eject herself from a social encounter more than she did at this moment. Between running into April and listening to two drunk socialites discuss their fitness schedules, she was sure she could actually feel bits of herself dying inside.

"Anyway," Kathryn continued, "I used to flip through the channels on Saturday mornings, and whenever I'd come across your show I'd stop. Jim used to joke that watching food shows while on the treadmill seemed like a form of torture, but I told him at least *your* food was healthy!"

"Right?" Barb said. She took a sip of her drink. "That's what I'm saying. Now all they have is this, you know, extreme stuff—

bacon-covered fried cheese dipped in cream sauce or whatever. They need to bring you back. A year or two without your kind of show is too many."

"I think it's been more like five," April cut in.

"No," Barb gasped. "Has it really?"

"I think so," April said before Lizzie could answer.

"So wait," Kathryn said, pointing her finger between Lizzie and April. "How do you two know each other?"

"We were roommates at Penn," Lizzie said, hoping to keep the conversation as civil as possible.

"Shut up! *Roommates?*" Kathryn didn't try to mask her surprise. "So you ladies really *know* each other, huh?"

"You could say that," April replied.

"And now you're running into each other here, at our party! How funny is that? Though, Lizzie, I guess you probably knew that April is now working for Jim."

"I didn't."

"Really? I guess the roomies aren't as in touch as they used to be!" She winked.

"Not exactly," April said. She locked eyes with Lizzie.

"Well, April is now part of the corporate and digital communications team. Jim brought her on after all the fabulous work she did at NBC in New York. It isn't every day that you can snag one of *Forbes*'s Thirty under Thirty! Though I guess you aren't under thirty anymore."

"Thirty-one in August," April said, giving a mock frown.

"Oh, please—what I wouldn't give to be thirty-one again!"

"Sing it, sister," Barb said, raising her now nearly empty glass in the air.

"But wow, between the two of you... One had a show on the Food Network; the other is blazing a trail in the digital space. You ladies haven't wasted any time, have you? And now you're both working for Jim! How funny is that?"

"Very," April said, but Lizzie just stood mutely staring into April's eyes, not finding any of it funny at all.

CHAPTER 10

Linda,

Sorry I still haven't returned your call. Everything has been crazy, and I'm still trying to wade through it all.

To answer your question: Yes, they're sending me for a biopsy. The doctor says it's probably nothing—these sorts of things show up on mammograms and ultrasounds all the time—but it's worth checking out, just to be safe. Apparently the procedure is pretty quick and straightforward, but I won't be able to lift things for a bit afterward (not that I lift anything particularly heavy on a regular basis, but it'll probably interfere with my gardening for a little while).

Anyway, I haven't said anything to Gary yet. I'm not sure what to tell him, to be honest. When do you start sharing medical information? I can't remember when Frank and I started talking about those sorts of things. We were young, so I guess there really wasn't much to talk about. Maybe a case of the runs, or a sinus infection. But when

you're our age . . . well, the medical history is
longer, and there's more stuff that can go wrong. Is
it Gary's business? It isn't not his business. I mean,
we're sleeping together. That's pretty personal! But
somehow this feels . . . more personal. I don't know.
I don't want to worry him for nothing. And the
doctor said it's probably nothing. What do you
think?

In other news . . . Lizzie seems to be enjoying
her job with the Silvesters. Kathryn sounds like a
talker! And you'll never guess who she ran into last
week at their Memorial Day barbecue—her college
roommate! Remember her? The one who produced Lizzie's on-campus show? As you may recall,
they had a bit of a falling-out once Lizzie's show hit
it big. Lizzie didn't go into a lot of detail, but she
sounded as if the whole encounter took her by surprise. Thankfully it doesn't sound as if there were
any fireworks (the figurative kind—I actually do
think the Silvesters set off some fireworks at the
end of the party). Who knows? Maybe the two of
them will finally be able to patch things up.

Shoot—gotta run. The neighbor's dog is peeing
on my plumbago again. But I'll call you tomorrow
to fill you in on the biopsy details. I've scheduled it
for Thursday. Think positive!

xxoo

S

CHAPTER 11

After the Memorial Day barbecue, Lizzie's first three weeks in Avalon flew by without a hitch. Or at least not many hitches. There were a few. The "wok station," she concluded, was not meant for a novice, and she had the singed eyelashes to prove it. And one afternoon she stumbled across Kathryn and Barb lying topless by the pool, Barb's breasts suspiciously upright, defying the laws of gravity, while Kathryn's flopped beneath her armpits like saggy beanbags. Lizzie tried to act blasé about the whole situation (*Pretend you're European,* she told herself. *You are Cecile! You spend summers in Biarritz!*), but inside she was dying a little and was certain she would never be able to expunge the image of Kathryn's drooping breasts from her memory.

But other than a few minor problems, the weeks passed without incident. Lizzie was getting used to living and shopping in Avalon, and she was enjoying herself. There was something about being close to the beach that was so relaxing, even if the only time she was able to relax was after Kathryn disappeared for the evening. Any time Lizzie started to feel frazzled, she could simply look out one of the Silvesters' many windows and watch the waves crash into the shore and the tall reeds swoosh back and forth in the breeze and almost immediately she'd feel the tension loosen. Even though she'd never been the type who enjoyed lying on the beach all day, she could see why people came here summer after summer. The salty air, the squawking gulls, the glittering ocean—it was a tonic for the soul.

Lizzie's initial fears about dealing with a lonely, garrulous Kathryn were only partially borne out. Yes, there were the evenings where Lizzie had to listen to Kathryn prattle on, ping-ponging from one topic to the next until Lizzie thought her ears might fall off. But to Lizzie's surprise, those nights were in the minority. Most times during the week, if she wasn't eating at the Yacht Club, Kathryn invited a gaggle of her girlfriends to join her for dinner and cocktails, so her never-ending monologue was directed at them and not Lizzie. Many of them were nearly as talkative as Kathryn— an astonishing phenomenon Lizzie considered worthy of scientific study—meaning Lizzie spent much of her evening cooking to a soundtrack not dissimilar from the sound of cackling hens.

Mornings tended to be a quiet, peaceful time, when Lizzie could make her shopping lists, visit the markets, and collect her thoughts before launching into her prep work for lunch and dinner. Kathryn awoke much later than Lizzie, and they often didn't see each other until later in the day. Lizzie didn't have much involvement with weekday breakfasts anyway. Kathryn regularly received a delivery of cold-pressed juices that she would drink for breakfast, usually on their own, occasionally with a hard-boiled egg and small bowl of "Paleonola" that Lizzie left in the refrigerator. So even when they did see each other, it was usually in passing, as Kathryn floated through the kitchen in a gauzy cover-up on her way to the refrigerator, trying to decide whether to start her morning with juiced beets or kale.

But on Lizzie's third Friday morning in Avalon, something in the air changed. She started her day as she usually did, munching on a piece of toast while she planned her menus for the weekend. Jim would arrive in the late afternoon, and according to Kathryn he wanted scallops again for dinner. But whereas normally Lizzie could count on several uninterrupted hours before having to see or deal with Kathryn, on this Friday Kathryn blew into the kitchen before Lizzie had even finished her toast.

"Ah, there you are," she said. The characteristic effervescence in her voice had been replaced by a more serious edge. Lizzie wondered what she had done wrong.

"Everything okay?"

"What? Oh—yes. Everything's fine." She smoothed the front of her white, sleeveless, linen tunic, which she wore over black capris. This was the first morning Lizzie had seen her in anything but a cover-up and the first time she'd seen her awake before 10:00 a.m.

"I hard-boiled more eggs last night, so there are plenty in the fridge."

"I'm not very hungry, but thanks," Kathryn said. Her eyes darted around the room.

Was Lizzie in trouble? Kathryn's sudden reticence struck her as both odd and concerning.

"Are you sure there isn't a problem?"

"A problem? No, no. There isn't . . . I'm just trying to sort everything out before Zoe arrives. You know she's coming today, right?"

"I thought she was coming next week."

"No, today. I could have sworn I told you. Then again, I have a goldfish brain these days, so anything is possible."

Lizzie expected her to leap into a soliloquy about the origins of the phrase "goldfish brain," which is precisely what Kathryn would have done on any normal day, but today she left it and simply shrugged. Something was definitely wrong.

"What time is she planning to get here?"

"Well, that's the thing. . . . I'm not exactly sure. I think she'll be here for dinner. But she also said she wants to catch up with some old friends when she gets into town, so . . . maybe not? She could also show up for lunch, like she did last year. Or even breakfast! I just don't know. . . ."

She seemed so anxious and jittery. Lizzie didn't understand why Zoe's arrival time was such a mystery. How hard was it to tell your mom when you planned to show up? *I'm leaving at X o'clock. I should be there by Y.* Lizzie admitted her own journey had been unexpectedly long and harrowing, but potential traffic didn't seem to be the source of the uncertainty.

"Is there anything I can do to get things ready for her?"

"About a million things," Kathryn said.

"Maybe I can start with two or three," Lizzie joked.

Kathryn didn't smile. "Well, first of all, is her cupboard ready?"

"The one in the butler's pantry? I was told not to go in there."

"For ingredients. Right. But you can check to make sure things aren't out-of-date, and that she has enough to get started."

"Enough . . . what, exactly?"

"The kinds of things she likes to eat and cook with," Kathryn said, as if Lizzie had any idea what those things were. "I don't know, I can barely keep track of her favorites these days. But things like sprouted almonds, buckwheat groats, calendula tea, bee pollen, gluten-free oats, something called—what was it? Maca powder? She put that in lots of stuff last summer. And then there are all of the refrigerated things she likes. Nut butters, almond milk, lots of fruits and vegetables. Last summer she kept asking for reishi and astragalus, but Bob couldn't find either, and none of the rest of us were even sure what she was talking about, so . . ."

She raised her eyebrows at Lizzie, as if she hoped Lizzie might reply, *Ah, yes! Reishi and astragalus! I know exactly where to go.* But Lizzie just stared back blankly because she was as clueless as the rest of them.

"Why don't I take a quick look through her cupboard and check the dates on whatever is in there, and I'll restock as necessary, just to get her started. I can pick up a few things for the fridge, too."

"That would be wonderful," Kathryn said. She wrung her hands. "I just want everything to be as close to perfect as possible when she gets here. If we start fresh, on a high note . . . or at least try . . . well, I think it would be good for all of us."

Lizzie nodded in pretend agreement, but as she studied Kathryn's taut expression something told her Zoe's arrival wouldn't be good for anyone at all.

By four o'clock, Lizzie had done all of her shopping and there was still no sign of Zoe. Kathryn paced around the house, continually checking her phone and peering out the windows, her nervous energy electrifying the air. The entire scenario struck Lizzie as strange and highly dysfunctional (Why couldn't Kathryn just call Zoe and ask her what time she'd arrive? Why couldn't Zoe give a straight answer?), but none of it was really her business.

What was her business was getting dinner on the table, and the cloud of uncertainty over Zoe's appearance made it difficult for Lizzie to plan. Did she need to prepare something for Zoe to eat? Or could she stick with the scallops, beans, and cauliflower purée she intended to make for Kathryn and Jim? She didn't know what to do, and every time she broached the topic Kathryn's anxiety seemed to boil over, launching a new round of cell phone checks and hand-wringing.

When another hour passed without any word from the Silvesters' daughter, Lizzie decided to get on with her prep work. Even if Zoe showed up at six o'clock, Lizzie would still have time to cobble something together for her, since Jim and Kathryn didn't eat until seven. Fridays tended to be early evenings, which suited Lizzie just fine. Jim was usually tired from a long week at CC Media and only wanted to eat dinner and kick up his feet on one of their deck chairs while he caught up on *The Economist* and *Businessweek.* Kathryn typically sat next to him, jabbering about her week, as he nodded with the occasional, "Uh-huh . . . Really . . . ?" Lizzie wondered if Kathryn knew he wasn't really listening. If she did, she didn't seem to care.

Lizzie trimmed the beans, tossing the ends into the compost bin that Manuel regularly emptied for the gardener to use. She couldn't believe she was working for someone who had a gardener. The novelty of the Silvesters' extensive staff still hadn't worn off. To whatever extent Lizzie thought the house might feel empty during the week without Jim, the constant bustle of maids, gardeners, pool cleaners, and drivers proved her wrong. Some days she felt as if she were living in a modern-day Downton Abbey.

She tossed the beans into a bowl and eyed Zoe's dedicated cabinet. Earlier, she'd replenished the almonds, cashews, and pumpkin seeds, all of which were several months out-of-date, and added a few other odds and ends she thought Zoe might enjoy. She couldn't believe how much food Zoe had left to spoil—entire bags of nuts and seeds and powders, some of them never opened. Having scrimped and saved for the last year she lived in New York, Lizzie couldn't imagine having such a full cupboard, much less one so carelessly maintained. And anyway, even if she had all the money in the world, Lizzie couldn't let so many perfectly good—and expensive!—ingredients go to waste. She took pride in always being able to find a use for something, whether it was a lonely carrot or a bag of walnuts.

The minutes ticked by until it was well past six, at which point Kathryn poked her head into the butler's pantry.

"Jim is here," she said. "So we're still on track for seven."

"Just the two of you . . . ?" Lizzie didn't want to mention Zoe's name because every time she did it set Kathryn off. But for the sake of her job, she needed to know how much dinner to make and for whom.

"I . . . well, I guess so." She heaved a sigh as she checked her phone for what must have been the thousandth time that day. "She would have texted by now if she were coming. Unless her phone died. But that doesn't seem likely. She has a charger in the car. Maybe there's something wrong with her car. Jim said he took it for a spin last week, but no one had driven it in ages. I wonder if it broke down. Or got a flat. Oh, God—can you imagine? Zoe changing a flat? She'd have to call Triple A. Unless her phone died. Do you think her phone died?"

She went on and on in circles, asking questions that Lizzie had no ability to answer and that seemed more rhetorical than anything else. By the time she'd repeated the question about Zoe's phone dying for the fifth time, Lizzie thought Kathryn's head might spin off.

"Why don't I plan on dinner for just you and Mr. Silvester, and if Zoe arrives . . . we can cross that bridge then."

"Yes. Okay. That should work. Unless . . . no, no, never mind. That will be fine."

She glanced at her phone one more time before shaking her head and leaving. Lizzie set to work, caramelizing the shallots for the green beans and boiling the cauliflower for the purée. She was a little bored with this meal—Jim seemed to request some variation of it every time he visited—but she knew the importance of keeping the boss happy, and on some level she was glad he had enjoyed it enough the first time to keep asking for it.

When she finished plating the food, she picked up both plates and carried them into the dining room, where she found Jim and Kathryn sitting in what seemed to be their assigned seats. Lizzie found it a little funny: twenty seats, and they chose the same ones every time. But she also understood. When it had been just her and her mom, they always sat in the same seats, too. Granted, the table in their Glenside kitchen was tiny—barely big enough for four— but there was no reason they couldn't have rotated positions or sat on the other side of the table. They just never did. Lizzie supposed they liked the predictability, especially when so much in their lives had been up in the air.

"It's ridiculous," Jim snapped as he unfolded his napkin.

"Maybe something happened. . . . I mean, there's no reason to jump to conclusions—"

"I'm not. I'm saying it's ridiculous. Because it is."

Given their tone, Lizzie suspected they were discussing Zoe. In the three weeks she'd worked for them, Lizzie noticed their tone changed when they discussed their daughter. Kathryn got defensive, and Jim got exasperated, and they both seemed on edge. Lizzie always pretended she didn't notice, but she did and had so many questions.

"It isn't *ridiculous,*" Kathryn said. "Or, I don't know, maybe it is a little, but you know how she—Ah! Would you look at those scallops!"

As usual, Kathryn changed the conversation as soon as she noticed Lizzie approaching the table. Lizzie was tempted to say, *No, no, please continue. I'm dying to hear more.* But she was staff, and if she'd learned anything over the past three weeks, it was that staff were meant to be seen and not heard.

"She's done it again!" Kathryn trilled. "Crisp and golden, just the way you like them."

She was trying so hard to seem cheerful. It made Lizzie a little sad.

"Thanks," Jim said as Lizzie put his plate in front of him. "They look great."

"Enjoy."

She had turned to go back to the butler's pantry when she heard the clickety-clack of heels on the stairway. She assumed it was Barb, who'd decided to crash their dinner plans (she regularly turned up unannounced and almost seemed to live at the house when Jim wasn't around), but instead, a lissome blonde with long, wavy hair appeared at the top of the stairs. She wore a sheer, floaty white maxi dress and what looked like fifty different bangle bracelets, some thin, some thick, some covered with jingly charms. The dress was slit up the side all the way to her mid-thigh, and she still hadn't removed her oversize brown sunglasses, even though she was inside. She clasped a slouchy leather purse over her shoulder.

"Zoe!" Kathryn cried, clapping her hands together. "You're here!"

"I told you I was coming today." She had an unexpectedly deep voice, rife with ennui.

"But you didn't say when. Did you get any of my texts?"

"I don't know. What did they say?"

"I guess it depends on the text—I sent a bunch, and some were longer than others. . . . Actually, thinking about it, some were probably a little *too* long. Maybe that was part of the problem—"

"They asked what time you might grace us with your presence," Jim cut in, obviously annoyed.

"Well, I'm gracing you now."

"Excuse me?"

"I said I'm gracing you now. Mystery solved."

"Watch your tone."

"Oh, so you're the only one who gets to be snippy?"

"Now everyone calm down," Kathryn said with a nervous smile. "The weekend is just beginning! Let's not start off on the wrong foot. Zoe is here now, and that's all that matters. Zoe, dear, we were just sitting down to dinner, if you'd care to join us?"

Zoe cast an unimpressed look at the table. "What is it?"

"Scallops, green beans, and cauliflower purée. I know you don't eat scallops, but I'm sure Lizzie would be happy to make something else for you."

"Who's Lizzie?"

Kathryn smacked her forehead. "I'm sorry—I haven't introduced you. Zoe, this is Lizzie, our cook for the summer."

Lizzie waved and attempted a friendly smile. "Nice to meet you."

Zoe just stared back. "Same," she finally said.

"Could I make you something to eat?" Lizzie asked. "Maybe something to go with the beans? Those are vegan."

"What's in them?"

"Caramelized shallots and some salt and pepper."

"They look greasy."

"Zoe!" Jim snapped.

"I'm just saying."

Lizzie flushed. She didn't know what to say. She also kept eyeing the beans. Did they look greasy? She didn't think so. She hoped they tasted okay.

"I'm sure Lizzie would be happy to make you something else," Kathryn said.

"Anything you want," Lizzie said, though the more time she spent in Zoe's presence the less inclined she felt to do anything for her at all.

Zoe tapped her fingers against her lips. "I think I'm going to meet up with some friends at The Princeton," she said. "I'll take a pass tonight."

"Are you sure?" Kathryn asked. "Lizzie is a wonderful cook—I'm sure she could make you something."

Zoe rummaged through her purse and pulled out a lip gloss, which she slicked over her lips. "No thanks—I'm good."

She popped the gloss back in her purse, and as she skipped down the stairs Lizzie couldn't help but think "good" was the last word she'd use to describe her.

CHAPTER 12

When Lizzie awoke Sunday morning, she had a text on her phone from April Sherman:

Funny running into you the other week. Hope all is well.

Lizzie stared at the message. According to the log on her phone, the last time she and April had communicated via text was five years ago. It was a message from April that read: "Karma's a bitch, huh?" Lizzie suddenly felt queasy.

Her finger hovered over the keyboard on her phone as she contemplated what to say. The truth was, she missed April. She missed a lot of the friends she'd lost, ones who'd ditched her when her star began to fall or others she'd let drift away when her star was rising. But of all of them, she probably missed April the most. For most of her time at Penn, she considered April her best friend. Then Lizzie had hit it big, and April felt left behind, and Lizzie knew that was mostly her own fault.

She tapped out a response:

Great seeing you. Would love to catch up at some point. Any chance you'll be in Avalon again this summer?

She knew her suggestion was a long shot—both that April would be in Avalon again and, if she was, that she'd have any interest in catching up with Lizzie. But Lizzie also realized this might be her last opportunity to extend an olive branch, so she should make the most of it.

She slid her phone back onto the nightstand and threw on a T-shirt and pair of denim shorts. It was nearly eight thirty, which meant the Stone Harbor Farmers Market would be up and running for its opening weekend. Lizzie wanted to head out before it got too crowded. She pulled her hair into a ponytail, grabbed her purse, and tossed her phone inside before slipping on a pair of flip-flops and heading out the door.

She made her way toward her car, which was parked next to a graphite BMW Z4 convertible. Zoe's car, if she had to guess. She hadn't seen Zoe—or her car—since their first interaction Friday night. Where had Zoe been the past day and a half? Lizzie had no idea.

The car's metallic finish sparkled in the light from the morning sun. Lizzie was jealous. Not that she didn't appreciate her mom's 2007 Honda, but next to Zoe's car it looked so . . . boring. Ordinary. How Lizzie imagined she might look if she stood next to Angelina Jolie or Heidi Klum. Lizzie had obviously been attractive enough to appear on TV, but even on her best day she couldn't compete with the bombshells. She secretly wondered if her TV career would have ended so abruptly if she were a pneumatic blonde. She kept herself in decent shape, but she could only work with the genetic material she'd been given. Same with the Honda. To whatever extent her mom kept up the maintenance on her vehicle, it would never be a fifty-thousand-dollar sports car.

Her mom had, indeed, maintained the Honda, which was part of the reason Lizzie was so surprised when her mom offered it to her for the summer. Surely her mom couldn't survive in the suburbs without a set of wheels. But apparently her new boyfriend (or special friend, as she tended to call him) lent her the off-road Jeep he used for weekend adventures, so she would have transportation after all. It struck Lizzie as odd, both that her mother would date someone who was into off-roading and that she would drive a vehicle suited for such activities. She had driven sedans her entire life—Hondas and Toyotas and Fords. What did she know about driving through gravel, mud, and rocks? She didn't even like driving on a street with a lot of potholes. She said it gave her headaches. But if she was willing to part with her practical and reliable Accord, Lizzie was willing to take it.

She backed out of her spot and turned south on Dune Drive as she headed for the farmers' market. Renata had recommended it as a good place to pick up fresh vegetables, along with specialty goods such as pies and olive oil and cheese. The market took place in a plaza next to the town's water tower, just off 95th Street, and Lizzie managed to find a parking spot on 96th, right in front of a shop called the Bread and Cheese Cupboard.

As soon as she stepped out of the car, she sniffed the air. Cinnamon buns. Fresh, hot cinnamon buns. She'd know that smell anywhere. She peered in the window of the shop and saw trays of huge, pillowy buns slathered in creamy white frosting, along with other trays filled with raisin-studded sticky buns, freshly glazed doughnuts, and streusel-topped muffins. A long line of families waited with impatient little ones, who eagerly awaited their vacation morning sugar rush.

Lizzie bypassed the shop's temptations and made her way to the plaza behind the shop, where the farmers' market was in full swing. She saw a few young children running around with bacon on a stick and freshly fried doughnuts. She strolled past vendors selling homemade dog treats and homemade pies until she happened upon tables overflowing with fresh produce: lettuces and peas and spinach and cherries. It was still a little early for her summer favorites—the sugary-sweet corn and juicy tomatoes—but she knew in a matter of weeks these tables would be buckling under the weight of summer's bounty.

Jim wasn't leaving until early Monday morning, so tonight would be his last dinner, and he'd requested turkey burgers. Kathryn wouldn't eat a bun and Zoe wouldn't eat anything but the vegetable toppings, so Lizzie needed to make sure there were plenty of sides to make everyone happy. She wasn't actually sure Zoe would be joining them. No one ever seemed to know Zoe's plans. When would she arrive? Would she be joining them for dinner? Had she slept at home last night? Where was she? The family dynamic was completely dysfunctional, and Lizzie sensed Kathryn and Jim knew it. But Kathryn in particular seemed hesitant to criticize Zoe about anything.

"Let's focus on the *positive,*" she kept saying to Jim, though she never managed to articulate what those positives were. Jim didn't seem to know either, because inevitably he replied with a huff or an eye roll.

Lizzie grabbed a smattering of green vegetables that she would turn into a side dish, along with some beets that she'd toss with avocados and scallions in a salad. Everything would be vegan and safe for Zoe, assuming she chose to join them. Lizzie wasn't holding her breath.

Before she left she also bought a bag of cherries for dessert. There was nothing quite like fresh cherries at their peak. As a little girl, before her parents divorced, she and her dad would share a bowl of cherries on the back patio, holding a contest to see who could spit the pits the farthest. Her dad almost always won, but Lizzie got pretty good at it, to her mother's chagrin. Lizzie doubted the Silvesters ever held similar competitions. She could barely picture Kathryn spitting out toothpaste, much less a cherry pit.

As she headed back to her car, she pulled her phone from her purse. The cherries reminded her of her parents and how she hadn't been in touch with them in a while. She'd talked to her mom after the Memorial Day barbecue, but something about the conversation seemed off to Lizzie, and the more time that passed, the odder it seemed. Her mom sounded distracted, only half-engaged in what Lizzie was telling her about Kathryn and April and the other guests. She obviously was listening because she sounded genuinely surprised at the mention of April's name, but there was something in her voice . . . Lizzie couldn't quite put her finger on it. Maybe she had mixed feelings about Lizzie being a glorified servant for the summer. *All that college tuition, at an Ivy League school, and now she's doing this?* She could understand her mom's disapproval, assuming that's what it was.

Maybe Lizzie was just projecting, as she often did.

She was toying with calling her mom to check in when another text from April appeared on her screen:

I'll be in Avalon for the 4th. Assume the Silvesters will be doing another party? Could maybe catch up then. Though I guess you'll be working?

Did Lizzie detect some smugness in that last question? Of course she did. Why wouldn't April feel smug? She had a plum position at Jim's company and Lizzie was his cook, and it all seemed like a perfect case of poetic justice. But Lizzie decided to rise above her insecurities and texted back:

I'll be working but could probably hang out after. Would love to reconnect.

—even if she knew she was probably the only one who felt that way.

Later that afternoon, as she was scrubbing the beets, Lizzie looked up to see Zoe in the doorway of the butler's pantry. The thin strings of her turquoise bikini peeked out from beneath her sheer black cover-up, which hit at mid-thigh. Her sunglasses rested on the top of her head, holding back her tousled blond waves like a headband.

"What are you making?" she asked. She had a way of speaking that bordered on aggressive, as if she were interrogating Lizzie and not simply trying to make conversation.

"Roasted beets," Lizzie said. "For a salad."

Zoe inched closer, narrowing her eyes as she examined the beets. "What kind of beets?"

Lizzie studied the vegetable in her hand. "Regular red ones."

"Are they organic?"

"I . . . think so? Maybe? I bought them at the farmers' market."

"Just because they're local doesn't mean they're organic."

Lizzie wasn't sure what she'd done to antagonize Zoe, but already they seemed to be at odds. They'd spent less than ten minutes together the entire weekend. What could Lizzie possibly have done to rub Zoe the wrong way? Nothing, as far as Lizzie was concerned. She knew it shouldn't matter. Kathryn had hired her, not Zoe. And anyway, Lizzie had taken an almost instant dislike to the Silvesters' daughter from the moment they met Friday night. If she didn't like Zoe after such a short time, then surely Zoe had every right to dislike her. But here her lifelong character flaw reared its head once again: She couldn't stand being the target of anyone's disapproval, even if she disapproved of that person herself. It was a foible she couldn't shake. The fact that she'd ended up working in television—on camera, no less—was laughable to anyone who knew her. No career was more savage than one on TV. Lizzie had always tried to accept criticism with maturity and grace, but she'd hated every second of it and felt as if a piece of her died inside with each nasty e-mail.

"Sorry—I didn't check. Next time I'll ask."

"Please do. Because I only eat organic."

Lizzie tried to content herself with Zoe's use of the word "please." She wondered if this meant Zoe wouldn't touch any of the food at dinner.

Zoe pulled the sunglasses from her head and gnawed on one of the arms. "I used to watch your show sometimes," she said.

"Yeah?"

"Yeah. It wasn't half-bad."

Lizzie brightened, then hated herself for it. Why should she care whether Zoe liked her show or not? But she did, and more than a little.

"Some days that feels like a lifetime ago," Lizzie said, scrubbing the dirt and grime off another beet.

"I was still in high school, so yeah. Long time." She watched as Lizzie finished cleaning and seasoning the beets. "What have you been doing since then? This?" She waved her hand around the butler's pantry.

"Sort of. More personal chef work than private chef work."

"What's the difference?"

Lizzie stuck the pan in the oven. "Personal chefs have several clients, and you don't have to be at their house all the time. I'd leave a week's worth of meals in the fridge with a note, and that would be that. A private chef works for just one person or family, and . . . well, I'm still learning how that goes."

"So you had, like, a business? Must not have been doing that well if you're here now."

"I got by." *Barely.*

"Must be a huge bummer, though. To go from TV star to this."

There was a tinge of glee in Zoe's voice, as if she was hoping those wounds were still a little raw. It was similar to the way April spoke of Lizzie's fall from grace, except there was a reason April sounded that way. Lizzie supposed Zoe had a reason too. She just didn't know what it was.

"To everything there is a season . . ." Lizzie said.

Was she quoting the Bible now? And if so, did that line even make sense? Zoe didn't look entirely satisfied with this as an answer, and Lizzie couldn't blame her. At the same time, Lizzie wasn't willing to give her the satisfaction of knowing, *Yes, it was a huge bummer, and if I'm being honest, I still haven't fully come to terms with it.* She hadn't admitted that out loud to anyone, and she wasn't about to make Zoe her first confidante.

"Anyway," Lizzie continued, "I still have a bunch of prep work to do before dinner. I assume you'll be eating with your parents?"

"I guess." She sounded thoroughly unenthusiastic about the prospect. "What time are they eating?"

"Six thirty, I think. Your dad has to get up early tomorrow morning to head back to Philly, so he wants an early night."

"Big surprise there."

"Sorry?"

"Nothing. My parents are lame. But I should be at dinner. Assuming there's something I can eat."

"For sure. The greens are all organic, and I'm pretty sure the beets are too." This was a lie, but she didn't want to be the source of more tension between Zoe and her parents. Kathryn, in particular, wanted Zoe to join them for pretty much any activity—a meal, a walk on the beach, a few minutes by the pool—and seemed continually disappointed when Zoe either rejected her invitations or wasn't even present to hear them. If lying about the provenance of tonight's vegetables would keep the family peace, Lizzie was willing to do it. She wondered if Zoe could tell.

"I guess that's fine. It'll make my parents happy. And then I can tell my friends I ate a meal prepared by a former Food Network star, which is pretty cool, if you're into that kind of thing."

Lizzie smiled, feeling pretty pleased with herself, until Zoe added, "I mean, hanging with a has-been doesn't really do it for me, but other people might be impressed."

And just like that, Lizzie felt her good spirits evaporate, and if Zoe's expression was any indication that had been her intention all along.

Lizzie watched as Renata set the table, laying Zoe's place at the head, between Kathryn and Jim. Lizzie admired Renata for the care she put into even the most menial tasks, the way she buffed the water spots off the knives or positioned the place mats so that they were even with the edge of the table. Depending on what Lizzie had made for dinner, Renata would select coordinating plates and cutlery (the Silvesters had a few different sets) and would infuse jugs of spring water with fruits and herbs that complemented the meal—watermelon and basil to go with grilled fish, pineapple and mint to go with turkey burgers. Lizzie sensed Renata did all these things not out of fear of retribution but because she actually enjoyed making things nice for a family she'd known for many years, a family that, from what Lizzie had seen, treated Renata more like a relative than an underling.

Back in the kitchen, Lizzie put the finishing touches on the beet salad, sprinkling a handful of chopped scallions over the top. She scraped the sautéed spinach, peas, and asparagus into a bowl before stepping out the side door to take the turkey burgers off the grill. Renata helped her carry all of the platters into the dining room, where Jim and Kathryn had already taken their seats. Zoe wasn't there.

"Look at all this!" Kathryn said as Lizzie and Renata laid the platters and bowls on the table. She glanced at her watch. "Zoe should be here any minute. . . ."

"What time did you tell her?" Jim asked.

"Six thirty," Lizzie and Kathryn said in unison.

"So she had two people tell her and she's still managed to be late."

"It's six thirty-one," Kathryn said. "I'd hardly call that late."

"Considering she's nowhere in sight, I wouldn't call it on time."

Kathryn's cheeks flushed, and she smiled tightly. "Can we please not do this now? She'll be here. She promised."

"Don't you trust me, Daddy?" Zoe appeared in the dining room, a weighty DSLR camera slung over her shoulder. She'd changed out of her bathing suit and cover-up and was now wearing a navy romper.

"There you are!" Kathryn cried. She eyed Jim and smiled. "See? I told you."

Zoe slid into her chair. "So what is all this?"

Lizzie inched closer to the table and gestured at each dish. "Turkey burgers and toppings. Beet and avocado salad. Early summer sauté, with spinach, peas, and asparagus."

"Isn't it a little late for peas and asparagus?"

"They had some at the farmers' market, so . . . I guess not?" She hoped she didn't sound too snippy, but after only two days her patience with Zoe was wearing thin. She wondered if every meal would involve Zoe giving her the third degree.

"Huh. Weird."

"Well, whatever the season, it looks delicious," Kathryn said. She had reached for the serving spoon when Zoe reached out to stop her.

"Hang on—let me get a photo first."

She removed the lens cap and took a series of photos of everything on the table, rotating bowls and platters in different directions and, at one point, standing on her chair to snap a few aerial shots. The entire episode struck Lizzie as a little odd—Jim and Kathryn just sitting there while their burgers got cold as Zoe turned the meal into a photo op.

"Zoe has a blog," Kathryn said as she sat awkwardly with her hands folded in her lap.

"You mentioned that at the interview," Lizzie said. "What is it called?"

"I'm not . . . Zoe, sweetie, what is your blog called? I can never remember. . . ."

"That's because I don't like to talk about it."

"I'd love to take a look sometime," Lizzie said, trying to sound encouraging but really hoping Zoe would bring the photo session to a close. The turkey burgers were getting colder by the second, and although Zoe wouldn't eat them, they were the main component of her parents' dinner.

Zoe snapped the lens cap back into place and slung the camera over the back of her chair. "Okay," she said. "Let's eat."

Lizzie let out a sigh of relief and headed back to the kitchen. At least they were eating. She did wonder about Zoe's blog, but not enough to delay dinner any longer than Zoe already had. Would every meal be like this? And would Zoe be posting those photos to her site? The thought hadn't occurred to Lizzie as Zoe snapped shot after shot, but as Lizzie rinsed the cherries under the tap she wondered whether Zoe would credit her with the food and, if she did, what the context would be:

Dinner with a former Food Network star!

My lame dinner by a washed-up Food Network star . . . womp, womp.

Ever wonder what happened to Lizzie Glass? Of course you didn't.

This is what failure tastes like.

Lizzie tried to shake the headline images from her mind. It was just a silly blog. Who cared? Frankly, at this point Lizzie viewed any mention of her name as a good thing. It was a way to keep her relevant, to keep her name alive in the food world. Any publicity was good publicity, right? Zoe might not even mention Lizzie at all. But as that thought chased the others away, she suddenly felt disappointed, as if another opportunity to resurrect her career had slipped through her fingers, even if the opportunity had been nothing but a figment of her imagination. And that's when she realized: Yes, it was just a silly blog, but she did care, and for reasons that, at this moment, didn't make her particularly proud.

CHAPTER 13

The week that followed wasn't nearly as bad as Lizzie thought it might be, but that was mostly because Lizzie had envisioned living under some Zoe-led totalitarian regime and, as it turned out, Zoe wasn't around all that much. She'd pop in for the occasional meal, which she almost always photographed with her digital camera or iPhone, sometimes both. But that only happened two or three times, and when it did it came as a surprise to both Kathryn and Lizzie. Kathryn pretended she was fine with Zoe's capricious (and, Lizzie thought, disrespectful) ways, but Lizzie saw through her act. Was she putting it on for Lizzie? Or herself? Lizzie couldn't tell.

When Friday morning arrived, Kathryn burst into the butler's pantry full of excitement. Jim's college friend Sam Offerman was coming for the weekend, and she wanted Lizzie to plan a few menus for his stay.

"Maybe a Mexican night. Or Italian! Although I guess that's a little tricky, since I can't have pasta and Jim shouldn't have garlic. No, Mexican would be good for one night. And maybe splurge on lobster for another. Lobster is Paleo, isn't it?"

Lizzie had no idea. She somehow didn't picture cavemen dining on crustaceans, but what did she know?

"Well, even if it isn't," Kathryn continued, not waiting for an answer, "Jim loves it, and so does Sam if I remember correctly, so I say let's do it. Oh! And for lunch one day, could you make that beet salad again? Or a variation on it. It doesn't have to be exactly the same. Maybe you could add arugula or something. Listen to me! Telling you how to cook again. Ignore me. I don't know what I'm talking about."

"Arugula would actually be really nice," Lizzie said, feeling slightly dizzy, as she often did in conversation with Kathryn. "Maybe with some nuts for crunch."

"I think Sam is allergic to nuts. Or is that someone else? I'll check and let you know."

"How many nights will he be here?"

"Just tonight and tomorrow. He leaves Sunday after breakfast. Oh, breakfast! Jim asked if you could whip up a few special breakfast treats for Sam's stay. Maybe some scones or muffins or that kind of thing."

"Should I make them grain-free so that you can eat them?"

"Oh, God no. Jim won't touch them if he thinks they're diet food, and Sam will just tease me. Mind you, last time I saw Sam he looked a little like a muffin himself, if you catch my drift. A grain-free diet might actually do him some good. But it isn't my place to say anything. That would be his wife's domain—or should I say *ex*-wife's."

She raised her eyebrows conspiratorially, as if she'd just passed along a juicy piece of gossip Lizzie should be delighted to learn. But Lizzie didn't know Sam and barely knew the Silvesters. Hearing that one of their friends had gotten a divorce meant nothing to her. And anyway, after her parents' divorce she couldn't think of any failed marriage as titillating news. Divorce was sad and hard and sometimes ugly, and no matter how gory the details, they were really no one else's business.

However, given the look on Kathryn's face, she clearly didn't see it that way. "Affairs," she said, leaning in. "On her side. Lots of them. Apparently the latest was with her tennis instructor. Big surprise there. I met him once when we visited their place in Montauk, and the first thing I said to Jim was, 'Watch out for that guy—he's trouble.' Charming, tan, fit. *T-r-o-u-b-l-e!*"

She went on to describe the various ways in which this now ex-wife was terrible and why she'd always known the marriage would never last. Lizzie let it all wash over her as she let her mind drift to what she might make this weekend, which she decided was more important and relevant than hearing about the charges Sam's ex-wife had made to his credit card and the damage she did to his Jaguar convertible. Maybe some cherry streusel muffins? Or a blueberry coffee cake? She could also make some yogurt and granola parfaits to leave in the refrigerator. If Kathryn wasn't planning to eat any of it, anything was fair game.

"Mind you, Sam is hardly the innocent," Kathryn continued. She was still talking. How was she still talking? "There's a reason she was wife number three. He's a huge flirt. HUGE. Just wait—you'll see."

Lizzie had no interest in seeing and wished Kathryn would steer the conversation back to more pertinent subject matter. Did they want lunch by the pool or in the house? How many people should Lizzie expect for dinner?

"So about the weekend . . ." Lizzie cut in when Kathryn paused to catch her breath.

"Right! The weekend. Let's do Mexican tonight and lobster tomorrow. Tonight can be like a fiesta—margaritas, fish tacos (no tortilla for me, of course!), lots of avocado and salsa and that kind of thing. Oo-o-oh, and we can eat outside!" She clapped her hands excitedly. "I'll tell Renata to light the tiki torches."

"Will Zoe be joining you?" Lizzie immediately regretted asking the question when she saw the expression on Kathryn's face. On the one hand, Lizzie needed to know how much to cook and how much of that needed to be organic, gluten-free, and vegan. But Kathryn's stress levels seemed to rise at every mention of Zoe's name, which only made her talk faster. Lizzie could barely keep up as it was.

"I think so. She hasn't seen Jim since Sunday, and she always gets a kick out of Sam—Uncle Sam, as she calls him. Plus, I'm sure she's dying to pry details out of him about the divorce. Zoe loves that kind of stuff."

Other people's misfortune? Lizzie wondered. *Or just gossip in general?*

"So, yes, count on Zoe. And Barb! Can't forget Barb. Between you and me, I would *love* to set her up with Sam. I mean, yes, okay, he's a flirt, but he's a very successful property developer, and at this point I don't think either of them is anxious to get married again. It could just be for fun—a summer fling! At our age, can you imagine? Not that I'm looking for anything like that. Jim is all the man I ever need, trust me. But for Barb . . . Anyway, that's five including Barb, and then I think my friends Diana and Wendy are planning to swing by tonight, too, so that makes seven. Three single ladies— Sam will really have his pick of the litter!"

Lizzie smiled and played along, but the more Kathryn talked, the more dreadful this dinner sounded, and if she weren't contractually obliged to be a part of it she would happily take a pass.

With only a few hours until Sam Offerman's arrival, Lizzie plopped down on her bed, scanning a few different apps on her phone for inspiration. She often took to social media when she wanted to spark an idea or two, if not for an actual recipe, then for a beautifully composed photo that would get her culinary synapses firing. These days, there was no shortage of people posting photos of their meals, whether it was a dish they'd made themselves or one they'd eaten at a restaurant.

As Lizzie flicked through various #beetsalads and #tacos on Instagram, she was reminded of how much the culinary landscape had changed since she'd started her public-access TV show in college. Back then, food blogs were growing in popularity but hadn't quite reached the omnipresence of a few years later, when it seemed anyone with an Internet connection and moderate interest in cooking had started an online food diary. Now having a food blog seemed almost passé, and it certainly wasn't enough to land you a book deal, unless you also had a huge following on Instagram and Pinterest and Snapchat and whatever other social media app was the Hot New Thing.

Lizzie was a part of that world, but she also wasn't. She'd signed up for all of those services as they became popular, but in many cases the timing coincided with her post-TV life. Who cared about following a has-been? There were hundreds of other people who'd already filled the void she'd left behind, for whom technology wasn't an afterthought but rather the lifeblood of their careers. It all made Lizzie feel so old and out of touch, even though she was only thirty.

She was scrolling through images of #beetsalads for something enticing when she stopped abruptly at an appealing photo. It had all the elements from the salad she'd made the other night, which Kathryn said she wanted her to repeat: beets, avocados, scallions. But as she looked at the photo more closely, her interest morphed into confusion. The salad didn't look a little like hers; it looked *exactly* like hers, right down to the platter on which it was served.

When Lizzie clicked on the photo to enlarge it, she discovered it was posted by someone with the username "@thecleanlife" with the caption "Can't get enough of this amazing #beetsalad. Recipe coming soon to the blog!" The caption was followed by a string of emojis and about ten different hashtags, ranging from #cleaneating and #plantbased to #eeeeeats. The closer Lizzie looked, the more certain she was that it was, indeed, her beet salad. The table surface, the cutlery, the place mats . . . everything looked just like the Silvesters'. Was this Zoe's Instagram? Was The Clean Life the name of her blog?

Lizzie opened @thecleanlife's profile and felt her stomach somersault. The beet salad wasn't the only photo that looked familiar. Wasn't that the roasted vegetable platter she'd made the other night? And didn't that look just like her green vegetable sauté? All of the recognizable dishes were accompanied by reassurances that the recipe would be "coming soon" to the blog, as well as the Clean Life app, which had just launched. Lizzie scrolled back to the top and saw that The Clean Life had more than 150,000 followers. She didn't consider herself a social media guru, but she knew that was a lot of followers—not Kim Kardashian levels of fame but enough to entice companies to send whoever ran The Clean Life free samples and pay for sponsored posts. Was Zoe making money off of Lizzie's food?

The profile didn't give the author's name. All it said was "Whole Foods. Whole Spirit. Whole Life," with a link to the accompanying Web site. Lizzie clicked on it. When the site loaded, Lizzie found herself looking at a stylish, crisp site, with bright images of beautifully photographed food. The latest post was titled "What Work

Looked Like This Week" and featured all the familiar photographs
Lizzie had seen on Instagram, along with a few others that Lizzie
didn't recognize. In succinct prose, the post talked about the author's need to hit the reset button after splurging on her trip to Europe:

> I managed to eat my body weight in
> socca while I was in Nice. If you've
> never had socca, it's a crepe made
> with chickpea flour, and it is A-
> MAZING. And vegan! And totally good
> for you! But when you eat it six
> times a day...well, yeah. Time to
> detox.

Europe. Nice. The beet salad. The roasted vegetable platter.
This had to be Zoe's site. It was all too coincidental.

Lizzie clicked on the "About" tab. There she found a long, detailed story about the site's mission and origins:

> The Clean Life isn't just a blog.
> It's a lifestyle. A creed. An
> approach to cooking and nutrition
> built on the knowledge that foods can
> not only nourish but also heal.
> I should know. Six years ago, I
> received a phone call that forever
> changed my life. My best friend,
> Marie, called to tell me she'd been
> diagnosed with cancer. Not only that—
> the cancer had spread to her spleen,
> liver, and blood. The doctors gave
> her two to three years to live.
> My heart stopped beating. I couldn't
> breathe. How could this be? She was
> only 18. She was an athlete. She had
> just been accepted to the college of
> her dreams.

I refused to accept her diagnosis.
I refused to listen to the doctors
who told her there was nothing to do
but manage the disease until it eventually took her from this world. I
refused to let her go.

I started reading as much as
possible about cancer cures and
alternative medicine, and that's when
I learned about the amazing healing
powers of food and diet. Although the
doctors claimed Marie's cancer was
terminal—and couldn't pin down an
exact cause other than bad luck in
the genetics department—I discovered
that her disease was caused by the
buildup of toxins in her system,
which led to a pancreatic enzyme de-
ficiency. If those toxins were
flushed out with a clean diet and
clean lifestyle, she had a very good
chance at survival.

With my help, Marie adopted a
clean diet of healing foods—entirely
gluten-free and dairy-free, with no
processed sugar or soy. She drank raw
juices, took natural supplements, and
went for coffee enemas. I joined her
on this journey, and let me tell
you, it was a tough transition. But
I knew I had to do it. Her life
depended on it.

Almost immediately, Marie's health
began to improve. She looked better,
but more important, she felt better.
And so did I. I realized I'd been
walking through a fog for years, but
by removing the toxins from my system

```
I could see the world clearly again.
A veil had been lifted. I couldn't
believe how amazing I felt. That ache
in my left knee? Gone. My monthly mi-
graine? Vanished.
    Against all odds, Marie beat her
cancer diagnosis. That's right: The
doctors told her she wouldn't live
more than three years, and six years
later she is not only alive but
cancer-free.
    We now live thousands of miles
apart, but we have stuck with our
clean diet and haven't looked back.
Some people have called us wellness
gurus. I like to call us wellness
warriors.
    If you, like me and Marie, are
frustrated with conventional medicine
and its advocates (most of whom, by
the way, are funded by the pharmaceu-
tical industry) I invite you to join
us on this journey.
    Food is medicine.
    Food heals.
    It saved Marie's life and, in a
different way, it saved mine. It
could save yours, too.
    Peace and love
    Z
```

"Z." Zoe. It had to be.

Lizzie read the story once more before laying her phone on her bed. She suddenly cared less about Zoe claiming the beet salad as her own and more about the emotional story behind the site's genesis. So *that's* why Zoe was so fanatical about what she ate. It was all starting to make a lot more sense.

Lizzie put herself in Zoe's shoes and tried to imagine what it would have been like if, at the peak of their friendship, April had announced she'd been diagnosed with cancer. Lizzie would have lost it. And, like Zoe, she probably would have looked for any way to keep her best friend alive. Lizzie wasn't sure about the coffee enemas (Did they shoot a Venti Americano up there? It sounded terrible.), but grief and fear often led you to do crazy things. Who was Lizzie to judge?

If she was being honest with herself, she wasn't entirely convinced the so-called clean diet cured Zoe's friend. It could have been a coincidence. Correlation, causation, blah blah blah. Then again, as someone who'd had a show promoting healthy campus cuisine, Lizzie knew firsthand the benefits of eating well. She wasn't fanatical about it and she was always skeptical of trendy diets like Kathryn's, but Lizzie's entire claim to fame was that cooking and eating healthy food instead of eating processed crap meant you'd look, feel, and study better. Was it such a stretch to think that, if you ate so that your body was performing at its peak, you could help yourself heal? Maybe not.

She picked up her phone again and stared at the photo of Marie that "Z" had posted next to the story. The photo was tightly cropped, but the girl looked to be about fifteen or sixteen and was standing in front of a fat tree trunk. Lizzie tried to enlarge the picture but started as someone tapped at her door.

"Knock, knock?" It was Renata.

"Come in," Lizzie said, putting down her phone.

Renata cracked the door and poked her head inside. "Mrs. Silvester wanted to know if you need help with the shopping for tonight."

Tonight. Sam Offerman's visit. Lizzie had gotten so sidetracked with "Z's" Web site that she'd forgotten why and how she'd ended up there in the first place.

"I don't think so. I'm still making my shopping list."

"Let me know if you need anything. I will handle the wine and liquor. Mr. Offerman . . . let's just say he enjoys more than a glass or two. . . ."

"I know the type." Lizzie glanced at her phone, whose screen had gone black. "Did you . . . I mean . . . you said you've known the Silvesters for ten years, right?"

"Yes."

"So Zoe would have been, what, thirteen when you first met her?"

"I think so." Renata looked at the ceiling as she counted silently. "Yes, that sounds right. Why?"

"I was just wondering. . . . Did she ever talk about her friend—"

"Renata?"

Kathryn's voice sounded down the hallway, cutting off Lizzie. Renata held up a finger and peered over her shoulder. "Yes, ma'am?"

"I'm sorry to bother you," Kathryn said, her voice coming closer. "We have an issue with Sam's room. Whoever last stayed there left a hideous stain on the pillow. I have no idea what it is, but you can see it through the pillowcase. Could you get him a new one? He'll be here in a few hours."

"Certainly."

Kathryn poked her head in Lizzie's room. "All okay here?"

"Yep. Just making my shopping list."

"Fantastic. Sorry to pull Renata away. I hope you weren't in the middle of something?"

"No, not really," Lizzie said.

"Not really . . . oh, dear. Sounds to me like maybe you were. Well, Renata should be finished helping me in a few minutes, and then you two can continue discussing whatever you were discussing."

"It wasn't anything important," Lizzie said. "Honestly."

"Important or not important—I'm still interrupting. Which is so like me, I know, and it's for a good reason—you should *see* that pillow—but I still feel bad. So hold that thought, and you can bring it up again later."

"Will do," Lizzie said, even though she had no intention of doing so.

CHAPTER 14

A storm front moved in just before dinner, dashing the plans for an outdoor Mexican fiesta. Lizzie wasn't sure who was more disappointed: her or Kathryn. As hostess, Kathryn was hoping for tiki torches and lively salsa music by the pool, and while all of that sounded nice to Lizzie, she was most looking forward to some peace and quiet inside while she cooked. But to make up for the change in ambiance, Kathryn decided to turn dinner into a performance, where Lizzie was the star.

"We'll set up the bar over there, and then everyone can watch you cook over here! Obviously you can do the messy work in the pantry, but I know Sam would love to watch you put the finishing touches on everything. It's a shame the grill isn't closer, but . . . No, that's fine—you'll grill back there, and then you can assemble everything here. You don't mind, do you? What am I saying—of course you don't! You used to be on TV. What's a little dinner for seven when you used to cook in front of millions?"

Lizzie was tempted to clarify that her show wasn't live and that really she was only cooking in front of a cameraman and a producer. Also, she was pretty sure her viewership was never in the millions or anywhere close. But despite Kathryn's misplaced enthusiasm, Lizzie didn't want to rain on Kathryn's already-rained-out parade. Lizzie wasn't thrilled at the prospect of being put on display in front of Jim and Kathryn's friends, but she knew it came with the territory.

"Sam is changing in his room, but once he comes down—*andale!* Barb, Wendy, and Diana will be here any minute. Well, Barb will. The other two are always late. But I've never known them to miss a free margarita, so they will be here soon. And Zoe . . . well, I think you know by now that Zoe shows up when she shows up. But she'll be here. She promised."

Kathryn scurried off and left Lizzie to set up her prep station. Lizzie scanned her checklist and put an asterisk next to tasks that were performance worthy. Skewering raw shrimp: no. Making fresh guacamole: yes.

Lizzie headed back to the butler's pantry, removed the marinating shrimp from the refrigerator, and began threading them on long metal skewers. The menu would be simple and fresh, with plenty of options for everyone to accommodate a panoply of dietary restrictions: grilled shrimp tacos, shredded pork tacos, and a bunch of fun sides such as grilled Mexican street corn and arroz verde.

Once she had finished with all of the dirty work in the back, she donned a pair of potholders and carried the hulking Le Creuset filled with braised pork into the main kitchen. The aroma was intoxicating. *How would I have described this on* Healthy U? Lizzie wondered. Her producers were obsessed with telling the audience how things smelled.

"Bring them into the kitchen with you," they'd say. "People can see what you're making, but they can't smell it. Make them feel as if they're right next to you. Heighten the experience—make your cooking come alive!"

Lizzie understood and agreed, but she also found herself commenting on ingredients that weren't exactly known for their pleasant aroma or, in some cases, that barely had a scent at all.

"M-m-m-m, sour cream . . . so tangy."

"These cucumbers smell so . . . fresh."

"And then you add the dried cranberries, which smell really. . . . cranberry-ish."

To this day, she was still embarrassed about that last one. *Cranberry-ish?* That's the best she could do? She'd tried to think of something better, but dried cranberries were sort of sweet and sort of tart and didn't really have a smell. *Yummy?* She hated that word and had already used it to describe six different ingredients in that episode. So "cranberry-ish" it was.

She placed the pot of pork on the stove and took a big whiff as she lifted the lid. *Smoky,* she thought. *Spicy. Rich. Porky.* Porky? *Whatever.* It was better than "cranberry-ish." Anyway, she wasn't on TV anymore, a fact numerous people had reiterated during her time in Avalon. She didn't need to think in adjectives anymore. She could just cook.

As she laid out the ingredients for the guacamole, she heard a loud *thump, thump, thump* as someone came down the stairs. A rotund man in khaki shorts and a pink polo shirt appeared in the living room, his belly hanging over his leather belt. *Speaking of porky,* Lizzie thought, then immediately felt guilty. She never liked to comment on people's weight. If she were going to comment on anything, it should be his hair. She wasn't sure what color to call it. *Apricot? Peach?* For some reason, the only descriptors she could come up with were stone fruits. It was also styled in a way that Lizzie found very distressing. His part began an inch or so above his ear, and the long, brittle pieces that he'd dragged across the top of his head seemed to be held in place with hairspray. Why? Why had he done this to himself? Lizzie didn't understand. Could he not see how terrible he looked?

He trundled over to the kitchen island and smacked his belly with his hands. "So what's on the menu, sweetheart?"

"Tacos," Lizzie said, trying to ignore the condescension in his voice. "Mexican."

"*Muy bueno,*" he said. He craned his neck across the counter. "Got any tequila back there?"

"Ah, Sam, you're down!" Kathryn hurried from across the room. "Renata will fix you up with something to drink. Renata?"

As if by magic, Renata appeared next to Lizzie with a tray of drinks.

"What do we have here?" Sam asked.

"Classic margaritas on the rocks."

"Don't mind if I do," he said. He lifted a glass off the tray and raised it at Renata. "Thanks, doll."

Sweetheart, doll—Lizzie knew Sam Offerman's type, and she didn't like it one bit. She'd encountered plenty of men like him in New York: entitled, loud, chauvinistic. She'd always assumed those men were compensating for some sort of deep insecurity or feelings of inadequacy, but after a while she realized some of them were just narcissists. She wondered where Sam fell along that divide.

"Hell*o-o-o-o-o!*" Barb appeared in the living room, announcing her arrival with the usual fanfare, waving her hands above her head as her gold bangles clattered against one another. She wore a strapless black jumpsuit that looked fabulous on her, even if Lizzie thought the style might be a touch young. Barb was in great shape, though as far as Lizzie could tell, staying in shape was pretty much all Barb did. Everything about her was well maintained, aside from her skin, which had gone from a golden tan at the Memorial Day barbecue to what was now a leathery brown. It reminded Lizzie of Sam's skin, which was also leathery, but more orange than brown. Maybe Barb and Sam really were meant for each other.

"Barb, baby, you look better than ever." Sam leaned in and kissed Barb on the cheek, lingering a beat longer than Lizzie thought was polite, but Barb didn't seem to mind.

"Oh, please, I feel like a cow lately—I haven't been to the gym in two days."

Two days? Lizzie hadn't been to the gym in two years. Three, actually, the more she thought about it. She could barely afford her Equinox membership even when she was still on TV and making decent money, so when that income dried up she downgraded to a cheap plan at Planet Fitness. But once the cookbook royalties dwindled and she had more and more trouble finding personal chef work, a gym membership was one of the first expenses on the chopping block. She still tried her best to stay in shape, but if two days without a workout made Barb a cow, Lizzie wondered what animal she might be. A hippo, maybe. Or a sloth.

"Whatever you're doing, it's working," Sam said. "Here—have a cocktail. You deserve it."

"Well, if you *insist*." Barb winked. Lizzie couldn't remember ever seeing Barb without a cocktail or a glass of wine.

Soon Diana and Wendy arrived, and the party was officially in full swing. Lively music pumped through the Silvesters' sound system as Renata ferried cocktails back and forth from the butler's pantry. Lizzie set to work on preparing the guacamole, using a *molcajete* the Silvesters had purchased on a trip to Riviera Maya.

"Oh, look, Lizzie is making the guacamole!" Kathryn cried as she shepherded everyone toward the kitchen island.

"I am obsessed with guacamole," Barb said, trading her empty glass for a full one. "You shouldn't let me near it—I swear I'll eat the whole bowl myself."

"How do you make it?" Diana asked.

Lizzie felt the crowd's eyes on her and took a deep breath as she switched into performance mode. "Well, first you start with a bunch of perfectly ripe avocados."

She explained to everyone how to spot a ripe avocado (yields to firm gentle pressure, is green under the stem) and began slicing open the avocados and removing the buttery green flesh. She felt the personality she'd cultivated on TV return, describing each step carefully before moving on to the next and peppering her performance with amusing anecdotes. This was what she'd been trained to do: keep them listening, put on a show, avoid awkward silences, and cover up any mistakes. Before now, she had almost forgotten what it was like to be the center of attention, to have the spotlight on her as the expert and star, but as the Silvesters' guests hung on her every word she realized she missed it.

"And there you have it," she said as she scraped the guacamole into a large serving bowl. Renata swooped in and placed the bowl at the center of a platter that she'd already filled with tortilla chips.

"Bravo!" Barb said as she reached in for a chip. She scooped up a large dollop of guacamole and shoveled it into her mouth. "Oh my God. Take it away. I'm not kidding. Take it. Now. I'll eat the whole damn bowl."

Sam tried some next. "Yeah, baby. That's what I'm talking about." He nodded at Renata. "You give her a few tips?"

Renata looked puzzled. "No. . . ."

"I get it—better keep those family recipes a secret, right?"

It took a minute for Lizzie to catch on, but once she did she was offended on Renata's behalf. She was pretty sure Renata was Bolivian, not Mexican, and anyway, what kind of thing was that to say? But to Lizzie's surprise, Renata didn't look bothered, and that almost upset her more. Was this the kind of behavior she put up with on a regular basis? Would Lizzie be expected to do the same?

Lizzie had begun tidying her station when Zoe appeared in the living room. "Did I miss the show?"

Everyone turned around, and Zoe raised an eyebrow as she smiled and waved, as if she were uncomfortable being the center of attention, even if that had been her objective. She wore a floaty pink dress with an uneven hem that came to the floor in the back and her mid-calf in the front. Lizzie had to admit: For all of Zoe's quirks, she was beautiful and seemed to look good in just about everything.

Sam whistled. "Jim, you better look out for this one. If I were a younger man . . ."

Kathryn nudged him with her elbow, and Zoe rolled her eyes.

"If you were a younger man, I wouldn't let you anywhere near my daughter," Jim said. Everyone laughed.

"Would you listen to this guy? Like I didn't know you back when. You were worse than I was!"

"I don't think that's possible."

"Oh, really? Maybe it's time for a few stories from our trip to Miami circa 1973—"

"I don't think anyone needs to hear those stories," Kathryn jumped in. Lizzie wasn't sure if it was the margaritas or Sam's threats, but Kathryn's cheeks had gone a little pink.

"No, no—by all means," Zoe said, rubbing her hands together as she approached the island. "I'd love to hear more. Sounds to me like this party is just getting started."

Her parents' friends laughed, and in the blink of an eye Zoe became the funniest and most interesting person in the room.

The party continued for several more hours. The booze flowed freely, and the menu was a hit, and Lizzie felt comfortable saying the latter wasn't entirely due to the former. Even Zoe seemed to enjoy the things she could eat, though she never explicitly said so. Lizzie wondered if Zoe had taken any pictures. She'd been too busy to notice.

Lizzie cleaned up the butler's pantry while the Silvesters and their friends took turns whacking a piñata shaped like a dollar sign in the living room. She wondered if, instead of candy, there was actual money inside and, if so, how she could get in on the action. As a chorus of hoots and hollers filled the house, Lizzie removed a fruit platter and tres leches cake from the refrigerator in preparation for dessert. She suddenly heard footsteps behind her, but before she could turn around she felt a hand on her back.

"That pork was out of this world, sweetheart," Sam said. He was slurring his words a little, and even without facing him Lizzie could smell the liquor on his breath.

"Thanks..." she said. She couldn't bring herself to turn around. At the same time, she couldn't leave the refrigerator door open forever, so she awkwardly slipped to the side with the platters in her hands, squeezing past Sam before sliding the desserts onto the counter.

"What do we have here?" She could feel him moving closer, and before she knew it he was peering over her shoulder. His stiff, apricot hair grazed her cheek. She shuddered.

"Fruit, and pastel de tres leches."

"Oo-o-oh, I love it when you *habla espanol.*" He rested his hand on her shoulder. Lizzie thought she might throw up.

"Listen, if you don't mind"—

"Uncle Sam, stop being gross."

Zoe appeared in the doorway, a glass of wine in her hand.

"Aw, come on, Zo. You know I'm a gentle giant."

"So you say.... Why don't you go hit on someone your own age? Barb looks pretty lonely out there."

Sam smirked. "And we can't have that." He gave Lizzie's shoulder one last pat. "Another time, sweetheart. Keep up the good work."

He lumbered toward the doorway, giving Zoe a peck on the cheek before leaving the room.

"Sorry about that," Zoe said.

"Not your fault. But I appreciate the help."

"Any time. My parents' friends are pretty lame. Barb is okay, but the rest..." She took a sip of wine and pointed at the cake. "My dad will love that. He's totally into anything rich and creamy. Basically, if it's unhealthy and might give him a heart attack he wants it."

Lizzie wasn't sure if Zoe was complimenting her dessert or dissing it, but she was too tired by this point in the evening to care. "Well, I hope he enjoys it. And if he feels like being virtuous, there's always fruit."

"Which is all the rest of us will probably eat, except for my dad and Sam, who could probably eat the whole cake themselves. Or at least Sam could. That belly..." She leaned against the door frame. "So what do you think of the gig so far?"

"I like it," Lizzie said.

"Must be pretty different from what you're used to."

"Yes and no. Cooking in front of everyone tonight reminded me a lot of my old show."

"Really?"

"I was surprised. But it's funny—once my show got canceled, I actually had to get used to cooking in silence again. I'd been so used to talking as I cooked that I found myself saying, 'And now add a squeeze of lemon juice...,' even though no one else was there."

"I guess the difference tonight is that no one here really wants to learn how to make any of this themselves. They all have other people cook for them. I bet they don't even know how to turn on their ovens. I mean, I do, but Barb? Wendy? No way."

Lizzie laid a serving spoon on the fruit platter. "Speaking of cooking, I've been meaning to ask...."

She hesitated. Did she really want to bring up Zoe's blog? What difference did it make if she posted photos of Lizzie's food and claimed credit for herself? Did it really matter? But that was the problem: It did matter, at least to Lizzie. Those were her recipes and her meals, and even if their provenance wasn't a matter of life and death, it bothered Lizzie that Zoe would imply she'd made them herself.

"Yes?" Zoe prompted, her eyebrows raised.

"I think I came across your blog."

"Oh." An uncomfortable silence hung between them. "Sorry—you said you had a question. Is that a question?"

"No, I just . . . I saw some of the photos. Of my food."

Zoe stared back at her. "Like what?"

"My beet salad, the roasted vegetable platter, a few other things . . ."

"Oh. Right." She took a sip of wine. "Okay . . . so what's the question?"

"Did you . . . I mean, you seemed to suggest those were things you made, and I wasn't sure . . ." Lizzie tripped over her words. Why was she pussyfooting around the issue? Something about Zoe's demeanor made it very difficult for Lizzie to say what she wanted, which wasn't a question at all: *I don't appreciate you claiming my recipes as your own, and I'd like you to stop.*

"You weren't sure what?"

"I wasn't sure if you planned to add those recipes to your site, since you didn't actually make them yourself."

Zoe swirled her glass and didn't say anything for what, to Lizzie, felt like a long time. "I was sort of using them as placeholders," she said eventually. "I mean, hello, you're in the kitchen all the time. When am I supposed to do any cooking myself?"

"Oh—well, if you ever want to use the kitchen, just tell me. It's your house."

"It's my parents' house."

"Right, but by extension . . ." Lizzie remembered the whispered conversations between Jim and Kathryn about wiring money to Zoe. Even though Zoe was twenty-three (and by all accounts had been flitting about Europe over the past year, exploring the likes of London, Budapest, Zagreb, and Nice on her own), their financial lives still seemed inextricably linked, and from what Lizzie could glean, the only one who had a problem with that was Jim.

"Yeah, I guess, but if you need to make my dad lunch it's not like I can kick you out."

"True, but I'm sure we could share the space. All you need to do is ask."

Zoe shrugged. "Sure, okay. Next time I'll do that."

"And if you want to post photos of my food ... could you at least credit me with the recipe? I'd be happy to contribute a guest post sometime, if you want."

"Most of my audience probably doesn't even know who you are. It's not like you're famous anymore."

Lizzie knew she'd set herself up for that, but the words still stung. "That doesn't mean I couldn't write a post—"

"Oh, I get it. You want to tap into my readership. Get a little name recognition from a new crowd."

"No, that isn't it at all."

"Please, I know how this works. Most people don't remember who you are, and the ones who do don't really care, unless they're lame like my parents' friends. So you figure you can ride my coattails."

"That isn't what I'm trying to do."

"Really? You don't wish you had your old job back?"

"No." But even as Lizzie said the words, she wasn't sure they were entirely true. If her old producer, Nick, called her up today and offered her another show, would she accept? In a heartbeat. Regardless, her reasons for wanting recognition on Zoe's site had nothing to do with a desire for fame.

"I find that hard to believe," Zoe said. "But whatever the case, I don't really do guest posts, so that wouldn't work anyway. I can mention you in one of my posts, though. Maybe if you give me the recipe for the beet salad, I can tell people you developed it."

Lizzie hesitated. "Okay. That works."

She couldn't believe she was negotiating with someone seven years her junior, who'd probably never had a summer job, much less an actual career. Yet Zoe had a domineering personality that always made Lizzie feel as if she needed to apologize, even when she'd done nothing wrong.

"You can e-mail me the recipe. Or just leave it for me in the kitchen or something."

"I don't think I have your e-mail."

"Considering you found my site, it shouldn't be that hard to figure out. My e-mail is right there."

"Oh, right. Sorry." Lizzie drew a cake knife from one of the drawers and laid it on the cake platter. "By the way, I'm really sorry about your friend Marie."

Zoe blanched. "What?"

"Your friend Marie. The one mentioned on your site. You said she had cancer . . . ?"

"Yeah, so?"

"I'm just sorry she had to go through all that, and that you did too. It must have been a really tough time."

Zoe stared at her for a long time. "You don't know anything about it," she finally snapped, and then she turned around and left without saying another word.

CHAPTER 15

Linda,

Sorry I hung up so abruptly earlier, but I'm still trying to process all of this. I know you're upset, but trust me when I say you aren't even half as upset and confused as I am. Obviously I always knew at the back of my mind this was a possible outcome, but the doctor had seemed so sincere when he reassured me it was probably nothing that I convinced myself he was right. If he'd used the word "possibly" instead of "probably," I would have braced myself a little more, but nothing I can do about that now.

Like I said, it's pretty small (only 7mm), but apparently it's an aggressive type (triple negative—ugh). So while the surgeon said they often just do radiation and hormone therapy after a lumpectomy with a lump that small, he thinks the oncologist may want to take a more aggressive approach. You know what that means: chemo. I'm waiting to hear what the oncologist says, but I'm just not sure I can bring myself to do it. I'm all for getting rid of the cancer cells (obviously), but chemo is just thoroughly, horribly brutal. We've both watched friends go through it, so you know what I'm talking about. And sometimes it doesn't even work. Remember Alice White? Six rounds, and she lost her hair and all of her energy, and in the end the cancer still came back. I remember at the time thinking, "What a waste." Imagine all of the other things she could have been doing during that time. And then, of course, I think of Ryan and everything he went through as a baby. Hell of a lot of good "modern medicine" did him.

Anyway, I haven't decided yet what I'm going to do. But now I really do need to say something to Gary. It was different when it was probably nothing, but now that it's something, I can't keep him in the dark. It isn't fair. I wouldn't want him to keep something like this from me. Our relationship has gotten serious pretty quickly, so if I expect him to stick by me through this, I have to be open about what's going on. In a lot of ways, it's more important for him to be in the loop than Frank. (I am going to tell Frank, by the way. Don't ask me why—I guess I still feel connected to him, given all we went through.)

Having said all of that, I have one request of you: Do NOT say anything to Lizzie. Please. She's been going through a rough time lately, professionally and personally, and the last thing I want is for her to worry about me. She needs to sort herself out first. I don't want this diagnosis to throw her life off track, too. Obviously I will tell her once I have a treatment protocol, but until I decide how and when, please keep this news to yourself. Promise?

I'll give you a call later to talk about all of this in more detail. But for now, please don't worry. I'm doing enough of that for the both of us. Just be there for me, like you always have been. I need you now more than ever.

xxoo

S

CHAPTER 16

The rest of Sam Offerman's visit passed without incident, much to Lizzie's relief. She could tolerate Barb's drunkenness and Kathryn's loquaciousness, but she had a much harder time putting up with Sam's arrogance and chauvinism. Every time he entered the room, Lizzie stiffened, praying he wouldn't make another pass at her or say some horribly offensive thing that would force Lizzie to bite her tongue until it bled. When he left Sunday, she felt her shoulders relax, as if they'd been carrying a heavy weight all weekend.

"Isn't Sam a laugh?" Kathryn said once she'd seen him off. She pulled up a chair along the kitchen island.

That's one word for it, Lizzie thought.

"Lucky for us, we get to have him back in two weeks!"

Lizzie tried to mask her disappointment. "Oh? What's the occasion?"

"Only the birth of our great nation!"

The Fourth of July. Lizzie had almost forgotten. For as long as Lizzie could remember, Independence Day had snuck up on her. In her mind the holiday took place in the middle of summer, when really it was closer to the beginning. But somehow summer always felt like a big hill, where you climbed and climbed until you reached the

Fourth of July at the peak, and everything that followed was a clumsy roll and tumble toward Labor Day.

Lizzie thought back to her text exchange with April and her mention of a party. "So what's the plan? Are you thinking of something similar to the Memorial Day barbecue?"

"Oh, no, no—I mean, yes, there will be a party, and yes, there will be lots of people and food and drinks, but the menu has to be totally different. Many of the guests will be repeats from the barbecue, so I don't want them thinking we're a one-trick pony. Speaking of ponies . . ." She tapped her lip as she drifted off in thought. Lizzie couldn't imagine where she was headed.

"Ponies . . . ?"

Kathryn snapped back to attention. "Sorry—I was just thinking. One of Jim's friends might bring his granddaughter in the afternoon—before the party really gets going obviously—and I was wondering if we should hire someone to do pony rides. She's only nine months, so I guess that's a little young. Do you think?"

Lizzie knew nothing about babies, but she was almost certain pony rides were meant for toddlers and school-age children. "Probably. Can a nine-month-old sit up?"

"Oh, sure. At least I think so? It's amazing how quickly you forget these things. I mean, it seems like just yesterday Zoe was a baby, but if you asked me when she started to sit up or roll over or talk, I couldn't tell you. My gosh, at this point it feels as if she's been talking forever!"

"I know the feeling," Lizzie said. "So back to the party."

"Right! The party. We are expecting about fifty people, and as I said, a lot of them came to the Memorial Day celebration. So no chicken or shrimp or beef kebabs. Last year we did the traditional burgers and hot dogs, which worked well, but again—no one-trick ponies here! Let's try to come up with something different."

"Different as in grilled swordfish and chicken teriyaki, or chili dogs instead of plain hot dogs?"

"See, this is why I hire a cook—I just don't know! I guess it's our country's birthday, so we should stick with a very American menu. Our party will not be where patriotism goes to die. I've never liked chili dogs—they give me the most *horrible* gas—but I like how you're thinking. Is there another kind of fancy hot dog you could make?"

"It isn't fancy, but I could do Chicago-style hot dogs: poppy seed buns, tons of toppings, that kind of thing."

"Oh, that sounds interesting. Sam will love it. Did you know he's from Chicago originally? His midwestern accent has all but vanished, but he's a Chicago boy through and through."

Lizzie wondered if that meant he supported the Cubs or that his business ethos was reminiscent of Al Capone's.

"And with all those vegetables," Kathryn continued, "it sounds like I'll be able to enjoy a dog myself—without the bun, of course."

Lizzie wasn't sure why Kathryn always felt the need to stress the restrictions of her diet. They both knew what they were. Lizzie couldn't figure out if it was a means of keeping herself on track, or of making herself feel virtuous, or a combination of the two.

"As for the burgers," Lizzie said, "I could do a riff on a regular burger, like an Asian burger flavored with soy sauce and ginger—"

"Oh, no, I don't really think that would be appropriate. Do you?"

"Why not?"

"It's Independence Day—*American* Independence Day," Kathryn said.

"Right...." Lizzie wondered if Kathryn was confused and thought America had won its independence from the Chinese. "Is there something wrong with soy sauce?"

"There's nothing wrong with it. It just doesn't feel very American, you know?"

Lizzie was tempted to argue that more Americans probably ordered Chinese takeout on a weekly basis than had ever eaten a Chicago-style hot dog, never mind the fact that a sizable proportion of the U.S. population was of some sort of Asian descent. But she sensed a "melting pot" themed Fourth of July party would not be Kathryn's style.

"Okay, well, what about . . ." Lizzie stopped herself.

"What?"

"Never mind. I hadn't really thought the idea all the way through."

"That's okay—I'm open to anything! Well, not anything. But

you know what I mean. I can't shoot down an idea if I've never even heard it."

Exactly, Lizzie thought.

"I was just thinking . . . you can't get more American than Mc-Donald's, so maybe I could do a riff on a Big Mac? With only one burger instead of two, and maybe even turkey instead of beef, if that's what you're into. And I could do a veggie burger version, too, for Zoe and any other vegetarians."

Kathryn brightened. "I love it. Love it! Zoe will be thrilled. Mind you, I'm not sure how much she'll attend. Apparently a bunch of her friends are throwing parties that weekend. But she said she'd stay at least for a little bit, especially if you're cooking. She seems very happy with your food."

"Really?"

"Oh, definitely. You couldn't tell?"

"She can be a little . . . difficult to read."

"That's true. But she really does seem pleased—such a change from last summer. I guess things did start off on the right foot with Bob, but they went south pretty quick, as you know."

Lizzie didn't know, other than whatever vague allusions Kathryn had made in their previous conversation on the matter. But before she could ask Kathryn to clarify, Kathryn changed the subject.

"Anyway, I'll send you the final numbers once I have them. Nate threatened to come in for the party, but it looks like he'll be too busy in DC. In fairness, I guess Washington really is the place to be to celebrate our country's birth. Not that I think that has anything to do with his reasons."

It was the first time Kathryn had mentioned Nate since the interview at her house in Gladwyne. "He'll be coming later in July, though, right?"

Kathryn sighed. "So he says. Hopefully he will spare you the headaches he gives the rest of us."

Lizzie shared Kathryn's wish, because if Nate was anything like Zoe she had a long, hard road ahead of her.

"Oh, and I forgot to mention—I think your friend April will be joining us as well."

"That's what she said."

"You two still keep in touch then?"

"A bit," Lizzie said. That was only true as of the last few weeks, but she didn't feel like clarifying.

"Oh, good. Because at the Memorial Day barbecue, I got the sense that you'd maybe had a falling-out . . . ?" She raised her eyebrows expectantly, hungry for a juicy scrap of gossip.

Lizzie's falling-out with April wasn't a big secret—anyone who'd known them in college knew they'd stopped speaking once Lizzie's show took off and April was no longer a part of its production—but Lizzie couldn't bring herself to indulge Kathryn's unrelenting appetite for rumors and scandal. So instead, she simply said, "Nothing as dramatic as that," because even if that wasn't entirely true, she didn't think she owed it to Kathryn to elaborate.

When Lizzie met April Sherman on her first day at Penn, she wasn't sure they'd be friends. April burst into their Hill House dorm room, a small chamber with two lofted extra-long twin beds and very little space between them, and announced her arrival with the sort of fanfare one might expect from a Hollywood star.

"I'm here!" she exclaimed, as if everyone on the floor had been waiting for her to show up and could now relax.

It was a brutally hot August day, and Lizzie and her mom were sweating as they attempted to unpack Lizzie's things. The room wasn't air-conditioned, something Lizzie had been prepared for more in theory than practice. She'd brought a fan, but whatever relief it brought was minimal.

Lizzie wiped her brow with the back of her arm and extended her hand toward April.

"Hi, I'm Lizzie," she said. "Sorry about the mess—there's even less space than I expected."

April shook her hand and surveyed the room. "You can say that again. Where am I supposed to put all of my sweaters?"

Sweaters were the last articles of clothing on Lizzie's mind as she stood in a room whose temperature seemed to hover somewhere around ninety-five degrees. But April had arrived with a wardrobe big enough to clothe half of Philadelphia and was quickly realizing that four small drawers beneath the lofted bed weren't going to cut it.

"Daddy?" Her father, a tall black man with horn-rimmed glasses, appeared in the doorway, lugging one of April's suitcases. "Daddy, I think you're going to need to take one of those back home with you. There isn't enough space. See?"

He dropped the suitcase at his feet and heaved a sigh. "Didn't I warn you . . . ?"

"I know, but I didn't think it would be *this* small."

Her dad shook his head and then smiled at Lizzie and her mom. "Sorry—Steve Sherman. April's dad."

"Susan Glass," Lizzie's mom said, wiping her hand on her shorts before shaking his.

"My wife, Kate, should be here any second," he said. "She's un-loading more stuff from the car."

Lizzie wondered if he was waiting for her mom to say some-thing like, *So is my husband,* but she wouldn't be saying that be-cause she was divorced, and Lizzie hadn't wanted her dad to come. It's not that she didn't want his help or for him to be a part of this life moment. She just knew moving into her dorm would be stress-ful and chaotic, and she didn't want to layer her parents' awkward post-divorce relationship on top of that. She had enough on her plate as it was. Given the cramped space and stifling heat, Lizzie thought she'd made the right choice.

Moments later, April's mom showed up with yet another suit-case. She was a petite brunette, with olive skin and shoulder-length straight hair, and her brown eyes widened in disbelief as she sur-veyed the room.

"Seriously? We're paying more than forty grand for *this?*"

Lizzie and her mom laughed because they'd been thinking the same thing themselves, even if the bulk of Lizzie's tuition was being covered by loans and scholarships. Lizzie appreciated Kate's blunt-ness, a trait that, as Lizzie would learn, had been passed on to April in spades.

The two families crammed into the tiny space and did the best they could to make it livable. When Lizzie had found out over the summer that she'd been assigned to Hill House and not The Quad, where most freshmen lived, she was disappointed. She wanted the college experience she'd seen when she'd visited the year before— the Tudor Gothic architecture, the grassy courtyards teeming with undergrads reading books and playing Frisbee. She didn't want to live a half mile away in what looked like a brick fortress, marooned with a fraction of the freshman class. She tried to convince herself it would be fine, but as she dripped in sweat and watched April unpack more pairs of jeans than seemed possible or necessary she wasn't so sure.

April was . . . well, she was just so different from Lizzie. For starters, April's parents worked for the State Department, so April had lived all over the world until her parents eventually settled down outside Washington, DC. Kenya, Russia, Brazil—Lizzie could barely keep track of all the places April had called home. Meanwhile, Lizzie hadn't lived anywhere but Glenside her whole life. And April was so outgoing and outspoken. Lizzie didn't consider herself a shrinking violet, but next to April she could almost feel herself disappear. Everything about April was exotic—she was striking and unconventionally beautiful, well traveled, and worldly in a way Lizzie had always wanted to be. Lizzie didn't see what they could possibly have in common.

But what Lizzie quickly discovered was that they had one very important thing in common: Hill House. To whatever extent Lizzie felt isolated from the rest of the freshman class by her living arrangements, April felt that way, too, even more so, given her convivial nature. And so they became fast friends, leaning on each other for support as they navigated the joys and sorrows of freshman year. Even when they went to different parties and different bars, they'd meet in their room at the end of the night or in the wee hours of the next morning and rehash the evening's events: who'd made out with whom, who'd gone where, who'd drunk and eaten what.

It was during one of these late-night, alcohol-fueled conversations that April and Lizzie had come up with the idea for *Healthy U*. One night in February, April had stumbled in with a greasy slice of pizza from Lorenzo's and Lizzie rolled her eyes, knowing the next morning April would bitch and moan about needing to go on a diet and yell at Lizzie for letting her drunkenly binge on cheese and carbs. April hadn't gained the dreaded "freshman fifteen," but she'd put on about five to ten pounds since they'd first met in August.

"Don't roll your eyes at me," April had slurred, taking a bite of the pizza. "It's de-e-e-elicious."

"I'm sure it is. And you'll be complaining about it all day tomorrow."

She stared down at the oily slice. "Thas-s-s . . . true."

"Want me to get you something a little healthier?"

"Like what?"

"I don't know. I think I have carrots and hummus in the mini fridge."

"Do *you* feel like eating carrots and hummus when you're drunk?"

"No," Lizzie conceded.

"I want carbs-s-s-s-s-s."

Lizzie sighed. She wasn't as drunk as April, but she wanted carbs too. "I think I have some pita bread. If we can find some cheese and tomato sauce, we could make pita pizzas. It isn't exactly health food, but it's better than the grease bomb you're holding in your hand right now."

Lizzie couldn't remember exactly how it happened, but they scrounged their hall for pizza ingredients and made their way to the communal kitchen, and before she knew it she and April were scarfing down hot, cheesy pita pizzas, which were surprisingly easy and delicious.

"Oh my God, these are so go-o-o-o-o-od," April groaned as she tucked into hers.

"And now you can make them for yourself anytime, instead of resorting to Lorenzo's. You saw how easy they were to make, right?"

April nodded, then looked at Lizzie with narrowed eyes. "You know . . . you should have a show. Like on TV. *The Glass Kitchen. Cooking with Lizzie. Sizzle with Lizzie.*"

Lizzie laughed. "You've pretty much described my dream job."

"I'm not kidding. It's not just drunk idiots like me. Half of these clowns would be a lot better off if they knew how to make a pita pizza."

"You're probably right."

"Not probably. Definitely."

"Okay, so who's producing this show?"

April wiped the corners of her mouth. "I am. And you're in front of the camera. And we'll shoot it right here in this kitchen, and everyone will love it."

"Can I invite guest chefs?"

"Of course."

"And use the word 'spatchcock'?"

"Obviously."

"Then I think we have ourselves a hit!"

They laughed, but really, neither of them was joking. Lizzie had loved to cook since she was a little girl, and she credited it with getting her through her parents' divorce. At first, the batches of chocolate chip cookies and Duncan Hines brownies were a way to occupy herself so that she didn't have to think too much about her father's absence. But once she'd come to terms with that, she carried on cooking and baking not because it was a distraction but because she actually enjoyed dumping a bunch of ingredients into a bowl or pot and creating something delicious. Having her own cooking show would be a dream come true.

April may not have dreamed of producing a cooking show, but she'd always dreamed of working in TV. She often talked about how after college she planned to move to New York, where she'd work for one of the networks or MTV or CNN or, frankly, anyone who was willing to hire her so that she could get her foot in the door. She already had a summer internship lined up with NBC, which impressed Lizzie, who still hadn't managed to sort out her summer plans. A cooking show would be a perfect addition to April's already dazzling résumé.

In the months that followed, they continually brought up the idea as a joke, usually when they were drunkenly cooking in the communal kitchen after a night of partying. But soon they started joking in moments of sobriety as well, until it was no longer a joke and they began thinking through what they'd actually need to do to get a show on the air: camera, editing software, a channel on which to air the finished product. What at one time seemed like a gag or a fantasy began to crystallize into an actual thing, and by sophomore year that thing was a campus cooking show on the Penn Video Network.

It took two years for the show to take off, but by Lizzie's senior year her thirty-minute cooking program was the most-watched student-produced program on Penn's campus. And that's when things started to get crazy. First the *Daily Pennsylvanian* ran an article on Lizzie and April. That article raised their on-campus profile, but it also attracted the interest of a food writer for the *New York Times,* who happened to be a Penn alum. The reporter featured Lizzie and her show on the front page of the dining section, in a story about the rise in campus cooking. Other schools and students were mentioned, but Lizzie's *Healthy U* was the main focus and her picture was splashed across the paper—and, eventually, the Internet, as the story was tweeted and retweeted and shared hundreds of times.

In a matter of days, Lizzie had been contacted by dozens of people who'd read the *Times* piece: agents, editors, *Bon Appétit* magazine, *The View,* the *Today* show. Lizzie could barely keep up with the volume. Before she knew it, she had a book agent, a film agent, a book deal, and a meeting with executives at the Food Network about a potential show.

Initially, April acted as if she didn't mind that Lizzie was getting all of the attention, though she was always quick to provide cautionary balance to Lizzie's elation.

"Be careful—these people have their own agendas. At the end of the day, they're looking out for themselves."

But Lizzie was so swept up in the excitement that she figured April was just jealous. April's name appeared once or twice in the *Times* article, but Lizzie was clearly portrayed as the star, and in subsequent profiles in other media outlets April rarely got a mention. Lizzie did talk about April in interviews, but as the media circus took on a life of its own people seemed less interested in Lizzie's off-camera partner in crime and more interested in leveraging Lizzie's on-camera personality. Lizzie felt a bit guilty—the idea for a show had, admittedly, been April's, and April was the one who'd always dreamed of a career in television—but the onslaught of attention came fast and furious and swallowed Lizzie up before she realized what was happening.

By the time Lizzie met with the Food Network during the second semester senior year, no one asked about April anymore and Lizzie had stopped trying to include her in interviews and meetings. At first, Lizzie figured April didn't mind. Or at least she convinced herself that was the case. The truth was, they had come to a point in their friendship where they hadn't really spoken in months. April was so busy interviewing for jobs—with NBC and MTV and CNN but also less competitive PR firms and ad agencies—that she wasn't home most of the time, and Lizzie was constantly taking the train into New York for meetings. Lizzie told herself they were as close as they'd ever been, even if deep down she knew that wasn't true.

When the Food Network finally offered her a show, she rushed into April's room as soon as she got off the phone with her agent.

"It's happening!" she cried. "Thirteen episodes. Saturday mornings at nine thirty. We start taping next month!"

April slipped her laptop into her bag and slung the bag over her shoulder. "Good luck," she said in a steely voice. She brushed past Lizzie and left their off-campus house without saying another word.

Looking back on it, Lizzie didn't know why she was at all surprised by April's reaction. What did she expect? That April would jump up and down in excitement? "Yippee! I'm so thrilled that you ditched me and will now be making lots of money off my idea!" Thinking about it now made Lizzie cringe. But at the time, she was genuinely hurt and had only just begun to realize that their friendship would probably never be the same again.

That was the last conversation she had with April before leaving Penn. Within a few weeks, Lizzie had packed up her belongings in their house on Spruce Street and moved to New York to begin work on the pilot episode. The two of them never had a knock-down, drag-out fight, but every time Lizzie reached out she was met with radio silence. Lizzie had dropped all of her classes that semester and thus wasn't eligible to graduate in May with the rest of her class (a fact she'd kept from her producers), but she expected at least a few invitations to the various graduation parties on campus. And a few did come. But when she saw photos on Facebook of April's own party, from which Lizzie had been conspicuously absent and excluded, she knew April's snub had not been an accident.

After that, Lizzie stopped trying to get in touch with April and the two of them never spoke again—until they ran into each other at the Silvesters' Memorial Day barbecue. Lizzie wanted to believe that enough time had passed to heal any wounds she'd inflicted on their friendship. After all, it had been nearly a decade. So much had changed. But if April's demeanor at the barbecue was any indication, Lizzie knew that was wishful thinking. There was still hurt and resentment on both sides, and if they had any hope of starting fresh it would take more than a little conversation at a Fourth of July party.

Nevertheless, once Kathryn had finalized the menu and guest list for the party Lizzie shot off a text to April:

Really looking forward to seeing you on the 4th. It's been too long.

All of that was true. Lizzie was looking forward to seeing April, and too much time had passed since they'd had a meaningful conversation. But a bland, semi-conciliatory text was also a lot easier than what Lizzie really wanted to say and somehow couldn't, which was: "I'm sorry."

CHAPTER 17

July 4 arrived, and the Silvesters' house was a hub of activity. Deliverymen shuttled decorations into the house—balloons, streamers, table arrangements, pool décor—all tastefully but unquestionably patriotic. Kathryn was running around like a Tasmanian devil, ensuring every centerpiece and tiki torch was in its right place.

"Oh, this looks fabulous—fabulous!" she crowed as she centered a glittery arrangement of hydrangeas, roses, stars, and ribbons. "Ken has outdone himself yet again."

Lizzie didn't know who Ken was, but Kathryn spoke as if she should, so Lizzie smiled and nodded because whoever he was, he'd gone all-out with the décor. There were hundreds of toothpicks festooned with American flags, star-spangled linen napkins, and red, white, and blue guest towels in the bathrooms along with French-milled star-shaped soaps. Even the enormous inflatable swan in their pool was adorned with a sparkly red, white, and blue crown, which looked as if it had been made specifically for that purpose. Lizzie wondered where Ken had found it. Did they make accessories for pool accessories? These were the sorts of questions Lizzie had found herself asking ever since she moved in with the Silvesters for the summer. Some days, she almost didn't recognize herself.

Lizzie spent the morning prepping ingredients in the butler's pantry. Unlike the dinner party two weeks prior, tonight Lizzie's cooking would not be the entertainment. The Silvesters had hired other people to fill that role for the evening: a pyrotechnic crew to set off fireworks, a juggling mixologist to whip up signature cocktails, and, from what Lizzie overheard a few days earlier, a mime. Lizzie had never understood the appeal of mimes. Even as a little girl, she'd wonder, *Why are you pretending to be stuck in a box?* It didn't make any sense. Not to mention all that makeup. The white faces, the blackened eyes—it was kind of terrifying. She supposed the only appeal was that they didn't speak. After dealing with Kathryn for more than a month, Lizzie did not take this attribute for granted.

The morning wore on, and Lizzie worried she was getting behind. She had made the potato salad and special burger sauce and had shaped the veggie and turkey burgers, but she still needed to prepare all of the hot dog toppings and finish the side dishes, many of which couldn't be dressed and garnished until the last minute. None of the dishes on the menu were overly elaborate, but the quantities were dizzying. The Silvesters were expecting about fifty-five guests, so Lizzie found herself quintupling many of her tried-and-true recipes, and those were the ones that already made large quantities. Others she found herself scaling up by a factor of ten. At one point, as she heaved twenty pounds of potatoes onto the counter, she felt as if she were cooking for an army.

The other problem was that, unlike the Memorial Day barbecue, this time Kathryn wanted to make sure Lizzie accommodated her guests' many dietary restrictions. Apparently, although Lizzie's menu had been popular, there had been a few complaints from those on special diets. Some were Paleo like Kathryn or vegan like Zoe, but then there were the ones with nut allergies and soy allergies and the ones who were gluten-free. A few were on a macrobiotic diet and another was pre-diabetic. One of the more perplexing cases was a friend who was "experimenting" with kosher.

"He isn't Jewish," Kathryn explained. "But he appreciates the kosher ethos. I think he's been studying the kabbalah."

Lizzie didn't have a problem with any of these diets in theory, but combining them all in practice meant she had to make lots of extra dishes to make sure everyone had something to eat. When had something as traditionally low-key as a summer barbecue gotten so complicated? She half-jokingly worried someone would request the beef for the burgers come from cows who'd been sung lullabies and fed bottled water.

As she set about slicing tomatoes for the burgers and hot dogs, Kathryn blew into the kitchen, her hands in the air.

"Of course he would pull this a few hours before the party," she said. "Typical!"

"Who?"

She grimaced. "Nate. Apparently he had a last-minute change of plans and will be visiting for the Fourth."

"Oh." Lizzie wasn't really sure what to say. "Well, there's plenty of food. I made extra of everything. What's one more, right?"

"Normally I'd agree, but Nate is . . . I mean, never mind that I see Jim's ex every time I look at Nate's face. Those eyes." She shivered. "But I'm just not in the mood for another fight! The two of them, every time, like clockwork. It all starts off fine, and then—bam!—fireworks. And not *nearly* as nice as the ones I've paid a fortune to see tonight."

"Is there . . . a specific issue? Or they just don't get along?"

Lizzie knew her question might be too personal, but given Kathryn's penchant for dishing dirt, she figured it might be within bounds.

"They get along fine, most of the time. If it weren't for Nate's ridiculous career choices, there probably wouldn't even be an issue. But he's so headstrong." She huffed. "I wonder where he gets *that* from."

Lizzie couldn't tell whether Kathryn was implying the answer was Jim or his ex-wife.

"What does he do for a living?"

Kathryn rolled her eyes. "God knows. It's a question I've asked myself a million times."

Lizzie arranged the tomato slices on a platter. "How long is he staying?"

"Until tomorrow. At least it's a quick trip this time. Although he'll be back in a week for his vacation. I seriously do not understand the point of visiting now for, what? Twenty-four hours? What's the point? I'd understand if he'd switched up his vacation days and were staying through the week, but no. This is a surprise visit, just for the heck of it. It doesn't make any sense at all, unless the entire point of his visit is to torture us, in which case, bravo! Mission accomplished."

Lizzie was trying to give Kathryn's stepson the benefit of the doubt, but she was beginning to dread his visit as well. Kathryn hadn't given Zoe nearly this much of a negative preamble, and Zoe seemed pretty terrible.

"Does he have any dietary restrictions?" Lizzie braced herself but figured it was worth asking—if not for today's party, then for his visit in seven days.

"Pizza," Kathryn said.

"He doesn't like pizza?"

What kind of person didn't like pizza? It was probably the world's most-liked food, followed closely by chocolate.

"No, he loves pizza. He could eat it for every meal. Sorry, I should have clarified. That isn't a restriction. It's a necessity. He'll request it for at least one meal while he's here, if not several—mostly to annoy me and Zoe because we can't eat it." She paused, and Lizzie braced herself for what she knew would follow. "Unless it's Paleo."

"Right."

"Anyway, don't trouble yourself with whipping up a pizza for this party. I assume there isn't time. And even if there were, he can't spring a visit on us like this and then expect the royal treatment. He will survive without his *quattro formaggi*."

Lizzie had so many questions, the first being, *Does he only eat pizza?* And the second being, *Does it have to be plain cheese?* Because now the pendulum had swung the other direction and she worried she'd be cooking for a guy who only ate pizza, and plain pizza at that. She'd cooked for such people before, but they were also usually fans of Thomas the Tank Engine.

Before Lizzie could ask any more about Nate's dietary idiosyncrasies, Renata appeared in the doorway. "Excuse me—Mrs.

Silvester? The ice sculpture has arrived, but you might want to come see. The eagle . . . something doesn't seem quite right."

"Oh, dear. Lizzie, I'm sorry, but we will have to continue this conversation another time. Just . . . whatever. Nate will eat what you serve. And for breakfast tomorrow . . . well, he can eat leftover hot dogs for all I care." She headed for the door. "Now, Renata, what seems to be the problem with the—oh! Oh, my! Are you . . . Is that . . . What is in his *mouth?*"

She rushed out of the room, and Lizzie couldn't decide whether this would be the worst Fourth of July party she'd ever encountered or the absolute best.

The ice sculpture was, indeed, not quite right. From what Lizzie could piece together from the snippets of conversation she overheard, Ken had requested a bald eagle perched atop a cliff. The artist had delivered that representation but had also included a snake in the eagle's mouth, thinking it added to the bird's majesty. However, when the delivery crew arrived to pick up the sculpture they, being of Mexican descent, informed the artist that an eagle with a snake in its mouth was Mexico's coat of arms. Upon hearing this, the artist panicked and attempted to whittle down the snake to what he hoped resembled a ribbon, but the tail fell off in the process and the delivery crew grew sick of waiting and whisked the sculpture away, and so what was left in the eagle's mouth resembled a limp phallus.

"Is there any way to remove it?" Kathryn shrieked into the phone. She had called Ken, who was off-site at another event. "Well, could you call him? What do you mean he's not picking up? How many times have you tried?"

She paced up and back in front of the sculpture. Lizzie couldn't see how anyone could fix it without lopping off the eagle's face or beak in the process. As inappropriate as an eagle with a cock in his mouth might be, she didn't think a decapitated eagle would be much better.

"Well, I'm not paying for this, Ken. I'm not. You saw the photo. It's obscene! What am I supposed to tell my guests? I'm not letting the delivery crew leave until someone fixes this. Well, they can take it away, then. No. No. No—I don't care how fabulous and sought-after he is. He could be fucking Brancusi, and it wouldn't change the fact that there is an eagle in my living room with a PENIS in his mouth! Do you hear me? *Do* you?"

Whatever goodwill Ken had built up with the swan tiara and patriotic toothpicks had vanished in the face of an X-rated ice sculpture. Lizzie thought the entire situation was hilarious and, if it were her party, she would leave the sculpture front and center. If nothing else, it made for a unique conversation starter. Kathryn, however, did not share this view.

"Renata!" she cried once she'd hung up on Ken. "Renata, tell these men to load the sculpture back onto the truck. I'd rather have no sculpture than...*that*." She turned her head away, as if she couldn't bear to look at it.

Renata spoke to the deliverymen in rapid-fire Spanish, and as Lizzie peered through the door in the butler's pantry she saw lots of gesturing and shrugging.

"They say they aren't authorized to remove it," Renata said.

"*What?*" Lizzie thought Kathryn's head might actually spin off her body. "I'm authorizing them. Me."

"They say the problem is at the other end. They cannot return it to the designer because they cannot get ahold of him."

"Then tell them to take it somewhere else. They can throw it in the ocean for all I care! Just get it out of here."

More high-speed Spanish. More hand waving and shrugging.

"I'm sorry, it seems—"

"Is it a matter of money? Because obviously that isn't a problem. Jim!" she called out. "Where's Jim? We'll cut them a check. How much? Would two hundred do it?"

Lizzie suspected it wasn't so much a matter of money and more a matter of hauling an enormous, heavy sculpture back onto a truck, with nowhere to take it. But as Kathryn tossed out higher and higher figures, Lizzie realized Kathryn would get her way. Frankly, for five hundred dollars Lizzie would happily come up with a plan to dispose of the sculpture, though hers would likely involve a hairdryer and a lot of towels.

"Oh, thank *God*," Kathryn sighed, collapsing onto one of the barstools as the deliverymen surrounded the statue and prepared to transport it back onto the truck. Lizzie had come into the kitchen to start arranging the finger foods. "Lizzie, I'm telling you right now—if you're coming out here to talk about a problem, I'm not sure I'll be able to handle it. I've already had more bad news today than I can take."

"I'm just plating the crudités and chips."

"Fabulous. Music to my ears. There's only so much drama one woman can take."

"What's the problem now?"

Lizzie turned to see a man in khaki cargo shorts and a white T-shirt standing at the top of the stairway. He wore a faded Washington Nationals baseball cap, which covered a mop of wavy brown hair, and he held a beat-up gray backpack over one of his shoulders.

"Nate. You're here." Kathryn couldn't have sounded less enthusiastic if she tried.

"I made great time. I'm kind of still in shock—that's never happened before, especially on the Fourth."

"I guess there's a first time for everything. . . ." She looked him up and down. "Though I guess not when it comes to improving your wardrobe."

"Aw, come on Kathryn. You like that I'm a little rough around the edges. It's part of my charm."

"So you say." She let out a deep sigh. "Listen, I can't really talk right now. Things have not been going as planned this morning."

"Oh?"

"Don't get too excited. I'm not in a place to talk about any of it right now."

"You? Not talk about something? Wow, this really must be serious."

"Nate, please. I am not in the mood."

"Okay, okay. Sorry. I'll go unpack my things." He caught Lizzie's eye. "I'm Nate, by the way. You must be the new chef?"

"Lizzie. Nice to meet you."

"Likewise. Maybe later you can fill me in—since Kathryn is feeling uncharacteristically taciturn today."

"Nate, I'm giving you ten seconds to get out of here before I officially lose it."

"Okay, sorry—I'm outta here." He gave Kathryn a salute. Be-

fore he turned to go downstairs, his eyes landed on the deliverymen, who'd taken hold of the platform holding the ice sculpture
and were getting ready to lift it.

"Whoa, hang on a second . . ." he said, narrowing his eyes to get
a better look. "Is that eagle holding a dick?"

The men managed to get rid of the ice sculpture just in time. No
sooner had they loaded it back onto the truck than the first guests
began to arrive. As with the Memorial Day barbecue, the Silvesters
had hired a small army of helpers to assist with passing out food
and drinks and cleaning up. White-clad servers milled around the
living room, porch, and pool deck, picking up empty cocktail
glasses and passing around pigs in a blanket that Lizzie had made,
with help from three mute women who were part of the temporary
staff. Lizzie wished they'd been around for the past two days, when
she had to boil twenty pounds of potatoes and chop so many
onions she wondered if her eyes would ever stop watering. She
knew it was her own fault for claiming she could do larger parties,
but she hadn't realized how thoroughly draining it would be to run
a catering operation.

Renata ordered the servers around, making sure every dish was
properly arranged with the coordinating label and that each label
clearly identified whether the item was vegan, kosher, gluten-free,
nut-free, dairy-free, and/or Paleo. Lizzie had given Kathryn a list of
what was what a few days ago, and Kathryn had passed the list
along to Ken, who managed to deliver gorgeous star-spangled
cards with all of the information written in festive calligraphy. It
was another triumph for Ken, but even combined with all of the
other successes, Lizzie doubted it was enough to make up for the
ice sculpture.

The crowd steadily grew as the afternoon wore on, and Lizzie
worked feverishly to replenish the snacks and hors d'oeuvres as she
prepared to transition to the main meal of hot dogs and burgers.
She had more help today than she did at the last party and was able
to turn over the grilling responsibilities to two men named Luis
and Jon, while she dressed the salads and garnished the side dishes.

Even with the help, she was sweating like crazy. Despite the hot and humid temperatures, Kathryn had insisted Lizzie wear her chef's coat ("It's more professional, don't you think? And safer. No burns on my watch!"). Lizzie couldn't argue with Kathryn that a starched, white coat was both more polished and protective than, say, a bathing suit, but as beads of sweat raced down her back she wished she were cooking in a bikini.

As Lizzie brought out a platter of pickled vegetables, she scanned the room for April. Given Kathryn's hysteria earlier in the day, she hadn't wanted to ask what time April might arrive. Kathryn probably didn't have any idea, and knowing April, she'd be fashionably late (though Lizzie always thought April's idea of what was "fashionable" bordered on rude). Lizzie hoped April wasn't *too* late, or they might not have a chance to talk. Not that it mattered, really. After all this time, Lizzie didn't really expect to patch things up in an evening. But the more she'd thought about the way they'd left things, the worse she felt and the more she wanted April to know she felt that way. Even if it didn't change anything, even if they never became friends again, she at least wanted April to know she was aware she'd been a shitty friend. Recently this had become very important to Lizzie, though she wasn't entirely sure why. Perhaps the downward spiral of her career had made her more reflective and self-aware, as if the person she was now and the person she was then were so different that she could view that younger woman with fresh, dispassionate eyes. Or maybe so many people had now cast her aside that she saw their relationship from April's perspective and realized what a crappy friend she'd been. Or maybe she was just getting older.

The crowd was thick, so Lizzie couldn't easily pick out faces, but from what she could tell, April hadn't arrived yet. The only person she could identify so far was Zoe, who appeared at the top of the stairway just as Lizzie was heading back to the butler's pantry. Zoe wore a maxi dress in a bold Hawaiian print of bright blues, greens, and yellows, her blond hair tumbling over her shoulders in long, sparkly waves. She stood next to a young man about her age, whose defining characteristic, at least to Lizzie, was that he was both shirtless and shoeless.

Lizzie slowed her step and tried not to stare, but she couldn't help it. He had the sort of rippled abs she'd only ever seen in Calvin Klein underwear advertisements, and his skin was a deep butterscotch. She wasn't attracted to him. She was more fascinated that he obviously thought it was appropriate to show up almost naked to an adult party thrown by multimillionaires. He was probably only twenty-two or twenty-three, but his age didn't fully explain his nakedness. Maybe he was a relative? It was possible, but that didn't explain it either. Lizzie may not have grown up in Gladwyne, but she knew showing up without a shirt or shoes was pretty tacky, even if he were the Silvesters' own son.

But to whatever extent Zoe's shirtless and shoeless friend scandalized Lizzie (and, if their expressions were to be believed, many of the Silvesters' guests), he thrilled Zoe, who appeared to revel in everyone's shock.

Ah, Lizzie thought. She wondered if it had been his decision to show up this way or if Zoe had goaded him into it. Zoe seemed to love getting a rise out of people, her parents in particular. Her only disappointment was probably that he didn't have any weird piercings and that he didn't show up completely nude.

Zoe caught Lizzie's eye, and though Lizzie tried to look away and pretend she hadn't been staring, it was too late.

"Did you put out the burgers yet?" she asked, making her way toward Lizzie, her shirtless friend at her side.

"Not yet. Soon."

"You made vegan ones, right?"

"Yep. And the special sauce is made with Vegenaise."

"Cool. Trevor is a vegan, too." She gestured to her friend. "Trevor, this is our cook for the summer, Lizzie."

"Hey." He raised his hand in a way that made Lizzie unsure if he was saying "hi" or waiting to give her a high five. She kept her focus on his eyes, trying very hard not to let them wander to his exposed stomach.

"Wait . . . I've seen you before," he said.

"Oh, yeah, she used to have a cooking show," Zoe said before Lizzie could answer. "*Healthy U.* It got canceled a while ago."

"No, no—I mean around here."

Lizzie studied his face. He didn't look familiar. "I don't think so," she said.

"You sure? I could swear I've seen you somewhere. Have you been hanging at The Princeton? Or Jack's?"

Lizzie shook her head. She hadn't been hanging anywhere but the Silvesters' house, at least not with any regularity.

"What about—"

"Jesus, Trevor, let it go. She's my parents' cook. She doesn't party. You probably saw her pumping gas or something." Zoe looked at Lizzie. "Trevor works at the Sunoco on Ocean Drive."

"The one across from Avalon Seafood?" Lizzie asked.

Trevor nodded. "Pumping gas like a boss."

"That's probably where you saw me. I got gas there the other week."

Trevor elbowed Zoe. "See? What'd I tell you? Trevor never forgets a face."

Zoe rolled her eyes, but her attention quickly shifted to her mother, who was flitting around the living room, in perfect hostess form.

"Looks like Mom is making small talk," Zoe said, though if Lizzie had to guess, nothing about Kathryn's talk was small. "Let's go and say hi. I'm sure she'd love to meet you."

But before Zoe and Trevor could make their way to Kathryn, Kathryn caught sight of them and made a beeline toward the kitchen.

"Zoe," she said, her smile tight at she reached them. "I didn't realize you were bringing a friend."

"You said I could invite people."

"I did. But you told me everyone you knew already had better plans—though honestly I don't know what could be better than this!"

"Kind of anything?"

Lizzie couldn't understand why Zoe acted like a bratty teenager so much of the time. She seemed to want it both ways—the respect and independence of an adult but also the financial support and attitude of a child. When would she realize she wasn't entitled to the former if she insisted on the latter?

"Anyway, some of Trevor's plans fell through, so. . . ." Zoe gave her mother a supercilious look. "I can tell him to leave if it's a problem."

"Of course it isn't a problem," Kathryn said. "You are both welcome."

"Really? Because you don't exactly seem—"

"It's fine. Honestly." Kathryn's eyes quickly ran up and down the length of Trevor's body. Her smile tightened, as if she was willing herself to be fine—fine!—with his exposed chest and bare feet. "I'm sorry—Trevor, was it?"

"Yup," he said, nodding slowly.

"Trevor, welcome. I'm Kathryn. Feel free to help yourself to some snacks—Lizzie here has whipped up some delicious hors d'oeuvres. And there's lots more coming. Burgers, hot dogs, potato salad. A real Fourth of July feast!"

"Sweet."

Lizzie waited for him to add a, *Thank you,* but he didn't.

"I'm not sure how long we'll stay," Zoe said. "There are a few other parties I want to hit up before the fireworks."

Kathryn brightened. "You're coming back for the fireworks?"

"No, not yours—the ones in Stone Harbor."

"Oh. Are you sure? Because Ken told me they would be fabulous this year. Not that Stone Harbor's won't be nice, but to be able to see them from your own house . . ."

"We're meeting people."

"You're welcome to bring them back here."

"Mom—get over it. We're not staying."

Kathryn sighed. "Well, obviously you'll stay long enough to eat a little something." She scanned Trevor's body a second time, barely masking her disapproval. "And maybe take a dip in the pool?"

"Probably not," Zoe said. "We'll grab a quick bite, but then we need to head out."

"There's no need to make it quick—you can stay as long as you like. And Trevor, if you need a place to change, our pool house has a shower and plenty of space."

"Nah, thanks, I'm good."

Kathryn blinked rapidly. She clearly didn't think he was good at all. "Are you sure? Because if you're worried about privacy, I promise, no one can see in. We made sure of that when we built it.

Though I guess maybe you aren't too worried about people see-ing ... well, you know. Not that you should be. I'm just saying. Whether you're worried about privacy or not, the shower is there, and you are more than welcome—"

"Mom, let it go. He doesn't want to shower."

"Or change into something else?" she asked.

"Not that either."

"Are you sure?"

"Do you have a problem with how he's dressed?" Zoe raised an eyebrow, willing her mom to engage. But Kathryn, having probably traveled down similar roads many times in her many years as a mother, backed down.

"Not at all. I hope you two have fun, wherever you end up going." She took a deep breath and turned her attention to Lizzie. "Now, Lizzie—how much longer on those burgers?"

CHAPTER 18

By the time the Silvesters were ready to set off the fireworks, Zoe and Trevor had long since gone and April was still nowhere in sight. The crowd gathered around the pool, eagerly anticipating a pyrotechnic display that Kathryn assured them would be absolutely *fabulous*.

Lizzie wanted to join them, but she had to set up the ice-cream sundae bar on the kitchen island, so the best she could hope for was a glimpse through the floor-to-ceiling windows. She'd always loved Fourth of July fireworks. When she was a kid her parents would take her to the township's annual display at Abington High School, and as a teenager she'd take the train downtown to watch the city's show on the Benjamin Franklin Parkway. Her favorites were always the ones that looked like fluffy white dandelions, the sparkles falling to the ground like downy seeds. For most of her youth, the entire holiday weekend was characterized by the distant rapid-fire *pop-pop-pop* of fireworks, many of them set off by people who had no business doing so.

"Hear that?" her mom would say. "That's what a trip to the emergency room sounds like."

She always said this as if Lizzie somehow needed dissuading from setting off her own fireworks display, when all Lizzie wanted to do was watch. But her mom always needed to underscore the risk of any potential hazard, whether it was an explosive or a hot beverage. Danger lurked everywhere, even in places you hadn't thought. Lizzie wondered if her mom had been this way forever or only since Ryan died. It didn't matter, really, since either way, she'd acted this way for as long as Lizzie could remember. She just wished her mom would occasionally enjoy an experience like the Fourth of July fireworks without needing to comment that someone somewhere had probably lost a limb.

As the crowd around the pool thickened, Lizzie finished scooping the ice cream into three large glass bowls. She stacked the balls in a big heap, vanilla in one bowl, blueberry in another, and strawberry in the third. Lizzie had suggested swapping chocolate for the blueberry, but Kathryn insisted the red, white, and blue theme carry through to the dessert. There were huge bowls of fresh strawberries and blueberries and big vats of whipped cream and Marshmallow Fluff. Lizzie had also made hot fudge, caramel, and wet walnut sauces to go on top.

"Better hurry up or you'll miss the show," said a voice over her shoulder.

She turned around and saw Kathryn's stepson, Nate, standing in the doorway. He wore the same cargo shorts and Nationals hat as earlier but had changed into an American University T-shirt.

"I don't think the show is meant for me."

"You're here, aren't you?"

"Yeah, but I'm cooking."

"You're here. Which means it's for you."

"I don't think—"

"Trust me. When Kathryn asks you about it later, she's going to want you to tell her how amazing it was, so you're better off watching it than not." His eyes landed on the ice cream. "You need help taking that out?"

"They hired other people to do that." She craned her neck, looking over his shoulder. "Though to be honest I'm not sure where they are at the moment."

"Probably getting ready to see the fireworks. Which, like I said, is what you should be doing, too." He lifted the bowl of vanilla ice cream and reached for the hot fudge. "Come on. I'd say we've got this in three trips. Four max."

The two of them shuttled the ice cream and toppings into the kitchen and set up the sundae bar while Renata, who once again had appeared as if by magic, arranged all of the calligraphic signs.

"Renata, how's it going?" He reached in and gave her a hug. "I haven't gotten a chance to talk to you since I got here."

"I know," she said, giving him a squeeze. "I'm good. We've missed you."

"Maybe you've missed me. I'm not so sure about Kathryn."

Renata smiled. "Silly boy. Everyone loves you."

"Are you sure we're talking about the same family . . . ?"

"Well, I love you, and I've missed you. So there."

He wrapped his arm around her shoulder and kissed the top of her head. "Renata is the best," he said, looking at Lizzie. "But I'm sure you've figured that out by now."

"Nate just likes me because I buy him doughnuts."

"Aw, come on, that isn't the only reason. Though now that you mention it . . . some Kohler's tomorrow morning would be most excellent."

"I can pick some up," Lizzie offered. "Kohler's is that bakery at Twenty-Seventh and Dune, right?"

"Whoa, hang on—are you telling me you've been in Avalon for six weeks and haven't tried a Kohler's cream doughnut yet?"

"Guilty as charged."

Nate pressed his hands against his lips and took a deep breath, in a way that Lizzie found more than a bit overdramatic. "Renata, our mission is clear. Tomorrow. Breakfast. Kohler's. Yes?"

Renata patted his back. "Yes."

"Good. Excellent. Thank you. Make sure you buy enough for everyone, including Lizzie."

"You don't have to do that," Lizzie said.

"Yes, we do." Nate gave her a probing look. "Unless you don't eat doughnuts."

"I definitely eat doughnuts."

His shoulders relaxed. "Thank God. For a second there I thought maybe you were into one of those diets like Kathryn or Zoe. What is Kathryn's thing this year? Paleo?"

Lizzie nodded.

"Right. And last year it was gluten-free, and a few years before that it was South Beach and Atkins, and at some point I remember her eating nothing but cabbage soup. My dream is that someday she'll just eat food like a normal person. Not that I dream about Kathryn." He cringed. "Oh, God. Now I'm totally going to dream about Kathryn, aren't I?"

Lizzie tried not to laugh. "Probably."

"Great. With my luck, it'll be an eight-hour dream where she doesn't shut up the entire time. Christ."

"Better than eight hours in real life, right?"

He met her eyes and smiled in a way that Lizzie found reassuring, as if she was no longer alone in bearing the weight of Kathryn's voluminous speech.

"I'll get the rest of the serving pieces," Renata said, and disappeared in the butler's pantry.

Lizzie glanced at Nate's T-shirt. "American University. Very patriotic. Did you buy that especially for the Fourth?"

"This? No, I've had this for years. I actually bought it just after I—"

"Nate, my man!"

Sam Offerman stumbled into the room, a tumbler of whiskey in his hand. His skin looked even more orange than the last time Lizzie had seen him, and his hair was as puffy and stiff as ever.

"Sam. Hi. Long time no see." Nate did not sound thrilled to see his father's friend.

"I'll say. You still bumming around our nation's capital, or have you finally decided to get a real job?"

"I have a real job."

"Sure, sure—if you say so."

Nate rolled his eyes. "My dad put you up to this?"

"Jim? Nah. He's too busy worrying about all that CC Media nonsense."

"What CC Media nonsense?"

Sam took a sip of whiskey. "Nothing. Never mind. See, this is what happens when you're old and drunk. You say things you probably shouldn't." He gestured toward Lizzie. "In front of the help, no less."

Nate cleared his throat. "Hey, I think the fireworks are about to start. You'd better get out there."

"Same goes for you." Sam's eyes flitted toward Lizzie. He grinned. "Ah, I see. . . . Don't worry, I get it. If I were your age I'd try to tap that, too. Frankly, even if I weren't your age—"

"Better get going, Sam."

"All right, all right—I'm out of here."

Sam raised his hands in the air as he headed back outside, weaving back and forth with an unsteady gait.

"Sorry about that," Nate said. "Sam is . . . well, he's . . ."

"We've met before."

"Oh. So then you know."

"Unfortunately."

"I've never understood why he and my dad are still friends. I think it's one of those friendships that endure because they've known each other for so long. Like, the past is what's keeping them together, not the present or the future, if that makes sense."

Lizzie thought about April. In their case, the past was keeping them apart. Lizzie hadn't seen April all evening and wondered if she'd decided not to come.

"Anyway," Nate said, "I'm heading out there. You coming?"

"In a sec'. I just want to put the finishing touches on everything so that dessert is ready once the fireworks are over."

"I'll save a spot for you by the tiki bar." He made for the door but slowed his step before he reached it. "By the way . . . contrary to what Sam said, I'm not trying to 'tap that.' Don't get me wrong—you seem nice and all, but that really isn't my style."

"Understood. See you by the tiki bar."

"Looking forward to it."

"Me too," Lizzie said, and to her surprise, she meant it.

The fireworks were some of the most beautiful Lizzie had ever seen. There were the traditional red, white, and blue bursts, the explosions speckling the sky like stardust. But there were more exotic ones, too, whose glittery streams would crackle and flash like confetti or explode into small constellations that would fall through the sky in formation. One looked like a heart with an arrow through it. Another burst into the shape of a shooting star. During the finale, the crew shot off a series in which the cascading tail of each firework detonated into another firework, until the entire sky above the Silvesters' property was alight. Lizzie couldn't believe the Silvesters—or, more specifically, Ken—had arranged all of this for a private party. The cost must have been astronomical.

To whatever extent the fireworks enthralled Lizzie and, afterward, the sundae bar thrilled the guests, both reactions paled in comparison to Lizzie's reaction the next morning when she tried her first doughnut from Kohler's.

"Oh. Oh, wow."

She took another bite, standing over the sink in the butler's pantry so that the mountain of powdered sugar wouldn't cover the floor. The doughnut was soft and pillowy, filled with a thick, white cream filling. She could almost feel the sugar rushing straight to her brain.

"See? What did I tell you?"

Lizzie looked up to find Nate standing in the doorway. She quickly wiped the powdered sugar off her face. He was the first to arrive for breakfast, and Lizzie and Renata hadn't finished preparing everything. Renata had only just returned with the order from Kohler's.

"You were right," Lizzie said. "These are pretty amazing."

"I hope you saved some for the rest of us?"

"Plenty. This is my first. Though I'm guessing it won't be my last."

"Please say Renata picked up some sticky buns, too." He approached the counter and lifted the lid to one of the boxes. "Yes-s-s-s-s. Save room for one of these. You won't be sorry."

"Until she gets diabetes."

They both looked toward the kitchen door, where Zoe stood with one hand on the frame. Her hair was wet, as if she'd just swum or showered, and although she didn't appear to be wearing any makeup, her skin seemed to glow.

"Leave it to you to ruin all the fun," Nate said.

"You know it's what I do best." She nodded at Lizzie. "What I don't understand is how you can call yourself a healthy cook and then eat crap like that."

"Just because I cook healthy doesn't mean I always eat healthy—"

"Obviously. But don't you think that's a little hypocritical?"

Nate clicked his tongue. "Pots and kettles, Zo . . ."

"What are you talking about?"

"Never mind. I don't want to start something."

"Of course you do. You always do. All I'm saying is that she hosted some show called *Healthy U* that was all about healthy eating and she doesn't even eat healthy food. Is that why it got canceled?"

"No. And I do eat healthy stuff. But sometimes I also eat unhealthy stuff. . . ." She took another bite.

"Apparently." Zoe glanced at her phone. "Anyway, Nate, weren't you supposed to be leaving first thing? That's what Dad said yesterday."

"That was wishful thinking on his part. But as it turns out, I do need to hit the road—though not before grabbing a few of these." He pulled a doughnut and sticky bun from the box.

"What, is there some sort of sociological emergency that requires your immediate attention?"

He rolled his eyes as he took an aggressive bite of sticky bun. "You too? I get enough grief from Dad and Kathryn, thanks."

"Please. They've been driving me nuts lately. You need to take some of the heat."

"You're joking, right? They've been on my ass for years."

"Not without justification." She looked at Lizzie and gestured toward Nate. "Mr. Doughnuts here is a 'sociology professor.' " She used air quotes, which confused Lizzie. Was he actually a professor of sociology? Or was that some sort of code for "drug dealer" or "pimp"?

"I'm sorry, remind me what you do again?" Nate asked Zoe.

"I run a lifestyle Web site."

"You mean a blog."

"No, a Web site. And an app. Which, by the way, makes me a fair amount of money."

"So you say. . . ."

"So I know."

"Whatever. I just don't see why being a professor of sociology at a respectable university is taken less seriously by this family than writing some blog about . . . eating seaweed or whatever it is you write about."

"Oh—so you're actually a professor?" Lizzie cut in.

"Yeah. Why?"

"I just thought . . . the way everyone talked . . ." She trailed off.

"What? That I was a stoner who couldn't quite get my life together?"

Lizzie flushed. "Something like that."

"Nice. So apparently my family thinks what I do is so lame that they make total strangers think I'm a loser without a job." He took another bite of sticky bun. "Well, then I'd better get back to wasting my life."

He yanked a square of paper towel off the kitchen roll and used it to wrap up the rest of his baked goods. "Lizzie, nice meeting you. I'll see you in a week—unless I get so busy with my lame, do-nothing job that I can't make it."

"Aw, Nate, but then you couldn't mooch off your rich dad." Zoe mimed a pout.

"Stay bitchy, Zo. You do it so well."

He turned and stormed out of the room, and Zoe watched him leave, her expression unreadable. "Watch out for that one," she said. "He's trouble."

Funny, Lizzie thought. *I bet he'd say the same thing about you.*

Later that afternoon, once the out-of-town guests had left and Lizzie had tidied the kitchen and pantry, Kathryn knocked on Lizzie's bedroom door.

"I hope I'm not interrupting," she said, though Lizzie suspected she didn't really care one way or the other.

Lizzie slid her phone onto the nightstand. She'd been checking social media to see if April had posted anything about her July Fourth activities. She never showed at the Silvesters' party, but she hadn't texted Lizzie and there was no indication, on the Internet at least, that she had done something else instead.

"Nope—just trying to decompress."

"You deserve it. What a weekend! Jim and I are thrilled with the way everything turned out. Except for the ice sculpture—don't even get me started. But you had nothing to do with that. All the food was wonderful. Those burgers! And everyone raved about the ice-cream sundaes. A must for the menu next year. Speaking of which . . ." Kathryn moved farther into the room and shut the door behind her. She lowered her voice. "It's a bit early to discuss next year, I know, but Jim and I have been talking, and given how well everything has gone so far this summer, we were thinking . . . maybe you stay on with us after Labor Day back in Gladwyne."

Lizzie tried to mask her surprise. "Full-time?"

"Or part-time. We are open to discussion."

"Wow. I don't know what to say."

"You don't have to decide now. This isn't a formal offer. We'd have to negotiate a salary and all of that, and of course our lifestyle is a bit different at home than it is at the beach—fewer big parties, more dinner parties, a bit less loosey-goosey, et cetera. But it's something for you to think about. We'd compensate you well—certainly better than what we're paying now."

What they were paying now was more than Lizzie had made at any of her gigs in New York combined, other than her TV show. She wasn't entirely sure she'd want to be a member of the Silvesters' "staff," but if the job paid better than this one she wasn't sure she'd be able to turn it down. She still had school loans to pay off, and the interest payments were growing so fast some days she wondered if she'd ever be able to keep up with them.

Kathryn clapped her hands together. "Anyway! I just wanted to thank you for your hard work this weekend. An excellent job all around. I hope you were at least able to enjoy yourself a little bit."

"I did. The fireworks were incredible."

Kathryn beamed. "Weren't they? I told Ken, 'You are one lucky man,' because if they hadn't been so completely fabulous, he wouldn't be hearing from me ever again. But he claims the ice sculpture was a onetime mistake, and everything else was A-plus, so for now he is back in my good graces. He promised me I'll have an ice sculpture for Labor Day, but I warned him—if anything even looks vaguely inappropriate, he's finished. I mean, honestly. That eagle!" She shuddered. "Luckily we have two months until Labor Day, so he has plenty of time to find a new artist. Though to call the man who sculpted that atrocity an 'artist' is a stretch, if you ask me."

Lizzie hadn't asked, but Kathryn was clearly still traumatized by the penis-eating eagle and, if Lizzie had to guess, probably would be for some time.

"By the way," Kathryn said, "I'm sorry your friend April wasn't able to make it."

"Me too," Lizzie said. "I'm not sure what happened."

"I am—sounds like Jim has her working overtime these days. Something to do with changes at the company."

Lizzie thought back to Sam's comment to Nate about all the "CC Media nonsense." She had little to no interest in company business, but she was curious what was so pressing that April needed to work Fourth of July weekend. A small part of her hoped that, whatever the issue was, it was fully responsible for April not even having time to send a text letting Lizzie know she wouldn't make the party. It seemed plausible, though just as plausible as April having no interest in reconnecting with a friend who'd treated her badly all those years ago.

"What kind of changes?" Lizzie asked.

"God knows. I stay out of company business. I mean, sure, I love gossip as much as the next person, but when it comes to information that could impact corporate results—no, thank you. I don't want that on my conscience." She glanced at her watch. "Anyway, given how crazy this weekend has been for you, you deserve the evening off. Sound good to you?"

"Are you sure?" Lizzie asked, though as soon as she did she regretted it. She desperately needed some downtime. If Kathryn suddenly changed her mind, Lizzie might actually cry, mostly because it would be her own fault.

"Absolutely," Kathryn said. "Jim and I will eat at the club, though between you and me, I won't be eating much of anything after all the holiday indulgences. Time to get back on track. Summer isn't even halfway through! Not that your food isn't worth every calorie. Thank goodness you have a background in healthy cuisine."

Lizzie smiled, but now that she knew she had the rest of the day off all she wanted was for Kathryn to leave. She wasn't sure whether she wanted to nap on the beach or read a book or stare at the wall, but all sounded very appealing.

"I'm sure you have plenty to keep yourself busy," Kathryn continued, "but if you need any recommendations on places to eat or things to see, just ask. Frankly, Renata is your best bet. She knows everything when it comes to this town. You two should talk!"

"Will do," Lizzie said, even though Lizzie already had a list of things she wanted to do and talking was most definitely not one of them.

Lizzie searched for the best word to describe her six hours of freedom and decided on *blissful*. She napped under an umbrella on the beach, read four chapters of her book, napped some more, and bought an ice-cream cone from Sundae Best. There was something so perfect about an ice-cream cone in the summer, especially at the beach. She ordered two scoops, and as she licked the top of the cone she felt like a kid again.

She walked along Dune Drive, devouring her ice cream as she looked up at the sky, which was streaked with pinks and blues and purples as the sun began to set. She'd walked the thirty blocks from the Silvesters' house, figuring she could use the exercise, and with the entire evening stretched before her she was in no hurry to get anywhere.

Renata had recommended Sundae Best as "the" spot for ice cream in Avalon, declaring it just as good as and closer than the famous Springer's in Stone Harbor. As she finished her helping of It's All Good, a signature flavor of vanilla ice cream studded with chocolate-covered pretzels and swirled with creamy peanut butter, Lizzie had to agree. It was some of the best ice cream she'd ever eaten. When it came to local suggestions, Renata was like a walking edition of Yelp or Google. Lizzie could always count on her for the perfect recommendation.

Lizzie checked on her car when she returned to the Silvesters' house, turning on the motor and letting it run for a few minutes to keep the battery in good condition. As she let the motor run, she glanced out the window and saw Zoe's car parked in its usual spot. Had it been there when she left? Lizzie didn't think so, but in all the excitement over her free afternoon and evening she hadn't paid much attention. She'd been meaning to follow up with Zoe about her Web site and ask why she never posted the recipe for the beet salad. Lizzie had sent it to her more than a week ago, but Zoe never confirmed she'd received it and it hadn't appeared on the site.

Lizzie also had a lot of questions about what *had* appeared on the site—mostly gorgeously photographed meals whose origins Lizzie couldn't ascertain. There were amethyst-colored acai bowls striped with chia seeds, almonds, and goji berries; lush arugula salads studded with yellow peaches and juicy red tomatoes; and verdant tangles of zucchini noodles slicked with puréed avocado sauce. One dish was more enticing than the last, but Lizzie couldn't figure out when and where Zoe had made them. Were these things she'd made while she was traveling in Europe? Or maybe before she left? It seemed unlikely, if only because several of the meals involved produce that had only just come into season. But Lizzie could say with almost absolute certainty that Zoe hadn't prepared these meals in Avalon. The kitchen was Lizzie's domain, and she saw and heard everything that went on there.

Regardless, what struck Lizzie most was how perfect Zoe's life appeared online when, in reality, even Lizzie knew Zoe's life was far from ideal. Sure, her family had money and she came and went as she pleased, but her relationship with her parents was highly dysfunctional, and in the few encounters they'd had Zoe never seemed particularly happy. Whatever personality she conveyed on her site was carefully curated to portray a version of Zoe that didn't actually exist.

Lizzie turned off the car and headed back toward the house, which twinkled in the dusky evening light. She didn't want to confront Zoe, if only because she didn't want to admit she'd been stalking her site. But something about The Clean Life felt off to Lizzie—first the photos of her own food, now photos of dubious origin, not to mention the way the entire thing seemed at odds with reality. If it weren't for the fact that Zoe had admitted to Nate she'd made money from it, Zoe's site wouldn't hold much interest for Lizzie. Okay, so Zoe claimed credit for a few recipes that weren't really hers. So what? But with almost two hundred thousand followers on Instagram and probably just as many on her Web site, Lizzie was beginning to think maybe it did matter. People were following Zoe because they believed she was a wellness warrior. They were signing on to her lifestyle, and she was making money off their interest. What if that lifestyle wasn't really hers?

When Lizzie got back to her room, she loaded Zoe's site again. There was a new post, titled "Sad News":

> I've been struggling for the past few weeks with how and when to share this news with all of you because I haven't fully made sense of it myself. And on top of it all, it isn't really my news to share. But I talked to Marie last night, and she gave me the green light, so here it goes:
>
> Marie's cancer has returned. Her knee and hip started aching a few months ago and she figured it was just from running, so she cut back and started swimming instead, but the pain didn't go away. She went to the doctor, and they ran a few tests, and that's when she discovered she had cancer in her bones. It had also spread to her blood, but luckily (if I can even use that word) it hadn't spread to her liver or brain.
>
> Of course they recommended more toxic and invasive therapies, but given the success she had with alternative therapies last time around, she doesn't want to go that route (and who would?). So we are back where we started. Only this time, we already have all the tools we need. We just need to use them.

Zoe went on to describe the dietary changes Marie would make and the protocol she'd follow to treat herself: coffee enemas, an intense course of supplements that included green tea concentrate, capsaicin, and baking soda, and regular visits to an herbalist who would recalibrate her system and rid it of toxins. Lizzie was skeptical, but she also knew cancer was a complicated disease, with many modes of treatment. Part of her wondered if Marie's cancer had returned because she hadn't used conventional treatments the first time around, but Lizzie also knew of many cases—both personally and anecdotally—where a person's cancer recurred even after chemo, radiation, and drugs. If alternative medicine worked for Marie the first time around... well, Lizzie supposed there was no harm in trying again. As a general rule, Lizzie tried to keep an open mind about these sorts of things.

In the post, Zoe also included a quick note from Marie, in which she thanked all of Zoe's readers for their "amazing support over the years":

> I'm a pretty private person, which
> is why I let Z be my proxy in our
> little health crusade. But please
> know how much it means to me that you
> keep reading and promoting this site.
> The lifestyle she writes about on
> here really does change lives, and
> thanks to her passion and enthusiasm
> I have no doubt I will be on my feet
> again in a flash.

There was another photo of Marie embedded in the post. She looked thinner in this photo, though not that much older than in the photograph Lizzie had already seen. Now Lizzie felt bad bugging Zoe about the recipes on her site. In the scheme of things, did it really matter? If anything, Lizzie felt bad for Zoe. She decided to send her an e-mail instead of confronting her face-to-face:

Hey, Zoe,

Just wanted to make sure you got the recipe I sent you. Did it make sense? Let me know if you have any questions.

Also, I saw the news about Marie. I'm so sorry. If there's anything I can do, let me know. I have a lot of healthy recipes in my collection, so I can send a few your way or even develop a few with you especially for Marie. Happy to help in any way I can.

Hang in there,
Lizzie

Happy to help. Was she? *Willing* was more like it, and if she was being honest with herself she was barely that. But whether it was genuine concern or morbid curiosity, Lizzie wanted to know more about Marie's story, so she hit Send and, though she hated to admit it, really hoped Zoe would reply—or, at the very least, wouldn't delete the e-mail without ever reading it.

CHAPTER 19

Linda,

Thanks for sending along Dr. Rosenfeld's information. I really appreciate your concern and hear he is one of the best oncologists in Philly. However, after doing a lot of soul-searching (and a lot of reading), I'd really like to go another way.

I know, I know—I can already hear your objections. But there are so many alternative options out there, and I'd like to explore them. I promise this has nothing to do with vanity. We both know you got all the good hair genes in the family. I even joked with the doctor after my diagnosis that I'd probably look better in a wig than I look with my real hair. But I just can't bring myself to do chemo. I'm sorry, I can't. So I've agreed to a lumpectomy and will follow that with a course of alternative, more natural therapies.

I have to say, Gary has been an absolute savior when it comes to researching treatments. He's pointed me to all sorts of useful Web sites and information—so many and so much that I can barely wade through it all. I had no idea how many possibilities there were aside from chemo and radiation, which is all you ever hear about. Demuth, Kelley, Contreras—and those are just the beginning. You're probably scratching your head and asking, "Demuth? Who's that?" I was, too. But as Gary told me, that's because the Medical Industrial Complex has suppressed these options because they would cut into the profits of doctors and hospital systems and pharmaceutical companies. He said, "When you're a hammer, everything looks like a nail. All doctors want to do is operate and medicate. But what about treating the underlying cause? What about fixing whatever toxic conditions created the problem in the first place?" Makes a lot of sense, if you ask me.

I'm still trying to figure out which approach is best for me, but this week Gary is taking me to meet with a doctor who specializes in Demuth therapy. From what I gather, the Demuth protocol is pretty intense (lots of organic juices, enemas, things like that), but when you hear from people who've done it the results sound pretty amazing. We'll see. I guess a part of me feels like it couldn't hurt. I mean, is anyone really going to tell me eating more fruits and vegetables is a bad idea? And once they've cut out the lump, the cancer is gone anyway, so all I'd be doing is flushing out all the bad, toxic stuff in my body and beefing up my immune system so that the cancer won't come back.

Anyway, thanks again for looking out for me. I really do appreciate your concern. You're the best baby sister a girl could ask for (and yes, I still get to call you my baby sister—don't fight it). But I've come to a point in my life where I am trying to live with fewer "shoulds" and instead am doing what makes sense for me. After losing a child, going through a divorce, and dealing with all of the other crap I've had to deal with, I think I've earned that right. I hope you understand.

Love you tons, and I'll let you know how the consultation goes this week.

xxoo
S

CHAPTER 20

The morning after Lizzie e-mailed Zoe, Zoe disappeared. Lizzie knew referring to Zoe's absence as a "disappearance" was a little melodramatic, but she couldn't think of a better way to characterize it. One day Zoe'c car was there, and the next day it wasn't, and neither was she, and no one seemed to know where either had gone.

Vanishing without so much as a good-bye seemed to be Zoe's specialty, but whereas before Lizzie simply found it odd and a little rude, she now took it personally. Did her e-mail prompt Zoe to take off? The timing seemed fishy. Now there was no chance they'd run into each other and Zoe could ignore Lizzie's note indefinitely.

Lizzie tried to pretend she didn't care (she was just trying to be nice, after all), but she did, and it drove her crazy. Why couldn't Zoe at least reply to thank Lizzie for offering to help? Probably because Marie's health was none of Lizzie's business. But that's what rubbed Lizzie the wrong way. Zoe had effectively made it everyone's business when she posted the news on her site, and given Lizzie's background in healthy cuisine, Zoe's silence felt like a slap in the face. Was she threatened by Lizzie? Was she afraid Lizzie would usurp her role as wellness guru? Because Lizzie had no interest in doing that. As much as she missed her days as a healthy cooking star, she didn't see a role for herself in the world Zoe inhabited. It was too affluent and privileged.

That said, as much as it bothered her to admit it, Lizzie saw some of herself in Zoe. She'd been the twenty-three-year-old "expert," dispensing advice to the masses about how to eat and cook healthily even though she had no background in diet or nutrition. She always felt a pang of guilt when she received an e-mail from a viewer asking for specific diet advice ("I've been a yo-yo dieter for years, and I'm sick of it! I'm ready to make a real change. Please help!"). What business did Lizzie have telling people what to eat and what not to eat? She wasn't a nutritionist. She knew as much as any interested young woman knew about dieting: cut back on sugar and carbs; don't drink too much; eat lots of fruits and vegetables and fish and lean meats. Beyond that . . . well, she didn't really know what else to recommend.

Maybe Zoe knew more than she had, but somehow Lizzie doubted it. No matter how much research Zoe had done—and from the looks of her site, she had obviously done a lot—she was still only twenty-three. Aside from the fact that Zoe hadn't studied nutrition or, as far as Lizzie could tell, ever held an actual job, she was barely an adult. She had clearly gone through a trying experience with her friend Marie, but otherwise Zoe had lived a fairly sheltered life under the Silvesters' roof. Lizzie didn't think age necessarily correlated with expertise, but she also knew from her own experience that the word "expert" was often used without much to back up such claims. The only thing Lizzie considered herself an expert in these days was peaking too early in one's career. She wondered if that's why Zoe was keeping her distance, as if confiding in Lizzie would cause her own career to befall a similar fate.

The week passed, and still there was no sign of Zoe. Renata didn't have any insider information, and Lizzie had learned not to ask Kathryn about Zoe—or anything, really—unless she wanted to lose at least thirty minutes of her life. As the week went by, all Kathryn seemed interested in discussing was Nate's return and how much she hoped his trip would fall through.

"Apparently he is still coming," she lamented Friday morning as she sipped a kale-apple juice in the kitchen.

"Tomorrow?" Lizzie asked.

"Around lunchtime. At least that's what he told Jim. Traffic will probably be terrible, so unless he is leaving Washington at the crack of dawn I don't see how he'll make it for lunch, but then Nate is the master of wishful thinking. . . ."

"I didn't realize he was a professor," Lizzie said, recalling her conversation with him and Zoe.

"Of 'sociology.' "

She used air quotes, as Zoe had done when referring to Nate as a professor. What was it with this family and air quoting Nate's career? To become a sociology professor was a legitimate professional choice. Didn't they know this? Did they also throw air quotes around "financial" "planners" and "kindergarten" "teachers"? Lizzie didn't understand.

"He studies neighborhoods. Neighborhoods! How is that a real job? The only people who need to study neighborhoods are ones who are looking to buy a house. It's ridiculous."

"I'm guessing he looks at things like demographics and gentrification," Lizzie said, trying to be polite but also trying to emphasize to Kathryn that neighborhoods were a legitimate area of study. She had taken a course on that topic during her sophomore year at Penn, and it was one of her favorite classes.

"Probably. Who knows. It just seems like such a waste. With his brains and talent, he could be doing something high-powered and meaningful, but instead he spends his days talking about 'communities.' "

Again with the air quotes. "I took a class like that in college and loved it, so—"

"At least that was at *Penn*. If he were at an Ivy League school, that would be a different story. I mean, I still say no one needs to learn about neighborhoods, but if it were Yale or Penn, we could point to that as an achievement. But he's at American. I mean, seriously? I know he loves DC, but come on. He couldn't even get a job at Georgetown or GW? Jim went to GW, so Nate is a legacy. He should have been a shoo-in."

Lizzie couldn't believe Kathryn's intellectual snobbery. Had she even gone to college? And maybe Nate didn't want to work at GW.

From what Lizzie knew of their relationship, Nate's legacy status would, if anything, be a turnoff.

"A friend of mine from high school went to American," Lizzie said. "It's a very good school."

"Oh, I'm sure it's a fine place for some people. But after two degrees from Princeton, it just seems so . . . meh."

"Better than selling drugs, right?"

"At least then he'd be making money. . . ." Kathryn caught Lizzie's eye and blushed. "I'm kidding. Obviously." But given her expression, Lizzie guessed she wasn't.

Kathryn slurped down the rest of her juice and glanced at the clock on the wall. "Right. Time to get moving. Barb is coming to hang by the pool and will stay for lunch, and Jim will be here by dinnertime. He's requested turkey London broil. Well, actually, he requested London broil, but we both know that isn't happening! Not after all the burgers and hot dogs on the Fourth. If he keeps eating like this, his cholesterol will be off the charts. I've seen his numbers, and let me tell you, they aren't good. I keep telling him he should talk to Zoe about trying a vegan diet for a while, but he won't hear it. Oh, but speaking of Zoe . . . you may have noticed that she hasn't been around this week."

Lizzie tried to downplay her interest. "I did. What's she been up to?"

"I don't know. Something about a friend of hers. I only heard from her today. But apparently she is coming back sometime this weekend, so plan on stocking some of her usual favorites—greens, avocados, nuts, that kind of thing."

"Will do." Lizzie took Kathryn's empty glass and washed it in the sink. "Maybe she was visiting her friend Marie," she suggested, looking up at Kathryn as she dried the glass with a towel.

"Marie?" Kathryn looked confused. "No, I think it was . . . Actually, now that you mention it, I don't think she specified. Maybe it was Marie. I can't keep track—Trevor, Kai, Yvette, Sasha. Too many names to keep straight."

"Marie is the one who was sick. Or I guess is sick again."

Kathryn's expression hardened, and she stared at Lizzie for a beat. "Oh. Then no. No, I don't think it was Marie." She looked at the clock again. "Sorry—I have to go. I'll see you at lunch."

Then she turned and left, her sudden brevity ringing in Lizzie's ears like an alarm bell.

As lunchtime approached on Saturday, Lizzie found herself both looking forward to and dreading Nate's return. On the one hand, despite the Silvesters' misgivings, he seemed like the most sane member of the Silvester clan. On the other, his presence promised to ratchet up the household drama by a factor of about a thousand and Kathryn would probably be even more frazzled and frantic than usual. He also, by definition, possessed Silvester DNA, so after a week of having him around Lizzie knew she might decide he was just as crazy as the rest of them.

She spent the morning restocking the pantry and preparing for the week ahead. Kathryn had requested a big chopped salad for lunch ("Lots of veggies—dressing on the side, please!"), so Lizzie set to work chopping a mound of lettuce, cucumbers, and tomatoes. Lizzie wasn't clear on how many people would be at lunch. No one seemed to know when Zoe would arrive, and everyone agreed hoping for a lunchtime arrival on Nate's part was overly optimistic. Add to that the frequent surprise visits by many of the Silvesters' friends (particularly Kathryn's) and Lizzie didn't know whether to make enough salad for two or twenty. She suspected the number would be closer to four or five, so she made enough for twice that number to give herself a buffer.

As she dumped the chopped cucumber into a bowl, she heard footsteps behind her and turned around to see Nate walking through the kitchen toward the butler's pantry. She noted the time: 11:45.

"Impressive," she said. "No one thought you'd actually make it in time for lunch. Kathryn will be . . ."

"Thrilled?"

"Not the word I would have chosen, actually."

He smiled. "Must be fun, dealing with the dynamics of our crazy family."

"Another interesting word choice. But sure. Let's go with 'fun' "

"Dad seemed really happy with the way things have been going, so you must be doing something right."

"There's no magic to it. I keep my head down and do what I'm told."

"Hey, competence is rarer than you'd think. If my research assistants kept their heads down and did what I asked them to do, I wouldn't be so worried about making my deadline."

"For?"

"A book. Or, at this point, a bunch of stuff on my computer that I'm supposed to turn into something people actually want to buy and read."

"About 'neighborhoods'?" Lizzie used air quotes and tried not to laugh.

Nate furrowed his brow. "Yeah. Good guess."

"Kathryn mentioned that's what you study—using air quotes, because apparently that's the right way to talk about what you do."

"In this family, yes. I'm a 'professor' of 'sociology' who 'teaches' and 'studies' 'neighborhoods.' "

"And 'communities'?"

"You bet."

"I told Kathryn I took a class on all of that when I was at Penn. I think it shocked her a little when I said it was one of my favorites."

"Oh, yeah? Who taught it?"

"Peter Goldberg."

"For real? Goldberg is a rock star. I cited him a lot in my dissertation."

"He's published a lot of research to cite."

"That's for sure." Nate watched as Lizzie chopped a pint of cherry tomatoes. "So, I have to ask. If you took classes with the likes of Peter Goldberg . . ."

"What am I doing here, cooking meals for rich people?"

Nate blushed. "Well . . . yeah."

"I don't think we have enough time before lunch for that story."

"Sorry. I hope I didn't . . . or, you know, I didn't mean . . ."

"It's fine. Trust me when I say you aren't the first to ask that question. I've asked it myself, many times."

"I feel like that kind of makes my asking worse, not better."

"Not worse. Don't worry."

"Okay, but if not worse, then at least annoying."

Lizzie grinned. "Sure. I'll give you 'annoying.' That's fair."

"You don't actually have to tell me the whole story. I was just curious. I can guarantee you are the only person in this house who has even heard of Peter Goldberg. That may not seem like a big deal to you, but it's a big deal to me. The house suddenly feels less . . ."

"Hostile?"

He smiled. "Yeah."

"Ah, so we've agreed on another adjective? That's two in a row."

"I guess so. Feels worthy of a celebration."

"Someone bust out the Veuve." She scooped up the tomatoes and tossed them into the salad bowl. "In all seriousness, though, I need to get lunch on the table. I didn't realize you'd be here this early, so I'm a little behind."

"I'll get out of your way. I need to say hi to my family anyway." He took a deep breath and looked toward the pool, where the family and some friends had suddenly appeared. Kathryn, Barb, and Diana were sunning themselves on chaise lounges, and Jim was sitting at a table beneath an umbrella, talking on his phone. "And so it begins."

Lizzie scattered a handful of toasted pine nuts over the salad and reached for a ripe avocado. "Okay, I really do need to get to work, but now I have to ask you a personal question: Why do you come if it's always so . . ."

"Tense? Complicated? Stressful?"

"Yeah."

He shrugged. "Because he's my dad, and as tricky as our relationship might be, he's the only one I've got. And part of me hopes one of these trips will end with us accepting each other's life choices and moving on."

"Let's hope it's this trip, then, eh?"

He pressed his hands together and looked at the sky. "*Inshallah.*"

"Maybe this will be the summer of healing. You and your dad, you and Kathryn, Zoe and . . . everyone, I guess."

"Ha!" Nate shook his head. "It'll take more than a summer to heal what's wrong with Zoe."

"You never know. People can surprise you."

"What I mean is . . . Zoe . . . how can I put this . . . She's not quite—"

"Nate! You're here." Kathryn appeared in the pantry, her sunglasses perched atop her head. "You must have left before dawn."

"Anything to be able to spend more time with you, Kathryn." He reached in to kiss her cheek.

She pulled away. "Did I overhear you talking about Zoe?"

Nate cleared his throat. "Lizzie was just asking about, you know, family stuff."

"Let's not trouble her with all of that, hm-m? She has plenty to keep her busy." She glanced at her watch. "Lunch at twelve thirty?"

"Sure," Lizzie said.

"Great. Now, Nate, why don't you come and say hi to your father."

She placed her hand on the small of his back and, without even trying to look gentle, pushed him out of the room.

CHAPTER 21

Sunday morning, Lizzie headed to the farmers' market first thing. From experience, she knew the crowd thickened as the day went by, so she hoped to beat the late-morning crush.

Kathryn had planned a "clambake" dinner party for that evening: ten people and lots of seafood on their terrace overlooking the dunes. Originally she wanted it on the beach but decided that wouldn't be private enough. The beaches in Avalon were open to anyone with Avalon beach tags, so there was no way to keep interlopers from gaping at the Silvesters' heaping platters of shellfish and corn.

"And they *will* stare," Kathryn said.

Lizzie agreed this was probably true, given how much food Kathryn had requested. The plan was for her, Jim, and four other couples to have drinks at the Avalon Yacht Club and then return to the Silvesters' house, where a seafood feast would be waiting for them.

"I want everything hot and ready to eat as soon as we get back," Kathryn said. "After a few drinks at the club, we'll be hungry. Jim will want to eat at seven o'clock sharp!"

She'd outlined, in great detail, what she wanted the clambake to entail: huge platters of clams, mussels, shrimp, lobsters, and crab legs, mixed in with boiled corn, baby potatoes, and platters of fresh vegetables. Lizzie had suggested also including grilled kielbasa, but Kathryn objected.

"Not with Jim's cholesterol. He can't help himself—he'll eat it even though he knows he shouldn't! Maybe some chicken sausage instead?"

As Lizzie strolled through the market, she scanned the tables for the juiciest tomatoes, the fattest ears of corn, and the greenest sugar snap peas. She wasn't sure which of Jim and Kathryn's friends would be joining them, but she knew for certain Nate wasn't invited to the clambake.

"*No* children," Kathryn emphasized at least six times. Considering Nate was in his mid-thirties, Lizzie had trouble thinking of Nate as a "child," even though technically he would always be Jim's. It was less of a stretch for Zoe, but she hadn't returned yet, so Kathryn's "no children" rule seemed designed specifically to exclude Nate. Lizzie was pretty sure he would gladly take a pass.

On the way back from the market, Lizzie stopped by Avalon Seafood to pick up the shellfish she'd special ordered the day before. She loaded the seafood into a cooler in her trunk and slid back into the driver seat, but when she turned her car back on the gas light illuminated. The tank was nearly empty.

She pulled into the gas station across the street and lowered her window. She glanced out and realized Zoe's friend Trevor was walking toward her.

"Regular, please," she said. She avoided making eye contact. She wasn't in the mood to make small talk with one of Zoe's friends.

Trevor began filling up the tank, and Lizzie grabbed her phone to occupy her. She decided to load Zoe's site to see if she'd posted any updates. Sure enough, she'd written a new post this morning, and to Lizzie's delight, it featured her beet salad. Or, rather, what looked like her beet salad. As she scrolled through, she saw no mention of her name or the fact that she'd developed the recipe.

"Seriously?"

"Sorry—did you say something?" Trevor approached the window.

"No, I was just talking to myself," Lizzie said.

Trevor hunched over and looked through the window. "Hey . . . don't I know you?"

Lizzie tried to act surprised. "Oh . . . hi. . . ."

"Wait . . . don't remind me, I've got this." He stared at Lizzie. "Last week at Jack's, right?"

"No, the Silvesters' party," she said.

"The Silvesters?"

"Zoe's parents." She waited for him to acknowledge her, but he just stared at her for a beat. How dumb was this guy? The party was only a week ago.

"Oh-h-h, ri-i-i-i-i-ight," he finally said. "The cook, right? Sweet party. Food was awesome."

"Thanks," Lizzie said. She handed him her debit card.

"I haven't seen Zoe since the party, actually. I should give her a shout."

"She hasn't been around for the past week or so, but I think she's coming back tonight."

"Oh, yeah? Where's she been?"

"Your guess is as good as mine."

"Zoe, man. She's so mysterious. Always disappearing and shit."

"Yeah? I thought that was just from her parents."

"Nah, she's always, like, taking off to do her own thing. She's a fun girl, but you can't really tie her down. She's like a free spirit. Only, like, darker."

"Darker?"

"Maybe not darker. Just, like, complicated. You know?"

Lizzie signed her receipt. "So I'm learning."

"Definitely tell her I say hey if you see her. I'll shoot her a text later to see if she wants to hang. And hey, if you're ever looking to party . . ."

Lizzie offered the least horrified smile she could muster and raised her window. "Thanks," she said. "I'll definitely keep that in mind."

Lizzie worked at a dizzying pace all day to get everything ready for the clambake. She scrubbed clams, peeled shrimp, debearded mussels, and monitored the lobsters and crabs, which she'd stored in a big tub of water. As soon as she completed one task, she moved on to the next—shucking corn, trimming snap peas, marinating peppers—until she worked her way to the bottom of her To Do list. Even then, there was still so much to do before the Silvesters returned with their friends, and since this was merely a dinner party and not a full-fledged fete, she had only Renata and one or two others to help her.

Renata set the table on the terrace, using a set of nautical-themed china Lizzie had never seen. Was it new? Possibly. Lizzie was still getting used to living with people who had so much money they could buy china on a whim, simply because the pattern fit the theme of a dinner party. When she was growing up, her mom had only one set of everyday dishes, along with the wedding china she occasionally used on holidays. Lizzie knew her mom hated referring to it as "wedding china." She once heard her tell Aunt Linda, "At this point I should probably call it 'divorce china'—we certainly broke enough of it in the process." Lizzie wasn't exactly sure when all of this breaking happened. She never witnessed any loud, tearful fights where dishes were thrown and shattered, like she'd seen in the movies. But she also knew her parents well enough to suspect such fights happened when Lizzie wasn't around. For all of their faults, her parents had done a decent job of shielding her from their rancor.

As Lizzie chopped and sliced and minced, she thought again about her parents and the fact that she hadn't heard from either in a while. When it came to her dad, that was nothing particularly new. Ever since the divorce, their relationship had been . . . well, complicated. She knew much of that was her own doing. At nine years old, she was too young to understand the complexities of marriage—that sometimes a tragedy can bring two people together, but other times it can tear them apart, and when the latter happens there's often no way to fix it. She understood that now, but twenty-one years ago all she knew was that her dad moved out and moved in with someone else and started a new family. No matter how many times he told her he loved her and she would always be his number one girl, she still felt passed over. He'd chosen another family over hers, and it burned.

Initially, Lizzie was the one who encouraged the distance between them. On the weekends she was supposed to visit him, she'd pretend she was sick or choose an activity like going to the movies so that she wouldn't have to talk to him. But as she got older and he became increasingly busy with his new wife and kids, he stopped trying to win Lizzie back. That, too, felt like a betrayal. She knew now that wasn't entirely fair. She was the one who'd pushed him away for years. But part of her felt that if she were really his number one girl he would have fought for her, and he didn't. So their phone calls and visits grew more infrequent, and now they spoke a handful of times a year, usually on big occasions like birthdays and holidays or major events like presidential elections or the Olympics. Lizzie noted that he'd called more often when she'd had a show on the Food Network, which could have been a coincidence, but part of her felt that he, like everyone else, lost interest when she was no longer a hot commodity.

Her mom, however, had become even more important to Lizzie in the years following the divorce. Ryan had been dead for more than five years when her dad left, so it was just her and her mom, and often Lizzie felt as if it were them against the world.

"You're the most important thing in my life, you know that?" her mom would say, and Lizzie felt the same way. Even when Lizzie was living a high-flying life in New York, she spoke to her mom on the phone almost daily and they were always texting and e-mailing each other. But ever since Lizzie started working for the Silvesters, their communication had been less frequent, and uncharacteristically, that was mostly her mom's fault. Lizzie had called and texted and e-mailed, and although her mom had responded to a few of those attempts, she hadn't to all, and when she did reply her tone was a little strange. Was something wrong? Lizzie began to suspect it might be. She'd been meaning to write Aunt Linda to make sure everything was okay, and as she blanched the snap peas in one of the Silvesters' stainless-steel pots she made a mental note to do so once the clambake was over.

Time seemed to race onward, until it was nearly six thirty. The Silvesters and their friends would return in about half an hour, which meant that was all the time Lizzie had to get everything on the table. Using four of the six burners on the Silvesters' cooktop, Lizzie layered the potatoes, sausage, and shellfish atop a pile of sautéed onions and leeks, dousing each pot in a healthy shower of white wine. The mélange steamed beneath tittering lids while Lizzie used a fifth burner to bring a big pot of water to boil for the corn. Renata ferried platters of heirloom tomatoes and snap pea salad to the table, and once the corn and seafood finished cooking she helped Lizzie scoop everything into huge wooden bowls with twine handles. When they laid the last bowl on the table, Lizzie looked at the clock and noted the time: 7:00 on the nose. She'd nailed it.

"The smell!" Renata said, smiling. "So good. Kathryn will be thrilled."

"I couldn't have done it without you. The table looks amazing."

It did—worthy of a splashy spread in a lifestyle magazine. The table was covered in a blue-and-white-striped tablecloth with shells and starfish scattered across it, and linen napkins cinched with rope napkin rings sat atop the nautical china. There were rustic wooden bowls heaving with shellfish, lanterns filled with flickering candles, and a miniature sailboat perched in the middle of the table. Lizzie tried to be humble, but she thought she and Renata deserved a standing ovation.

"So I guess they'll be here any minute . . . ?" Lizzie was trying not to sound worried, but she couldn't help it. Kathryn had been adamant that the meal be ready at 7:00, but it was now five past and she and her guests were nowhere to be found.

"Yes. I'm sure," Renata said. But there was doubt in her voice.

Lizzie's heartbeat quickened. "They wouldn't . . . I mean, Kathryn is usually punctual, right?"

"Yes." A beat. "Usually."

"What do you mean . . . usually?"

"Most of the time. On occasion . . ." She trailed off.

"On occasion what?"

Renata took her time, as if choosing her words very carefully. "On occasion, when she is at the club, she gets talking and . . . well, things can get a bit . . . delayed."

"How delayed?"

Renata shrugged. "It depends. As I said, it's only on occasion."

"But she specifically said she wanted everything hot and ready to eat at seven o'clock sharp."

"Yes. Of course. And I'm sure they will be here very soon."

But something in Renata's voice said otherwise, and as Lizzie watched the steam pour off the heaping platters of food she had a sinking feeling the evening was about to take a very unpleasant turn.

CHAPTER 22

Thirty minutes passed. Then another fifteen. By the time fifty minutes had elapsed, Lizzie wanted to vomit.

"Where are they?" she cried. She held a hand over the shellfish. No steam. Nothing. Was it even safe to let shellfish sit out like this? Probably not. *Great,* she thought. *Not only will everything be cold; they'll also get food poisoning.*

"Help me take everything back inside," she told Renata.

Renata looked at her watch. "They could be here any minute."

"They could also be another hour, at which point nothing will be edible. At least now I can salvage some of this. Though, to be honest, I'm not sure how."

"Can't you reheat it?"

"Shellfish?" Lizzie ran her eyes over the perfectly arranged pile of lobsters, shrimp, clams, and crabs. She wanted to cry. "No. It'd be rubbery and disgusting."

"Oh. Oh, dear." Renata pressed her hands to her cheeks. "Then what will you do?"

"I don't know. Just help me carry the platters inside, and I'll figure something out."

Renata helped her shuttle the bowls and platters back into the house, laying the seafood, corn, and tomatoes on the counter in the butler's pantry. Lizzie stuck the snap pea salad in the refrigerator and turned around to face the surfeit of food. She blinked back tears.

"Perfect," she said, holding her head in her hands.

"Ah, so this is where all the food is."

Lizzie looked over her shoulder and saw Nate standing in the doorway. She couldn't even muster a smile.

"Whoa, if looks could kill . . ."

"Not now," Lizzie said. She wasn't in the mood for banter.

"Sorry, I didn't mean . . . I was just hungry and came looking—"

"If you are going to ask me to make you a pizza right now, I honestly might start crying."

"I wasn't. But now that you mention it . . ."

Lizzie felt the blood rush to her face. "*Seriously?*"

Nate raised his hands apologetically. "No—I was kidding. But apparently the joke didn't land."

"Not even a little."

"Apologies." He glanced at the food on the counter. "What's the problem? Everything looks great."

"Too bad it's all cold."

"Cold? Why?"

"Because Kathryn told me to have everything ready at seven o'clock sharp and it's now eight."

Nate shook his head. "Classic."

"Classic? As in this happens a lot?"

"Not this specifically. More like . . . Kathryn lives in Kathryn land and doesn't always think about how her actions impact others."

"Well, this time it's going to affect her because she isn't going to have any dinner."

"Sure she will. Assuming you want to keep your job for the rest of the summer—which, by the way, I wouldn't blame you if you didn't."

"No, I do." She took a deep breath. "I just don't see how I can save this sorry excuse for a clambake."

"I wouldn't call it a 'sorry excuse'—"

"It wasn't an hour ago. An hour ago, it was perfect. But now? It's basically a pile of room temperature seafood that, in a few more minutes, will be borderline dangerous to eat."

"Are you suggesting you could poison Kathryn? Because if so, I have to say—"

"No."

"I was joking."

"Badly."

"Again. Sorry."

Lizzie sighed. "It's fine. Or not really. But either way it doesn't matter. I need to figure out how to turn many pounds of shellfish into something edible."

"Couldn't you . . . I don't know, make a salad out of it or something?"

"I mean . . . yeah. But it wouldn't be a clambake. Which is what Kathryn requested."

"Okay, but it sounds like what Kathryn requested isn't an option, unless you're planning to microwave all of that, which even I know wouldn't work."

"True."

"So just work your chef magic and turn it all into a seafood salad or something and convince Kathryn that's what she wanted all along." He looked over his shoulder and lowered his voice as he turned back to face Lizzie. "Between you and me, if they're this late, it means they've been drinking, so you could probably serve McDonald's and they wouldn't even notice."

"I somehow doubt that."

"Okay, maybe not McDonald's. But a fancy seafood salad? Sure. As long as it's good."

"And Paleo."

He smiled. "Right."

Lizzie surveyed the mounds of shellfish. There was just so much of it. It would take her ages to peel and shell and chop it all. "I just don't see how I can do it in time."

"I can help."

She eyed him skeptically. "Oh, really?"

"What, you don't think I can crack a few lobster claws?"

"I have my doubts."

"Oh, it's on." He rolled up the sleeves of his blue-and-white gingham shirt and made his way toward the counter. "Move over. It's time for Nate Silvester to show you how it's done."

*   *   *

Lizzie had never seen someone peel seafood so fast. Or at least someone who wasn't a professional cook. Nate cracked and shucked his way through claw after shell after claw, tossing the cooked meat into a bowl before moving on to the next. Lizzie decided she would follow his suggestion and make a big marinated seafood salad, into which she'd fold the cooked baby potatoes and corn she'd shaven off the cob. Would it be the best meal she'd ever cooked? No. But it would be better than a rubbery clambake and certainly better than food poisoning (though she suspected Nate's glee over the latter prospect hadn't actually been a joke).

"So where did a guy like you learn to pick crabs like that?" she asked as he tossed some crabmeat into the bowl.

"A guy like me? What's that supposed to mean?"

"Rich guy. Born with a silver spoon in his mouth. Et cetera."

"First of all, I wasn't born rich. Zoe was, but not me. My dad didn't start making serious money until I was about five, at which point he divorced my mom and married Kathryn. And second, it may shock you to know that rich people eat a lot of lobster. And shrimp. And clams."

"I guess. . . . But picking crabs?"

"My mom grew up in Baltimore."

"Ah. Now it's all making sense."

"More to the point, am I correct in assuming this is your veiled way of complimenting my skills?"

"Nothing veiled about it. You're good. I stand corrected."

"Glad you approve."

Lizzie began chopping a handful of chives for the vinaigrette. "I'm doubly impressed, given that you also basically only eat pizza."

"What? Since when?"

"That's what Kathryn said." Lizzie thought back to their conversation. "I guess she didn't specifically say you only ate pizza, but she made it very clear it was your favorite food."

"I mean, it's *one* of my favorite foods. But I eat lots of different stuff. And anyway, who doesn't like pizza?"

"Lunatics."

"Exactly. It's sort of a litmus test: If you don't like pizza, there's probably something wrong with you."

"Kind of like puppies."

Nate's eyes widened. "You eat puppies?"

"No, I mean *looking* at puppies. If you can look at a puppy and not think it's even a little bit cute, you are probably a psychopath."

"Fair."

Lizzie shot Nate a sideways glance. "Does Zoe like puppies . . . ?"

"Ha, good question. She doesn't seem to like pizza, so that should set off some alarm bells for you. . . ."

Lizzie waited for him to go on, but he didn't. "It's weird that she disappears like she does."

"Not going to argue with you there."

"Has she always been so . . ."

"Odd? Prickly?"

"I was going to say 'mysterious,' but those work too."

He shrugged. "I don't know. I guess? We're twelve years apart and half siblings, so we've never been super close. But I do remember her getting weird around the time she left for college."

"Weird?"

"Maybe 'weirder' is a better way of putting it. She's always been a bit of an odd duck. But there was all sorts of shit that went down around the time she graduated from high school, so that was probably part of it."

"Shit like . . ."

"Well, for starters—"

"They're here!" Renata burst into the butler's pantry. "I just saw a car pull into the driveway. How close are you to being ready?"

Lizzie panicked as she looked at the bowls of seafood. She and Nate had managed to shell half of it, but they still had a lot to do and now that they'd started peeling everything there was no turning back.

"Shit," Lizzie said.

"We'll be fine," Nate said. "Renata, maybe you can open a few bottles of wine to keep everyone busy."

"I could, but I am sure they've been drinking for hours. . . ."

Nate and Lizzie looked at each other. Renata was right. More alcohol was probably the last thing they needed.

Lizzie eyed the platter of tomatoes on the counter. "I can chop those up and turn them into bruschetta."

"But Mrs. Silvester... she doesn't eat bread.... And I don't think some of the other ladies do either."

"Then I'll put their tomatoes in lettuce cups or hollowed-out cucumber or something. Just... give me a second."

Lizzie ran to the refrigerator and rummaged through the hydrator. She'd bought a bunch of cucumbers at the farmers' market that morning with the aim of turning them into a cucumber salad later in the week, but she could always scrap that idea and make something else instead.

She gathered up the cucumbers and laid them on the counter and darted across the room to the bread basket, where she found a day-old baguette.

"Renata, could you grab some basil from the herb garden?"

Renata headed out the side door while Nate continued peeling shrimp and lobsters and Lizzie began slicing the bread. It was dry and a little hard, but since she'd be turning it into toast, it didn't really matter.

"Hey, Nate—new line of work?"

They both turned to see Zoe in the doorway. She wore a floaty navy sundress, her long blond hair tied in a low ponytail.

"Where'd you come from?" Nate asked, ignoring her attempt to goad him into a spat.

"I just got back. Where is everyone?"

"What do you mean? They aren't parking in the driveway?"

"They weren't two minutes ago when I pulled in."

Lizzie's shoulders relaxed. "Thank God."

Renata reappeared, a bunch of basil in her hand. "What's happening?"

"The car you saw was Zoe's. Kathryn and Jim still aren't back."

"Oh—I'm so sorry. All this panic for nothing."

"Don't apologize," Lizzie said. "We still need to hurry. I'm just relieved we have a little more time."

"Wow, really down to the wire, huh?" Zoe said. "Must be pretty bad if you're asking Nate to help."

"You could always make yourself useful, too," Nate snapped as he tossed an empty clamshell into the trash bowl.

"I don't touch anything with a face."

"If that includes people, humanity thanks you."

"Sometimes I can't believe you're responsible for shaping young minds. It's truly frightening. Though I guess sociology majors aren't planning to rule the world someday—"

"Remind me what you majored in again, Zo? Food, folks, and fun?"

"American studies, thanks."

"Glass houses and stones, Zo. Glass houses and stones."

Zoe let out a belabored sigh. "Anyway, I would help, but I'm meeting some people at the Golden Inn. Gotta run."

Nate glanced at the clock. "Wow, a whole five minutes before disappearing again."

"I'm not disappearing. I told you—I'm going to the Golden Inn. It's reggae night."

"Ah. Of course. How could I forget?" His voice was dripping with sarcasm.

"Don't get pissy with me just because you don't have a social life."

"My social life is fine, thanks."

"Debating gentrification with other PhDs doesn't count."

"Says who? The party police?" He dumped the last of the lobster meat into the bowl and wiped down the counter with a damp paper towel. "And anyway, if you are detecting any testiness in my voice, it's because you basically vanished for a week, stressed out your mom, and now can't stay put for more than five minutes so that she knows you're here and okay. Where were you, anyway? No one seems to know."

"What business is it of yours?"

"None. That doesn't mean I can't ask."

"And I'm under no obligation to tell."

Nate's weariness was almost palpable. "Fine. Whatever. Run weapons for the Russian mob. I honestly don't care."

"Sounds like you do, actually."

"No, really, I don't. But I will say this: I find it interesting that someone with such a supposedly happening social life doesn't seem to have any close friends who know anything about her. And don't waste your breath telling me that isn't true because we both know it is."

Zoe clenched her jaw. "Fuck you, Nate."

She stormed out of the room, and Lizzie stood frozen beside the counter, her head full of questions she didn't have time to ask.

Kathryn, Jim, and their friends didn't return until almost nine fifteen, and when they did they were all unquestionably drunk. They tittered and guffawed as they paraded into the house, weaving with unsteady gaits as they made their way from the top of the stairs to the living room. Kathryn, in particular, looked completely wasted, her eyelids sagging as she smiled stupidly at no one in particular.

"Les-s-s-s keep this pardy moo-oving," she slurred as she waved everyone onto the terrace. "A clambake feast awaits!"

The drunken herd plodded toward the door, and as they filed outside, Lizzie snuck up beside Kathryn and whispered in her ear, "Could I talk to you in the kitchen for a second?"

"Sure," Kathryn said in a stage whisper. She smelled of wine. "Jus-s gimme two seconds." She held up two fingers and wiggled them for what seemed to Lizzie like an unusually long time. She then cupped her hand beside her mouth. "I have to go pee pee."

She scampered off to the bathroom, and Lizzie slipped back to the butler's pantry, hoping Kathryn still possessed the wherewithal to figure out where she'd gone. She'd never seen Kathryn like this, and she knew the evening could go one of two ways: high comedy or painful disaster.

When Lizzie returned to her station Nate was wiping down the counters, a clean dish towel slung over his shoulder.

"Renata and I will take care of that," Lizzie said. "You should relax—you've already done more than your fair share tonight."

"No worries—I'm almost finished anyway." He tossed a damp paper towel into the trash can.

"You have no idea how much I appreciate your help."

"My pleasure. And hey, it gave me something to do."

"Other than . . . how did Zoe put it? Debate gentrification with other PhDs?"

Nate shook his head. "God, she is the worst at times. Sorry you had to witness that."

Lizzie was contemplating whether to ask Nate what he meant when he'd said Zoe didn't have any close friends when Kathryn staggered into the room.

"*Na-a-a-ate?*" She sounded completely befuddled. It was as if she'd stumbled across him naked in front of the freezer, eating a pint of ice cream straight from the container.

"Whoa, Kathryn—wild night?"

Kathryn clicked her tongue as she tried to focus her eyes. "We've been having *fun*. Not that you'd know anything about that. But it's okay. I'm not mad. Y'know what, though? I think I found a girl for you. No, stop. Stop. No. I'm serious. She's . . . d'you remember Sam? 'Course you remember Sam, duh-h-h-h. No one forgets Sam. Didjou know he and Barb are a thing now? Mm-mhm-m. Oh, yeah. Hot and heavy. All thanks to guess who?" She gestured at herself with her thumbs. "That's right. *Moi.* Anyway . . . what was I saying . . . ?"

Lizzie honestly had no idea. Kathryn was obviously trying to set Nate up with some woman, but as difficult as it was to keep up with Kathryn's rambling monologues under normal circumstances, her inebriation had demolished any semblance of structure.

"You know, I'm not really sure," Nate said, "but considering you're more than two hours late for dinner, I think you'd be better off discussing the menu with your cook."

"Are we really that late?" Kathryn looked at the clock with narrowed eyes. She gasped. "Oh, I din-n even . . . see, Sam an Jim got into one about . . . whatever, business stuff . . . an then Barb was pissed 'cause Sam wasn't, y'know, fussing over her an' whatever, s'then Sam bought a few more bottles, an' before we knew it . . ." She made an exploding sound while miming a mushroom cloud with her hands. Lizzie wasn't exactly sure what that was supposed to mean, but she assumed it meant they drank a lot.

"Well, the thing is. . . ." Lizzie cleared her throat. "I know you were counting on a clambake, and I had everything ready at seven like you asked, but then you were late and everything got cold. So I hope you don't mind, but I turned it all into a big seafood salad."

Kathryn frowned, then hiccupped loudly. "Oh-h-h-h-h, boy."

"I'm really sorry, but it was the only way to salvage everything."

"No, no, is-sfine, is-sfine. I mean, I promised everyone a clambake, but they've all had a lotta wine. . . . Y'know what they say, when life gives you lemonade . . ." She grasped for the right idiom but, unable to find it, simply shrugged. "Whatever, I don't know, add vodka or something."

Lizzie tried her best to keep a straight face. She refused to meet Nate's eyes. "Everything is in the refrigerator. Renata will help me bring it out whenever you're ready."

"I'm ready!" Kathryn winked deliberately and gave a thumbs-up.

"By the way, Zoe is back," Nate said.

Kathryn's expression brightened, and she looked over her shoulder toward the pool. "Where?"

"She's at the Golden Inn. She was here for all of about six minutes before she took off again."

"But she's here? In Avalon?"

"Yes. At least for now."

Kathryn heaved a sigh and leaned against the door frame. "Oh, thank God. I jus-s worry. How'd she seem . . . ?"

"Her normal, prickly self."

"Oh, good. I mean that she's herself. I jus-s never know. Er-ry-thing was fine, but then the other day Lizzie said something 'bout Marie, and I thought, 'Oh, Jesus, here we go with all *that* again. . . .'"

Nate frowned. "Marie?"

"I know. Don't gemme started." Her eyes moved lazily in Lizzie's direction, and her expression changed, as if she suddenly remembered Lizzie was standing there. "Anyway, Nate, I know this dinner's not for you, but come say hi to Sam—he can tell you about that girl. . . ."

"Girl?"

"Woman, whatever. She's an . . . anthromopologist? Archaeologist? Something. Sounded right up your alley."

"Because an -ologist is an -ologist, right?"

"*Ex-x-xactly.*"

"I'll be out in a sec'. I think Lizzie could use an extra set of hands."

"I'm sure she's fine. Renata? Renata, come help Lizzie get er-ry-thing ous-side, okay? Nate, thisaway."

She grabbed Nate by the elbow and, swaying back and forth with him as her hostage, dragged him as far away from Lizzie as she could.

CHAPTER 23

Linda,

Sure, 12:30 at JG Domestic works for me.
Lunch downtown—what a treat! A perfect way to
spend the day before my surgery.

I can tell you more about this over lunch, but
Dr. Konovsky was amazing. He trained with the
Demuth Institute and is a certified expert in
Demuth therapy. We've come up with a pretty intense regimen that I'll follow immediately after the
lumpectomy and will continue with for up to two
years, depending on how I respond. It involves lots
of freshly pressed juices and coffee enemas. Can't
say I'm too excited about the latter, but I'm sure it
beats chemo. And when Dr. Konovsky took me
through the process and how it works, the results
spoke for themselves.

He also pointed me toward some really useful
reading material, both in print and online. I've
been reading like crazy! Some of the Web sites are
really inspiring—lots of personal stories of people
who've followed protocols like mine and are now
cancer-free. And lots of these cases were way more

advanced than my own. One site in particular talks about a girl who got cancer as a teenager. As you can imagine, this was very difficult for me to read, but it ended up really inspiring me. Her best friend runs the site and put her on a very Demuth-like program and basically cured her. In the latest post, I saw that the cancer has returned, but she was cancer-free for something like five years and, even though it has returned, she has it under control. I wish I'd known about these alternatives to conventional medicine when Ryan was a baby. My heart breaks over and over when I think about what we put him through.

Anyway, like I said, we can talk about some of this over lunch—though I'd love it if we could spend the bulk of the time talking about something else. I'm a little burned-out on the c word these days, as you can probably imagine.

I'd love to pick your brain about Lizzie. I'm having a really tough time talking to her lately. Actually, I should clarify: We haven't talked in a long time because I'm not sure what to say. I just feel so guilty keeping all of this from her. I know, I know—it was my choice. And I stand by it. But I miss her, and I'm not sure how much longer I can screen her calls. Ugh. I don't expect you to have a solution for this (mostly because I'm sure it will involve telling her the truth sooner than I'd like), but you've always been a good listener, so I'm counting on you for that.

Okay, gotta run. Gary is taking me to some new yoga class in Jenkintown. I swear, if it weren't for the cancer, I'd say I'm currently in the best shape of my life, and it's all thanks to him.

See you tomorrow!

xxoo

S

CHAPTER 24

The Silvesters' non-clambake clambake was a success, and Lizzie tried to tell herself that wasn't because everyone was so drunk they probably didn't know what they were eating. The party wore on past 1:00 a.m., at which point Sam Offerman was naked in the pool and another guest was passed out on the living room couch. Lizzie couldn't believe how hard these people could party. They were around her parents' age. How did they have the energy? She knew that was probably an ageist question, but she was only thirty and had already lost the ability to drink much past midnight. In another twenty or thirty years? Forget it. She'd be in bed by nine.

Lizzie helped Renata clear plates and glasses that had been left around the pool deck, shielding her eyes to avoid an accidental glimpse of Sam's anatomy. She was convinced that seeing his naked body up close would leave deep mental scars, from which she would possibly never recover.

"Hey, cutie, why don't you join me in here?" he called to Lizzie. "The water is per-r-r-rfect."

"No, thanks," Lizzie said, her eyes trained on the small table in front of her.

"Aw, come on. Don't leave me in here all alone."

"Maybe I should find Barb."

He pretended to purr like a cat. "Sassy. I like that."

Lizzie heard splashing behind her and the smack of wet feet on the pool deck. The footsteps came closer, but she refused to turn around and instead walked quickly toward the house, a pile of dirty plates in her hands.

"Hey, where you running off to? I promise I don't bite." Lizzie waited for the inevitable punch line. "*Hard,*" he added before exploding with laughter.

Lizzie hustled into the house without turning back and shivered as she closed the door behind her. Was it the air-conditioning or Sam's lecherous advances that sent chills up her spine? She wasn't sure. He was just so thoroughly unappealing—the fake tan, the peachy hair, the brash chauvinism. The fact that Barb was sleeping with him baffled Lizzie. Was she really that desperate?

Lizzie dumped the dirty plates in the sink in the butler's pantry. Part of her hoped to run into Nate, but she hadn't seen him since Kathryn lured him away earlier and she wasn't sure where he was. He hadn't eaten with the Silvesters' friends, but she wasn't sure whether he'd left or gone to bed. She knew she shouldn't care—she was effectively being paid to cook for him—but she did. He was kind and smart and funny, and he was the closest thing she had in this town to a friend.

Renata came into the kitchen carrying a tray full of dirty wineglasses. "I'll put all of this in the dishwasher if you wouldn't mind gathering up the rest of the napkins and other trash," she said.

Lizzie agreed and headed outside. She prayed Sam had put clothes on or gone to bed, but as she approached the glass doors she could hear him bellowing into the night about how he could have been an Olympic swimmer.

"You don't even know. I'll race ya. I'll frickin' race ya right now. Don't be such a pussy—come on."

Lizzie averted her eyes as she walked onto the patio and began gathering up crumpled cocktail napkins and empty bottles.

"Hey, sugar tits—you believe me, right?"

Lizzie knew nothing would be gained by answering one way or the other, so she kept her head down and continued picking up bits of trash.

"Oh, so now I get the silent treatment? Please. I'm more man than you'll ever meet in this town. Where do the young chicks hang out these days? The Whitebrier? The Princeton?" She heard the *splish-splosh* of wet feet on the pool deck. "That's where the boys go. You need a real man. Tell me, can those boys do this?"

She heard a loud splash, followed by silence. Then a scream.

"Blood! *Blood!*"

Lizzie whipped her head around and saw a red cloud blooming in the deep end of the pool. Sam lay at the bottom. He wasn't moving.

"Oh my God," Lizzie said. She dropped the pile of trash on the ground and rushed into the house. "Renata!" she shouted. "Call nine-one-one!"

Renata came running into the kitchen. "What's happened?"

"Sam hit his head on the bottom of the pool. I don't know how. But he isn't moving, and there's blood."

Renata's eyes widened. She ran for the phone and dialed 911.

Lizzie hurried back outside, where two of the men had pulled Sam out of the pool and onto the pool deck. "He's breathing!" one of them shouted. "Sam! Sammy boy!" He slapped Sam's face. "Wake up!"

Sam let out a loud groan as water spurted out of his mouth. Blood trickled onto the pavement from a large gash on his crown. He was also still naked, but to Lizzie's infinite relief his blubbery belly rose high enough to obstruct any view of his penis. She couldn't help but think he looked like a beached whale, though given the unnaturally orange shade of his hair and skin, it was more like a beached orangutan.

"An ambulance is on its way!" Renata called from the doorway.

In a flash, the ambulance arrived, and a team of paramedics heaved Sam's naked body onto a stretcher, covering his lower body with a white sheet. They pushed him on the stretcher to the ambulance and whisked him away in a cacophony of sirens and bells, the red and white lights illuminating the night sky.

"What happened . . . ?"

Barb stumbled into the living room. Her dark hair was matted to one side of her face, and she had rings of mascara beneath her eyes. She looked as if she'd just woken up, only she was fully dressed, minus a shoe, which led Lizzie to believe she'd passed out somewhere in the Silvesters' house.

"Sam cracked his head on the bottom of the pool," Lizzie said. "He's on his way to the hospital."

"Oh!" Barb covered her mouth, her eyes wide. "Oh, Sammy!"

She hobbled toward the stairs, alternating heeled and bare feet with a *clack-thump, clack-thump, clack-thump.*

"Sammy!" she called. "Sammy, wait!"

"They're gone," Lizzie said.

"Then I'll meet him at the hospital. Where are my keys?" She patted down her body. She was wearing skintight jeans and a tight black tank top, so Lizzie doubted her keys were anywhere on her person. She was also clearly still drunk, so no matter where her keys were, Lizzie thought her driving anywhere was a very bad idea.

"I can take you," Lizzie offered, though as soon as she did she regretted it. What was she thinking? Did she really want to spend all night at the hospital with Sam and Barb? She'd rather chew on rusty nails.

"I'm fine—I can drive myself. I just need to find my keys."

"You don't have any keys, dear," Renata said. "Sam drove you. Remember?"

"Oh. Right. Whatever. Then where are his keys?"

"I don't think you are in the best shape to drive," Renata said.

"I'm *fine.*"

"No, you're not," said a stern voice. Nate descended the stairs from the second floor. He wore red boxers and a gray T-shirt and looked as if he'd just woken up. "Look at you—you can barely stand upright. Let Lizzie take you." He met Lizzie's eyes and seemed to read her misgivings. "I'll come, too. To keep you guys company."

Barb began to protest but, apparently too tired and drunk to put up much of a fight, ultimately relented. "Fine," she said. "Let me just get my other shoe."

Barb got her shoe and Nate threw on clothes while Lizzie ran to her room to grab her keys and purse. They all met in the driveway and piled in Lizzie's car, Nate riding shotgun and Barb in the backseat.

"Thanks for tagging along," Lizzie said as she started up the car.

"No prob." He lowered his voice. "I figured you might need moral support, given the players involved."

"Much appreciated. Sorry to have disrupted your evening."

"Eh, it's just sleep, right?"

Lizzie smiled.

"*Hello-o-o-o-o!* Can we get going?"

"Sorry—here we go." Lizzie threw the car in reverse and pulled out of the Silvesters' driveway.

"Thank God," Barb said. Then she frowned as she sniffed the air. "Is it me, or does this car smell like piss?"

Fifteen minutes later, Lizzie pulled in front of the entrance to the Cape Regional Medical Center. Barb bolted from the backseat, teetering in her strappy stiletto sandals as she ran toward the sliding glass doors.

"Sammy! Sammy, I'm coming!"

Lizzie stared in amazement. "Wow."

"Are you marveling at her ability to run in those shoes? Or the fact that she is so emotionally invested in Sam's well-being?"

"Both."

Nate laughed. "There's parking in the lot over there. We should probably stick around to make sure he's okay."

"Aren't they going to need a ride home?"

"That's your call. You were nice enough to drive them here. At their age, if they can't figure out how to call a cab that's their problem. The two of them are drunker than some twenty-two-year-olds. It's ridiculous."

Lizzie parked the car in the lot, which was pretty empty, though at two o'clock on a Monday morning she wouldn't have expected otherwise. She and Nate walked through the entrance and approached the registration desk.

"Hi, we're here for Sam Offerman?" Nate said.

The receptionist typed at her computer. "I believe he is being seen by the doctor at the moment. He already has one companion, so only one of you can go back. We have a two-person maximum."

Nate and Lizzie looked at each other. Neither of them had any interest in being that person.

"You know what? We'll both hang here in the waiting room. Give us an update when he's talked to the doctor."

Nate gave his name, and then he and Lizzie found two seats in the waiting room. Lizzie collapsed into one as she let out a loud sigh. "What a night."

"Not exactly what you expected when you took the job, huh?"

"Not specifically."

"Still insist you want to work for them for the rest of the summer?"

"Yep. And into the fall, if they'll have me."

"Seriously?" He shook his head. "I know it isn't really my place, but I have to confess: I don't get it."

"What's to get? The pay is good, and I don't have any other options."

"I find that hard to believe."

"Believe it."

"Come on—you had a show on the Food Network."

"Five years ago. People's memories are short."

"Okay, but you graduated from Penn. That has to count for something."

Lizzie gulped. She could feel her cheeks turning pink. "It isn't quite that simple."

"I guess. You just seem way too smart and competent to have to put up with this kind of bullshit." He gestured around the waiting room.

"You're here, too, thank you very much."

"True. But Sam and Barb are almost family, at least as far as my dad and Kathryn are concerned. I can't really avoid them. But you—you don't *have* to deal with these people."

"If it weren't them, it would be another pair of crazies. Trust me. Some of the people I dealt with in New York . . . One guy made me cut all of his food into bite-size pieces for him. Another lady had a separate freezer filled entirely with Arctic Zero. Like, at least fifty pints."

"Arctic Zero?"

"It's this terrible low-calorie, non-dairy ice cream. It tastes like hunger and tears."

He laughed. "Still doesn't sound quite as bad as sitting in a beachside ER at two a.m., waiting for a drunken sixty-something chauvinist to get staples in his head."

"When you put it that way . . ." She slid down in her seat and sighed. "Jesus."

"Sorry—I didn't mean to pour salt on the wound."

"No, listen, it isn't your fault. I'm the one who put myself in this position. I just . . ." She sat back up, wondering how much to confide in Nate. "When you're on top of the world, you don't think there's anything that can bring you down. At least I didn't. I thought the ride would last forever. I was twenty-two, and that's how twenty-two-year-olds think. I wasn't worried about career stability or longevity. I mean, on some level I guess I knew I wouldn't be hosting a college cooking show when I was forty, but forty sounded so far away. Frankly, thirty sounded far away, too, and yet here I am."

She played with the hem on her shirt. She typically hated talking about the demise of her career, but tonight it felt good to articulate all the thoughts that had been weighing on her for years.

"Anyway, it just kind of sucks, because on some level I feel like I had my shot, and I blew it, and now I don't have a lot of choices left."

"Sure you do. Maybe not as many as when you were twenty-two, but you always have choices."

"I guess. I just sometimes wish, if I had it all to do over again . . ." She trailed off.

"What? You'd do something else instead?"

"No. But I'd plan better. More backstops and safety nets." She thought about it more. "Actually, maybe I would do something else. I don't know. Sometimes it feels as if I peaked too early. Like, if I had just been patient and put in my time, I would have built a career that would last, instead of one that would flame out before I hit thirty."

"I wouldn't say you've flamed out."

She gestured around the emergency room. "Need I remind you where we are . . . ?"

"I'm the one who brought that up to begin with. But I only did that because you still have a star quality. And to be honest, if you don't mind me saying so, you kind of seem like you're settling."

"It's not settling when it's the only option on the table."

"This isn't the only option."

"It is at the moment. And before you tell me I can always get back into TV, let me assure you: I can't. That isn't how it works. That door has closed, at least for a while."

"I hate to break it to you, but having doors close is part of getting older. That's just a fact. I'm thirty-five, and already I know I'll never be on the Supreme Court or the Olympic swim team or serve as president of the United States. But that's because I made choices a long time ago that ruled those options out. That doesn't mean all doors have slammed shut. I could still start a business, or become an author, or take up competitive poker. Okay, maybe not the poker in my case, but you get the idea. Hell, I could even go to culinary school and become a chef."

"At which point you, too, could cook for crazy millionaires."

He laughed. "You get what I'm saying. It isn't over at thirty. Even if it feels that way sometimes."

"I guess." She felt her lip start to quiver and tried hard to tame it. If she started crying—*oh, God*. What if she started crying? Part of her knew it would feel good. So good. Better than anything had felt in a long, long time. But then there was Nate, whom she barely knew, and all these strangers in the waiting area. Was she ready for them to see her ugly cry? Because it would be ugly. She'd held on to these feelings for so long, and if she let them out all at once it would be a huge, hideous catharsis, the likes of which these people had probably never seen. But the more she thought about it, the more she wanted it—the immense satisfaction of an explosive cry, with wailing and moaning and rivers of tears and snot. Right now, she wanted it more than anything, more than sex or money or chocolate.

"Nate Silvester?"

Lizzie's fantasy was interrupted by a young nurse who entered the waiting area. Nate jumped up, and Lizzie followed him to meet her.

"The doctor is just finishing up with Sam. He has a two-centimeter laceration on the crown of his head. We're finishing up his staples now while we wait for the results of his CT scan."

"CT scan?"

"To make sure he doesn't have a brain bleed or a fractured spine."

"Jesus."

"It's standard procedure when anyone his age comes in with a head injury. In all likelihood, it's just a mild concussion."

"How much longer until he gets the results?"

"Probably another forty-five minutes or so."

"Forty-five minutes?" Nate groaned. "Is Barb still back there with him?"

"You mean the woman in the heels?"

"And tight pants. Yeah."

"Yes, she's still there."

Nate met Lizzie's eyes. "They could take a cab," he said in a low voice.

"Yeah, but . . ." Lizzie wasn't sure why she was about to oppose Nate's idea. Maybe it was because she felt guilty. Or maybe it was because she knew waiting for them would mean more time with Nate and she was enjoying his company.

"You really want to wait around for these clowns?" he asked, incredulous.

"No, but I feel bad. The guy has a concussion. And staples in his head."

"None of which is your fault."

"True, but we're already here. I'm sure we can entertain ourselves for another forty-five minutes."

Nate sighed. "Okay, how about this: I'll leave my number for Sam, and he can call us when they release him. In the meantime, we can find something else to do."

The nurse smiled politely. "I'm happy to give him your number, but I'll warn you . . . it's almost three in the morning. There isn't a lot to do around here."

Nate grabbed a scrap of paper and jotted down his number. "We're less than five miles from the ocean," he said, smiling as he handed the nurse the paper. "I'm sure we can find something."

*   *   *

Nate helped Lizzie navigate from the hospital to Stone Harbor's 96th Street beach. She parked in one of the metered spots on 96th and followed Nate up the boardwalk. Part of her couldn't believe she was going for a walk on the beach at three in the morning with a man she barely knew while she waited to pick up a sixty-something who'd injured himself while drunkenly skinny-dipping. Had she lost her mind?

Nate kicked off his flip-flops once they reached the sand and headed for the edge of the water. Lizzie did the same and shivered as the ocean rushed over her toes.

"Cold?"

"A little," Lizzie confessed.

"You'll get used to it. Left or right?"

"Left," she said, for no reason in particular.

They started walking, the nighttime silence punctuated by the sound of waves crashing against the shore. The beach looked eerie at night, dark and deserted, the sand dimpled with shadows in the moonlight, looking itself like a lunar landscape. The edge of the ocean glinted like frothy lace. The air was thick and salty.

They continued following the edge of the ocean. Lizzie looked up at the sky. "So many stars," she said.

"Much easier to see out here than in the city. I'm sure New York is even worse than DC."

"Probably." She sidestepped a mound of seaweed.

"Listen, about earlier . . . when we were talking about your career . . . I didn't mean to overstep."

"You didn't. No need to apologize."

"You sure? Because I kind of feel like I took you to a bad emotional place, and then we got interrupted by the nurse, so I didn't get a chance to fix it."

"There's nothing to fix. Honest."

"I guess I was just trying to give you the confidence to reinvent yourself if you wanted to."

"Oh, so now I lack confidence?"

"No, no—that isn't what I'm saying."

"Then what are you saying? That I need to 'reinvent' myself?"

"No. God. See? This is why my teacher evaluations always come back that I'm 'overly critical.' I'm really bad at giving pep talks. What I'm trying to say is, keep doing what you're doing if you love it. But if you don't, and you're tired of dealing with the likes of my crazy family, you don't have to keep doing it. You have at least thirty-five years of your career left, maybe even fifty. You still have time to do lots of different things, maybe even the thing you'll be known for."

"You mean other than being a washed-up Food Network star?"

"See, this is what I'm talking about: You're letting that one experience define you. You tried something in your twenties, and it didn't work out. So what?"

"So what? So I failed at something in front of *everyone*. This isn't like, 'Oh, I tried a new syllabus, and the students really hated it, so I had to scrap it and start again.' This was my name and my brand becoming synonymous with 'has-been' and having every future employer ask about it."

"Yeah, but memories are short. You said so yourself. People are probably more impressed that you ever had a show on the Food Network than they are dismissive that it didn't last."

"I think that depends on who you're talking to."

"Listen, on some level I get it. These days, people feel like failures if they haven't invented Facebook by the time they're thirty. But that's ridiculous. Sure, some people hit it big right out of college. But others don't hit their stride until their forties or fifties."

"I guess. But then I look at people like Zoe. . . ."

"Who what? Have some lame little Web site?"

"It's more than a lame little Web site. Have you seen it?"

"Honestly? No. I've just heard she has one."

"It's really polished and professional. And she has tons of followers—something like two hundred thousand last time I checked Instagram."

"Seriously? Wow. Way to go, Zo."

"That's what I'm saying. She has a brand, and she's growing that brand in a way that could last. Mind you, having met her, I think there's something about her site that isn't entirely . . . authentic."

"Yeah, well, that's Zoe for you. Let me guess: Her life looks totally fabulous and easy, as if you ripped it straight from a lifestyle magazine."

"Pretty much. Never mind that she claims credit for stuff she had nothing to do with."

"Like?"

"Some of the food I've made, for starters. She posted photos of all these dishes as if she'd made them herself, and when I called her out on it she basically blamed me for hogging the kitchen."

"Even though that's your job."

"Exactly."

"Typical."

"So I'm learning." The water rushed over Lizzie's toes. It felt warmer now. "Don't get me wrong—I feel bad for her friend Marie."

"Marie? You mean her friend who died?"

Lizzie stopped short. "What?"

Nate stopped, too, and turned around. "Marie. The one who died when Zoe graduated from high school."

A wave crashed against the shore, but Lizzie barely heard it. "No . . . the one who has cancer."

"Right. Zoe's friend from sleepaway camp. She had osteosarcoma and died the summer before Zoe went away to college."

"But . . . on Zoe's site . . ."

"She talks about Marie?"

"That's like the entire point of the site."

"As a tribute to her or something?"

"No, as in, her entire brand is based around the fact that she helped her friend Marie go into remission by cleaning up her diet and following some sort of alternative protocol with juices and natural supplements and stuff."

"I don't think so. Unless she has another friend named Marie who also got cancer."

"Maybe she does."

Nate raised an eyebrow. Lizzie had to admit: Such a coincidence was extremely unlikely.

"Marie's death was a big effing deal for Zoe. She had a really hard time getting over it."

"But . . . that doesn't make any sense. Why would she claim she saved Marie's life if Marie actually died?"

"Honestly? I have no idea. Like I said, she had a tough time with the whole thing."

"What happened?"

Nate shrugged. "I'm not up to speed on all the details, but from what I know, she met Marie at overnight camp in the Adirondacks when she was about fifteen or so and they got really close. I think Marie was Canadian—from Montreal, maybe? Anyway, they were super close and stayed in touch, but about two years later she was diagnosed with cancer, and then about a year after that she died. Zoe sort of fell apart. Lots of weird behavior."

"Weird like . . . ?"

"Claiming Marie had been reincarnated in the neighbor's puppy, disappearing for days and weeks at a time, going on strange diets. That's when all of the 'clean eating' stuff started."

Lizzie stared at Nate in disbelief. "So let me get this straight. Marie died five years ago, and yet Zoe claims she cured her—and is still curing her, actually—and is encouraging other people to follow the same diet to cure themselves?"

"I guess? I've never been on her site."

"Nate—think about this for a second. There are people out there who legitimately have cancer who are reading the information on Zoe's site and saying, 'Oh, hey, that sure sounds better than chemo—I think I'll give it a try!' Do you understand how dangerous and irresponsible that is?"

"Of course I do. I've studied mortgage fraud for years. I know what a scam looks like."

"Did Marie even try the stuff Zoe claims she did?"

"I have no idea. It's not like Zoe and I are super close. She didn't exactly bare her soul to me when all of this was happening. I always suspected there was a little more to their relationship than just . . . friendship. But we didn't talk about it. It's not as if she was flying up to Montreal all the time when Marie was sick. That much I know. Frankly, until she died, I'm not sure how much Kathryn and Dad even knew about her. Maybe Zoe feels guilty for not having done more to help? Or maybe Marie did follow Zoe's advice and died anyway. I'm not sure."

"Whatever the case, thousands of people are now following her advice, and it's all a big lie."

"Hang on—you don't know that thousands of people are actually doing what she suggests."

"Even if it's only ten people. Even if it's only one! It's wrong, Nate. And you know it."

"I agree. So what are you going to do about it?"

"I don't know. I was thinking I'd talk to her and tell her to stop lying."

Nate huffed. "Good luck with that."

"What's that supposed to mean?"

"Zoe does whatever she wants. And if you try to get in her way, forget it. She has a history of being . . . how do I put this? Unstable."

"So she talks about dog spirits and disappears for a while. So what?"

"It's not just that. She also does stuff like . . . okay, last summer? When that guy Bob was working as the chef? I'm not clear on the whole story, but he saw her out one night after most of the bars had closed, and my guess is she was with another woman and got embarrassed or something, because the next thing I knew, Zoe was accusing him first of drinking my dad's whiskey and then of trying to break into Kathryn's safe. So my dad and Kathryn fired him."

"Did they have any proof that he'd done either?"

"Nope. But that's how they are when it comes to Zoe. They are so afraid of pushing her off the deep end that they'll do anything to keep her happy. And anyway, they are both so uptight that when Bob implied Zoe was lying because she didn't want them to know she might be gay or bisexual or whatever they refused to believe him."

"But this is different. She is endangering people's lives."

"I get it—trust me. What I'm saying is that she can be vindictive and malicious, so a confrontation isn't necessarily going to end the way you want it to. And anyway, throughout her life, she's gone through phases and fads. It's what she does. This Web site is probably another one of those things. In a few months, I bet she'll lose interest, and the site will disappear. She doesn't stay interested in anything for long."

"Maybe this is the exception."

Nate shrugged and opened his mouth as if he were about to say something, but his phone rang and interrupted him. "Hello?"

Lizzie could hear a loud voice yammering on the other end. Nate covered the receiver with his hand. *Sam,* he mouthed.

"Yep. Okay. We'll be there in ten or fifteen minutes. See you then." He hung up and nodded over Lizzie's shoulder. "Time to head back. We can continue this conversation another time."

Lizzie turned and followed Nate back up the beach, but she had no plans to continue their conversation because there was nothing more to discuss. She had already made up her mind: She was going to confront Zoe.

CHAPTER 25

By the time Lizzie returned to the Silvesters' house, it was nearly 4:00 a.m. Barb had fallen asleep in the backseat, her face pressed against the fat cervical collar around Sam's neck. He hadn't sustained any serious injuries, other than the cut on his head and a mild concussion, but the nurse recommended he wear the collar for a day or two for protection. Lizzie hadn't thought it was possible for orange-skinned, peach-haired Sam to look any more ridiculous than he already did, but the cervical collar proved her wrong. He looked like a court jester or an Elizabethan cartoon. She probably would have found it funnier if his antics hadn't cost her a night's sleep.

She turned off the engine and noticed that Zoe's car wasn't there. It hadn't been when they left either, so she must not have made it home. Where did she sleep when she stayed out late like this? In all the photos on her site, Zoe looked so bright and well rested. Where and when was all of this rest happening?

"Barb, babe, wake up. We're here."

Sam nudged Barb in the side, not entirely lovingly, Lizzie thought. Barb awoke with a snort and a start, the left side of her face pink from the pressure of Sam's cervical collar.

"What time is it?" she asked.

"Three fifty-seven," Nate said.

"Hey, the night's just getting started, right?" Sam caught Lizzie's eye in the rearview mirror and winked.

"Maybe for you," Lizzie said. "For me, this is the end of the line."

"Okay, okay." He lowered his voice to a stage whisper. "Apparently chef-y can't take a joke."

Maybe the collar made him think he really *was* a jester, Lizzie thought. A really bad one, in a hospital onesie. Since he'd been naked when they hauled him into the ambulance, he didn't have any clothes to change into, and so they'd sent him home in what Lizzie overheard one of the nurses refer to as a "bunny suit"—a long-sleeved jumpsuit made of stiff, papery blue cotton, which zipped from the crotch to his neck. It looked like a Halloween costume, or a hazmat suit.

"Come on, sleepyhead, out ya get." Sam poked Barb in the side.

"I'm going, I'm going." Barb yawned as she unfolded herself out of the car. "Where are your car keys?"

"Why? You going somewhere?"

"Home, silly."

"Let's just sleep here tonight. All my clothes are here, and they've got plenty of room." He leaned toward Nate, who was climbing out of the passenger seat. "They've got some beds made up, right?"

"I honestly don't know."

"Sure they do. And if not, what's-her-face . . . Renata? She can always throw some sheets on."

"Pretty sure Renata is sleeping." Nate's voice brimmed with impatience. He'd clearly had enough of Sam's bullshit for one evening.

"Pretty sure you can wake her," Sam snapped back. "She works for you, remember?"

"She works for my dad and Kathryn."

"And I'm their friend, and I'd like to stay here."

"Sammy, baby, just come back to my place. It was good enough for you last night."

"Last night I didn't have staples in my head."

"You can both sleep on the couch for all I care," Nate said. "Just don't wake up Renata, or anyone else, for that matter."

Sam sighed as he looked at Barb. "I don't even know where my keys are. I'll make a hell of a noise trying to find them. Let's just crash here for the night. I'm sure chef-y has a primo breakfast planned for us anyway."

In fact, Lizzie did not have any special breakfast plans, mostly because she'd been too preoccupied with Sam's hospital shenanigans to arrange anything. But the Silvesters would expect a decent breakfast, especially if some of their drunk friends had spent the night—which, from the Mercedes and BMWs filling the driveway, it looked as if they had.

Lizzie slid out of the front seat and closed the door behind her. Sam remained in the backseat.

"Sweetheart, give me a hand, would you? I can barely move with this damn collar."

Lizzie took a deep breath and let it out slowly as she opened the back door. She reached out her arm, which Sam grabbed a little too tightly as he swung his legs out of the car.

"Ready? On the count of three: one, two . . ."

Lizzie pulled with all of her strength as she tried to hoist Sam out of the car. It was like trying to lift a three-hundred-pound sack of potatoes. He barely moved.

"You're going to have to help me a little," Lizzie said. "Either that, or Nate will have to lift you out."

"But his skin isn't nearly as smooth."

He rubbed her arm with his thumb. She felt as if she were being attacked by venomous spiders.

"Nate?" She nodded at Sam. "A little help."

She managed to extract her arm from Sam's grip, and Nate slid in front of her. As if by some miracle, Sam grabbed the side of the car and lifted himself out without Nate's assistance.

"Aw, Sammy baby, look at you." Barb pouted as she tottered toward him. She held his hand. "Let's get you inside."

The two of them hobbled toward the house, Barb in too-high stilettos and Sam in a foam collar.

"Look at those two," Nate muttered in Lizzie's ear.

"A match made in heaven," Lizzie said.

"Hey, you're welcome!" Nate called after them.

Sam slowed and turned around step by step until he faced them. "What's that?"

"I said, you're welcome."

He stared at Nate quizzically, then offered a half smile. "Oh. Right. Sure."

He slowly pivoted back around, and it was then that Lizzie realized neither he nor Barb had even once said thank you.

As exhausted as she was, Lizzie couldn't sleep. All she could think about was Zoe. She was going to confront her, but she didn't know how or when and she wasn't exactly sure what she was going to say. Her lifelong dislike and avoidance of confrontation had left her completely unprepared. But she had to do it. She didn't care what Nate said. Frankly, she was a little disappointed in him for counseling her to leave the issue alone. Was he really so weak? He seemed like such a nice guy.

Unable to sleep, Lizzie slipped out of her bedroom and headed upstairs to the kitchen. If she wasn't going to get any rest, she might as well work. The Silvesters would expect a nice breakfast for their friends, and doing some of the prep work now would save her time later in the morning, when she would probably be a zombie.

The house was dark and still. Lizzie shivered. She wasn't used to seeing the Silvesters' home like this, and even though she knew she was allowed to roam the kitchen whenever she wanted, she felt like a trespasser.

She tiptoed into the butler's pantry and flicked on the light. Renata had cleaned up while Lizzie and Nate were at the hospital, and the entire space was immaculate, as if there'd never been a clambake at all (which technically, Lizzie reminded herself, there hadn't been). The surfaces gleamed, and all of the dishes and glasses had been washed and returned to the appropriate cupboard.

Given all that Renata had done, Lizzie felt bad making her run out first thing in the morning to buy bagels or doughnuts, so she opened the refrigerator to see if there was enough food to cobble together a decent breakfast. There were two cartons of eggs and a little cheese, and Lizzie knew the Silvesters grew lots of herbs in their garden. Combined with some leftover fruit and maybe some homemade muffins, it would be enough—nothing spectacular, but passable, especially given the circumstances.

Lizzie searched the pantry for flour for the muffins, but all she found was a gluten-free blend and a bag of almond meal. Could she make muffins with that? Possibly. She slunk into the main kitchen, where the signed copy of Martha Stewart's *Entertaining* sat on the shelf. Maybe Martha would have some ideas. Granted, gluten-free wasn't even a thing in 1982, or at least not something that was written about in mainstream cookbooks. Nevertheless, Lizzie pulled the cookbook from the shelf and brought it back into the butler's pantry.

She scanned the pages and found no inspiration as far as muffins were concerned, but she found plenty to keep her interest. The book was so gloriously retro: the formal font, the elaborate food styling, the lace tablecloths and fancy china. And Martha's hair! It was vintage 1980s, fluffy and voluminous, yet Martha still managed to look gorgeous and perfect in her belted shirtdresses and crew-neck sweaters. Lizzie wasn't sure she'd ever make anything from the book (one recipe made enough eggs for forty and called for eighty eggs and four sticks of butter), but she was still envious that the Silvesters had a signed copy. It was the kind of artifact that any cook would want to own, and part of her felt it deserved a home with someone who actually appreciated it.

Lizzie continued flipping through the pages but looked up when she heard footsteps shuffling toward the kitchen. Zoe peered through the doorway.

"Oh. It's you."

Lizzie wasn't sure why Zoe sounded disappointed. Who else would be in the kitchen at this hour? And why did Zoe care?

Zoe's eyes landed on the cookbook. "What are you doing? It's like five a.m."

"I couldn't sleep."

"So you're hanging out in the kitchen?"

"I'm just doing prep work. Better than staring at the ceiling."

"I guess."

Zoe moved farther into the room. She wore the same navy sundress as the night before, but her hair was now loose, the blond waves tumbling over her shoulders. She also had noticeable circles under her eyes, though Lizzie wasn't sure how much of that was just mascara that had run. Was she drunk? Lizzie wasn't sure. Whatever the case, she didn't seem entirely lucid.

"Why can't you sleep?" Zoe asked.

"A lot of reasons," Lizzie said, though she wasn't sure why. There was really only one reason, and that reason was Zoe. Why couldn't she say so?

"I get insomnia too. That's why I stay out so late. If I'm not sleeping, I might as well be doing something."

"What kind of things do you do . . . ?"

"This and that." She came closer and glanced at the cookbook. "Why are you looking through my mom's Martha Stewart book?"

"I thought maybe I'd find a muffin recipe I could use."

"You aren't supposed to cook out of that. It's a signed copy. Mom would freak out if it got dirty."

"Don't worry. I'm putting it back." Lizzie closed the book and put it back on the shelf in the main kitchen. When she returned to the butler's pantry, she saw Zoe picking through the ingredients Lizzie had laid out.

"You know this gluten-free flour is mine, right?"

"No, I didn't, actually. Could I borrow it?"

"I guess. Just replace it."

"I will." Lizzie came closer to the counter. "Listen, there's something I need to talk to you about. . . ."

Lizzie steeled herself. This was an ideal moment to confront Zoe. They wouldn't be interrupted, and with everyone else in the house asleep, neither of them would want to raise her voice. It was the perfect opportunity.

"I'm not much for talking at the moment," Zoe said. "It's been a long night."

"I'll keep it brief."

Zoe's eyes flitted to the almond meal. "I think that's mine too."

"I'll replace both. So what I wanted to say was—"

"Make sure it's blanched almond meal. I don't like the other kind."

"Noted. But about—"

"Make sure you don't use any nutmeg, by the way. If you make muffins. It gives Barb a mild reaction. Granted, I think a lot of that is in her head, but whatever. I mean, I'm sure she won't touch muffins anyway. She's always dieting. But just in case she decides to cheat—"

"*Zoe.*"

Zoe's eyes flashed. "Jesus. You don't have to yell. What?"

"I know about your site."

Zoe frowned. "Uh, yeah. Duh. We've talked about it before. You gave me a recipe."

"No, I mean I know about Marie. That she died."

Zoe stared at Lizzie. Her expression was unreadable. "What are you talking about?"

"Marie. I know she died before you left for college."

"So?"

"So . . . on your site, you say she's still alive. That you cured her with your diet."

"I did."

Lizzie's brow furrowed. "How could you have cured her if she's dead?"

"What business is it of yours?"

"You run a Web site where you put all this stuff out there publicly, so . . ."

"Doesn't make it your business."

"Why not?"

"Because you work for my fucking parents and you should keep your head down and do what they're paying you to do."

"That's exactly what I'm doing."

"No, you're asking me personal questions that have nothing to do with you." She narrowed her eyes. "Are you stalking me or something?"

"Stalking you? What are you talking about?"

"You seem to know an awful lot about me, considering we've only spoken a handful of times."

"I hardly know anything about you. That's the point."

"Why should you? You're our private chef. Honestly? I don't think my parents will be thrilled to know you're trying to dig up dirt on me."

"I'm not. I just asked a question."

"Right. And I'm sure you have no agenda whatsoever."

Lizzie shook her head in disbelief. "How am I in the wrong here? Your Web site is a totally public thing—which, you may re-call, I only discovered because you'd posted photos of my recipes as if they were your own. I gave you a beet salad recipe that you said you'd post, so I followed up to see if you had. That's when I saw that Marie was sick again—or, I guess, that you claim she's sick again."

"See, that's what I'm talking about. You're trying to make me sound so shady."

"Well? *Is* Marie sick again?"

"What business is it of yours?"

Lizzie clenched her fists and pressed them against her eyes. "Jesus! This is ridiculous. We're talking in circles." She pulled her hands away and looked directly at Zoe. "It's my business because I am the public and the public thinks you cured some girl of cancer, but you didn't because she's dead."

"It isn't my fault she died."

"I never said it was."

"You implied it."

"Are you insane?" Lizzie immediately regretted asking the ques-tion because Zoe's eyes went wild with rage. Whether that was be-cause she was insulted or, indeed, completely insane Lizzie wasn't sure.

"Sorry," Lizzie blurted out before Zoe could explode. "What I meant was . . . I do not think, nor did I mean to imply, you were re-sponsible for Marie's death in any way. I don't even know the full story."

"Exactly. So stay out of it."

"I wish I could, Zoe, but you are endangering people's lives. I can't just look the other way."

"Endangering people's lives? That's a stretch."

"Not really. If Marie is dead, then there are people out there who actually have cancer who are drinking carrot juice and blasting coffee up their asses thinking it will cure them when it won't."

"Oh, so you're a cancer expert now?"

"I never said I was an expert."

"Well, that's good, because you're not. You're a cook."

"And you're what, then? A twenty-three-year-old with a Web site and too much time on her hands?"

Zoe turned puce. "You have no fucking idea what you're talking about. The stuff I write about—it works. Just because you've been brainwashed by the pharmaceutical industry like almost everyone else doesn't make you right."

"Just because you read something somewhere on the Internet doesn't make you right either. You have no evidence to back up any of the supposed cures on your site."

"I am the evidence—I live this lifestyle every day."

"But you aren't sick."

"Exactly."

"Your friend is dead!" Lizzie realized she was shouting now.

Zoe looked as if she'd been slapped. "Fuck you," she said.

"I'm sorry," Lizzie said, lowering her voice.

"No, you're not."

Lizzie took a deep breath. "All I'm asking is that you take the site down. Or at least stop writing misleading posts that give people false hope."

"Take the site down?" She stared at Lizzie, wide-eyed. "You'd love that, wouldn't you? You can't stand looking at my success when your own career is a joke."

"This has nothing to do with my career."

"Doesn't it, though? I know all about your fall from grace—not to mention the people you stabbed in the back along the way."

"What are you talking about?"

"You know exactly what I'm talking about. I had a nice, long conversation with April Sherman. It was very enlightening."

Lizzie almost took the bait but then stopped herself. "The fact that your site is based on a lie has nothing to do with me. Shut it down, or I'll do it for you."

"Like you'd even know how."

"Maybe I should talk to your parents about this."

Zoe let out a sharp laugh. "You're going to tell on me? Are we four?"

"No, Zoe, we're not. We're adults. Maybe it's time you started acting like one."

Zoe started to speak, but was interrupted by a sound coming from the living room. "Good luck with your muffins," she said, and walked out of the room.

"Zoe, wait!" Lizzie called after her. She hurried into the kitchen and followed the noise into the living room, expecting to find Zoe there. Instead, she gasped as she came across Barb, whose head was bobbing up and down as she performed fellatio on Sam, who was lying flat on the couch, his neck still immobilized in the foam cervical collar. He was also still wearing the hospital onesie, though Barb had unzipped it so that his erect penis poked through.

"Oh! Oh, God!" Lizzie cried. Barb flushed with embarrassment. Lizzie turned away and headed for the stairs. "I'm sorry! I'm so, so, so, so sorry!"

"Hey, where you going?" Sam called after her. "There's always room for one more."

Lizzie rushed down the stairs, chasing after Zoe, but by the time she got to the bottom it was too late. Zoe had disappeared.

This time when Zoe disappeared, she didn't do so for days or weeks. Technically, she may not have disappeared at all, because only a few hours later she was at the breakfast table, sitting between Kathryn and Barb. Lizzie was shocked to find all of the guests up and ready for breakfast, given the antics of the previous night, but apparently a night of drinking and drama had made everyone hungry.

"Good morning!" Kathryn called out as Lizzie brought a basket of muffins to the table. "Can I even say that? After the night we all had? My God. Lizzie, we can't thank you enough for your help.

Without you . . . well, none of us was really in a state to drive, put it that way."

"Nate was a big help, too," Lizzie said, nodding toward the other end of the table. She met his eyes, which were ringed with red. He looked exhausted.

Kathryn's smile tightened as her eyes flitted in Nate's direction. "Yes. Well. Thanks to you, too, Nate."

"Anything for you, Kathryn."

"It wasn't for me. It was for Sam! And Barb. Poor Barb. Look at you. You must be bone tired."

"*That's* for sure," Zoe muttered under her breath. Lizzie's and Barb's eyes met, and they both turned bright red.

Kathryn caught Barb's expression. "Did I miss something? What happened?"

"Nothing you want to know about," Zoe said, unfolding her napkin onto her lap.

"Barbie, what did you do?" Kathryn elbowed her playfully in the side.

Barb's cheeks reddened again, and she shrugged coyly. Sam was engrossed in a conversation on his other side and so, to Lizzie's great relief, didn't fill in the blanks. He was dressed in normal clothes now, the lavender polo and chinos he'd been wearing the night before, but he still wore the cervical collar, and Lizzie was pretty sure the image of Barb giving him a blow job would be tattooed on her brain forever. She was already contemplating how much therapy she would need to get over it.

"You little sexpot," Kathryn whispered. "We'll talk later. I need details. Not *too* many—as they say, some things are better left to the imagination."

You can say that again, Lizzie thought, though what she witnessed a few hours earlier wasn't something she ever would have tried to imagine either.

Lizzie returned to the butler's pantry to finish making the frittata, and with Renata's help she brought it to the table along with a big fruit platter.

"Ta-da!" Kathryn crowed. "What did I tell you? She's a genius.

There's a reason we want to hold on to her. The Food Network's loss is our gain."

"Oh, that's right," said one of the guests, whose name Lizzie couldn't remember. "You had that show. Barb and Kathryn started telling us about it last night, but with all of the activity . . . It's the one that airs on Saturday mornings, right?"

"Aired," Zoe cut in. "It got canceled like six years ago."

"Five," Lizzie corrected her. "But yes, it aired on Saturday mornings."

"Goes to show how behind the times I am," the guest said. Lizzie was pretty sure her name was Christine. "Anyway, I think I do remember you! The Ivy League graduate with a cooking show, right?"

Lizzie nodded, but before she could speak, Zoe cleared her throat. "That isn't *exactly* right, is it, Lizzie?"

Lizzie's face grew hot. Kathryn laughed nervously. "What? Of course it is. Right?"

"Yep," Lizzie said, a little too quickly. She didn't think this was the appropriate time to explain she hadn't actually graduated from college. She scanned the table. "Whoops—forgot the orange juice. I'll be right back."

She hurried back to the pantry. She could feel Zoe's eyes on her the whole time. Lizzie wasn't sure what Zoe knew or thought she knew, but whatever it was, Lizzie sensed Zoe was sending her a message: *Don't fuck with me.*

The thing was, Lizzie didn't want to fuck with Zoe. She didn't want to fuck with anyone. That wasn't how Lizzie was built. She sometimes wondered if she might still have her job if she were more inclined to fuck with people, but it was one of those questions she didn't linger on because she didn't want to be that kind of person. When she'd threatened to talk to Kathryn and Jim about Zoe's site, Lizzie wasn't trying to cause trouble. She just wanted to impress upon Zoe how serious her lies were.

Lizzie brought the pitcher of orange juice to the table, and as she set it down she overheard one of the Silvesters' friends ask Zoe about her post-graduation plans.

"I have a few irons in the fire," she said.

"Like? Are you going to work for your dad?"

"God no. That would be a disaster."

Kathryn clucked. "It wouldn't be a disaster. Zoe just has other interests. Have you told them about your Web site?"

Zoe's and Lizzie's eyes met. "No . . ." Zoe said.

"Well? Tell them about it!" Kathryn leaned toward the table. "To be honest, I don't know much about it myself—Zoe is very private about the whole thing—but if she's running the show, I'm sure it's fabulous. Isn't that right, sweetie?"

Zoe chewed on a small slice of plum. "I guess."

Lizzie cleared her throat. "It's about healthy eating, right?"

Zoe shot her a cautionary look. Lizzie stared back. She wanted to throw up or run away, but she wasn't about to let Zoe change the subject.

"Yeah," Zoe finally said.

"That's fab, Zo," Barb said. Her eyes suddenly widened, as if a lightbulb had illuminated. She pointed to Lizzie and Zoe. "Hey, the two of you should talk! I bet you could collaborate on something."

"I don't think so . . ." Lizzie said.

"I'm serious! Your show was about healthy cooking; her site is about healthy eating. There's a lot of potential for . . . what do you call it? Hey, Jim? Jim!"

Jim was engrossed in another conversation and didn't hear her.

"Jim, honey?" Kathryn snapped her fingers to get Jim's attention. "Barb is talking to you."

Jim broke off his conversation and turned to Barb with raised eyebrows. "Yes?"

"What are you always calling that thing over at CC Media? You know, where like all of your different channels and services help each other."

"Synergy?"

"Synergy! Yes!" She turned back to Lizzie and Zoe. "You girls could have a lot of synergy together."

"I highly doubt that," Zoe said.

"Why? You seem like a perfect match."

Lizzie's and Zoe's eyes met again. Neither of them knew what to say, even though they both knew the answer. Lizzie decided to speak first, before Zoe could undermine her. "I think our styles are probably too different."

"What, you mean like you're too old for Zoe's followers?"

That wasn't what Lizzie meant, but now she felt self-conscious about her age. How old did they think she was?

"Not exactly," Lizzie said.

"You probably are, actually," said Zoe.

Lizzie felt as if she were engaging in a virtual game of chess, and if that was the case Zoe just left her knight open to attack. "I guess your readership probably does skew really young," Lizzie said. "At this point in my career, I'd be looking for a broader, more serious audience."

Zoe's expression hardened. "My audience isn't the problem. People in their fifties and sixties regularly visit my site."

"You're kidding!" Barb crowed. "Oh my God, send me the link, will you? You know I'm always trying to lose a few pounds."

"It isn't that kind of site," Zoe said.

"What kind of site is it, exactly?" Lizzie asked. It hadn't been her plan to out Zoe in front of her parents and their friends, but if that's what it took. . . .

Zoe stared coolly at Lizzie. "I think we're out of cucumber water. Could you go make some?"

Lizzie didn't want to let Zoe off the hook. But she also knew her role, and that role was private chef. So unless she wanted to lose her job, all she could do was smile and say, "Sure," before heading back to the kitchen.

Most of the guests cleared out by lunchtime. Some went to their own homes and others headed straight for the beach, but they all planned to meet up again for afternoon cocktails and dinner. Lizzie tidied up the pantry and began the prep work. Since breakfast had turned into more of a brunch, she wasn't responsible for feeding people a midday meal.

As she toasted some pine nuts in a small frying pan, Lizzie pulled out her cell phone. She was going to text April. At this point, Lizzie had given up on making this the summer of atone-

ment, though she still hoped she and April could bury the prover-
bial hatchet. But she didn't like the idea of Zoe cozying up to her
former roommate. April knew too much about Lizzie's backstory,
and Lizzie feared what Zoe would do with those tidbits.

She sent April a message:

Hey! Sorry we still haven't been able to meet up. Lmk what the
rest of your summer looks like. Btw, Zoe mentioned you chatted
recently? Curious how that came about!

Lizzie knew the odds of April replying were low and of her doing
so with any useful details were even lower. But Lizzie couldn't shake
the nagging feeling that Zoe might know something unflattering
about her and would do something even less flattering with that information. Was Lizzie being paranoid? Maybe. Still, she didn't
trust Zoe and didn't want to get caught in her web of lies.

Lizzie slid her phone back onto the counter and sniffed the air.

"Shit!" She grabbed the frying pan off the burner, but it was too
late. The nuts were burnt. "Damn it."

She dumped the nuts into the sink and rinsed the pan under the
faucet. There was a loud hiss as the water hit the hot surface.

"Everything okay in here?"

Kathryn stood in the doorway. She had changed into a bathing
suit and sheer black cover-up and wore a floppy black-and-white
sun hat that Lizzie hadn't seen before. She seemed a bit jittery.

"Yeah, sorry—I just burned some nuts."

"Oh, no. Do you need Renata's help? Or someone else? I
thought I smelled something. Our old cook at home was famous
for burning nuts. He once nearly set the oven on fire with a tray of
walnuts. Or maybe not on *fire,* but there was enough smoke that
there should have been. And . . . well . . . hm-m-m." She wrung her
hands.

"I don't need help, but thanks for asking."

"Oh. Good." She was blinking a little too quickly.

"Are you okay?" Lizzie asked. "You seem . . . upset. Or bothered."

Kathryn cleared her throat. "Well, if I'm being completely honest, I am. Upset and bothered."

"Did Zoe do something . . . ?"

"Zoe? No, no, no. Zoe is fine." She looked over her shoulder. "Ah—here she is! We had a good chat this morning, didn't we, sweetheart?"

Zoe sidled up behind her mother and nodded. Lizzie couldn't quite place the expression on her face. The word *smug* came to mind.

"Anyway, we talked about lots of things, but one of the things we discussed was my Martha Stewart cookbook."

"The signed one?"

"Yes." She glanced at Zoe, who now stood beside her, then looked back at Lizzie. "It's missing."

"Missing? I just saw it earlier this morning." Lizzie dried her hands and went to the display shelf in the main kitchen, but as soon as she did she saw Kathryn was right: The book wasn't there. She returned to the butler's pantry, completely confused. "But that doesn't make any sense. . . . I put it right back. . . ."

"See? I told you she'd say that." Zoe raised an eyebrow.

"Say what?"

"That you put it back. But you didn't."

"Yes, I did. You saw me."

"I think I'd remember."

Lizzie started to talk, but Kathryn interrupted. "So you admit you took it from the shelf."

"I flipped through a few pages for inspiration. Then I returned it."

"And when was this?"

"I don't know. About five in the morning?"

Kathryn's and Zoe's eyes met. "What were you doing up here at five in the morning?" Kathryn asked.

"I couldn't sleep, so I thought I'd get a head start on breakfast."

"By using a precious artifact whose value would be greatly diminished if it got a single stain on it?"

"I wasn't planning to use it. Like I said, I was just trying to get ideas. I put it back."

"And yet it's nowhere to be found," Zoe said.

Lizzie retraced her steps in her mind, as if she were fast-forwarding through a video of the morning's events. "No, I'm one hundred percent sure I left it where I found it."

"I just don't see how that's possible," Kathryn said. "It isn't there, and you were the last person to touch it."

"Maybe Renata moved it when she was dusting. Renata?"

Lizzie made her way toward the kitchen, but Kathryn and Zoe blocked the doorway. "I've already spoken to Renata," Kathryn said. "She didn't move it and hasn't seen it."

Lizzie turned and began lifting up random platters and cutting boards in search of the book. She wasn't quite sure why—she remembered returning the book to the shelf and hadn't removed it again. But maybe one of the other guests had glanced through it and accidentally put it in the butler's pantry instead of the kitchen. She scoured the counter, rifled through drawers, and combed every shelf. The cookbook was nowhere.

"This doesn't make any sense—I literally had it in my hands a few hours ago."

"The thing is . . . I hate to do this because it's so awkward, but . . ." Kathryn wrung her hands. "I'm going to need to check your room."

"My *room?*" Lizzie felt as if she'd been punched. "Why?"

"Because . . . well, think of it from my perspective. Renata says you made a big fuss when you saw the cookbook for the first time, especially once you found out it was signed by Martha herself, and then Zoe saw you sneaking it into the butler's pantry this morning—"

"I wasn't sneaking. I was very open about what I was doing."

"Zoe said you were acting very odd when she caught you looking through it; didn't you, Zoe?"

Zoe nodded.

"*I* was acting odd? *Me?*" Lizzie could barely control herself. "*She's* the one—"

"Excuse me," Kathryn interrupted. "Lower your voice, please."

"Don't try to pin this on me," Zoe said.

Lizzie tried to calm herself, but she was having a hard time. "I think you have this backwards. You're accusing me of stealing, when I've done nothing wrong."

"I'm sure you *think* you've done nothing wrong—"

"I don't think—I know. I didn't take that book. I flipped through a few pages, and then I put it back. End of story. The only reason you're pointing the finger at me is because—"

"Let's not start blaming this on Zoe," Kathryn said.

"Why not? She's the one blaming me."

"Because she saw you with the book."

Lizzie felt as if she were going crazy. They were talking in circles. "She did see me with the book. And then she saw me put it back."

Kathryn looked at Zoe, who was shaking her head.

"I'd like to check your room," Kathryn said.

Lizzie started to object, but before she knew it she was chasing Kathryn down the stairs. She was enraged. Was this really Zoe's plan to stop her from talking to Kathryn and Jim about her site? Because if it was, it was having the opposite effect. Now all she wanted to do was expose Zoe as a fraud, to anyone who would listen.

Kathryn opened the door to Lizzie's room and began searching through every drawer and across every surface. As expected, she found nothing.

"Well, this just doesn't make any sense," she said.

"Did you check under the mattress?" Zoe asked.

Kathryn nodded. "This would be a lot easier if you just told me where you put it."

"I told you—I put it back on the shelf."

"Here we go again...." Kathryn gestured toward the door. "Let's go look for the hundredth time, shall we?"

They headed back upstairs, and when they got into the kitchen the empty space on the shelf stared back at them.

"What do you know—still not there," Kathryn said.

"Zoe, I know you saw me put it back. Two seconds afterward we started talking about your flour and almond meal, and—"

"Oh, right, that's another thing, Mom—she was using ingredients that belong to me."

"You were?" Kathryn looked shocked, as if Lizzie had just been accused of drinking their liquor. "Didn't I tell you her cupboard is off-limits?"

"I was going to replace the ingredients."

"Just like you replaced the cookbook?"

Lizzie clenched her jaw. She was losing patience. "Do I really have to keep defending myself? I didn't steal your stupid cookbook."

"It isn't stupid," Kathryn said. "It's a signed first edition!"

Lizzie felt as if she were losing her mind. Before she could once again make a case for her innocence, Zoe pushed past her and walked into the butler's pantry. She searched the same drawers and shelves that Lizzie had gone through herself, but when she peeked into one of the canvas shopping bags hanging by the door she raised an eyebrow. "Now what would Mom's cookbook be doing in here?"

She pulled the book from the bag and held it high.

"I-I have no idea," Lizzie stammered. "I didn't put it there."

"Sure you didn't."

"I swear. Someone else must have put it there."

"It is a little interesting that you didn't check there the first time around," Kathryn said.

"I guess I didn't think the book I had returned to its proper shelf would be in my shopping bag."

Kathryn closed her eyes and took a deep breath as she pressed her fingertips against her temples. "I don't have the energy to go over this for the umpteenth time. Zoe, bring me the book. Lizzie, Jim and I would like to have a conversation with you later this afternoon. Meet us in the living room at two."

Zoe handed her mom the cookbook, and as she followed her mother out of the room Lizzie swore she heard her whisper, "Gotcha."

CHAPTER 26

Linda,

Yes, the coffee enema is literally brewed coffee that I insert into my you-know-what. I know it sounds gross (and it is, I won't lie), but is it really any grosser than all those chemicals you pump through your veins for chemotherapy? At least we can pronounce the word "coffee" and know where it comes from. The process isn't comfortable (I have to hold about two cups of coffee up there for 12-15 minutes, and then I need to do another 2 cups for the same amount of time—yikes), but then no one said fighting cancer was pleasant. I'll admit I occasionally have misgivings about going this route and wonder if I'm doing the right thing, but if I keep second-guessing myself I'll go crazy. That's what Gary says, anyway, and I agree.

Otherwise, I'm doing . . . okay. I'm still sore from the surgery, but I'm trying not to overdo it on the pain meds, especially since I'm trying to phase them out (don't tell Gary—he thinks I've already stopped using them). I'm basically doing the enemas and juices, along with the occasional Motrin. I found some excellent juice recipes on that Clean Life site Dr. Konovsky recommended, and Gary has been kind enough to make them for me. He offered to help with the enemas too, but brewing the coffee is pretty much as far as I'm willing to take that for now. I mean, talk about killing the romance.

Anyway, my arm is really stiff, so I can't write more at the moment. I'm doing the exercises the surgeon gave me, but everything is still very tender, which makes it tough. Give me a call when you're home from work, and I can fill you in on the rest. I'll preempt your question about Lizzie by saying: No, I haven't called her yet. I'm working on it. Maybe later this week. Or next.

xxoo

S

CHAPTER 27

At 1:59 p.m., Lizzie sat on the couch in the Silvesters' living room, waiting for Kathryn and Jim to appear. She felt sick. Her job was on the line, and she knew it, and to make matters worse, it was for an offense she didn't even commit. From the bits of hushed conversation she'd overheard, Lizzie knew Jim in particular considered Zoe's behavior bizarre and unpredictable, so in Lizzie's mind he was her only hope. If she could appeal to him and convince him this was yet another instance of Zoe gone wild, maybe he would override Kathryn's misplaced faith in their daughter.

Lizzie picked nervously at her cuticles as she kept an eye on the clock above the mantel. Part of her hoped Kathryn would appear, sun hat in hand, and apologize for the entire misunderstanding. Actually, what Lizzie really wanted was for Zoe to get her just deserts, but Kathryn probably didn't even understand the concept, and the mere utterance of the phrase would prompt her to ask if they were Paleo or gluten-free.

The Silvesters' house was uncharacteristically quiet and empty. Had they told their staff and guests to leave for an hour? Lizzie hoped not. That meant they anticipated yelling—maybe even tears. Not that Lizzie planned on crying. Oh, who was she kidding? Of course she would cry. That's what happened every time she was involved in a heated argument. She was just so bad at it. Instead of her diffusing the situation or one-upping her adversary with additional facts and logic, something inside her would crack and she'd disintegrate into a heap of tears and apologies. It was so embarrassing. Why did she do it? She wasn't sure. One of the guys she had briefly dated in college said it had something to do with her balance of estrogen and progesterone, to which she took great offense, but then the argument got heated and, inevitably, the tears came, and that was pretty much the end of their relationship.

Lizzie steeled herself as she heard footsteps on the stairway behind her. She glanced over her shoulder and saw Kathryn and Jim making their way toward the living room. Kathryn had changed into white capris and a navy tunic, and Jim was wearing his usual combination of chinos and polo shirt. They both wore stern expressions, though Jim's bordered on annoyance.

They sat on the couch opposite Lizzie, with a good foot between them. Lizzie sat tall, her hands folded in her lap. She refused to look guilty.

"So Jim and I wanted to talk to you about what happened this morning," Kathryn said. "How, exactly, did my book end up in your shopping tote?"

Lizzie could feel her heart racing. "Honestly? I have no idea."

"Is that really 'honest'? Because I think you must have *some* idea."

"The only idea I have is Zoe."

Kathryn cast Jim a sideways glance. "See? What did I say?"

Jim shushed Kathryn with his hand. "Maybe it would be best if you took us through the morning, from the time you looked at the book until the time Zoe found it in your bag."

Lizzie took a deep breath and tried to maintain as even a tone as possible, even though she wanted to stomp her feet and scream. She recapped every step of her evening and morning, a sequence of events she felt she'd already summarized far too many times.

"There seems to be a lot of unexplained time between when you first looked at the book and when Zoe found it," Kathryn said, ignoring Jim's pleas for her to let him do the talking.

"It's not really unexplained. I was preparing breakfast and otherwise doing my job."

"Barb seems to think you and Zoe had an argument."

Barb. Lizzie had wondered if she would say anything. What had Barb overheard? Lizzie didn't see how she could have caught much of anything, given that her face was buried in Sam's crotch. But she saw Lizzie chasing after Zoe, so at the very least Barb knew some sort of squabble had occurred.

"We had . . . a disagreement," Lizzie said.

"About the book." Kathryn turned to Jim. "See? Zoe says she told Lizzie to leave the book alone, but Lizzie wouldn't listen."

"It had nothing to do with the book."

"Then what was it about?"

Lizzie stared at Kathryn and Jim. She hadn't planned on bringing up Zoe's Web site, mostly because she doubted they'd believe her, given the circumstances. She knew how predictably defensive she would sound: *I'm not the liar—your daughter is!* But they weren't giving her much of a choice. Kathryn seemed hell-bent on believing everything Zoe said, and Jim looked weary of this entire exercise, as if he wished he could just fire Lizzie and be done with it so that he could turn his mind to more important matters.

"It was about her Web site," Lizzie finally said.

"Her Web site?" Kathryn looked at Jim, then back at Lizzie. "Why would you be arguing about her Web site?"

"Because . . ." Lizzie looked over her shoulder to see if Zoe was listening. She knew it shouldn't matter—wrong was wrong. Nevertheless, she was still a little afraid of Zoe and wasn't sure what would happen if she told Kathryn and Jim about The Clean Life.

"Because?"

Lizzie turned back around. "Because her site is a lie."

"A lie?" Kathryn laughed nervously as she looked back and forth between Lizzie and Jim. "What do you mean? It doesn't exist?"

"It exists. It's just . . . the whole story behind it isn't true."

"I'm sorry, I don't understand. What story?"

"Zoe claims she cured her friend of cancer by helping her follow a special diet, but that isn't true because her friend is dead."

"What friend?"

"Marie."

Kathryn's face went white. Jim narrowed his eyes. "Marie," he repeated. "Isn't that—"

"There are lots of people named Marie," Kathryn snapped. "It isn't necessarily—"

"The one she met at summer camp?" Lizzie offered.

They both turned and looked at her. "Who told you about that?" Kathryn asked.

"Nate."

"Ah. Nate." She huffed. "I should have known. Well, I hate to break it to you, but anything Nate says should be taken with a large grain of salt."

"So . . . Zoe didn't have a friend named Marie from summer camp?"

"I didn't say that. What I said was you should be careful throwing around accusations when Nate is your source."

"Okay, but I've talked about some of this with Zoe herself. Hence the five a.m. argument."

"Of course there was an argument. You're calling her a liar— she had to defend herself."

"Right. And then coincidentally, a few hours later, your cookbook goes missing and ends up in my bag. Doesn't that seem a little convenient?"

"I'm missing the connection."

Lizzie met Jim's eyes. "Really? Because it seems pretty straightforward to me. I confronted Zoe about her site being a scam and threatened to tell you about it, but before I could, she made me look like the liar instead."

"Oh, please," Kathryn groaned. "Like Zoe would go through all that trouble for some little Web site."

"It isn't little. She has almost two hundred thousand followers on Instagram. Her site is very popular."

Jim raised his eyebrows. "Two hundred thousand?"

"Give or take."

He nodded, his eyebrows still high on his head. "Impressive."

Impressive? Lizzie was speechless. She'd thought Jim would be her ally in this, but she was beginning to wonder if she'd misjudged him.

"I told you she had an entrepreneurial spirit," Kathryn said.

"I thought it was just some blog. I didn't realize she had a legitimate platform. With that big of a following, she could probably monetize aspects of her brand."

"How do you mean?" Kathryn asked.

"Well, aside from things like book deals and ad space, she could branch out into other media as well, particularly in the mobile space. I wonder if she's thought about an app."

"She already has one," Lizzie said. "It's on the Apple watch."

"Wow—really?" Jim smiled. "That's incredible."

Lizzie couldn't believe what she was hearing. "It would be if it weren't for the fact that a lot of the information on her site is bogus."

"Bogus how?"

"Like she claims her advice can help people beat cancer without having to go through conventional treatments like chemo and radiation."

Jim shrugged. "Well? Maybe it can."

"Except she has no evidence to prove it. The one story she gives is about a friend who, come to find out, died five years ago."

"You're talking about Marie?"

"Yes."

Jim sighed. "Listen. We know Zoe had a camp friend named Marie who died a few years ago. To be honest, I never knew much about her until after she died. I still don't know very much, but Kathryn and I recognized that Zoe was very upset about her passing. Her grief manifested itself in many ways, most of them unpleasant, which is why we've attempted therapy so many times. But if she's finally found a way to channel that grief in a positive way, well, I'd say we've turned a major corner."

"How is this a positive way? She's lying to people."

"Not necessarily—"

Kathryn turned to Jim. "That's right. Remember what Dr. Stephens said—if she truly believes it in her own mind, it isn't really a lie to *her*."

Lizzie was beginning to wonder if this conversation was actually happening. Maybe it was a dream and any second Jim would morph into an elephant wearing a bow tie and then she'd wake up. Because this couldn't be real. She couldn't be sitting in front of two adults who were explaining away their daughter's dangerous behavior and instead seeing it as an achievement.

"Does that really matter?" Lizzie asked. She was trying to be delicate—after all, this conversation had begun as an interrogation that might lead to her dismissal—but she was having trouble maintaining an even keel.

"I think so," Kathryn said.

"Really? Some lady in Kansas with colon cancer could stumble across Zoe's site and decide, 'Hey, I think I'll give this a try instead of chemo.' "

"That would be her decision to make," Jim said.

"But it would be a misinformed one."

Kathryn wagged her finger. "Says you, the woman who tried to steal my cookbook."

"I didn't try to steal your cookbook!"

"Right. Maybe it's like Dr. Stephens says. If you believe it . . ."

"I don't believe. I know. Don't you see? Zoe just wants you to think that because—"

"Ladies!" Jim held up his hands. "Enough. I don't have time for this. This is supposed to be my vacation. I'm already dealing with work calls every damn morning. I don't need to play referee on top of it. Whether Lizzie took the book or not, it's back in its rightful place now, so there's no point in going on and on about it. Lizzie, we like your food, and you helped my buddy Sam in his moment of need, so you can stay."

"Jim, don't you think we should discuss—"

He silenced Kathryn with a wave of his hand. "But know that we will be watching you, and if there is any more funny business, we won't hesitate to fire you. Understood?"

Lizzie nodded.

Jim slapped his knees and got up from the couch. "Good. Now, let's get back to vacation, shall we?"

He headed out the back door, and Kathryn followed him, looking unsettled but cowed. Lizzie sat on the couch, watching them through the floor-to-ceiling windows, before returning to the butler's pantry to continue with a job she was no longer sure she wanted.

The afternoon wore on. For most of it, Lizzie was in a daze. The conversation with the Silvesters didn't make any sense. They thought Zoe's Web site was a good thing? What was wrong with them? She suddenly felt uncomfortable being in their employ. If she took their money and they supported their daughter in her shady venture, then was Lizzie effectively complicit in the whole enterprise? The thought made her queasy.

She needed to find a new gig as soon as possible. Almost anything would be better than this. But until she did, she wasn't in a position to turn down the Silvesters' money. She had loans to pay off and overdue credit card statements to settle, so she couldn't afford to quit before she'd lined up something else. Could she work for another family in Philadelphia? Or would she do something else altogether? She wasn't sure, but she vowed to put out feelers this week.

Cocktail hour approached, and Lizzie hurried around the kitchen as she prepared the nibbles that would accompany the wine and prosecco. Kathryn had requested simple hors d'oeuvres—crudités, Paleo-friendly dips, nuts, and olives—so Lizzie didn't have much to do other than chop up some vegetables and whiz some ingredients in the food processor.

As Lizzie puréed a bunch of avocados, Nate knocked on the door frame. "You busy?"

"What does it look like?"

Lizzie realized she sounded snippy, which wasn't her intention. She liked Nate. A lot, actually. But the conversation with Kathryn and Jim had disrupted her equilibrium, and she was having trouble readjusting to reality.

"Sorry," he said. "Need any help?"

"I'm okay. Thanks, though."

He tapped his fingers against the frame. "Did something happen earlier? I heard one of the guests say something about a stolen book . . . ?"

Lizzie clenched her jaw. "Wow, news travels fast, huh?"

"Let's just say some of these people have a lot of free time on their hands."

"Too much, if I had to guess."

"So if you don't mind my asking . . ."

"In a nutshell? Kathryn's signed Martha Stewart cookbook went 'missing,' and then Zoe 'found' it in my bag and accused me of stealing it."

"And I'm guessing that isn't what actually happened at all."

"Correct."

"Care to set the record straight?"

"I tried earlier with your dad and Kathryn. Didn't exactly go as planned."

"What happened?"

"Well, to explain why Zoe would accuse me of stealing, I had to tell them what she and I discussed at five a.m. when we ran into each other in the kitchen."

"Which was . . . ?"

"I confronted her about her Web site. The whole Marie story."

Nate groaned. "Didn't I warn you not to do that?"

"Yeah, and I thought that was pretty lame, to be honest. She's basically peddling quackery. Maybe you're fine having that on your conscience, but I'm not."

"It's not that I'm okay with it. It's just . . . I know how she is."

"Which is what? Crazy?"

"That's a little strong, but . . . well, yeah. I mean, look what happened. You confronted her, and—surprise, surprise—she tried to get you fired, right?"

"For the record, it didn't work. I still have my job."

"So Dad and Kathryn believed you?"

"Kind of. I don't know. I'm pretty sure Kathryn still thinks I stole the book, but your dad seems skeptical."

"Dad is a little more levelheaded when it comes to Zoe."

"Not really. When I told them about her site, he was the one who seemed the proudest."

"Proud? Of what?"

"Something about her channeling her 'grief in a positive way.'"

In a flash, Nate's mood soured. "Fucking classic. I'm a professor of sociology at a legit university, and they basically think I'm a loser. But Zoe pens some bullshit blog about . . . what? Fairy dust? And she's the one doing something positive and meaningful."

"I think Kathryn used the word 'entrepreneurial.' "

"Of course she did." He pressed his palms against his eyes. "God, my family is so screwed up."

"I mean . . ." Lizzie trailed off as she realized there would be nothing to gain from agreeing with him, even though she did.

Nate gave a halfhearted laugh. "Bet you're super excited you still have your job, huh?"

"Listen, it pays the bills."

"So does working at Starbucks, and my guess is it comes with a lot less drama."

"But where's the fun in that? I wouldn't get to take midnight trips to the ER, or stumble across an old guy getting a blowie, or have these enlightening conversations with you."

"Wow. Good to know where I rank in the scheme of things."

"You're probably a small step above. Just a small one, though." She smiled. "In all seriousness, I appreciate the advice you gave me last night in the ER. You gave me a lot to think about."

"My pleasure." He glanced up at the clock. "Listen, I'm not sure what time you get off, but I was going to grab a drink with some friends at the Windrift later if you wanted to tag along."

"Wait, you have friends? I thought Zoe said . . ."

"Okay, okay—technically it's just one friend, and she's not even really a friend. It's that woman Kathryn and Sam are trying to set me up with."

"Whoa, whoa, whoa—you want me to be your wingman?"

"Wouldn't you be the wingwoman? Anyway, no, it's not like that. I think she's meeting some other people she knows too, and I've made it very clear this is not a romantic rendezvous."

"Unless she turns out to be attractive, right?"

"What? No. Give me a little credit."

"What makes you so sure you aren't interested?"

"Aside from the fact that she has a major endorsement from Sam Offerman?"

"I bet he'd endorse me. Am I so bad?"

Nate flushed. "No. But that's different."

"I don't see how, but whatever." She looked at the clock. "Dinner is at seven, but I will probably be finished by nine or ten. Where did you say you were meeting up?"

"The Windrift. It's like a five-minute drive. If you want, I could wait and give you a lift . . . ?"

"No, thanks. I'll be fine."

"You sure?"

"Yep. It sort of depends on how the evening goes anyway. If someone else splits his head open on the bottom of the pool . . . I may not make it."

"Understood."

He rubbed his hands together. It seemed like he wanted to linger but wasn't really sure what to say. Part of Lizzie wanted him to stay. She enjoyed the company, and his in particular. But she knew she'd enjoy it far more over a drink at a bar, so if she had any hope of meeting up with him later she needed to keep moving.

"Anyway, I guess I'd better let you get back to . . ." He eyed the puréed avocado in the food processor. "Whatever that is."

"Avocado dip."

"Paleo?"

"Do you even need to ask?"

He smiled. "I like you," he said. "I hope you can make it later."

"I'll try," Lizzie said, even though she knew she'd go, because the truth was, she liked him too.

To Lizzie's great relief, cocktail hour and dinner passed without incident. No drunken injuries, no stormy arguments. Kathryn still seemed leery of Lizzie, but she put on a happy face in front of her friends and Lizzie figured her distrust would wane over time. If it didn't . . . well, that was Kathryn's problem. Lizzie had nothing to hide, and with any luck she'd be out of there in a few weeks anyway.

Lizzie hadn't seen Zoe since she managed to find the cookbook that morning, and no one else had seen her since she'd left for the beach that afternoon.

"I think she's taking photos for her site," Lizzie overheard

Kathryn telling Barb. "Did you know she has more than *two hundred thousand* followers?"

Lizzie wasn't sure how "almost" had morphed into "more than," but she was pretty sure that by the end of the summer Kathryn would be telling people Zoe's site reached millions. Lizzie found it odd that Kathryn hadn't shown any interest in actually seeing the site itself or pointing others in its direction. She seemed more interested in bragging about it in the abstract. Maybe that's how she rationalized its existence in her mind. If she never visited The Clean Life, she wouldn't know for certain that Zoe's site was bullshit, and if her friends didn't visit either, they couldn't criticize it.

Once Lizzie had helped Renata clean up from dinner, she showered and put on fresh clothes and, though she hadn't made a habit of it this summer, some makeup. Back when she was on TV, she never left the house without wearing makeup, on the off chance she ran into someone who recognized her from her show. The one time she made an exception and popped into her local bodega without even a hint of mascara, she'd run into someone who was quick to inform her, "You look WAY better on TV. Like, a lot." After that, she didn't take any chances. Her big fear was that if there were a fire in her building in the middle of the night she'd have to run out to the street without putting her face on and a photo of her pale, bare mug would be splashed across the Internet. Maybe people would start to suspect her appearance wasn't the only thing she'd made up.

But once her fame fizzled, she cared less and less about getting dolled up, whether it was for a personal chef gig or a run to the grocery store. On some level, whenever she dabbed concealer beneath her eyes or swept blush across her cheeks the face staring back at her reminded her of the person she used to be—the star, the It Girl, the up-and-comer. That wasn't her anymore, and the fact that being that person involved wearing a mask of powder and gloss made her wonder if it ever had been. It's not that she no longer liked making herself pretty. It's that she'd spent so many years covering up her face that she'd forgotten there might be any natural beauty in it. She eventually grew used to seeing her bare reflection in the mirror. She didn't look like a TV star, but then maybe she never had.

Now, though, for a night on the town, she layered on the eye shadow, blush, and mascara. She wasn't doing it for Nate; she was doing it for herself. Did she want him to do a double take when he saw her? Maybe. Okay, yes. But she also wanted to draw the distinction between Private Chef Lizzie and Real Person Lizzie. Not that Private Chef Lizzie wasn't a real person. But that was her work persona, sweating over a hot stove and shoveling hamburgers or kebabs onto a platter. She was that person, but she was also a person who read books and drank wine and occasionally danced. She wanted to show Nate that side of her, but she wanted to remind herself of that side too.

She gathered her purse and keys and made for the driveway. She checked her phone to see if April had replied to her text, but she still hadn't. The more time that passed since the Silvesters' Memorial Day barbecue, the more foolish Lizzie felt for thinking she could reboot their friendship. April had moved on. What made Lizzie feel like an even bigger fool was her realization that April was probably the best friend she'd ever had. All of the "friends" she'd made in New York proved themselves to be hangers-on, and now she was thirty, and no one made new friends at thirty. Well, not no one. But it was hard, far harder than twenty-year-old Lizzie ever would have imagined. She was self-employed, single, and childless, and she had barely any time off. How and when was she supposed to meet people? And not just any people. The kinds of people she could call in an emergency or whose shoulders she would feel comfortable crying on. Would she ever make those sorts of friends again? It seemed impossible.

There was, of course, Nate. But he was her employer's son, and he was only in town for the week. And anyway, he lived in Washington, DC. There was no reason to think their connection would last beyond his stay. Also, despite her attempts to convince herself otherwise, Lizzie didn't necessarily think of him in a platonic sense. Every time he smiled or scratched his chin or cracked his knuckles, Lizzie felt something inside of her stir, like a bear awakening after a long winter hibernation. She'd had boyfriends over the years, sure.

Several, in fact. But none of them had really mattered. They made good dinner companions and gave structure to her social life, and the sex was generally good. But none of the men she'd dated or simply slept with had meant anything to her. She'd cared about them, in the way she cared about any human being, but she never felt her future weaving together with any of theirs. They had all been "good for now," if not actually good for her.

That was all fine until the last year or so, when she realized she wanted more than sex and a dinner date. She wanted a partner. She had been working so hard cobbling together a living that she could distract herself from this inner urge and suppress it by busying herself with drudgery. But occasionally, while she sautéed a pan of onions or chopped a bunch of celery, her mind would drift to a place in her heart, one that hadn't been filled by friends or family or an Internet date, and she'd wonder if anyone would ever fill it.

Did she honestly think Nate could be that person? Probably not. She barely knew him. And he was a Silvester—a huge strike against him. But she couldn't deny that she liked him. Beyond his boyish looks and obvious intelligence, he had a quality she couldn't quite put her finger on—a sense of composure that rubbed off on her when she was in his presence. She felt calmer around him. Even if her many worries—about her career, her finances, her future in general—still lurked beneath the surface, his company somehow tamed them. Even so, she knew it was unlikely he would ever amount to anything more than an acquaintance or possible one-night stand. And even if he did, after her parents' divorce she couldn't shake the notion that all relationships ended at some point.

She pulled out of the Silvesters' driveway onto Dune Drive, and as she crossed 53rd Street her phone rang. It was her dad. Her thumb hovered over the phone as she debated whether or not to pick up. On the one hand, she was both surprised and delighted he was calling her, considering he was supposed to be on vacation with his new family this week. Lizzie wasn't sure why she always thought of them as his "new" family. He'd been married to Jessica for twenty years now. That was longer than he'd been married to Lizzie's mother. But in Lizzie's mind, since she and her mom were his first family, they were the Original Glass Family—the OG Fam, as she sometimes called them—and Jessica and the kids would always be the newer phenomenon. Lizzie also thought of them as "new" because she sometimes felt as if she'd been traded for a newer model, one that was updated and improved and more deserving of his time.

But as pleased as she was that he was taking time away from the Glass Family 2.0 to call her, she also wasn't sure she felt like talking to him right now. Conversations with her dad inevitably dredged up feelings of abandonment and resentment that she usually tried to suppress, and chances were good she'd show up at the Windrift in a foul mood if the call went in its typical emotional direction. This was her first night out in months, and she wanted to have fun. She didn't want to think about her semi-screwed-up family. She glanced quickly at the screen and pressed Ignore.

She drove a bit farther, and then her phone chimed with a voice mail. Part of her wanted to listen right away, but she already knew what she would likely hear: *Hey, sweetie, it's Dad. . . . Been a while. . . . Just wanted to see what you were up to, so . . . uh, give a call when you get a second.* For years, his calls and messages featured a soundtrack of toddler and, later, adolescent screams, but now that the girls were grown (Madison was in college, and Ali was about to join her this fall), there was less background noise to contend with. Sometimes it was eerie how quiet it was, after so many years of audible chaos. Maybe that's why he could find time to call while on vacation. Now that his girls needed him less, he could finally make time for Lizzie.

Too little, too late, she thought as she pulled into the Windrift parking lot.

She slipped her phone back into her purse and got out of the car. She'd listen to the message later. Either that or she'd just call him back tomorrow. He was an early riser, so she could call him before breakfast.

She made her way to the Windrift's entrance and admired its elegant façade. Lizzie was pretty sure she stayed here once as a young girl with her mom, but in her mind it had been more like a really nice motel. It had clearly undergone a substantial renovation since then. Now the part of the building facing the ocean was modern and sleek, with stainless-steel railings, streamlined cedar siding, and clean white umbrellas dotting the terrace.

Nate had said he'd be in the Level 2 bar, so she asked someone at the front desk to point her in the right direction. When she reached the entrance to the bar, she felt her purse vibrate. She looked at her phone. It was her dad again. Was something wrong? He so rarely called, and for him to call twice in a row, after leaving a voice mail—

"Lizzie?" She looked up and saw Nate walking toward her. She slid the phone back into her purse. Nate smiled. "I barely recognized you without your chef gear."

"What, you mean without my knife?" She pretended to reach into her bag.

"Oh. I . . ."

Lizzie smiled. "I'm kidding. I come bearing neither tools nor weaponry."

"Oh. Good." Nate seemed to relax, though he still looked a bit nervous. "What I meant was . . . you look great. Not that you don't look nice in your chef's jacket and whatever, but in real people clothes . . ." He trailed off.

"In real people clothes . . . ?"

"I don't really know where I was going with that, to be honest. All I was trying to say was that you look nice. That's it. I didn't mean to make it . . ."

"Incredibly awkward?"

He flushed. "Yeah."

"You're an academic. If you weren't at least a little awkward, I'd worry you weren't very good at your job."

"Oh. Well . . . thanks? I guess?"

"You're welcome."

Her phone buzzed in her purse again. She glanced at it. Her dad, again.

"Jesus," she muttered.

"Everything okay?"

She stared at the screen for a beat, then ignored the call for the third time. "Yep," she said. "Just my dad, trying to make up for lost time. He can wait."

"Are you sure? There are plenty of quiet spots if you need to make a call."

Lizzie entertained the idea but then decided she was right: Her dad could wait. After years of being preoccupied with his second family, he could hold on for a few hours while she had fun for once. He'd already left a voice mail. If it really was an emergency, he could text.

"I'll call him back tomorrow," she said. "Now, which way to the bar?"

CHAPTER 28

Linda,

Well. Where do I even begin? I'm so enraged as I type this that my hands are shaking. SHAKING. I would have called, but I'm so furious with you that the sound of your voice would send me right over the edge. HOW COULD YOU GO BEHIND MY BACK AND TALK TO FRANK ABOUT MY TREATMENT? It's MY disease, and he is MY ex-husband. You have NO RIGHT to blab all of my private business to him and then gang up on me. I know you don't like that I'm doing all this alternative stuff, but guess what? It's my body, and I can do whatever I want with it. Just because you and Frank think I'm crazy doesn't mean I am, and it CERTAINLY doesn't give you permission to make any of this harder for me than it already is.

Oh, Linda, I am just so ANGRY. You're my sister. How could you betray me like this? All through the divorce, you stood by my side. And yet a small part of me always wondered if you had a little sympathy for Frank. I bet you didn't mean to, but sometimes your expression seemed to say, Wow, she still really can't let go. Well, guess what? I couldn't let go, and I still can't. You've never lost a child. You have no idea what it's like. All those "doctors" with their supposed "cures," and it was all for what? NOTHING. Frank always said I blamed them for something that wasn't their fault, and now I'm realizing you probably agreed with him the whole time. You know what? You two can go fuck yourselves. I'm doing this my way.

Don't bother trying to call me. I have nothing else to say to you right now.

S

CHAPTER 29

The bar was crowded for a Monday night. A sizable group stood around the counter, flagging down a busy bartender who shuttled back and forth with foaming beers and fizzy cocktails. Behind him, two broad windows took up nearly the entire wall and offered views of the beach and ocean. Whatever wall space wasn't covered by windows was painted a bright cerulean, illuminated by glowing spheres that dangled from the ceiling.

Lizzie slid onto one of the gray leather barstools and rested her purse on the granite counter.

"So where is your date?" she asked Nate.

"She isn't my date."

"Fine, your friend. Or setup. Or whatever you want to call her. And her friends, for that matter."

"They left."

Lizzie checked the time. "It's not even ten."

"Noted."

"Wow. Wild night, huh?"

"No need to rub it in."

"Sorry. Was it really that bad?"

"Not for me. But I guess even a fellow -ologist finds me a bit . . . bland."

"Impossible," Lizzie said.

"Evidence to the contrary." He shrugged. "Like I said, I wasn't interested in a romantic thing."

"Still. Never feels great to be rejected, even if you aren't interested. In some ways, it almost makes it worse."

"True. Dating is so weird."

"Luckily for you, this is not a date, so we don't have to deal with any of that nonsense."

"Thank God."

Lizzie reached for the cocktail list. "Ah, yes. A 'detox' cocktail. Because if you add freshly pressed apples and kale, gin will suddenly be healthy."

"I bet it sells like crazy. At least with a certain demographic."

"You're probably right. I'm sure Kathryn and Barb have drunk their fair share. Zoe, too, assuming she drinks. Does she drink? I guess that doesn't really fit with a 'clean' lifestyle. Not that anything on her site is legit anyway."

"I'm sure there's a kernel of truth to *some* stuff on there."

"There you go defending her again."

"I'm not defending her. I'm just—"

The bartender interrupted, asking if they were ready to order. Lizzie scanned the cocktail list a second time but decided to play it safe with a glass of sauvignon blanc. Nate ordered a beer.

"You were saying?" Lizzie prompted him. "You're not defending her?"

"I'm not. I'm just saying there is probably some truth to the information on her site."

"Such as?"

"Such as . . . the idea that diet can tame or exacerbate certain symptoms. There is some evidence to support that, depending on the disease."

"Sure. And it would be fine if Zoe left it at that. But she doesn't. She says: 'Screw modern medicine and eat these foods and drink these drinks instead.' "

"Right. And I agree that's a step too far. Trust me, I'm not condoning fraud. I encounter enough of that in my work. I spent like five years studying and writing about the subprime mortgage crisis."

"So why don't you say something?"

"To Zoe?"

"To anyone."

"It's complicated. She's family."

"Half family."

"We share a dad. I can't just throw her to the wolves."

"I'm not saying you have to throw her to the wolves. And even if I were, you and Zoe aren't exactly close. You've said so yourself."

"I know, and I agree she needs to stop what she's doing. But for me to be the messenger . . . I'd still have to deal with all of the blowback from my family. You must know what it's like. Don't you have siblings?"

"I did. He died."

"Oh." Nate turned red. "I'm sorry. I didn't mean . . ."

"It's fine. He died a long time ago. I was only three. I barely remember him."

"I don't know what to say. That's so . . . sad."

"It was. Is. He didn't even make it to his first birthday."

"Jesus."

Lizzie nodded, acknowledging Nate's inability to say anything more. Her heart ached a little. She hadn't spoken about Ryan in a long time. "I don't think my mom has ever been the same," she said.

"I mean . . . how could she be? The fact that she could function at all after something like that . . ."

"She didn't really 'function,' to be honest. It was rough for a while. For both of my parents, but especially my mom. She's better now, but that's after many years of therapy and a divorce."

"If you don't mind my asking . . . what happened? To your brother."

"He had a really rare condition—Pompe disease. Babies end up with enlarged hearts and usually die before they turn one, but the doctors told my parents about a clinical trial for an experimental drug that had potential. They got him into the trial, but the drug had all sorts of toxic side effects, and he ended up dying of a stroke. My mom always blamed the doctors for putting him on that drug, but my dad said he would have died anyway. It was sort of an ongoing argument between them."

Nate stared at Lizzie. He seemed to be holding his breath. Lizzie didn't blame him. What was he supposed to say? The story was so sad and terrible. No amount of sympathy could change what had happened, and words seemed wholly inadequate in the face of such a tragedy. That's why she rarely talked about Ryan. The story cloaked every conversation in sadness, and although she appreciated people's condolences, she didn't want people feeling sorry for her. She understood why they did. Was there anything more tragic than the death of a baby? But she didn't want the experience to define her, in the way it would define her parents for the rest of their lives. It was a part of her—a sad, dark part—but it wasn't the only part. She'd told April about him, along with a few other friends in high school and college, and now Nate, but otherwise, Ryan wasn't a topic she chose to discuss.

"I'm so sorry," Nate finally said. "I feel like such a jerk complaining about my family, when your family has gone through something like that."

"Don't. Your family has given you plenty to complain about."

"I guess. But still. I feel bad." He took a sip of beer. "You do understand what I'm saying about Zoe, though, right? I mean look what she did when you confronted her, and she barely knows you. She's known me her entire life. She probably has a list a mile long of ways she could make my life hell."

"So you're scared of your baby half sister?"

"I don't know that 'scared' is the right word."

Lizzie started clucking like a chicken. "Sure sounds that way to me—"

"Okay, okay." He elbowed her to stop her from clucking so loudly. Maybe it was the wine, or the way he gently nudged her, or the way he'd managed to pivot the conversation away from her dead brother, but she was starting to feel better. "I guess I am, a little," he admitted. "Aren't you?"

"Honestly? Yeah. She's terrifying. I don't trust her at all."

"See? So combine that with the fact that my dad and Kathryn think I'm the black sheep and you can understand why I'm hesitant to stir up trouble."

"Just because I understand your reasoning doesn't mean I can't think it's lame."

"Fair enough."

Lizzie began singing quietly to the tune of "Jingle Bells": "Lame, lame, lame. Lame, lame, lame. Lame, lame, lame, lame, la-a-a-a-ame."

"Stop."

"Lame, lame, lame. L-lame, lame, lame. L-lame, lame, lame, lame, lame. Lame!"

"Lizzie."

"Lame, lame, lame. Lame, lame, lame."

Before she could carry on with the song, he reached in and kissed her. At first, she was so surprised that she simply sat frozen on her barstool. But as his lips lingered, she felt herself relax into him before he finally pulled away. She stared at him, speechless.

"Well, I guess now I know how to shut you up," he said.

"If that's the case, I think I might feel another song coming on."

He smiled. "Don't tempt me."

"No? Probably for the best. You wouldn't want to ruin your chances with any of the other fine ladies here tonight." She gestured toward the tiki bar outside, where a large group of forty- and fifty-something women cackled loudly while drinking colorful cocktails. They all wore tight dresses and towering heels and enough makeup that Lizzie could see the eyeliner from where she sat.

"Ah, yes. The infamous Windrift cougars. Not for me, thanks." He narrowed his eyes. "I think some of those women are friends with Kathryn and Barb."

"Sounds about right."

He looked back at Lizzie. "You're much more my type."

"Which is . . . ?"

"Smart. Witty. Cute. Interesting. You get the idea."

"No, keep talking. I'd love to hear more."

He half-smiled and took a last sip of his beer. "Do you want to get out of here?"

"And go . . . ?"

"I don't know. Anywhere. I'd say my place, but my place is your place, so . . ."

"I'd suggest my car, but it's technically my mom's car, so . . ."

They looked at each other and smiled. Lizzie was trying to play it cool, but she had butterflies in her stomach. She hadn't openly flirted with someone like this in a long time, and it felt good. The fact that she was very attracted to Nate certainly helped.

"There's always the beach," Nate said.

Lizzie gulped down the rest of her wine, snatched up her purse, and slid off the barstool. "Well then," she said, leaving a generous tip on the counter. "Shall we?"

The sex was good. Better than good, actually. Lizzie might have gone so far as to say it was pretty spectacular, the involvement of sand aside. The whole escapade felt like the premise for a juicy romance novel: millionaire's stepson sleeps with the cook—on the beach, no less!—and scandal ensues. Lizzie made up the scandal part, though she was pretty sure Jim and Kathryn wouldn't approve, especially after the stealing allegations. Then again, they seemed to disapprove of nearly everything Nate did, so maybe they'd view his tryst with the help with little more than apathy. *Yet another poor decision by Nate.* Quelle surprise.

Lizzie gazed up at the stars as Nate ran his thumb across her bare stomach. "So did you really meet up with that professor woman," she asked, "or was that just a story to get me to come out so that you could sleep with me?"

"How dare you," Nate said. He didn't actually sound angry.

" 'How dare you' as in 'That couldn't be further from the truth' or 'How did you see through my ingenious plan?' "

"Couldn't it be somewhere in the middle?"

"Like?"

"Like, yes, I did actually meet up with her, but I also wanted to spend time with you in a venue that wasn't my dad's house or a hospital."

She ran her fingers through the sand, which felt deliciously cool against her skin. "I like it here," she said.

"On the beach?"

"In Avalon. There's something kind of magical about it."

"I know. I always feel like the rest of the world is on pause while I'm here."

"I wish I could work here year round. Not necessarily for your family, but maybe someone else in Avalon."

"Nah, in a couple of months, this place will be a ghost town. Almost everything shuts down. Part of what makes it special is that it comes alive for only a few months each year."

"And then it fades away, like everything else."

Nate turned his head to look at Lizzie. "Thanks, Debbie Downer."

"What's true is true."

Nate grabbed her arm and pulled her on top of him. He reached up and kissed her, and she kissed him back, gently at first and then more intensely. She felt him get hard as she pressed her hips into his. He ran his hands down her exposed back and slid his thumbs inside the lining of her underwear, lowering it in one swift movement. It was less awkward this time than the first, when they'd fumbled in the dark—her for his belt and fly, him for her shirt and bra. Then there was excitement and anticipation, but there was also the self-consciousness that comes with first-time sex. Would she embarrass herself? Would he come too soon? But those nerves had been supplanted by lusty desire. Lizzie wanted to wrap her legs around him again and scream into the still night air.

As he pulled her into him, her wild thoughts were interrupted by the sound of her phone ringing. It had rung twice more since they'd left the Windrift, but Lizzie had refused to see who it was. Now she began to worry. Was it her dad again? Because if so, she should pick up. He had never called this many times in a row. She looked toward her bag and felt herself tense up.

Nate followed her stare. "You okay?"

"My phone . . ." She trailed off.

"If you need to pick up, go ahead." She could tell he didn't mean it. He was still hard and held her close.

"I just . . . it might be my dad, and it's really unlike him to call this many times. This is more times than he's called this year, total."

"You should take it then."

He groaned as she rolled off and crawled toward her purse. She fished around for her phone, but by the time she found it, she'd missed the call.

"Oh," she said as she stared at the screen. "It was my aunt Linda."

She unlocked her phone and saw that the previous two calls had been from Linda, too. In some ways, that was even odder than having her dad call. She was close with Linda, but not so close that they regularly called each other to catch up. The only times they spoke on the phone was for birthdays. Lizzie's birthday had been in March. Linda's was in October.

"Do you need to call her back?" Nate asked.

"I don't know."

Her phone chimed with a voice mail. Lizzie held the phone to her ear and listened.

"Hi, Lizzie . . . it's your aunt Linda. Listen, I know your dad has been trying to get in touch with you. Could you give him a ring as soon as you can? There's something we—he needs to talk to you about. Okay? All right. I hope everything is going okay with the Silvesters. Just . . . give your dad a call, okay?"

She pulled the phone away and scrolled down to her dad's voice mail, which he'd left several hours earlier.

"Lizzie, it's Dad. Could you call me as soon as you get this? I need to talk to you about your mom. She's . . . well, I'll tell you when we talk, but I'm worried about her. I know you're probably busy with work and everything, but it's kind of important, so . . . yeah. Just call me. Doesn't matter what time. I'll pick up."

Lizzie sat frozen with the phone pressed against her ear. She suddenly felt queasy.

Nate crawled up behind her and rested his hand on her shoulder. "Is everything okay?"

Was it? She tried to downplay the situation with a, *Yeah, sure, it's nothing. Just my family being dysfunctional, as usual,* but she couldn't. It was more than that this time. She never doubted that her dad still cared about her mom, even after the divorce. They'd gone through so much together—marriage, parenthood, the death of a child. Even if sadness and bitterness had overtaken all of the other emotions, some semblance of solicitude lurked beneath the surface. But to whatever extent her dad might worry about her mom, Lizzie had trouble imagining a scenario that would require her own involvement, unless it was something really bad.

She replayed Nate's question in her mind: *Is everything okay?*

"No," she finally said, because now she was absolutely certain that it wasn't.

CHAPTER 30

Lizzie was too anxious to wait until she got back to the Silvesters' house, so she called her dad from the beach. She stood in front of the dunes while Nate stood at the edge of the water, looking over his shoulder every so often.

Her dad picked up after the first ring. "Lizzie?"

"Dad—hey. What's going on?"

He hesitated. "It's your mom. She's . . ."

Lizzie braced herself. She'd always feared a call like this. Had there been an accident? She felt her throat close up. She could barely speak. "She's what? What happened? Is she okay?"

"She's . . . well, she's okay right now, I guess. Technically speaking. It's just . . ." He trailed off.

She could tell he was having trouble, but she was losing patience. "It's just what? Jesus, Dad. You're freaking me out. Just tell me."

"She has cancer."

For a second, Lizzie stopped breathing. She crumpled to the ground, her hand over her mouth. She felt as if she'd been punched in the stomach. "Cancer . . . ?" Her voice cracked. "What kind?"

"Breast. They caught it early. But it's an aggressive type. Triple negative or something like that."

"When did she find out?"

"Sometime in early June."

"*June?*" A sharp pain tore through Lizzie's chest. "It's the middle of July. When was she planning to tell me?"

"I don't know. She hasn't told anyone, other than me and Linda and . . . whatever you want to call him. Gary."

"So she told Gary, but not me?"

Lizzie's initial shock and sadness began to morph into anger. After everything they'd been through together, how could her mom keep her daughter in the dark? Did she honestly think Lizzie wouldn't find out eventually? The fact that her mom had told Gary first felt like a slap in the face. She had only known him a few months. He probably didn't even know her favorite brand of chocolate (Ghirardelli) or her favorite musical artist (Joni Mitchell) or the fact that she hated the color peach. Did he even know about Ryan? Maybe, but even if Gary knew the story, he didn't know. Not the way Lizzie did.

"How *could* she?" Lizzie growled through clenched teeth.

"Well, now, to be fair, it's *her* disease. She can tell and not tell whomever she wants."

"If that's the case, why are you calling to tell me? She obviously didn't want me to know."

"The thing is, she's made a few choices about her treatment that . . . well, I'm not sure she's thinking straight. I'm a little worried about her."

"Why? What is she doing?"

"It's mostly what she's not doing. After your mom called to tell me about the diagnosis, I called Linda to say I was sorry to hear the news and was willing to help out if she needed some support. That's when Linda told me there wasn't really much to help with. The doctor recommended chemo after the lumpectomy, but your mom decided she didn't want to do that."

"She had a lumpectomy?" Lizzie felt dazed. Her mom had gone through surgery and hadn't said a word. What else was she hiding?

"She did. And from what Linda said, they got the cancer with clear margins. But it was an aggressive type, and apparently recent studies have shown chemo works really well in making sure the cancer doesn't come back. But you know how your mom is about doctors and medical treatments since Ryan died. So instead she's doing some sort of 'natural' alternative thing Gary put her on to."

"What do you mean 'natural'?"

"I don't know. Something about juices and coffee. Linda mentioned 'chelation therapy' as well. It all sounds like hocus-pocus to me."

"Is she seeing a doctor? Or is she doing this all on her own?"

"Linda says she's seeing a doctor, but we both agree he sounds like a quack. He's into something called Demuth therapy. That's where all the raw juice and coffee stuff is coming from. You should see some of the sites Linda has pointed me to. One more dubious than the last. The Cure Within. Heal Yourself Healthy. The Clean Life. I can't believe your mom has bought into all this nonsense."

Lizzie's heart nearly leaped into her throat. "The Clean Life?"

"Yeah, I should send you the link. Don't get me wrong—it's a beautiful site. They all are. But do I really think these people have been cured by drinking a few smoothies? Sorry, I'm not buying it."

"But Mom is." Lizzie felt sick.

"Oh, yeah. I wouldn't care if she were doing this on top of treatments that have actually been proven to work, but she isn't. She's convinced these alternatives are just as good. That's why I'm calling. I need you to talk to her."

"Me? I'm not even supposed to know she's sick. What about you and Linda?"

"We've tried, and we've gotten nowhere. I'm the asshole ex-husband, and Linda . . . well, I guess there's a bunch of sister history I'm not a part of. But she'll listen to you. She always listens to you."

"I wouldn't go that far."

"I would. The thought of adding to your stress—that's like her worst nightmare. The whole reason she didn't want to tell you about her cancer was because she didn't want to worry you. If you talk to her and tell her you *are* worried, but only because she's headed down a fool's path, she might change her mind."

Lizzie glanced over her shoulder and saw Nate staring at her as he kicked at a seashell. She wondered how much he'd heard. She turned back toward the dunes, her dad's plea echoing in her mind. Rationally, she knew it was her mother's right to refuse a treatment she didn't want. And yet, even if that were the end of the story, Lizzie would have trouble accepting her mom's decision. Lizzie doubted she'd be able to allow her mom to let go without a fight. But that wasn't what was happening. She *was* putting up a fight, but she was doing so with counterfeit weapons. If she truly wanted to live, if she wanted the absolute best shot that the cancer wouldn't come back, then she shouldn't be following the advice on Zoe's site.

"Okay, I'll talk to her," Lizzie said.

"I knew I could count on you."

It was the nicest thing he'd said to her in a long time. Lizzie only hoped she wouldn't let him down.

Dozens of questions raced through Lizzie's mind as she gathered up her belongings. What was her mom thinking? Did she really believe the information on Zoe's site? And what, specifically, could Lizzie say to change her mind?

From what Lizzie's dad had said, Zoe's site wasn't the only one her mom had visited. Even if she proved Zoe's story about Marie was bogus, Lizzie could already hear her mom's retort: *Why would other sites recommend the same sorts of treatments? Are you suggesting they're all in cahoots?* Lizzie wasn't sure how she'd counter that argument, other than to say lots of people believed things that weren't true. She worried that wouldn't be enough to sway her mom. Even if she tossed out historical examples, she somehow doubted bringing up Magellan and Galileo would make her case more appealing.

It doesn't matter, said a voice in her head, and she knew it was right. She needed to call her mom right away.

The phone rang a few times before going to voice mail. Lizzie left a message:

"Hi, Mom. It's Lizzie. I just talked to Dad. I'm worried about you. Could you please call me back? There's something you should know about these sites you're visiting about your treatment. I think you'll see you're making a big mistake. It's a long story, but it's really important that I talk to you. I'll be up for a while tonight and then early tomorrow, so call whenever. Just ... please don't believe everything you read, okay? I love you."

She hung up and breathed a sigh of relief. She'd braced herself for an emotionally fraught conversation, replete with tears and yelling, and now that she'd gotten away with a voice mail she felt as if a weight had been lifted. She knew a voice mail wasn't enough. The tense conversation she'd dreaded needed to happen, and soon. But after the emotional roller coaster of the past two days—an ER visit, cheating accusations, sex, cancer—she needed a moment to catch her breath. She knew she was being selfish, but at the moment she couldn't help herself.

"You okay?"

Nate appeared beside her. For a moment, she'd forgotten he was there.

"Not really," she said.

"Anything I can do?"

"I don't know. I'm still trying to process everything."

He reached out and held her hand. She could tell he wasn't sure what to do, and she didn't blame him.

"It's my mom," she finally said. "She's sick. Cancer."

"I'm so sorry." He squeezed her hand.

"They caught it early, but instead of doing chemo like the doctor suggested, she's using so-called natural treatments with the help of her new boyfriend."

"Natural?"

"Like the stuff on Zoe's site. Zoe's site happens to be one of her favorites. Perfect, right?"

Nate stared back at her. She couldn't place his expression. It was a mix of worry, fear, and guilt. "What are you going to do?"

"My dad wants me to talk to my mom. He says she'll listen to me. I'm not sure that's true, but I figure if I tell her what I know about Zoe, then I can at least sow a seed of doubt about what she's doing."

"How long has it been?"

"Since she found out? Or since she's been following Zoe's site?"

"Both."

"Apparently she was diagnosed in June, but I have no idea how long the juices and coffee enemas have been going on. A few days? A week? Longer? My dad was fuzzy on the details and time line."

"How long does she . . . I mean is there a window for . . . does she need . . ."

Lizzie knew what he was trying to say and understood why he was having trouble saying it. "You mean how much time does she have?"

"Sort of. Yeah."

"Honestly? I don't know. They cut out the lump, but apparently it was an aggressive cancer, so I'm not really sure what that means if she doesn't do chemo. Will it come back? And if it does, will it be worse? Part of me feels like she dodged a bullet by catching it early, but now . . ."

"You should call her."

"I did. It went to voice mail."

"Oh. Do you think she'll call you back?"

"Tonight?"

"At all."

"Of course. She wouldn't just . . . *ignore* me."

But even as she said the words, she wondered if they were true. Wasn't that exactly what her mom had been doing ever since her diagnosis? Until tonight, Lizzie figured she'd been busy. With what, Lizzie wasn't sure, but then Lizzie was so busy with the Silvesters that she didn't have much time to think about it. Now she knew why, and she wondered if her mom would shut her out in the same way she'd shut out Lizzie's dad and Linda.

"But if she did . . ." Nate was treading carefully. Whatever was going on between them—whether it was just sex or something more—they were only just getting to know each other, and their conversations were still buttressed by politeness and restraint.

"Ignore me?"

"Yeah."

Lizzie thought about it. "I don't know."

"Maybe . . . I'm just thinking out loud here, but . . ." Nate kicked at the sand. "You could get Zoe to come clean."

"To my mom?"

"To everyone. She could issue a mea culpa on her site. Explain how and why she started it—the whole Marie story, how hard all of that was for her—but warn people her advice isn't based on scientific fact."

"And how would you suggest I get her to do that?"

"We could talk to her. Together."

Lizzie frowned. "I thought you said that would end in disaster. That I should leave it alone."

"I did initially. But . . ."

"But what? Now you've slept with me, so you feel guilty?"

Nate flinched. "Hey. That isn't fair."

"Isn't it?"

"No. I mean, sure, I care about you, so if something upsets or hurts you, it's going to get my attention. But like I said, part of what I do for a living involves looking at how people are taken advantage of. Ever since we first talked about Zoe's site, I haven't been able to shake the thought that I'm being a huge hypocrite by not saying something. I keep trying to rationalize my behavior by saying, 'She's family, I shouldn't be the messenger, blah blah blah,' but deep down even I know that's bullshit."

"So you managed to grow a pair in the last hour?"

"No, it's more that I've been trying to figure out a way to step in, or to make the Web site magically disappear, but now with your mom . . . She's an actual person—a real person, who lost a son and got divorced and whose daughter I know and like. I guess the whole thing has become real for me in a way it wasn't before. I can't keep looking the other way while I try to come up with an easier solution."

"So would you come with me to talk to her now?"

"Now? Like now now?" He glanced at his watch. "Is she even home?"

Lizzie slung her purse over her shoulder and shrugged. "I don't know. Why don't we go find out?"

Zoe wasn't home. Lizzie was annoyed (why was Zoe conveniently absent whenever Lizzie wanted to talk to her?), but she was also a little relieved. Everything was happening so fast, and she was beginning to feel a little out of control.

Lizzie checked her phone obsessively to see if she had any missed calls or messages from her mom, but the answer was always the same: nothing. She wished there were a way to check whether her mom had listened to the voice mail. At least then Lizzie would know she'd planted a seed of doubt.

Nate offered to stay up with Lizzie, but by one in the morning Lizzie knew there was no point in staying up. Even if her mom had listened to the message, she would be in bed by now. She had never been a night owl, and now she was recovering from a lumpectomy. She would never call Lizzie at 3:00 a.m.

"What about Zoe?" Nate said.

"What about her?"

"She might come home in a few hours. Don't you want to catch her before she sneaks out again?"

Lizzie thought about it. She wanted to confront Zoe (at the moment, actually, she wanted to rip her head off), but she'd had so little sleep in the past two days that she couldn't contemplate another all-nighter. What if Zoe didn't come home at all? Lizzie would be a zombie, and for nothing. She still had a job to do. For Nate, this was vacation, but for her, this was just another workweek.

"I need to go to bed," she said.

"Okay. If you change your mind . . . you know where to find me."

"Do I?"

"I guess this house is pretty big. Top floor, fourth door on the right."

"Fourth? Out of how many?"

"I don't know. A thousand?"

"Sounds about right."

"Anyway, something in your face tells me I shouldn't wait up."

"Probably a good call. It's been a long couple of days."

"Understood." He rubbed his hands together. "See you at breakfast?"

"Considering I'm the one cooking it . . . yeah. I'll be there."

Nate smiled, a little awkwardly, and Lizzie regretted making a joke that highlighted their disparate roles. She knew it wasn't quite as "upstairs-downstairs" as *Downton Abbey,* but the fact remained: He was a Silvester, and she was their cook, and in a week he'd be back in Washington writing about gentrification and she'd still be in Avalon, rustling up Paleo snacks. She didn't feel sorry for herself—she'd chosen this path, after all—but she did wonder how their relationship, if she could call it that, would possibly last beyond this week.

"Well, good night," he said.

He kissed her on the cheek before heading upstairs. Lizzie followed him with her eyes, the sensation of his lips still tingling on her face, and then she slipped down the staircase to her room, where she peeled off her clothes and threw on her pajamas before sliding into bed. She checked her phone one last time. She wasn't sure why. She knew there wouldn't be a response from her mom. But before she hooked it up to the charger for the night, she decided to look at Zoe's site again. She pulled up the post about Marie's relapse and read through the comments: "Sending so much love xx," "Marie is so brave, don't give up!" "WE R PRAYING 4 U STAY STRONG!" Lizzie's face grew hot. People were *praying* for Marie? She suddenly felt a seething rage building inside her.

Her thumb hovered over the Comment button. Could she . . . ? Of course she could. The question was, did she want to? Taking on Zoe in the privacy of her parents' beach house was one thing, but doing so directly on Zoe's site would escalate their confrontation. Was she ready for that? *Yes,* she decided. She needed this job until she found a new one, but now knowing of her mom's condition, she didn't need it that badly. If Zoe got her fired, so be it. At least Lizzie would have left trying to do the right thing.

She began typing in the comment box, posting anonymously:

Am I the only one who thinks this story is pretty sketchy? Has anyone actually reached out to Marie directly? Does anyone have evidence she actually exists?

Lizzie realized the comment was a bit elliptical, but she knew if she came right out and wrote: "FYI, this is all a hoax," Zoe would immediately pin the blame on her. Eventually Zoe would probably do that anyway, but Lizzie wanted to buy a little time.

She posted the comment, and when she saw it appear on the site a thrill raced through her body. She felt emboldened—powerful, even—in a way she hadn't in real life. The Internet gave her a cloak of anonymity that allowed her to be the ballsy, hardened skeptic she'd always wanted to be but never was.

She pulled up another post, one about the detoxifying powers of ginger, and wrote another comment:

Z—do you know of any patients other than Marie who have been cured as a result of your advice? Why is "Marie" the only one we hear about?

And then she did it again:

Why aren't there any recent photos of Marie? She looks the same in all the photos you post. Hasn't she aged? Or have you also discovered the fountain of youth?

She kept posting and posting, sometimes multiple times on the same post, each comment a little snarkier than the last. Then she turned off her phone, plugged it into the charger, and, her rage having dissipated into the Internet ether, fell into a deep and much-needed sleep.

CHAPTER 31

Frank—

You ASSHOLE. I told you not to say anything to Lizzie. It's the one thing I specifically asked you NOT to do. And before you say, "I'm her parent, too," here's a news flash: A parent doesn't suddenly decide to act like one after two decades of being AWOL. And don't give me that crap about me getting custody. You had alternate weekends, and you blew them. You think Lizzie was really "sick" all those times she stayed home? The only thing she was sick of was you and your new family. You made her feel like you'd traded her in for something better, and if you didn't see that, you're an even bigger idiot than I thought.

Also, since when do you give a flying f&#% what kind of treatment plan I follow? You didn't care when I went through menopause, or the time I fell down the stairs when Lizzie was in high school. But suddenly now you're all hot and bothered because I'm not doing what YOU think is right? Funny how that works. This is why I didn't tell you about any of it. It's none of your business. It stopped being your business when you left me for Jessica. And don't give me that BS about, "Just because we aren't married doesn't mean I don't still care about you." If you really cared about me, you wouldn't have told Lizzie. To be honest, I'm not even sure why I told you I had cancer in the first place. I guess I felt vulnerable in the days after they diagnosed me, but apparently I also temporarily went insane. Telling you was such a mistake.

Don't think I don't see what you're trying to do, Frank. You're trying to use this as a way to resurrect your relationship with Lizzie. It's pathetic, and anyone with half a brain can see through your "concern." Can't you just be happy for me that I've made an informed decision for myself? Or are you jealous that I've finally met another man?

I could write ten more pages on how angry I am with you, but you aren't worth that much of my time. Save your worries for Jessica and the kids. And don't you dare try to talk to Lizzie about this again. If you think it will bring you closer together, you're delusional.

Susan

CHAPTER 32

When Lizzie woke up the next morning and checked Zoe's site, all of her comments were gone. Not just her comments—everyone's comments. All that remained were Zoe's posts, the latest of which had appeared overnight:

```
COMMENTS CLOSED

Dear friends,

    Last night, someone began posting
inappropriate material on several of
my posts. I've removed the offensive
comments, but until I figure out who
has been trolling my site and why, I
have temporarily closed comments to
everyone. I apologize and wish I
didn't have to do this. I know how
important this community is to all of
you. It's important to me, too. But I
cannot allow someone to ruin it for
the rest of us. Hopefully, I can set
things back to normal very soon.

    Peace and love

    Z xx
```

Lizzie stared at the screen. She wasn't sure whether to feel crushed or victorious. On the one hand, she'd clearly gotten under Zoe's skin. That felt, at the very least, like a small victory. But on the other hand, Zoe hadn't taken the site down or exposed her advice as bullshit. She'd merely closed the site to comments, precluding any chance that someone would challenge her. Had anyone even read Lizzie's comments? Probably not. She'd written them at almost two in the morning. She felt so stupid. If she'd really thought it through, she would have posted in the middle of the day or whenever site traffic peaked. Instead, she went on a commenting spree in the middle of the night, when the only beneficiary of her snark was her own ego.

Burned by your impulsive behavior yet again, she thought. Had she learned nothing from her post-college downfall?

She slid her phone back onto the nightstand and rolled out of bed. The Silvesters' guests had mostly left and Sam had slept at Barb's, but Jim would expect a decent breakfast, even if all Kathryn had was juice. Since this week was considered Jim's vacation, he tended to want more than his typical bagel and coffee.

Lizzie threw on clothes and headed up to the kitchen, where she found Renata refreshing a vase of hydrangeas.

"Good morning," Renata said. "How did you sleep?"

"Like a log."

"The Silvesters, they have kept you busy."

"The ER visit is what really put me over the edge. But now that I've had a little sleep, I should be back on track. At least I hope so." She watched Renata count out five place mats. "Five for breakfast?"

She grabbed another. "Possibly six."

Lizzie's shoulders tightened. She had expected Jim, Kathryn, and Nate, but there was no one else in the house—other than possibly Zoe. "Who's coming?"

"Let's see . . . Jim and Kathryn, of course. And Nate. Then I think she said Sam and Barb would stop by. And perhaps Zoe."

Lizzie's stomach soured. As much as she wanted to take on Zoe, she didn't fancy another tense, coded exchange across the Silvesters' dining table. She wanted to corner her in private, with Nate by her side.

"Should I have something special prepared, in case Zoe comes?"

Lizzie was asking less out of concern and more to see how likely Renata thought Zoe's appearance was. Renata frowned. "I don't think so. Miss Zoe is so particular. She can't expect you to go out of your way when so often she doesn't appear. I do not think she even made it home last night."

Lizzie left Renata to finish setting the table and proceeded to the butler's pantry to get out the eggs and smoked salmon. Renata had picked up bagels at Isabel's, and Lizzie planned to offer a few simple accompaniments like scrambled eggs and flavored cream cheese to go with them.

Jim and Kathryn returned from their morning walk around eight thirty, and by nine o'clock everyone was gathered around the table, ready to eat. Zoe's chair was conspicuously empty.

"I don't understand why it's so damn hard to be on time," Jim said. "At the office, this would never fly."

"It's a good thing we aren't at the office, then, isn't it, sweetie?" Kathryn tried to act lighthearted, but Lizzie could tell she was faking it.

"I don't think a little punctuality is too much to ask."

"Aw, Jimmy, come on, it's vacation," Barb whined. "You can't expect a young girl in her prime to wake up early on vacation."

"It isn't early. It's nine o'clock."

"That's early!"

"Maybe for you," Jim said. He left it there, but Lizzie knew what naturally followed: *And I don't want my daughter to grow up to be you.* On the one hand, Lizzie couldn't blame him for feeling that way. But on the other hand, given what she knew about Zoe, she'd take a harmless mutton dressed as lamb over a fraud any day.

Lizzie laid the platters of scrambled eggs and smoked salmon on the table while Renata passed around a basket of warmed bagels. As Lizzie reached across Nate's seat to lay a serving spoon next to the eggs, she felt his hand run up her thigh. Her stomach fluttered. She didn't think of their tryst as a secret, but she also knew it wasn't public knowledge and liked keeping it that way. Jim and Kathryn didn't need another reason to disapprove of Nate—or her, for that matter.

"Hey, sweetheart," Sam shouted across the table. "What's in the eggs?"

"Boursin and chives," Lizzie said. She still hadn't gotten used to Sam's brashness.

"Boar what?"

"Boursin. It's a French cheese, with garlic and herbs."

"Those French. Always so full of themselves."

Lizzie wasn't sure what adding garlic and herbs to cheese had to do with an entire country's self-image, but she'd learned that Sam had very strong opinions about certain cultural groups and nothing anyone said seemed to change his mind.

Despite Sam's dislike of the French and their egos, he managed to wolf down three helpings of eggs, along with two bagels and a sizable portion of smoked salmon, in a very short period of time. By the time breakfast was over, Lizzie estimated he'd eaten more than she sometimes ate in a day.

"What can I say, sweetie," he said as she cleared his plate. "I have a big appetite—for food, for money, and for women." He winked, in clear view of Barb, who proceeded to top up her third mimosa.

Lizzie took refuge in the butler's pantry, where she scraped the remnants of leftover smoked salmon into the sink and loaded the dishwasher. Zoe hadn't made it to breakfast, and the more time Lizzie spent in this house with the Silvesters' friends, the more she heard Nate's voice in her head asking, *What are you* doing *here?*

"Knock, knock?"

She turned around at the sound of Nate's actual voice and smiled when she saw his face. "Hey, stranger."

He glanced over his shoulder, then slid beside her and kissed the top of her head. "Egg-cellent breakfast."

She cocked her head. "Seriously?"

"Seriously was it a good breakfast? Or seriously did I just say 'egg-cellent'?"

"A little of both. Mostly the latter."

"Then yes, I was serious about both." He cracked his knuckles. "So Zoe is still MIA . . . ?"

"I guess." Lizzie cleared her throat. "I did something kind of stupid. Or maybe not stupid. I don't know."

Nate looked wary. "What did you do?"

"I started posting comments on Zoe's site."

"What kind of comments?"

"Questions about Marie and the whole story. Stuff that might make other people ask questions too."

"I thought we were going to talk to her together."

"Do you see her anywhere? If we wait on her, it could be October, and by then my mom's cancer could have come back."

"I know, but with Zoe . . . declaring war directly on her site might not be the best move. I guess there's a chance she hasn't seen your comments yet."

"Oh, she's seen them."

"How do you know?"

"Because she's closed the entire site to comments and has removed everything I wrote."

"Does she know it's you?"

"Maybe? I posted anonymously, so there's no way for her to prove it."

"You'd still have an IP address. She may be crazy and reckless, but she isn't stupid. I'm sure she could figure it out, if she hasn't already."

"Oh. Well, so what? We were going to talk to her anyway."

"True, but . . ." He drifted off in thought.

"But what?"

"Never mind. I'll handle it."

"Handle what?"

"Zoe."

"But I thought—"

"I know what you thought, but I'm telling you to forget about it. I'll take care of this. Don't you trust me?"

"Of course," Lizzie said.

"Good. Then go about your business, and pretend this conversation never happened."

Lizzie wasn't sure she could keep that promise, but she agreed anyway because, at the moment, she knew she didn't really have a choice.

That afternoon, Lizzie's mom called. Lizzie had barely said hello when her mom jumped in.

"Before you say anything, I want you to know that I'm sorry," she said. She sounded as if she were in a car, speaking on Bluetooth. "I should have told you about the lumpectomy. About all of it, really. I was just scared. I'm still scared, if I'm being honest. But when I found out, I panicked, and I knew you had a lot on your plate and didn't want to upset you. If I'd known you'd end up finding out from your dad . . ." She cleared her throat. "I didn't mean for it to go that way. I'm really sorry."

Lizzie took a deep breath. She was a bit taken aback by her mother's apology. Lizzie had developed a script in her mind of how the conversation would go when her mom finally called back: She would act defensive and tell Lizzie she was sorry but that it wasn't her business and she was sure she was doing the right thing, and Lizzie would say it *was* her business because she was sure coffee enemas were *not* the right thing, and her mom would say, *Says who?* and Lizzie would say, *Says the FDA and the American Cancer Society,* and her mom would say, *Oh, those liars,* and Lizzie would say, *You want to talk about liars,* and then she'd tell her about Zoe. It had all gotten very emotional and heated in Lizzie's head.

But her mom didn't sound angry. She sounded contrite and a little scared and, well, like the mom Lizzie knew and loved. So instead of launching into a detailed, point-by-point explanation of why her mother was headed down a fool's path, Lizzie simply said, "That's okay," even if deep down she still didn't fully feel that way. "I just wish you would have trusted me enough to tell me."

"Oh, sweetie, it had nothing to do with trust. Of course I trust you. It's more that . . . well, it's hard to explain. Someday when you have children you'll understand. I didn't want to burden you with my problems. I'm supposed to take care of you, not the other way around."

"But I want to help you."

"I know you do, sweetheart, and I appreciate that. But I'm fine.

I'm feeling much better, and I'm getting help from some really great people."

"I actually wanted to talk to you about that. Dad said you've been experimenting with alternative treatments."

"Hello? Lizzie?"

"I'm here. Can you hear me?"

"Sorry, sweetheart, I think you're breaking up."

Lizzie moved to the far corner of her bedroom. "What about now? Better?"

"I . . . oh, boy, I'm losing like every other syllable. Damn it. I'm using the Bluetooth in Gary's car, and I'm not . . . Hang on. Maybe if I pick up the phone." Lizzie heard rustling on the other end of the line. "How do you disconnect the Bluetooth? Do I press . . . oh, wow, no, that was definitely the wrong button. Why am I looking at a number pad? No. Back. Go back. Ugh."

"I hope you've pulled over the car," Lizzie said.

"What? I'm sorry, I still can't hear you. Maybe the problem is on your end."

"I can hear you fine."

"What's that? You think it's mine?"

Lizzie was losing patience. "No, I said I can hear you *fine,*" she shouted.

"It's all coming out like gibberish. I'd say I'd call you back, but I'm at my doctor's office and I'd be late for my appointment. Why don't we talk later, or maybe tomorrow?"

"Okay, but before you go I need to tell you something."

"Does that sound okay?"

"Mom!"

"Yeah?"

"The stuff you're doing doesn't work. That site you read? The Clean Life? It's all bullshit. There is no Marie. She died five years ago."

"Sorry, sweetie, I'm still not hearing you, but let's definitely talk later. Sorry again for not telling you about my diagnosis. I hope you understand. I love you so much."

"I love you too," Lizzie said, but her mom had already hung up.

* * *

Another day passed without any sign of Zoe. More disconcerting to Lizzie was the fact that by the next morning her mom still hadn't called her back. Was this Gary's influence? Lizzie's bemusement with Gary as a partner began to morph into animosity. *Screw him.* She had overlooked his quirks because he seemed to make her mom happy, but if he was the one behind her sudden aloofness—not to mention her experimentation with quackery—then Lizzie had no use for him.

Lizzie decided to take the reins and called her mom's cell. This time, it didn't even ring and went straight to voice mail. She left another message:

"Mom—it's me. We need to talk. I tried to tell you yesterday, but you couldn't hear me. I know the author of one of the sites you're reading—The Clean Life?—and she's a fraud. Don't believe all this stuff you're reading online. I can tell you more about it when you call me back, so . . . call me back, okay?"

She knew leaving a message wouldn't be enough, but she hoped she'd dangled enough details in front of her mom that a return call would be imminent.

The day wore on, the house eerily quiet without the Silvesters or their usual houseguests. Jim and Kathryn had taken Sam and Barb out on their boat for the day, and Lizzie hadn't seen Nate since dinner the night before. Kathryn had given Lizzie the day off, but with everything going on, Lizzie was having trouble relaxing. She tried to lie by the pool on one of the lounge chairs, but she found herself looking over her shoulder every few minutes, half-expecting to find Zoe staring at her through one of the windows. She relocated to the beach, but it was a brutally hot afternoon with a minimal breeze, so after twenty minutes she gave up and headed back to the house. After a failed attempt at taking a nap, she'd run out of ideas.

Ultimately she decided to use her free time to clean out the pantry. If she couldn't relax, at least she'd be productive. She pulled out a big trash can and began pitching stale crackers and tortilla chips. She was surprised at how many half-empty bags and boxes she found. She and Renata were pretty good about using up whatever items were already open before they opened something new. Had they really been so careless to let all of this go to waste? There were water crackers that had lost their snap and seeded flatbreads that smelled musty and sour cream and onion potato chips that probably would have been fine if they hadn't crumbled into a million pieces. There was even a half-eaten bag of Pepperidge Farm Goldfish at the back. When had they served Goldfish? Lizzie couldn't remember a single instance.

She chucked it all into the trash, and as she tied the top her phone trilled with a text message. She glanced at the screen. The message came from a Philadelphia-area number she didn't recognize:

Want to meet up tonight?

Was it Nate? Her instinct said yes, but Nate lived in Washington and, from what she knew, hadn't lived in Philadelphia for something like fifteen years. Would he really still have a Philadelphia number? She supposed she did, even though she'd lived in New York for nearly a decade. Before she could text back, her phone trilled again.

I'm thinking The Princeton at like 9 or so

Lizzie had never been to The Princeton, but she was pretty sure the crowd there skewed young. At the very least, it catered to more of a party crowd, not mid-thirties professors who studied gentrification. But then Nate had gone to Princeton University, so maybe this was his idea of a joke. It wasn't a particularly good one, but he had also used the word "egg-cellent" the day before, so already she had doubts about his sense of humor. She texted back:

That sounds good. Assuming this is Nate. This is Nate, right?

Yup its me, see you then

She stared at the screen. No apostrophe in *it's?* Nate was rapidly losing his allure.

Btw, how did you get my number?

Before she could wait for a reply, Renata came into the room. She seemed agitated. "Miss Lizzie, there is something I think you should see."

Renata led Lizzie down the stairs and through the mudroom into the driveway. The evening sun sat low in the sky, so Lizzie held up her hand to block out the glare. Zoe's car was gone, but Lizzie's mom's Honda sat in its usual spot. Renata guided her closer, and as Lizzie approached, she noticed huge scratch marks along the side, as if someone had keyed the passenger door. Most of the marks were wild squiggles, but Lizzie swore the drawing beneath the door handle said: "F U."

"WHAT?" Lizzie knew she was shouting, but she didn't care. "When did this happen?"

"I don't know. I just noticed it as I was clipping flowers for the kitchen."

Lizzie looked closer. Someone had definitely written: "F U."

"Zoe did this, didn't she?"

Renata frowned. "I don't think so. Her car has been gone all day."

"She could have walked."

"Why would she walk home and leave her car somewhere else? It doesn't make sense."

Lizzie knew Renata was right, but she couldn't think why anyone else would want to deface her car. The Silvesters' house was highly unpopular with Avalon locals, but it didn't take a rocket scientist to realize the 2007 Honda Accord didn't belong to one of Philadelphia's wealthiest families.

"I'm sure the Silvesters know a good body shop," Renata said.

"Oh, goody." Lizzie didn't want to contemplate how much a paint job would cost. "You know, if they'd closed their stupid gate, maybe this wouldn't have happened."

"Perhaps they will cover some of the cost."

"You think?"

Renata shrugged. "You never know."

Lizzie was pretty sure she did know, and what she knew was that the Silvesters would take one look at her beaten-up sedan and decide it wasn't their problem. She didn't have the funds to pay for all of the repairs herself, but she couldn't imagine asking her mom to kick in the difference, especially given what she was going through. *Hey, Mom, I think you should pay for chemo and radiation, and oh, by the way, could you pay to have your car fixed too? I kind of messed it up.*

Her phone buzzed in her pocket as she let out a sigh. It was another text from Nate:

Haha, sorry, I got your number from Katherine

Lizzie clicked off her phone and stared at her keyed car and was so distracted by the damage that she didn't even notice he'd misspelled Kathryn's name.

CHAPTER 33

Lizzie walked into The Princeton and looked for Nate, but he wasn't there. She was a few minutes early, so she tried to scope out a good spot to wait for him. The bar seemed like a logical location. It was big and rectangular and took up most of the room. But even at nearly nine o'clock, the counter was thick with tanned youngsters whose night of partying had already begun. The only hope she had of standing out was by the DayGlo paleness of her skin.

Nevertheless, she found an empty barstool at the far end and decided to claim it. She held her purse on her lap and ordered a glass of sauvignon blanc.

"You want to open a tab?" the bartender asked.

Did she? She wasn't sure she wanted to spend all night here or that Nate would want to either. The bar crowd made her feel old. It was hard to have a serious conversation in a place like this, and at one time that had appealed to her. But now she didn't want to shout over screaming drunk people or nod as she pretended she'd heard what Nate said when really she had no idea. She'd rather be somewhere quiet, like the beach or a restaurant or her room.

"No, thank you," she said before sliding a twenty across the counter.

She sipped her wine and scanned the room. Still no sign of

Nate. She wondered where he'd been the past day or so. Even before they'd slept together, they would pass each other in the kitchen and hallway or Nate would make one of his supposedly impromptu visits into the butler's pantry. But now he seemed to have pulled a Zoe. Was he avoiding her? She knew she shouldn't be surprised or offended. He was her boss's son. Things could get painfully awkward if he decided he wasn't interested. But he'd also given no indication he'd lost interest, and she couldn't think of another reason he would keep away from her. He'd also arranged this rendezvous, so he obviously wasn't trying to ditch her. Unless ditching her was the entire point of this meetup, which she supposed was a possibility.

She glanced at her phone. No messages or calls. Nate was only a few minutes late, so she wasn't worried (yet), but it had been more than twenty-four hours since she'd spoken to her mom. Until now, Lizzie had given her mom the benefit of the doubt (maybe she was rethinking her treatment and was meeting with new doctors), but now Lizzie was officially pissed off. She sent her mom a text:

Are you planning on calling me back? As in, this century?

Normally she would have called instead of texting, but it was too loud at The Princeton and the last thing she wanted was another bad connection where her mom could claim they'd spoken when really they'd merely talked across each other.

Lizzie laid her phone back on the bar. She felt a tap on her shoulder. She swung around expecting to see Nate, but instead she faced a blond twentysomething in a strapless black tube dress.

"Would you mind taking a picture of us?"

Lizzie peered over the woman's shoulder to see a group of women huddled together, each with a cocktail or glass of wine in her hand. They wore assorted colorful dresses and rompers, their hair ranging from glittery blond to coppery brunette. They were all white. For that matter, so was everyone in the bar. Actually, now that Lizzie thought about it, so was nearly everyone in Avalon. She was white, too—a blindingly pale shade, at that—but she wasn't used to such homogeneous surroundings. From her elementary school to her apartment in Brooklyn, she'd always lived among a diverse set of races and religions, if not cultures and classes. She wondered if that was why April hadn't been back. April hated being the token non-white face or having people look at her quizzically and ask, "So what are you, exactly?" Instead of replying "biracial," April used to stare at people coolly and say, "Bored," before turning around and leaving. Lizzie always loved her for that.

Lizzie took the woman's phone from her hand. "Sure," she said.

The woman scurried to join the group. Lizzie held up the camera. "On the count of three: one, two . . ."

Lizzie marveled as some smiled and others put on their best pout. Was this what she'd looked like with her friends when they'd gone out in their twenties? Probably. She hoped they'd at least been a bit less vain but knew that was wishful thinking.

She handed the woman's phone back and looked at her own. Still no word from Nate. Had she misread the message? She pulled up his texts. He definitely said The Princeton at nine. It was now nearly nine thirty.

"Hey, don't I know you?"

Lizzie looked up. Zoe's friend Trevor had slid between her and the stool beside her.

"Oh, hi," she said.

"Partying solo. I like it."

"I'm meeting someone," she said.

"Lucky dude." He leaned in. He smelled like booze and pot. "Or chick. I won't judge."

Lizzie forced a smile. Trevor was the kind of guy she had never liked: cocky, preppy yet poorly groomed, and seemingly only interested in partying and picking up women. Even in her college years Trevor's type had never appealed to her, and it certainly didn't now.

Lizzie checked the time. "It's a 'dude.' And he'll be here any minute."

"Got it. Well, since he isn't here yet . . ." He flagged the bartender. "Miller Lite for me. And for the lady . . . ?"

Lizzie had drunk less than half her wine. She nodded at her glass. "I'm good. Thanks."

The stool beside her opened up, and to Lizzie's dismay, Trevor took it. "How's that for timing?" he said as he lifted his beer bottle to his lips. He took a sip. "So where've you been? I never see you out."

"I'm usually working."

"Yeah, but I mean after that."

"I'm usually in bed."

"Seriously? Come on, girl. It's summer. Live a little."

"I'm a little old for that kind of thing."

"No way. You're only, what? Thirty-five?"

Lizzie tried not to flinch. "Thirty, actually."

"Really? Wow. That's definitely not super old. My mom was totally still partying at thirty. She's still partying now and she's, like, I don't know . . . fifty?"

"Good for her."

"Right? I ran into her at the Windrift the other week and was like, 'Dude, Mom's still got it.' "

Lizzie wished her seat had an ejection button. "I'm not sure I ever had it, to be honest, so . . ."

"Not true. Zoe said you were on TV or something, right?"

"A while ago. It was a cooking show."

"That's what Zoe said. It got canceled, right?" He took a sip of beer. "That must feel pretty shitty."

"Back then, sure, but a lot of time has passed. . . ." Trevor was possibly the last person she felt like confiding in.

"Still. Must've been a real kick in the ass to have everything taken away from you like that."

"I wouldn't necessarily say it was 'taken away'—"

"And then to have people like Zoe come along with new stuff on Insta' and Snapchat and whatever."

"Zoe's site is a separate issue."

"I guess. But I can understand why you'd feel pretty jealous of the sweet deal she has going. All those readers, an app, a deal with the Apple watch . . ."

"I'm not jealous of Zoe."

"Hey, listen, it totally makes sense. I get it. I'd probably be jealous, too. And when I get jealous, I sometimes do stuff I shouldn't. Like, I'm not thinking straight, you know?" He raised an eyebrow.

"Sure," she said. Something about Trevor was beginning to

creep her out. She looked at her phone and then around the room. Nate was still nowhere to be found.

"Sorry—touchy subject."

"No, it's fine," she said, even though it wasn't.

"So tell me about this dude you're meeting up with."

"He's just a friend," Lizzie said. She knew it was more complicated than that, but she couldn't be bothered to break it down for Trevor.

"Oh, yeah? Anyone I'd know?"

"I don't think so." She knew there was a good chance Trevor knew Zoe's half brother or at least knew of him, but she also felt her relationship with Nate was none of Trevor's business.

"What time were you supposed to meet?"

"Nine."

"Nine?" He pressed the button on Lizzie's phone. They both looked at the time: 9:43. "Girl, I hate to break it to you, but I think you got stood up."

Lizzie wished he'd stop calling her girl. "He's just running late."

"Has he called? Or texted?"

"No. . . ."

"And is he usually . . . what's it called? Punk . . . punk . . ."

"Punctual?"

He snapped his fingers. "That's the one."

"I guess so." She thought about Nate's arrivals: to the beach house, to the breakfast table, to dinner. "Actually, he's usually early."

"Right. So like I said: I think you got stood up."

Lizzie suddenly felt a little sick. Trevor was right that this was all very out of character for Nate. Had something happened to him? Or was he really standing her up? "Oh," she finally said. She took a long sip of wine.

"Hey—turn that frown upside down. Trevor is here."

This provided no comfort to Lizzie. "Actually, I think I'm going to go."

"Aw, come on, the night is just getting started."

"For you, maybe, but for me . . . I should probably try to track down my friend. Just to make sure he's okay."

"How'd you get here?"

"I drove."

"Then at least let me walk you to your car."

"I'm fine, thanks."

"Please, it would be my pleasure."

"Honestly, there's no need. I managed to snag a spot right out front, on Dune."

"No, I insist." He patted her shoulder, a little harder than Lizzie thought was necessary.

Lizzie slid off her chair. "Okay, fine, whatever."

She pushed her way out of the restaurant as Trevor trailed behind. She was glad she'd parked in clear view of those in and outside the restaurant and not on some dark side street. She crossed to the other side of Dune Drive and approached her car. Even in the dim light of the street lamps, she could still see the scratch marks and the "F U" beneath the passenger handle.

"So I hear Zoe's parents nearly fired you," he said as she slowed her step.

She turned around. "What?"

"Something about a stolen cookbook?"

"I didn't steal anything," she said.

"I'm sure." He peered over her shoulder. "And it looks like your car has taken a beating, huh?"

"Someone keyed it earlier today."

"Huh." It was dark, but Lizzie swore she detected something bordering on menace in his eyes. "Stealing accusations, a keyed car . . . Sounds to me like you'd better watch yourself."

"Sorry?"

"I'm just saying—if it were me? I wouldn't want to go out of my way to get other people in trouble. Like, talking to the press? That would be a really bad idea."

"I don't know what you're talking about."

"I think you do."

"No, really. Who's talking to the press?"

He shrugged. "Let's hope no one, eh? Because that? On your car? That's nothing. I promise it could get way worse."

Then he winked and turned around and headed back into The Princeton.

Lizzie's hands were still shaking when she got into the car. She pulled up Nate's texts and called the number. It went straight to voice mail, and when Lizzie heard the greeting her heart raced.

"Yo, it's Trevor; leave a message. Peace."

CHAPTER 34

Lizzie couldn't sleep. Every time she heard a sound—a creak in the ceiling, a rattle from the air conditioner—she bolted upright in bed, convinced Zoe or Trevor had entered her room and was trying to kill her. She knew her fears were a bit over-the-top, but Trevor's coded threats had rattled her.

As she lay in bed, she decided to channel her anxiety in a positive direction and started creating an action plan in her head. First thing in the morning, she would e-mail a few editors at prominent news outlets and tell them about Zoe's grand hoax. She still had a few contacts at *Savor, Cooking Light,* and even the *New York Times* food section. She wasn't sure how much they'd care about this kind of thing, but it was a start. She also planned to follow up with any past employers to see if they had any work for her so that she could make a swift and speedy exit. On that account, she wasn't holding her breath.

She eventually nodded off sometime between 3:00 and 4:00 a.m. and awoke just after 7:00 to the sound of her phone vibrating on her nightstand. It was her mom.

"Hello?" Lizzie's voice was scratchy with sleep, and she moved as if she were trapped in Jell-O. It had been a very bad week for sleep.

"Hi, sweetie. Did I wake you?"

"Yeah, but I needed to get up anyway. Breakfast approaches."

"Oh, right, of course. What time do they eat?"

"Depends. Usually around eight thirty."

"I'd better not keep you then."

"No, wait—I'm glad you called. I've been wanting to talk to you."

"So I guessed from your text. You know, I could live without the sarcasm and attitude. I'm going through some very serious stuff over here. You could cut me a little slack."

Lizzie sat up in bed. "Sorry. But I keep trying to talk to you about something, and every time you either cut me off or we get disconnected. I'm a little frustrated."

"Well, you have me on the phone now. So what do you want to talk to me about?"

"Your treatment."

Lizzie detected a sigh. "Of course."

"Dad says you've been doing some alternative therapies."

"I am."

"And that you've been reading a bunch of Web sites as part of that."

"Right."

"And one of those sites is The Clean Life."

"So?"

"That's what I wanted to talk to you about. The information on that site is bogus. There is no Marie. Or not anymore—she was a friend of the Silvesters' daughter, who runs the site. The real Marie died five years ago, and I'm worried that's what will happen to you if you follow the advice on that site."

"I know."

"You know? What do you mean you know?"

"For one, I know what you and your father and your aunt Linda think about what I'm doing. You have made that abundantly clear."

"Yeah, and for good reason—"

"Would you let me finish? I've seen the article, okay? Just because one site misrepresented itself doesn't mean none of this stuff works, and anyway—"

"What article?"

"The one on . . . what site was it? The Daily Beast?"

"When?"

"First thing this morning. I read it on my computer in bed, while I was having one of my—" She caught herself. "Well, whatever. I read it."

Lizzie jumped out of bed and grabbed her laptop. She pulled up The Daily Beast and scrolled down. Her heart raced as a bold headline stared her in the face:

POPULAR WELLNESS SITE PEDDLES BOGUS INFORMATION

Author never cured friend of cancer; info
on site can't be substantiated

"I assumed you already saw it."

"How could I have seen it? You woke me up, and it was only published this morning."

"Oh. I guess that's true. But then how did you know the information on the site wasn't true?"

"Because I'm living under the same roof as the author. It wasn't that hard for me to figure it out. And even if I weren't—come on. Curing cancer with fruits and supplements? How could that *not* sound at least a little fishy to you?"

"Here we go. I knew this would be your reaction. One site gets discredited, and now all of this stuff is crap."

"No, it was always all crap."

"Is that so? Then why would people promote these things?"

"Honestly? You'd have to ask them. I'm sure some of them actually believe what they're saying. Others, like Zoe, probably have their own agendas."

"God, between you and your father and your aunt Linda . . . I'm not an idiot, okay?"

"No one is saying you're an idiot. Cancer is a big freaking deal—I can't imagine how scared you must have felt when you found out. And after Ryan, I get that you have misgivings about modern medicine. But as tempting as it might sound to treat your-self 'naturally,' there's a reason things like chemo exist. People don't do chemo because it's fun. They do it because it works."

"Sometimes."

"More of the time than shooting coffee up your butt."

"It's my choice."

"I know it is. I'm not saying you have to do chemo if you don't want to. I'm saying don't do these other things and expect to have the same outcome."

A brief silence hung between them. "It's just . . ." She heard her mom's voice catch. "You don't know what it's like."

She was right: Lizzie didn't know what it was like. Not any of it. Not losing a child, not being diagnosed with cancer, not divorcing your husband and watching him start a new family while you cling to the memory of the one you once had. Lizzie hoped she never had to go through any of those things, but she also didn't want to lose a mother.

"I'd be lying if I said I didn't have moments of doubt," her mom continued. "Of course I do. Especially when I read things like that Daily Beast article. But then I read how horrible chemo can be and—"

"So stop reading."

"What?"

"Stop reading. About chemo, about alternative medicine, about all of it. Talk to a doctor—a real doctor, who cures patients. Not one patient or two patients—hundreds of patients. Thousands of patients. Then decide what you want to do."

"But Gary says—"

"Screw Gary. Gary sells insurance. What the fuck does he know about cancer?"

"His brother died of lymphoma."

"I'm very sorry for his loss. But excuse my insensitivity, that doesn't make him an expert. He didn't go to medical school. He doesn't have a PhD in molecular biology. He doesn't know what the hell he's talking about."

"And you do?"

"Not about curing cancer. That's why I'm saying you should talk to a medical professional."

"But Gary has been so supportive."

"And if he truly cares about you, he'll continue to be. The Clean Life is crap. Doesn't it scare you to think how much of the other stuff you're reading is, too?"

"Yes, but . . ." Her mom took a deep breath. "I need some time to think this over."

Of course she did. For as long as Lizzie could remember, her mother would say, when confronted with any decision, whether it was buying a couch or ordering dinner at a restaurant, "I need to think it over." She was, in many ways, the opposite of Lizzie, who'd jumped into decisions headfirst. Lizzie could see the advantages of her mother's approach (after all, look where Lizzie's rash behavior had gotten her), but she was also continually frustrated that her mom couldn't just *decide* sometimes. Lizzie wondered how much of her mom's contemplative nature was inbred and how much was a response to Ryan. Lizzie had heard her say dozens of times that maybe if she hadn't jumped so readily at the offer of a clinical trial maybe things wouldn't have ended the way they did.

"Anyway," she continued, "you probably need to get to work. I'm guessing things will be a little chaotic at the Silvesters' this morning. They must have seen the article by now. Don't you think?"

Lizzie wasn't sure whether they had or not. It was early, but then Jim, in particular, was an early riser. He also was on his phone or iPad constantly. Regardless, they would see the story soon, and when the time came Lizzie hoped she wouldn't be the one bearing the brunt of their rage.

As soon as Lizzie reached the kitchen she knew the Silvesters had seen the article. Jim sat at the dining room table, talking on his phone.

"I don't care what Mike says. I need you here. Tell him the inversion stuff can wait. . . . Yes, it can. None of the work you've done for the rollout will count for anything if we don't put the lid on this." He pinched the bridge of his nose. "He knows if I come in it'll just be a distraction. Did you show him the e-mail you got from the *Elle* reporter? . . . Others? What others?" He let out a sigh. "Jesus. Okay. Just get here as soon as you can." He hung up.

Lizzie tried to slip by undetected, but Jim called after her, "Hey—you. Get back here. I need to talk to you."

She stopped and turned around. Her heart raced. "Me?"

"Yes, you. I know what you did."

"I don't know what you're talking about."

"Don't bullshit me. I'm not Kathryn." His phone rang. He picked it up. "Mike? Hey. Hang on a second." He covered the receiver. "I need to take this. Don't go far. You're not off the hook."

Lizzie lingered, unsure what to say or do.

Jim stared at her. "Some privacy, please?"

"Sorry," Lizzie said. She turned and ducked into the pantry.

Did Jim know she'd left comments on Zoe's site? Or something else? And what was all the business about inversions and other reporters?

Lizzie tried to focus on pulling breakfast together, but she couldn't concentrate. As soon as she took the fruit from the refrigerator, she heard Kathryn babbling in the dining room. Lizzie lost every few words, but she got the general impression that Kathryn was very upset.

"But it's just so unfair . . . obviously has an ax to grind . . . for all we know she was hacked . . . looking to fill their twenty-four-hour news cycle . . . never even *asked* . . . what does that have to do with CC Media anyway. . . ."

It went on and on, as it always did, but this time the agitation in Kathryn's voice rose until she was nearly shouting. Lizzie wondered if Kathryn looked as manic as she sounded but wasn't quite curious enough to find out.

As Lizzie divided the fruit among parfait glasses, she heard footsteps behind her. She turned to see Jim in the doorway with Kathryn by his side. Kathryn did, indeed, look crazed. Untamed bits of her normally smooth and styled coif stuck out at the side, and her skin looked blotchy. Her hands sat on her hips, her eyes narrowed.

"Well," she said. "I hope you're happy."

"With . . . ?"

"Don't play dumb with me. Jim and I know you talked to the press."

"I did not."

"Oh, please. Do you think we're idiots? Three days after you tell us you don't approve of her site, the story magically appears online. What a coincidence!"

"It wasn't me. I—"

"You trashed her site. Zoe told us."

"I didn't trash her site. I wrote a few comments."

"It was more than a few comments, and you know it."

"I was only—"

"Stop," Jim cut in. "Enough excuses. I told you after the cookbook incident that you needed to watch it. You didn't listen. Do you have any idea how many problems this creates for me? Not just me. My family. My *company*."

"Your company?"

"I can't even begin to tell you how sorry you're going to be that you did this."

"Me? Your daughter is the problem."

"Lizzie, enough. You're only digging yourself into a deeper hole."

"I didn't do anything. I wanted to. In fact, I'd planned on e-mailing a few media outlets first thing this morning to expose your daughter for what she is."

"Which is what?"

"A liar and a fraud. But I didn't have the chance to do that because someone else beat me to it."

"And who would that be?"

"I have no idea. Anyone with half a brain, I guess."

Kathryn's eyes went wild. "You have a lot of nerve."

"*I* have a lot of nerve? That's rich."

Jim clenched his jaw. "Okay, fine. You want to play hardball? Let's play hardball. How about I sue you for defamation?"

"Are you joking?" A fierce pent-up anger was raging in Lizzie's chest. "I don't even know any reporters at The Daily Beast. And anyway, how can it be defamation if the story is true?"

"That's it. I'm calling my lawyer."

He had reached into the phone holster around his waist when a voice called out behind him, "I did it."

Jim and Kathryn turned around. Lizzie peered between them and saw Nate standing in the kitchen.

"I did it," he repeated. "I called a friend at The Daily Beast and told her to look into Zoe's site."

Jim slid his phone back into the holster. "Why on *earth* would you do that?"

"Because her site is bullshit?"

"It isn't bullshit."

"Yes, it is. And if you weren't so blinded by the dollar signs in your eyes and her hundreds of thousands of followers, you'd see that."

Kathryn huffed. "Right, of course, because making money is a crime."

"Making money isn't a crime. Neither, for that matter, is lying about saving a friend's life. But making money by lying about saving a friend's life? Maybe that isn't a crime either, but it sure as hell isn't right."

"You're just jealous that she was more successful than you," Kathryn said.

Nate's eyes widened. "I'm a tenured fucking professor. She wrote some stupid blog."

"It wasn't just a blog. It was a brand."

"I feel like I'm on Mars. Dad, is this really how you feel, too? That a popular yet fraudulent Web site is more of an accomplishment than getting tenure at a top university?"

Kathryn sniffed. "I wouldn't call it a *top* university—"

"Shut up, Kathryn," Jim snapped.

Everyone went silent. Lizzie had never heard Jim yell at Kathryn before, and by the looks of it, Nate and Kathryn hadn't either, at least not in front of other people.

"What you do is fine," Jim said.

"Fine. Wow. Don't sound too thrilled."

"Well, what do you want me to say? You write about neighborhoods. It isn't my thing."

"It doesn't have to be your 'thing.' It's my thing, and I enjoy it, and I would argue what I write about makes a contribution to society."

"And I don't?"

"I never said that. You employ thousands of people. You allow millions to get online and watch TV and do lots of other things we all take for granted. That's great. I might have questions about how you do business and whether some of your recent plans are a good idea, but I never said you don't make a contribution. I respect what you do. It would be nice if you did the same for me."

Jim stood in silence for what felt to Lizzie like a long time. She wished she could dissolve into the cabinetry. She respected Nate for everything he'd done and said—the way he stood up for his own career and also absolved her from blame—but she also knew she was witnessing a deeply personal confrontation that had been years in the making. She'd only recently inserted herself into the Silvesters' lives. She wasn't sure she deserved to watch Nate and Jim's relationship come to a head.

Jim eventually cleared his throat. "You're right. I'm sorry. I'll try to do better."

"It would be great if you could do more than try."

Kathryn groaned. "Typical. Always asking for more."

"Kathryn, I'm warning you," Jim said. He didn't look at her. "I'll do better," he said.

"Thank you."

"In the meantime, I need to clean up the mess you've made." He caught Nate's eye. "That Zoe made."

Lizzie could tell Kathryn desperately wanted to jump in, but after Jim's warning she instead crossed and uncrossed her arms and played with her frizzed hair. Lizzie thought she looked as if she might burst.

"Shouldn't Zoe be the one cleaning up the mess?" Nate asked.

"This is all a bit above her pay grade."

"Yeah, but come on. What did you used to tell me as a kid? 'You made your bed; now you have to sleep in it.' Or does that not apply to Zoe?"

"It would if this were strictly about a Web site. But unfortunately, now it's about more than that. People have started asking questions about the company."

"What does CC Media have to do with her blog?"

"It's complicated...I guess, technically speaking—" Jim's phone rang. He glanced at the number. "I have to take this. We can talk later. Kathryn, track down Zoe. Lizzie, have lunch ready at noon. April should be here by then."

Lizzie gulped. "April?"

"Sherman. From Publicity."

"She and Lizzie have a history..." Kathryn said.

Jim's eyes flitted from Kathryn to Lizzie and back to Kathryn again. "Yes, well, they'll have to save their singing of 'Kumbaya' for another day. This is a working lunch. Keep it simple. Nothing messy."

He answered his call and left. Kathryn looked Lizzie up and down. "It had better be Paleo," she said before turning on her heel in a dramatic huff and stomping out of the room.

CHAPTER 35

By the time April arrived, the Silvesters' house was a flurry of activity. Jim was on the phone constantly, toggling between calls with colleagues and lawyers, and Kathryn was on the hunt for Zoe, whom she could not find. Renata flitted from room to room, setting tables, watering plants, and otherwise ensuring the Silvester household wasn't falling apart, even if they felt as if their lives were. Lizzie, meanwhile, fantasized about blowing their house to bits as she pulled together lunch. If it weren't for the fact that she might finally get a chance to talk to April, she would have told the Silvesters to make their own damn lunch and walked out the door for good.

April rang the front doorbell, and Renata dashed off to let her in. Had April really climbed all of those stairs? Lizzie wondered. That alone qualified her for a pay raise. When it was combined with her willingness to drop everything and drive all the way to Avalon, Lizzie thought she probably deserved a promotion.

Lizzie busied herself in the butler's pantry, finishing off the frittata and salad she'd prepared for lunch. The velvety sound of April's voice echoed into the kitchen.

"Traffic was fine," she said. "Good thing Zoe's site went viral on a Thursday."

Lizzie knew that was April's attempt at a joke, and she wondered if it had landed. *Probably.* April always had a way of saying things others couldn't, and people rarely held grudges against her. April was also the queen of damage control. When she'd produced Lizzie's on-campus show, she'd bailed them out of numerous binds—bum microphones, bad lighting, a set that at one point was actually falling apart. Their friend and videographer, Sean, called her Mrs. Fix-It. Lizzie assumed she fulfilled a similar roll at CC Media.

That said, Lizzie was a little confused as to why someone in CC Media's corporate publicity department was being called in to handle the fallout from Zoe's site. Sure, Zoe's dad held a prominent role in the company, but that didn't entitle him to use company resources to manage a personal scandal. Did other people at CC Media know what he was up to? Or had Zoe inherited her loose ethical code from her father?

"Lunch on the patio," Jim called from the living room.

Renata helped Lizzie carry everything onto the patio. Jim sat at the head of the table, and April sat on one side and Kathryn on the other. April scribbled on a notepad, every so often checking one of her three devices.

"Okay, but who approached whom?" she asked.

"I didn't approach anyone. I mean, obviously I know Andrew, and he knows I have a daughter, but I didn't even know about the scale of her site until earlier this week."

"So she didn't approach them."

"No. At least not that I know of."

April started to speak but caught herself as Renata and Lizzie reached the table. She offered a weak smile as they laid the platters down.

"Yes?" Jim prompted.

April cleared her throat. Lizzie could tell April didn't want her overhearing. "It's just . . . I know some of this information is sensitive."

Jim waved at Renata and Lizzie. "Renata is family. And Lizzie is . . . well, at any rate, she knows about Zoe's site. And Kathryn says you know each other, so you can trust her."

"I wouldn't go that far."

Jim eyed Lizzie cautiously. He gestured at the frittata. "Could you slice that?" He looked back at April. "Carry on."

Lizzie picked up the platter and took it to the end of the table, where she could pretend she was out of earshot even if she wasn't.

April lowered her voice. "All I was going to say was . . . from what Andrew told me, someone must have approached his team about investing. It doesn't sound as if it was the other way around."

"That's ridiculous. I didn't say anything. Zoe didn't say anything. Who else does that leave? Marie?" He let out a bitter laugh.

"Well . . . I might have said a little something to one of Andrew's principals . . ." Kathryn said as Lizzie carried the platter back to their end of the table.

"What?" Jim's cheeks flushed. "You can't be serious."

"I just figured with a bit more capital . . . think where she could take this. You said yourself—two hundred thousand followers is an impressive start."

"Kathryn. Do you have any idea—"

"But CC Ventures is a separate division."

"It's a subsidiary."

"Right. So it has nothing to do with you."

"I'm the COO! It has everything to do with me. Do you have any idea how this looks?"

Kathryn folded her hands in her lap as Lizzie slid the platter onto the table.

"That'll be all, Lizzie," Jim said.

"If you need anything else—"

"I'll let you know." He waved her away and turned to April. "Now, tell me, how the hell do we spin our way out of this one?"

Lizzie only caught snippets of the conversation through the rest of the meal, but from what she could piece together, Zoe was in very early talks with CC Media's venture capital subsidiary about investing in the Clean Life brand. Even if Zoe's site hadn't been a sham, the relationship would have looked like nepotism, but now that The Daily Beast had revealed the lies behind The Clean Life, the scenario looked doubly bad. Journalists were now running with

Zoe's scandal and using it to look further into CC Media's affairs—something Jim clearly did not want.

"Because it isn't just this story," Lizzie overheard Jim say to Kathryn. "It's all the other investments CC Ventures has made. It's our finances. It's the upcoming inversion."

"The tax thingy?"

Jim sighed. "Yes. The tax 'thingy.' "

"But you haven't even announced that yet. I thought you were still working on it."

"We are. Hence the reason we don't want someone else getting the story first. We want to control the release, not the other way around."

There was a pause in the conversation as Lizzie and Renata reached in to clear the plates. Lizzie noticed the place she'd set for Zoe hadn't been touched.

"Do you want me to make her up a plate . . . ?" Lizzie asked delicately.

Jim and Kathryn locked eyes. "I don't know," Jim said. He sounded annoyed. "Should we, Kathryn?"

"I don't . . . no, I guess not."

"Should I expect her for dinner?" Lizzie asked. She wondered if they could see through her faux professional curiosity when what she really wanted to know was whether anyone actually knew where Zoe was.

"I . . . well . . ."

"Kathryn, I swear, if she isn't at dinner—"

"She'll be at dinner," Kathryn said. "I promise."

"And will April be staying as well?"

April waited for Jim to respond. "No, we'll wrap up our business at lunch," he said, "and then April will head back to the office to set the plan in motion." He looked up at Lizzie. "Any other questions?"

"No, that pretty much covers it."

"Good. I'll have a coffee when you have a second. Anyone else?"

"Coffee would be great," April said.

"Milk, no sugar, right?"

Lizzie thought she detected a hint of a smile. "Yeah. Good memory."

Lizzie took the plates into the kitchen and put the kettle on. She wondered where Zoe was and whether she knew how much trouble she'd caused—not just for her family but for an entire company. Lizzie somehow doubted she'd care. There was a good chance she'd even be quite pleased with herself.

While she waited for the water to boil, Lizzie grabbed her phone and pulled up Zoe's site. Instead of the traditional blog format, with regularly updated posts, the site was now a static front page that simply said: *Whole Foods. Whole Spirit. Whole Life.* above a beautifully photographed image of the beach and ocean. Lizzie tried to scroll down, but there was nowhere to go. Had Zoe erased all of her posts? There was no longer an "About" tab either. Everything was gone.

"Oh—sorry. I thought there was another bathroom in here."

Lizzie looked up and saw April standing in the doorway. "The bathroom is at the top of the stairway."

"Yeah, I remember from the Memorial Day party, but someone is in it. I thought there was a second."

"Given the size of this house, there should be. Did you try the pool house? I think there's one in there."

"Cool. Thanks. I'll check." She turned to leave.

"I'm really sorry," Lizzie blurted out.

April turned around. "For leaking the story?"

"I didn't leak the story. Nate did."

"Oh. The Silvesters seem to think you were involved somehow."

"I actually wish I could take the credit. But Nate beat me to it."

"Thought he'd impress you by showing he had friends in high places, huh?"

"I'm sure that had nothing to do with it."

"And that he wasn't like the rest of his family."

"No." Lizzie was getting annoyed. What did April know about Nate and his family? What did she know about any of it, other than what Jim had told her?

"Well? Why else would he go out of his way to throw his family under the bus?"

"Aside from the site being ethically problematic?"

"Ah, suddenly you're the bastion of moral uprightness."

"My mom has cancer."

April tucked a piece of hair behind her ear. "Oh." She cleared her throat. "I'm sorry."

"Me too. And she's been visiting Zoe's site and other ones like it thinking it will cure her." Lizzie saw a change in April's face. "Now do you see?"

"I guess—"

"You guess? April, you know my mom. You know she isn't an idiot. If she's buying this stuff, think of how many other people must be too. I know you haven't seen her in a while—"

"And whose fault is that?"

"Hey, you're the one who stopped—"

Lizzie cut herself off. She was so used to falling into her default defensive mode that she almost forgot she was talking to April. She started again.

"That's why I said I'm sorry. Not because I talked to Nate about Zoe's site, and not because I've indirectly caused some sort of trouble for the Silvesters. I'm sorry for the way I behaved when our show started getting a lot of attention. I screwed up our friendship, and I wish I hadn't."

"Hey, if wishes were horses—"

"Listen, I don't expect you to forgive me, okay? It's been a long time, and this apology is way overdue. But I wanted to tell you I know what I did wasn't cool, and I shouldn't have done it, and I hurt you, and I'm really sorry."

April stared at Lizzie. It was a while before she finally spoke again. "It's funny. For years I fantasized about you basically saying exactly what you just said. And then time passed, and you had this big public fall, and eventually I stopped caring. Like, watching the reason you ditched me completely blow up in your face was enough. But now, hearing you apologize, I'm realizing it wasn't enough. And this isn't either. Maybe it would have been five or six years ago. Who knows? But not now."

"What else do you want me to say? Because I'll say it. I was selfish. Too ambitious for my own good. Shortsighted."

April shrugged. "That's the thing. I don't want you to say any-thing. I just . . . don't care. Like, it's not even too little, too late. It's just too late. I've moved on. It's been almost ten years, Lizzie. I've made new friends—friends I barely have time to see, given my crazy work schedule. I don't have the time or energy to pine over our lost friendship. I'd rather save that for the people who've shown they give a shit."

"I give a shit."

April threw her head back and laughed. "Since when? Since you lost your show and realized all the friends you replaced me with were just hangers-on?"

Lizzie winced. "That isn't fair."

"Isn't it? Funny—I don't remember you showing any remorse three years ago when *my* mom had cancer."

"I had no idea—"

"Of course you didn't. Because we aren't friends."

"I know that. And I know we probably never will be again. That doesn't mean I can't apologize."

"Why? So you can feel better?"

Lizzie stomped her foot. She'd tried not to lose patience, but she'd had enough. "No! Jesus, April, when did you become so cyn-ical? Maybe you're lucky. Maybe in thirty years of life you've never made a mistake or done something you later regretted. But I'd bet everything I own that someday you will. Someday you'll screw up, and you'll hurt someone you care about, and it'll be messy and painful and ugly. And whether it's right away or much later, you'll want to apologize to that person—not because you think it will make you feel better but because you know they deserve it."

April was silent. Lizzie waited for her to say something, but she just stood there. The whistle on the teakettle sounded.

"Anyway, Jim is probably waiting for you, so you should go," Lizzie said as she poured the water into the French press. "I'm guessing the bathroom is free by now."

"Thanks," April said.

"You're welcome." She gave the coffee a quick stir.

"No, I mean . . . thank you. For your apology. Or, you know, saying I deserved it."

"Oh. Well . . . you're welcome for that too."

"And I'm sorry to hear about your mom."

"Thanks. Sorry to hear about yours. How is she . . . ?"

"Cancer-free, going on two years." She glanced over her shoulder, then looked back at Lizzie. "Your mom really shouldn't be looking at sites like Zoe's—"

"I know."

"Is she . . . I mean, has she seen the latest?"

Lizzie nodded. "I'm not sure it's changed her mind, but we'll see. I guess some of it will depend on how you guys 'spin' the story."

"I'm not spinning things to let Zoe off the hook."

"Really? Because it kind of sounded like it."

"Give me a little credit, okay? I work for CC Media. I don't work for Zoe Silvester."

"Where is she, by the way? Does anyone know?"

"Kathryn says she'll be at dinner, so . . ." April shrugged.

"April? Hello?" Kathryn appeared behind her. "Ah, there you are. Jim thought maybe you'd taken off!"

"I was looking for the bathroom."

"You won't find it in the butler's pantry."

"I was just saying a quick hello to Lizzie. It had been a while."

"Yes, well . . ." Kathryn smiled tightly. Lizzie noted Kathryn now offered her the same sorts of expressions she usually reserved for Nate. "Jim is waiting for his coffee," Kathryn said to Lizzie. "April, I'll show you where the powder room is."

"Great," April said.

Kathryn grabbed April by the shoulder and began directing her toward the hall bathroom.

"Good luck with everything," Lizzie called after her.

April turned around. She stared at Lizzie for a beat, then smiled. "You too."

And although there was no way for Lizzie to say for certain, she somehow knew in her heart that April meant it.

CHAPTER 36

Dinner approached, and Lizzie still hadn't seen any signs of Zoe. April had left around two, and Lizzie spent the time afterward tidying the kitchen. Now that she'd had some sort of closure with April, Lizzie couldn't think of a single reason to stay at the Silvesters', but she hadn't seen Nate since that morning and didn't want to quit or leave without talking to him. She also needed to have the last word with Zoe. She told herself she'd stay through dinner and that would be that.

She needed to pick up a few items at Avalon Market, so she grabbed her shopping bags and headed out. On her way to the car, she saw Nate walking up the driveway.

"Hi," she said as they met in the middle of the driveway.

"Going somewhere?"

Home, she thought. *Away from here.* But she couldn't bring herself to say good-bye yet. She still needed to find Zoe.

"Avalon Market," she said. "Want to join me?"

"Sure." He glanced at her car. "Want me to drive?"

"Are you embarrassed by my ride?"

"I'm more concerned that we'll come out to find a tire missing. You don't seem to be having great luck."

"Fair enough."

"Let me just grab my keys and I'll be right back."

Lizzie waited next to his car, a black BMW sedan. She hadn't noticed it before, probably because it blended in with the other luxury cars in the driveway.

"Nice set of wheels for a professor," she said as he returned with the keys.

"It's four years old, and I bought it used." He unlocked the doors.

"Still."

He shrugged as they both got into the car. "I didn't buy it to be fancy. I've always been a proponent of used cars, and I've found the nicer ones hold up better."

"I don't know. My mom bought a used Camry back when I was in high school, and that thing lasted forever."

He started the engine. "Then maybe next time I'll buy a Camry."

He pulled out of the driveway and turned right onto Dune. Was there a tinge of annoyance in his voice? Lizzie couldn't tell. Maybe it was her comment about his car, but she somehow doubted it. More likely, he blamed her in some way for the chaos that had ensued since Zoe's story broke.

"Thanks for standing up for me earlier," she said.

"About leaking the story? Don't mention it. Frankly, I was standing up for myself more than anything."

"Thanks anyway."

Why was everything so awkward all of a sudden? Had she completely misjudged the chemistry between them?

"So I was thinking," they both said at the same time.

Lizzie blushed. "Sorry."

"No, no—go ahead."

"No, it was nothing. Forget about it."

"Are you sure?"

"Definitely. You were saying?"

She braced herself. She'd known all along their relationship might end abruptly and awkwardly, but she had expected to make it to the end of the day. She still had dinner and the evening ahead of her.

"I was just thinking . . ." he continued. "I'm leaving Sunday, and I didn't have plans to come back for the rest of the summer. So that being the case—"

"I know," Lizzie jumped in. "You're right."

"Sorry?"

"You're right. It doesn't make sense, you and me. It would never work."

"Oh. Well, in that case . . . never mind."

"What?"

"I was going to say I'd like to stay in touch somehow, and maybe take you to dinner before I go."

"Oh."

"But obviously I'm barking up the wrong tree."

"No, no—I just assumed you weren't, I don't know. Into it. You seem really aloof."

"You think maybe that's because I just threw my family to the dogs?"

"See, this is what I mean. The way you're talking to me—it's like you're mad at me or something. You're the one who leaked the story. I didn't ask you to do that. I was perfectly happy to do it myself."

"I know; I just . . ." He pulled to the side of the road and put the car in park. He took a deep breath. "It's a lot to digest at once, that's all. Especially all the stuff with my dad."

"I'm sure. But I don't want you holding this over my head and resenting me."

"I won't. Honest." He rested his hand on hers. "So about dinner, I was thinking maybe tomorrow we could—"

"I'm quitting."

Lizzie wasn't sure if Nate looked relieved or surprised. "When?"

"Tonight. After dinner. I just want to wait until I've had one last conversation with Zoe."

Nate huffed. "Good luck with that."

"I know it'll get ugly, but I don't care. I need to look her in the face and—"

"No, what I'm saying is, good luck with looking her in the face. If I had to guess, she's long gone."

"What do you mean 'long gone'? Kathryn said she'll be at dinner."

"Of course she did. That's Kathryn. I'm not saying Zoe is on a flight to Mexico, but . . . well, by tonight? Maybe she's on a flight to Mexico."

"Please. Over this? She's not a fugitive."

"Maybe not of the law. But of her family. Of her followers and acolytes. I heard my dad talking earlier. The way they're spinning the story? He knew nothing about her site or its inauthenticity, nor did he know anything about a potential deal with CC Ventures. In turn, CC Ventures didn't realize the author of The Clean Life was Jim Silvester's daughter and, at any rate, had already determined they would not invest in the site due to some questions about its authenticity. Zoe is getting the help she needs, and the family would appreciate its privacy. All questions about the company can be addressed to April."

"But if Zoe is getting the help she needs . . ."

"Kathryn wants to send her to some 'retreat,' which I think is code for some sort of psychiatric facility, but there's no way Zoe will agree to that. Hence my hypothesis about her making a run for it."

"You think she already left?"

He shrugged. "I haven't seen her; have you?"

"No, but then how would she know about her parents' plans?"

"Zoe's no fool. She's pretty good at reading the tea leaves."

"But she can't just leave. She's the one who created this mess. She has to take some amount of responsibility."

"That would be a first."

Lizzie knew he was right but couldn't bring herself to accept Zoe's potential escape. She wanted Zoe to atone for her wrongs or, at the very least, apologize. But that would never happen if she disappeared for good. Worse, she could start anew somewhere else—under a different name and with a different life story—and peddle the same sort of crap that had gotten her in trouble before, or even new crap that was just as harmful, if not more so.

"I have to find her," Lizzie said.

Nate shook his head. "I don't think that's going to happen."

"Watch me." She placed Nate's hand back on the steering wheel and pointed ahead of them. "Drive that way and make a left at the light. I know someone who might know where she is."

Nate pulled into the gas station and furrowed his brow.

"I don't need gas," he said.

Lizzie didn't answer and peered through the front window. Three cars were filling up at the pump, leaving one available for Nate's car. "Pull in front of that one," Lizzie said.

Nate did as she instructed, even if he seemed baffled. He turned off the car and tapped his thumbs on the steering wheel while they waited. No one came.

"I'm sorry, what exactly are we doing here?"

"Sh-h-h." Lizzie glanced out the window. Her eyes brightened. "Here he comes. Roll down your window."

Nate lowered his window, and seconds later Trevor appeared in front of it. "What grade?" he asked.

Nate looked at Lizzie. "Uh . . . premium, I guess. . . ."

"You'll need to open the tank."

"Before he does that . . ." Lizzie cleared her throat.

Trevor hadn't noticed her sitting beside Nate, but when he ducked down to look in the car his expression changed. "Oh," he said. He stared at her coolly.

Nate frowned. "You two know each other?"

"Where's Zoe?" Lizzie asked, ignoring Nate.

Trevor shrugged. "How would I know?"

"Is she still in Avalon?"

"Like I said, how would—"

"Listen, I know you two talk. Nate seems to think she's skipped town."

"Nate?"

Nate raised his hand. "Me. What are you guys . . . how do you know each other?"

"Long story," Lizzie said. She pointed at Trevor. "So did she leave or not?"

"No idea. I wouldn't be surprised. Thanks to you, she'd have every reason to bounce."

"I didn't leak the story," Lizzie said.

"Sure you didn't."

"She didn't," Nate said. "I did."

Trevor narrowed his eyes and studied Nate. "Wait, aren't you like her stepbrother or something?"

"Half brother."

"And you ratted her out? Dick move."

"Listen, I'm not going to argue with a guy who thought it was totally appropriate to show up to my dad's Fourth of July party without a shirt or shoes."

"Fuck you, dude. You have no idea who I am."

"And who are you?"

Trevor stared at Nate. "If you don't know, I'm not going to break it down for you."

"What's that supposed to mean?"

"Let's just say I keep this gas station busy and leave it at that." He tapped the side of Nate's car. "Maybe you should fill up somewhere else."

Then he walked away and waited on the car in front of them.

They never made it to Avalon Market. Instead, Lizzie asked Nate to drive back to the house.

"What about dinner?"

"I'll make do with what I already have. It doesn't have to be great—I'm quitting tonight anyway."

Nate glanced in his rearview mirror for what to Lizzie felt like the fiftieth time as he drove up Dune Drive. "So who was that guy?"

"Trevor? He's Zoe's friend. I think they party together sometimes."

"Ah. That makes sense."

"What does? That she parties with gas station attendants?"

"No, that she hangs with a guy who probably deals drugs."

Lizzie stared at Nate. Was that what Trevor had meant about keeping the gas station busy? She supposed that made sense, but she wasn't entirely sure it suited Zoe's persona.

"Miss 'Whole foods, whole spirit, whole life'?"

"I know it will shock you to hear that Zoe is a huge hypocrite,"

Nate said. "She may condemn so-called chemicals in her food, but she has no problem consuming chemicals in other ways."

"And you didn't leak *that* to the media?"

"Listen, I'm not trying to completely destroy my family. The current story is plenty for now, thanks."

Lizzie leaned back against the seat and stared out the window. Every time she thought she'd figured Zoe out, she'd learn something new that would alter her perception. It was like staring through a camera lens and bringing the subject into perfect focus and then having her move ever so slightly backwards and to the right, blurring any sort of clarity. Lizzie doubted she'd ever fully understand Zoe. She wondered if Zoe would ever understand herself.

"I think she mainly takes stuff to self-medicate," Nate said after Lizzie had been quiet for a while.

They pulled into the driveway, and Lizzie noticed Zoe's car was still missing. Lizzie's car was there, but as she looked closer she noticed the tires on the driver's side were flat.

She waited until Nate had turned off the car and gotten out to survey the damage. She circled the car and saw the tires on the other side were flat, too.

"What's up?" Nate asked as he came up behind her.

"Someone let the air out of my tires."

"I told you this car was bad luck."

She stooped down and looked at the tire more closely. "But we just *saw* Trevor. He's still at the gas station. There's no way he could have done this."

"Who's saying he did it?"

"He's the one who keyed the side."

"Says who?"

"Him. Or I guess he didn't say that directly, but he alluded to having done it when he threatened me the other night."

"He *threatened* you?"

She waved Nate off. "It wasn't a big deal. Or, you know, I survived, so. . . ."

He lifted her to her feet. "I wish you'd told me—I would have pounded his face in."

"I can take care of myself, thanks."

He pulled her in for a hug, and she leaned into his chest and closed her eyes. For a brief moment, everything else fell away. There was no Zoe, no vandalized car, no Clean Life, no mom with cancer. She wished they could stay like this forever. She wrapped her arms tighter.

"Guess I can't quit tonight, huh? Unless I plan on walking back to Philadelphia . . ."

"I've seen your sneakers. I wouldn't try it."

She laughed, but the truth was she didn't find any of this very funny. She wanted to leave. Even if she didn't find Zoe, even if it meant leaving without having the last word, she was just so sick of it all.

"What a cluster," she sighed. She was still hugging Nate. It was as if she were afraid that if she let go everything would start falling apart, including herself.

"What can I do to help?"

"Figure out how to reinflate my tires."

"Done."

"And make all of this go away."

"Not so sure I can deliver on that one."

"Okay, then maybe just start with the tires."

He kissed the top of her head, but whatever brief moment of affection passed between them was interrupted by a gasp. Lizzie pulled away and turned around to see Kathryn standing behind them in the driveway.

"I should have *known*."

She looked furious, but Lizzie wasn't sure why.

Nate sighed. "Hello, Kathryn."

"Don't 'hello' me. The two of you—of course. It makes perfect sense. Scheming against Zoe to get her into trouble."

"Nobody was scheming," Nate said.

"Please. Do I look like an idiot?"

"Do you actually want me to answer that?"

Kathryn turned puce. "You can both go to hell. Wait until I tell Jim."

"Tell him what, exactly?"

"That you two are . . ." She waved her finger at the two of them. ". . . *doing it,* or whatever, and that's why you leaked the story. To impress her. Because the 'neighborhoods' thing clearly wasn't working, like it never does, which is why you're still single at thirty-five."

"Wow. Don't hold back. Tell me what you really think."

"What I really think? I think you're a *loser* who's been trying to get back in his dad's good graces for years because he's terrified of being cut out of the will. Well, let me tell you, I don't care that you and Jim kissed and made up this morning. I will make it my life's work to make sure you never get a penny."

"More for you and your plastic surgery, right?"

Kathryn's eyes went wild. "You have no idea what you're talking about, you little shit."

"Maybe not, but I'm pretty sure I know where Zoe got her crazy streak from—"

Something in Kathryn seemed to snap. She'd had enough. "Go fuck yourself!" she shouted at Nate. She turned to Lizzie. "And as for you—pack your bags. You're fired."

Nate huffed in disbelief. "Fired? She didn't do anything."

"Nate, it's fine; you don't have to—"

"She betrayed our family," Kathryn said. "I hired her to cook. Not to fuck you. Not to ruin our family's reputation. She should have kept her nose where it belonged."

"Up your ass?"

For a second, Lizzie thought Kathryn had stopped breathing. The scream that eventually came out of her mouth was so loud, Lizzie worried one of the neighbors would call the police, thinking someone was being murdered.

"GO TO HELL, YOU SON OF A BITCH!"

"If I'm a son of a bitch, then that would make Zoe . . . the daughter of a horrible human?"

"Enough!" Lizzie shouted. "The two of you. All of you. I can't take any more. You don't need to fire me because I *quit.*"

"It doesn't work that way, sweetheart. I fired you first."

"Fine. Whatever. I don't care."

"I don't believe that for a second."

"Seriously? Listen to yourself. Who on *planet Earth* would want to work for you?"

"Plenty of people, thank you very much."

"Oh, really? I guess that's why you were scrambling at the last minute and needed my aunt Linda's recommendation. Because so many people would kill for this job."

"It was late in the season, and all of the good people—clearly!—were taken."

"Did you ever stop and think that maybe it's because your family is so insane and horrible that no one wants to work for you?"

"You wanted to, didn't you?"

"Because at the time I didn't have other options."

"And why do you think that was? Maybe because you're a huge failure?"

"I'd rather be a failure than a phony or a fraud."

"Please. You'd have killed for Zoe's audience."

"No, I wouldn't have. And do you know why? Because my mom has cancer, and in the scheme of things page hits and bounce rates and click-throughs don't seem all that important."

"I'm sorry to hear about your mother, but don't try to make this about her."

"Why not? She's the kind of person Zoe's site targeted. Vulnerable people with a terrible disease who were hoping for other options. And Zoe gave them that gift, wrapped in beautiful paper with a fancy bow, only it turns out the box was empty inside."

"It wasn't *empty*."

"You know, you're right. Maybe we shouldn't make this about my mom. Let's make this about another mom—you. How can you continually turn a blind eye to everything she does?"

"I'm her mother."

"So? That's not what being a mother means. Where were you when her friend Marie was sick? Where were you when she died? Where were you when Zoe actually needed you?"

"Don't you dare lecture me on being a parent. You're single and thirty and childless. You have no idea."

"You don't have to be a parent to understand the value of a good one."

Kathryn raised her chin. "I think we're done."

"You know what? You're right. We're done. As soon as I pack my things and fill up my tires, I'm out of here. But don't kid yourself—you deserve some blame in all of this, too. You can't take credit and bask in her success when things are going well but then claim no responsibility when they aren't. It doesn't work that way. I don't care how many houses you own or how big they are. If you screw up your kid, nothing else really matters."

Lizzie stomped up the driveway toward the garage, and although she could feel both Nate's and Kathryn's eyes on her, she was too angry and exhausted to look back or care.

CHAPTER 37

Lizzie stormed into her bedroom and began shoving clothes haphazardly into her suitcases. She didn't bother separating dirty from clean or making sure things were properly folded. She just needed to pack everything away and she would deal with the rest later.

As she dumped her toiletries into another bag, she dialed AAA and held the phone between her ear and shoulder. Nate had promised to call someone to inflate the tires, but she couldn't wait for him to do that. She needed to leave as soon as humanly possible. Luckily, her mom had maintained her AAA membership, so someone would arrive shortly with a portable air tank.

Lizzie tossed her deodorant and brush in the bag but realized she'd left her toothbrush and toothpaste in the hall bathroom. She rushed down the hall, grabbed her things off the sink, and headed back to her room, but as she passed one of the unoccupied staff bedrooms that faced the front of the house something glinted in the hallway light and caught Lizzie's eye. She backtracked slowly and peered through the door. Her stomach curdled.

"Zoe?"

Zoe turned around. She had been staring out the window, which afforded a minimal view. How long had she been there? Had she overheard the fight between her and Kathryn? The window was open, and Zoe was smoking a cigarette and flicking the ash out the window. She didn't speak.

"How long have you been down here? Your parents have been looking everywhere for you."

She shrugged. "A few hours."

"But your car . . ."

"It's parked on Fifty-third. I don't need my parents up my ass. Don't worry, I'll be out of here in a minute or two. I just forgot my passport, but then all of you were in the driveway like assholes, so . . ."

"Out of here? Where are you going?"

She took a long drag of her cigarette. "Far away from this shit palace."

"Aren't you going to apologize?"

"To my parents?"

"And your followers."

"I already took down everything on my site."

"That isn't the same as an apology. Plenty of people read what you wrote before you took it all down. Now if they can't find the information on your site, they'll go looking for it somewhere else."

She flicked her cigarette. "And that's my fault?"

"Yes, it's your fault. You gave people false hope. You wasted precious time—time some people probably didn't have to lose—when they could have been doing something that had been proven to work. You owe them an apology. Frankly, you owe them more than an apology, but saying 'I'm sorry' would at least be a good start."

"How can you be so sure my advice didn't work for all those people?"

"How can you be sure it did?"

She blew out a stream of smoke. "Do you know how many e-mails I received from readers? Hundreds. Some of those people had been through everything—multiple rounds of chemo and immunotherapy and all that other stuff. You know what they said? 'Thank you. Thank you for illuminating another path.' For a lot of people, I was their last hope."

"And that's great for people who'd exhausted every other avenue. What did they have to lose? But for people who hadn't even tried the things that work for most people, the information you were pushing was dangerous. Don't you see that?"

"Why do you care? That's what I don't get. I've talked to April. You aren't pure as the driven snow. What gives you the right to lecture me on morals?"

"What I did to April was completely different. I hurt one person, and I've since apologized. I never put her life at risk."

"You were a shitty, shitty friend."

"Yep, that's right. But I guess you wouldn't know what that's like. You'd need to have actual friends to be shitty to them."

"I have friends."

"Like Marie?"

"I was a good friend to Marie," Zoe snapped. "Maybe if she'd fucking listened to me. I kept sending her . . . she was just so *stubborn*. And her parents, too. If I'd lived closer, I would have done more. I would have literally shoved the Demuth book in her face. But I was too far away, and there was only so much I could say." She took a puff of her cigarette. "I did everything I could, okay? I tried."

"Her death wasn't your fault," Lizzie said.

"Of course it wasn't. What the fuck? Why would you say that?"

"Because . . . you think it was."

"No I don't. I told you, I did everything I could. You can't make someone listen if they don't want to."

"Is that why you started your Web site? So that other people would listen, even though Marie and her parents wouldn't?"

"Are you trying to psychoanalyze me? You're a cook. A cook who didn't even graduate from college. That's it."

"I'm not trying to—"

"I mean, my parents have paid out their asses on shrinks and psychologists, but hey, what do you know, some washed-up TV chef has figured me out for free!"

"Zoe, would you just—"

"I don't need your 'help,' okay? I'm fine, and I'll be a lot better when I get away from my parents and people like you."

"My mom has cancer. Did you know that?"

"Of course I didn't."

"Well, as it turns out, she was one of your readers. She's been doing all sorts of things you recommended because she thinks they cured Marie and will cure her too."

"Good for her."

"No, not good for her! Breast cancer is curable, and they caught it early. But she's so scared and skeptical that when someone like you gives her an out, she'd rather take it than do chemo."

"Ah, so this is personal now."

"Even if it weren't, it doesn't change the fact—"

"It was personal for me too, okay? I loved Marie. More than you'll ever know."

"Then don't you owe it to her to take responsibility?"

"She's gone, and I shut down my site. It's over." She snuffed out her cigarette on the windowsill and tossed it out the window. "I'm sorry about your mom."

She grabbed a bag of her belongings off the floor and pushed past Lizzie.

"Where are you going?" Lizzie called after her.

"Away." She made for the garage door.

Lizzie chased her down the hall. "But your parents. Don't you think—"

"The only time my parents give a shit about me is when I'm making trouble for them."

"Okay, fine. Forget your parents. Think about your followers. You owe them more than a nonfunctional Web site. They trusted you, Zoe, and you broke that trust. They deserve to know why. Don't let this be Marie's legacy. If she really meant something to you, then at least give her that."

Zoe rested her hand on the garage doorknob. "I'll think about it," she said. "Tell my parents I said good-bye."

She opened the door, and before Lizzie knew it she was gone.

Fifteen minutes after Zoe left, the AAA truck appeared in the Silvesters' driveway. Lizzie went out to meet the driver, who surveyed her four flat tires.

"Somebody play a practical joke on you?"

"Something like that."

He shook his head. "We get these with high school kids all the time. Don't worry, we'll have you up and running again in no time."

He got to work on the car while Lizzie waited patiently beside the water feature. Nate and Kathryn had long since vacated the driveway, though she wasn't sure where either of them had gone. She felt bad for storming out on Nate, but she'd been so angry with Kathryn that she couldn't be in her presence for another second. She hoped Nate would understand.

She looked back at the house, which loomed high above her in the late-afternoon sun. She'd thought that perhaps after working for the Silvesters for a few months, their house would seem less obscene, but it still looked to Lizzie like a life-size sand castle. If anything, the Silvesters' Xanadu made her sad. Despite all the parties and gatherings, the mansion oozed sadness and loneliness. It was built with happiness but not for happiness, and whatever joy had passed through its halls during its construction had gone out with the tide long ago. Lizzie wasn't sad to leave.

As the technician refilled the first tire and moved on to the second, Lizzie felt a hand on her shoulder.

"Hey," Nate said. She turned around to face him. "So have you cooled off?"

"A little. Though I'm pretty sure if Kathryn appeared I'd go crazy all over again."

"Me too." He smiled. "You really gave it to her. I have to say, I was impressed."

"That may have been the first time I ever told someone off in my life."

"Really? Could have fooled me."

"I won't lie: it felt pretty good."

"Uh-oh. Have we created a monster?"

Lizzie raised an eyebrow. "Behave yourself and you'll never have to find out."

He laughed and watched as the technician inflated the second tire. "I would have called a tow truck."

"I know."

He looked back at Lizzie. "You just want to get out of here, huh?"

She nodded. He didn't press the issue. He understood, even if he didn't seem happy about her departure.

He reached down and held her hand, and they stood in silence as the technician finished his work. Lizzie closed her eyes and listened to the trickling of the water feature and the cawing of the seagulls. She wouldn't miss the Silvesters, but she would miss this: the sounds of the shore, the smell of the air. She wondered what her mother would say when she showed up later this evening. In all of the chaos, Lizzie hadn't told her she quit or that she'd be coming home. Would Gary be there? Lizzie hoped not. She hadn't seen her mother in the flesh since her diagnosis, and she didn't want Gary complicating what would already be an emotional reunion.

The technician finished fixing the tires and handed Lizzie a clipboard. She signed in the appropriate places and handed it back to him.

"Keep away from those pranksters," he said.

"I'll do my best."

He gave her a copy of the paperwork and left. Lizzie stuffed the papers in her bag and headed for the car. Nate followed behind.

"So I guess this is it," he said as she opened the car door.

"Depends what you mean by 'it.' "

"The last time I see you at my dad's house—though I hope it isn't the last time I see you, period."

"It's not."

Nate's shoulders relaxed. "Good."

"Things are going to be a little crazy on my end for a while, between my mom and my unemployment, and we don't even live in the same city—"

"We'll work it out. I'm patient."

"I'm not. But I'll do my best."

"Do you have my number?"

Lizzie thought about it. "No. I thought I did, but . . . Never mind. I don't."

They swapped phones and plugged in each other's numbers. They traded back, and Nate slid his in his pocket while she got into the front seat. She turned on the car and lowered the window. Nate leaned down and poked his head through. "Drive safe."

She started to make a quip about her fully inflated tires, even though she knew doing so was a mistake. The joke wasn't even fully formed in her head, and anyway, she'd never been particularly good at one-liners. She'd never been good at good-byes either, which was probably why she was making a foolhardy crack at a joke. But to her relief, Nate cut her off with a kiss, and she kissed him back as he held her face in his hands. A good-bye was easier when you knew it wasn't good-bye forever. She hoped she could at least make it back to Philadelphia without calling him.

He pulled away and stood back as she reversed the car out of its parking spot. She waved at him through the open window.

"Good luck with your mom," he called after her.

"Thanks," she called back, but her chest tightened as she steered down the driveway because she realized a confrontation even bigger than the one with Kathryn or Zoe lay ahead.

By the time Lizzie arrived in Glenside, it was dinnertime. She was shocked at how quickly she'd gotten home—less than two hours door to door. After her epic journey Memorial Day weekend, she'd forgotten how close Avalon was to home. Frankly, between that drive and the Silvesters' lifestyle, she felt as if she'd been living on a different planet for the past few months.

When Lizzie drove up her mother's driveway, she noticed it was empty. Her instinct had been to look for her mom's car, which made sense until Lizzie realized she was driving it. How would she explain the scratch marks? And how would she pay for them?

She parked the car and got out. Gary's off-road Jeep wasn't in the driveway or out front. Either her mom was out or, if she was home, Gary was using it. Or perhaps, Lizzie told herself, Gary was out of the picture altogether. She knew it was wrong to hope so— she didn't want her mom to be unhappy, and Gary seemed to make her happy—but she couldn't ignore the tinge of glee she felt at the prospect of Gary's dismissal.

She grabbed one of her suitcases from the trunk and wheeled it to the back door. She knocked twice, but when no one answered she fished the keys from the bottom of her purse and let herself in.

The house was quiet and still. It smelled of freshly laundered clothes and cinnamon. Her mom loved scattering scented candles and potpourri around the house, and so the air always bore strange combinations of Clean Cotton and Sparkling Cinnamon, often tinged with the likes of Ginger Spice Cookie and Sunset Breeze. To Lizzie, it smelled like home.

She left her suitcase by the stairs and headed toward the kitchen. As soon as she walked in the room, she noticed the counters. Every square inch was covered by fresh fruits and vegetables, juicers and blenders, numerous dietary supplements, and a tall stack of books. Lizzie scanned the spines: *Healing Naturally, Killing Cancer, The Demuth Bible.*

She picked up the top book—*Healing Naturally*—and had begun flipping through its pages when she heard a rustling sound in the hall behind her. She turned around. She and her mom screamed in unison.

"Are you trying to give me a heart attack?" her mother cried. She was holding an old tennis racket in one hand and clutched her chest with the other. "I thought someone had broken into the house."

Lizzie's eyes landed on the racket. "And so you were going to whack them with a tennis racket? That was your plan?"

"I don't know . . . maybe." She took a deep breath. "What are you doing here? Shouldn't you be in Avalon?"

"I quit. Or I guess they fired me. It was mutual."

"But what about . . . I mean, we still have six weeks or so until Labor Day."

"I'll figure something out. The relationship . . . it wasn't working anymore."

"Was it because of the daughter?"

"Yes and no."

Lizzie scanned her mother's figure from head to toe. She hadn't seen her since the diagnosis, and she looked thinner than Lizzie remembered. Her graying roots were about an inch long, made more noticeable by the fact that her hair was pulled into a tight, low ponytail. She didn't look sick. She just looked . . . different.

"How are you?" Lizzie asked.

Her mom shrugged. "I've been better. I mean, physically I feel fine. Still a little sore from the surgery, but otherwise, okay. Hungry some of the time. God, I do miss steak." She laughed weakly. "Mentally . . . well, I guess I'm still trying to process everything. I'd barely processed the fact that I had cancer, and then the story broke about that Web site. I'm feeling a little lost at the moment, to be honest."

"Have you thought any more about your treatment?"

"Of course I have. What else do I have to think about? It's *the* thing—the only thing."

"And . . . ? Have you made any decisions?"

She shook her head. "I know that isn't what you want to hear. But I need a little more time."

"To what? Facts are facts, and the latest scientific research shows—"

"I know what it shows. I'm not a fool. I know you think I am, especially after hearing about all this." She waved at the books and blenders on her counter. "But I'm not stupid. I'm just . . . scared."

Lizzie met her mother in the doorway. She reached out and hugged her. "I know. I am too."

Her mom squeezed Lizzie tight, her body shaking as she held Lizzie close. Lizzie felt hot tears trickle down her arm. She buried her face in her mother's neck and breathed in her scent. That smell—so specific to her mother, and no one else, like almond soap and fresh bread. How would she ever recapture that smell if her mom passed? She'd miss many things if her mom weren't around—the unconditional love, most of all, but also the advice, the outings, the silly birthday cards and panicked text messages ("Saw a news story about laptop fires—you turn yours off at night, right??? RIGHT???"). But that smell. Nothing was as comforting to Lizzie as that smell. She buried her face deeper.

"I don't . . ." She choked on the words. She took a deep breath and tried again. "I don't want to lose you," she said.

Her mom wept silently as she clung to Lizzie, and the two of them stood in the doorway, their tears mixing together, as they held each other up with strength they didn't know they had.

CHAPTER 38

The story about Zoe's Web site ended up having legs. First there were the followers and fans who'd paid for her app and demanded she refund the profits or donate them to charity. Then there were the people who threatened to sue. And then of course there were further investigations into CC Media's business dealings, which had nothing to do with Zoe per se but which her scandal had instigated.

When it came to Zoe giving the money back, Lizzie assumed most people didn't want their two ninety-nine so much as they wanted Zoe to atone.

"Good luck with that," Lizzie muttered as she read the latest rage-filled screed on an online news site. Like so many of Zoe's readers, the author of the post felt emotionally manipulated by Zoe's story about Marie.

```
    In some cases, she preyed on
people's sympathy. In others, she
preyed on their fear. In all, she
lied, and she used those lies to make
a buck. She didn't deserve a cent,
and she should give it all back.
```

Lizzie didn't disagree, but knowing Zoe as she did, she doubted Zoe would refund anything without a fight. Lizzie supposed that was where the lawsuits came in. Did those people have a case? Maybe. The fact that Zoe was merely selling advice and not a physical product definitely complicated the matter. And of course, no one—not reporters or followers or friends—seemed to know where Zoe was. A few stories even led with the mystery of her whereabouts ("Wellness Hack Goes MIA," "Clean Life Author Disappears in Face of Controversy," "Where in the World Is Zoe Silvester?"). The stories made for plenty of juicy speculation, but none of them succeeded in revealing her location or getting her to come forward. So the idea that she would pay back the money, much less appear in court, seemed like a long shot.

Zoe's absence aside, she wasn't the only one facing lawsuits. CC Media now had its own to contend with. At first, the press's interest in CC Media was mostly about the company's planned tax inversion, which was put on hold after the Treasury decided to throw up regulatory barriers to make such deals less financially advantageous. But once the media began poking around in CC Media's affairs, a reporter for the *Philadelphia Inquirer* discovered the company had padded its bottom line using deceptive fees and surcharges on customers nationwide. The company's so-called Service First Protection Plan claimed to offer free service calls and free repairs, but customers claimed they were still charged for both as somehow, coincidentally, the problems always managed to fall outside the parameters of the plan. In addition, thousands of customers claimed the plan was added on to their monthly bill, buried in the extra charges, even though they'd never signed up for it. Customers in Pennsylvania and Connecticut were suing CC Media, and there was talk of suits in other states. The stock was at its lowest level in five years.

As the media attention around both Zoe and CC Media heated up, Lizzie found herself suddenly in demand from journalists looking for an "inside scoop" about the Silvesters and their enigmatic daughter. Editors Lizzie hadn't heard from in months, who'd ignored her e-mails inquiring about potential job opportunities when her gig with the Silvesters started going south, now e-mailed and called with regularity. She'd only been in Glenside a few days when Jonah Sun, her former editor at *Savor,* gave her a call.

"Lizzie Glass—haven't heard from you in ages," he said.

"I e-mailed you last week. . . ."

"Did you? Man, things have been crazy over here with the new guy running the show. It must have gotten buried in my in-box."

"Ah."

"Anyway . . . so I heard you were working for Zoe Silvester's family when that whole story broke? Is that true?"

"Yeah."

"Wow. Nuts. You must have seen a lot of stuff, huh?" Lizzie didn't reply. "Anyway, we were thinking . . . how would you feel about writing an exclusive for us? 'My Summer with the Silvesters,' or something like that."

"I don't know."

"We'd pay you, obviously. Maybe not as well as the Silvesters were paying, but still." He laughed, but Lizzie didn't join him.

"I think I'll pass," she said.

"What do you mean you'll pass?" He was trying to sound relaxed, but Lizzie could tell he was annoyed. "You just e-mailed me asking if we had any work for you."

"You said you didn't see my e-mail."

"No, I mean . . . that's what . . . you said that's why you e-mailed me."

"No, I didn't."

"Whatever. Is it the money? Because I'm sure I could negotiate a good rate for a story like this. And if you nail it, there could be future work too."

"It isn't the money."

"You realize this is a huge opportunity right? And if you turn it down you'd totally be blowing it? You may never get another shot like this."

Lizzie had heard this spiel before: when she was offered her show on the Food Network, when she landed her cookbook deal, even when she was offered the cottage cheese gig with Queensridge Dairy. They were the words that shifted her anxiety into high gear. *If I turn this down,* she'd think, *I may never make something of myself.*

I may never work again! But she'd come to learn that wasn't true. She didn't regret hosting her show, and after much reflection this summer she could honestly say she was glad she'd done it. But if she hadn't, she would have done something else. There would always be opportunities, and she would always have a choice. If the offer felt right, she'd take it. If it didn't, she'd pass.

"I guess I'll have to take my chances," she said to Jonah.

"Seriously? I mean, listen, it's totally your call, but . . . I have to ask . . . why? Most people would kill for this kind of exposure."

"Not me. Not right now, anyway. I'm looking for work I can feel good about, and that kind of story isn't it, at least for me."

"Okay, I hear you." Something in his voice told Lizzie he didn't, but he was shrewd enough not to push her any further. Savvy New York editors never burned a bridge. Lizzie was trying not to burn any either.

She glanced out the window and caught site of her mother, who was watering her tomato plants, which had sprung high above their conical wire cages. As she shook the hose back and forth, she closed her eyes and lifted her face to the sky, letting the sun beat down on her cheeks. Lizzie couldn't be sure, but she thought she saw her smile. She looked happy. She had every reason not to, but she did. She had been through so much and would likely go through much more, and yet surrounded by her favorite things—her garden, her house, her daughter—she was content. She didn't ask for more. This was enough.

"Anyway, best of luck with everything," Jonah said. "I hope you find what you're looking for."

Lizzie watched as her mom opened her eyes and returned her attention to the tomato plants. "Thanks," Lizzie said. "I think I already have."

CHAPTER 39

Linda,

It was so good talking to you earlier. I've never been able to stay mad at you for long, and I'm glad you feel the same way. You mean the world to me. Everything has just been so scary and overwhelming that I haven't been at my best, but now that Lizzie is home, I feel more like myself again.

I've scheduled an appointment with Dr. Goodman for next week. He comes highly recommended and seems to take the integrative approach I'm looking for—combining more conventional treatments like chemo and drugs (you, Frank, and Lizzie will be relieved) with other things like mind-body medicine and nutrition therapy (Gary and I are very much looking forward to learning more about that). Actually, believe it or not, Lizzie has shown a lot of interest in learning more about nutrition therapy. It seems to combine her interest in healthy cooking with a vocation that helps people like me deal with the downsides of cancer treatments. She's meeting with someone at Penn and Fox Chase Cancer Center next week to learn more. I actually think it would be a great fit for her—kind of like a personal chef for cancer patients. Obviously I have a selfish interest in her running with this idea (if I end up doing chemo, I'll need all the help I can get), but for the first time in a long time, she seems truly excited about her career. I haven't seen her this enthused since she started her show at Penn. Can you believe it's been more than a decade? Seems like just yesterday.

Anyway, in the meantime, she has been helping me get the house in order, especially the kitchen. Gary is . . . well, let's just say he isn't bothered by clutter. You should have seen the kitchen when Lizzie got home—it looked like something had exploded. But Lizzie has helped me get it back in shape. She and Gary are still getting used to each other, but when Lizzie heard him say he'd support me no matter what treatment plan I chose I think we turned a page. I'm so relieved—the last thing I need is more conflict.

Shoot—gotta run. I promised Lizzie I'd take her to the King of Prussia Mall to look for a dress. Apparently a guy she met in Avalon is driving all the way to Philly to take her to dinner. Who says chivalry is dead?

Love you so much, and for the zillionth time: I'm sorry. Let's never fight like that again.

xxoo

S

EPILOGUE

Three Months Later

"Okay, I'm heading out!" Lizzie shouted up to her mom. "You sure you don't need anything?"

"I'm fine." Her mother's weak voice emanated from behind the bedroom door.

"If you change your mind, Linda's here. And I'm just a phone call away."

There was no response from upstairs, but then Lizzie wasn't surprised. She'd gotten used to her mom's silence ever since the chemo started. She was just so tired all the time. She didn't feel like herself either.

"My brain is all fuzzy," she'd say. "And my mouth—everything tastes like metal."

The doctors said she was responding well to the treatment, though they wouldn't know for many more months whether she was officially cured.

"And I mean cured," Dr. Goodman had said at the first appointment. "Not in remission. Cured."

He'd outlined all the latest studies and what he believed was the best course of action for making sure the cancer never returned.

"It won't be a fun year," he'd said, "but it will hopefully lead to many, many more that are."

Lizzie slipped her phone into her purse and kissed Linda on the cheek. "I'll be home for dinner. I left some things for Mom in the fridge. She never feels like eating much, but try to get her to have a little something."

"Last time it took a lot of persuading...."

"Whatever works." She squeezed Linda's hand. "Only a few more months to go."

Linda took a deep breath. "She's a tough cookie, your mom."

"The toughest." Lizzie opened the front door.

"Where does this client live?"

"Wyncote. The other two are in Blue Bell."

"It's really great what you're doing, you know. Your mom and I are really proud."

"Life has a weird way of showing you where you belong."

Her phone rang in her purse. She glanced at the screen. It was Nate. "I have to take this. See you tonight." She slipped out the door and answered the call. "Hey—you caught me just as I was running out the door."

"Sorry," Nate said. "I can call back."

"No, it's fine. I just wanted you to understand why I might sound like I'm out of breath."

"Are you *literally* running to your next job? Or are you just that out of shape?"

"Very funny. I'm driving, thanks."

"So how's your mom?"

"About the same. Chemo is awful, no getting around it."

"Need me to do anything?"

"Come visit me, for one."

He laughed. "Next weekend. I have to finish grading midterms this weekend."

"Okay, okay, if you must."

Lizzie smiled. Nate had already visited more than she could have hoped or expected over the past few months. If they were keeping score, it was definitely her turn to make the trip to DC, but with her mom's treatment it was too hard to get away. Linda had been helping, and even her dad had managed to pitch in by stopping by to clean up the garden and drop off groceries. Her mom was too exhausted to argue, and Lizzie suspected she appreciated the help, even if it came from her ex-husband. And of course there was Gary. Still, after all the years her mom had looked out for her, Lizzie felt responsible for making sure her mother was comfortable and well-fed. Washington wasn't far, but it wasn't next door either. If something went wrong, she would need at least three or four hours to get home. Nate seemed to understand, and she was grateful that he never complained or hinted that he wanted her to visit him instead.

"By the way, did I tell you Kathryn is hosting a benefit next weekend for the Leukemia and Lymphoma Society?"

"You're kidding." Lizzie walked toward the car but noticed a UPS deliveryman walking up her driveway with a package.

"Nope. Zoe still hasn't refunded the money or donated her profits to charity, so I guess this is Kathryn's attempt at setting things right."

Lizzie held the phone between her ear and shoulder and signed for the package. She noticed it was addressed to her. "A nice, if insufficient, gesture."

"Kathryn is full of them."

"I bet." Lizzie looked more closely at the package and noticed the return address was Brattleboro, Vermont. "Speaking of Zoe . . . have you heard from her?"

"Me? No. Dad thinks Kathryn knows where she is and has been sending her money, but I'm not sure."

Lizzie felt queasy as she held the package in her hands. She didn't know why, but she was certain it was from Zoe. She tore open the paper. Her stomach lurched as she stared at the contents: a copy of Martha Stewart's *Entertaining*. A small note fell from the inside:

> Saw this in a used bookshop up here and
> thought you might want it. It isn't a signed first
> edition, but whatever.
> Z

Lizzie stared at the note in silence. It wasn't an apology, at least not in the traditional sense, but then maybe in Zoe's warped mind it was. It certainly wasn't a threat. Lizzie knew there was a mental health facility in Brattleboro. Was Zoe there?

"Hello?" Nate had been talking for some time, but Lizzie hadn't heard any of what he'd said.

"Sorry—I . . ." She trailed off. Her eyes flitted between the note and the book. She wasn't sure what to make of any of it. The gesture, however thoughtful, didn't make up for all that Zoe had done. But then would anything ever offset that? Lizzie couldn't imagine anything would.

"Are you okay?" Nate asked.

Lizzie looked up at her mother's bedroom. The curtains were drawn, but a sliver of light peaked through. She saw Linda's shadow pass by the window, heading for the bed. It was hard to tell, through the rustling of leaves, as the crisp October air swirled through the piles lining the curb, but Lizzie swore she heard giggling, the sound of sisters, their easy laughter flowing through the window like birdsong.

"Yeah, I'm okay," she said. "We're all going to be okay."

She'd learned enough over the past few months to recognize that might not be true, that plenty could happen in the coming months and years to prove her wrong. But she somehow knew, deeply and with absolute certainty, that even if it wasn't true, it also wasn't a lie.

ACKNOWLEDGMENTS

Many thanks to my sharp-eyed editor, Esi Sogah, for believing in this book and making it a better one. Thanks also to everyone at Kensington Publishing for their hard work: Paula Reedy, Kristine Noble, Vida Engstrand, Steve Zacharius, and Lynn Cully. I feel lucky to work with such a great team.

This book would probably still be a document on my computer if it weren't for the hard work of Scott Miller and everyone at Trident Media Group. Thanks for all you do.

Thanks to everyone who gave me an insight into the life of a private and/or personal chef, especially Linda Rubin and Beth Kaufman.

To my mom: You are the strongest woman I know. I finished this book before you began one of your toughest trials to date, and you have braved it all with courage and grace. You are a rock star, and I love you so much.

And a big thanks to the rest: to Dad for the support, to Brian and Chelsea for the laughs, to Sophie for the advice, to Alex and Charlie for the joy, and to Roger for everything.

VIRTUALLY PERFECT

Paige Roberts

ABOUT THIS GUIDE

The suggested questions that follow
are included to enhance your group's
reading of Paige Roberts's
Virtually Perfect.

Discussion Questions

1. Several of the characters in the story are guilty of deception—both to themselves and to others. Is there ever an instance when lying is okay or even necessary? At what point does a lie cross a moral threshold?

2. Why do you think Zoe's many followers were so willing to believe the story on her site? Was the onus on her to provide the truth or on them to seek it?

3. In what ways does the Internet make it easier to spread false information, whether it's Zoe's story about Marie or fake news? As a consumer of information, how do you balance skepticism with open-mindedness?

4. A few characters, like Lizzie's dad and even Lizzie herself at times, refer to the sort of alternative medicine on Zoe's site as being "hocus-pocus." To what extent do you think that attitude fuels Zoe and her supporters?

5. Do you think there is a place for both conventional and alternative medicine?

6. If Lizzie's mom, Susan, had continued to follow Zoe's advice and the cancer ended up coming back and she died as a result, to what extent would Zoe be morally culpable? How much of the blame lies with Susan?

7. In her final confrontation with Kathryn, Lizzie says, "If you screw up your kid, nothing else really matters." Do you agree? How much responsibility does Kathryn bear for Zoe's actions?

8. Do you agree with Linda's decision to tell Lizzie and Frank about her sister's cancer treatment, even though she'd been

told to keep it a secret? How else might she have handled the situation?

9. Anyone with an Internet connection or mobile device can create a blog or a social media account. Do you think that allows for more diverse voices to be heard? Or do you think there is a self-selection bias?

10. At one point, Nate mentions that before Kathryn's "Paleo diet" she had tried Atkins, South Beach, and numerous other diet fads. To what extent does constantly changing dietary advice make it easier for novices or charlatans to seem legitimate?

11. An early tagline of this book was "Anyone can be a guru on the Internet." Do you think that's true?

Connect with U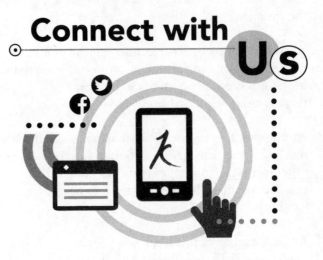s

Visit us online at
KensingtonBooks.com
to read more from your favorite authors, see books
by series, view reading group guides, and more.

 Join us on social media

for sneak peeks, chances to win books and prize packs,
and to share your thoughts with other readers.

facebook.com/kensingtonpublishing
twitter.com/kensingtonbooks

Tell us what you think!

To share your thoughts, submit a review,
or sign up for our eNewsletters, please visit:
KensingtonBooks.com/TellUs.